WITHDRAWN
UTSA LIBRARIES

The Election

The Election

☆ ★ ☆ ★ ☆ ★ ☆ ★ ☆ ★ ☆

by *SHERWIN MARKMAN*

Random House | *New York*

Copyright © 1970 by Sherwin Markman

All rights reserved under International and
Pan-American Copyright Conventions.
Published in the United States
by Random House, Inc., New York, and
simultaneously in Canada
by Random House of Canada Limited,
Toronto.

Library of Congress Catalog Card Number: 79–117672

Manufactured in the United States of America
by H. Wolff Book Manufacturing Co.

9   8   7   6   5   4   3   2

FIRST EDITION

To Marilyn, Steve, Nicki, and Stacy—with love

"*I have ever considered the constitutional mode of election ultimately by the legislature voting by states as the most dangerous blot on our constitution, and one which some unlucky chance will some day hit.*"

THOMAS JEFFERSON

1823

The Election

CHAPTER ONE

Stuart Brady came awake at once. The bedside signal corps phone was ringing and he quickly reached for it.

"Brady speaking."

"This is the duty officer in the Situation Room. They just called from the Mansion. The President wants you down here right away."

"Did they say what it is?"

"No, sir. Only that you and other members of the staff are to come directly to the President's bedroom."

"Thanks. I'll be there."

Stu sat on the edge of the bed for a moment, thinking about the unexpected call. It was not quite seven and a peremptory order to appear at this hour was unusual. It must have something to do with today's presidential election, he thought, but he was damned if he could think of anything more that could be done about that mess. Yet, here was the President summoning his staff almost before dawn.

Stu rubbed the back of his neck, beginning to feel the familiar tightening. He had worked at the White House long past midnight and the tension was still with him. He would probably have another headache today.

Sari was curled into a tight ball on her side of the bed, still asleep. It was just as well. Stu would probably have to work late again tonight and if he told her now it would just lead to another argument about his job.

He walked to the bathroom to shower and shave. As usual,

he had to wait for the hot water to come through the sputtering faucet, and he silently cursed the landlord. Living in a rented Georgetown apartment might be considered posh, he thought, but you paid for the privilege. Between the roaches and a landlord who couldn't care less, it certainly wasn't worth the rent. Sari wanted to live in the neighborhood, however, and this was the best they could afford.

When Stu returned to the bedroom, Sari was awake, sitting up in bed lighting a cigarette.

"Do you have to start smoking now?" Stu muttered. "Can't you lay off until after breakfast?"

Sari stared at him, inhaling deeply. "You make so much noise in the bathroom no one can sleep anyway," she said, ignoring his remark. "How come you're up?"

"The President wants me down there now."

"My God, Stu, isn't it enough that he keeps you there half the night? Does he have to get you early too?"

Stu's head was beginning to ache, and he struggled to keep his patience. "I work for the man, and I've got to be there whenever he asks. You knew that when you married me."

"Like hell I did," she said, angrily snuffing out her cigarette. "I thought I was getting a husband, not just some exhausted guy I see only late at night. We don't even get the weekends together, he's after you so much."

Stu finished knotting his tie. "You should have known what you were getting into."

"Maybe I should have, but I didn't," she said, lighting another cigarette. "I thought we'd have time together and get some fun out of your working at that place. I just didn't expect this at all. Never seeing you, never having a moment's peace from that man. He just owns you, Stu, and you let him do it." She was close to tears.

Stu sat beside Sari and reached for her hand. "It's almost over," he said. "Just a couple more months and he'll be out of office. Then I can go back to the newspaper."

Sari jerked her hand away. "What time are you coming home tonight?"

4

"How in the hell should I know," he said, angry again.

"Well, why don't you guess, so I can make some plans for a change."

"Probably goddamned late," he shot back, leaving the room.

He shoved a piece of bread into the toaster and started to boil some water for instant coffee. Marriage and the White House just don't mix, Stu thought.

He'd been with the President as Assistant Press Secretary for almost four years. Sari and he had been married two years ago. She had been working for the House Armed Services Committee and they met at a White House party for Hill staff people. Sari was unusually good-looking, with soft black hair and intense brown eyes set in a mobile, alert face. Stu had been instantly attracted to her and they began seeing one another steadily. Even then, however, he often had to break dates at the last moment or ask her to wait in the White House lobby while he finished some unexpected work. She should have known what marriage would be like, he ruefully thought, but in those days she had always seemed fascinated with the kind of work he was doing. She was interested in politics and political types, and seemed to enjoy the same people he did. She was intrigued by the Washington scene and would proudly tell people that her friend Stuart Brady worked at the White House.

Stu was thirty years old and they had known each other six months when they were married in a small Catholic church in Georgetown. Only their close friends had been invited, but, completely unexpectedly, the President and his wife had come to the wedding. Stu had been immensely pleased, and both he and Sari glowed from the President's warm praise as he stood, arms around them both, saying that they were like his own children and wishing them a lifetime of happiness.

The marriage had started off well, but Stu's work became increasingly demanding, and, during this campaign year especially, he was almost never home.

Stu had been accustomed to hard work even before he came to the White House. As the youngest member of the Washington

5

Bureau of the *St. Louis Post Dispatch*, he had driven himself hard. In fact, it was just this penchant for work that first brought him to the President's attention. Stu had been assigned to cover the President during his campaign for a second term and they had immediately hit it off. When the President had asked him to join the White House staff shortly after his re-election victory, Stu jumped at the chance. But nothing he had done before had adequately prepared him for the White House. In one sense it had been a magnificent experience, but in so many other ways it had been sheer hell.

He was a bit tired of it all, he thought, as he sipped his cof-fee. He meant it when he told Sari he was thankful it was almost over. Sari had learned to hate Stu's job and had become increas-ingly vocal about it. Yet, he really couldn't blame her. He was beginning to feel that way himself.

As Stu headed for the front door, the telephone rang again. This time it wasn't the signal line. He briefly hesitated, then quickly trotted to the kitchen to pick it up.

"Stu, baby, did I wake you? This is Charlie Jefferson."

"For Christ's sake, Charlie, it's practically the middle of the night. Too damned early for a good bureaucrat like you to be up and about."

"We at Justice never sleep, the price of liberty being eternal wakefulness or something like that."

"Charlie, I'm sorry, but I'm in a rush. What can I do for you?"

"Listen, Stu, I've been ordered to go to Oakland. I'm on an early flight and I didn't want to miss you. The F.B.I. thinks it's on to something hot involving the blacks out there, and the At-torney General . . . you know how he feels about the Director, especially when it comes to the ghettos . . . is sending me out there to check on it. Anyway, since you and I have been on this subject before, and times being what they are, I wanted to tell you that it might be very bad medicine. I'd like to be able to call you when I know something definite, if you don't mind."

6

"Sure, Charlie. I don't know what the hell you're talking about, but feel free."

"Thanks, friend. I'll let you go work on that Democratic victory."

"It doesn't look too good."

"I know, Stu, but good luck anyway."

Driving toward work, Stu thought about the two phone calls. The President's summons he could understand. But Charlie Jefferson was a different matter. Jefferson was a Deputy Assistant Attorney General in the Civil Rights Division at Justice. He was an able Negro lawyer, and he and Stu had become friends during the late nights they had worked together at the White House command post during the riots of the past two summers. Charlie was one of the coolest men Stu knew, which was why he was so valuable in a crisis, and Stu now wondered what in the world would necessitate a call at seven in the morning, simply about a trip to the coast.

Stu drove his battered Volkswagen slowly through rush-hour traffic. His job entitled him to a White House car with army driver but he rarely took advantage of this privilege, probably because, at thirty-two, he still felt ill at ease being chauffeured to and from work. He suspected that he would always remain a Midwesterner at heart, never shucking off his St. Louis upbringing despite his Columbia degree and his years in Washington. The Eastern establishment might naturally take to the accouterments of power, but Stu doubted that he would ever think of himself as anything more than a stranger temporarily on the scene.

There had been a time, though, when his penchant for driving his own car had brought the well-known wrath of the President down upon him. One Sunday evening Stu and Sari had gone to visit friends for an informal supper. As always, Stu had told the White House operators of his whereabouts.

They left their friends at about eleven o'clock but decided that the night was too lovely for them to go straight home. Stu drove up the George Washington Parkway and stopped at the

Overlook. The view down the Potomac toward the brightly lighted spire of the Washington Monument had been magnificent, and they sat for almost an hour quietly talking, as they had not done for months.

It must have been just after they had left the dinner that the White House operator had called for him. For the next hour and a half the operator rang Stu's house every five minutes, and the phone was jangling away when he and Sari finally walked in the door. When Stu picked up the signal line the nervous operator said, "It's the President. He's been looking for you for almost two hours." Then there was a silence, a click, and the familiar drawl came on: "Where in the hell have you been?"

The questioner really didn't want an answer, and to Stu's tentative response, "We were just out for a drive," the President shot back, "And what about the radios I buy for all of you? You're always getting them in my way when I don't need them, but the one time I have to find you, you just drop out of sight." Stu explained that he hadn't been in a White House car and didn't carry a radio in his own car. This explanation resulted in a short, pointed suggestion from the President that he wanted Stu to be available whenever he was needed, even if this meant riding in White House cars or installing a radio in his own.

When the President hung up, Stu had known precisely what was expected of him in the two-way radio department, but he never did find out what it was the boss had wanted to speak to him about. The President simply had failed to mention it.

Now, approaching the White House, Stu's thoughts turned back to the President's early morning meeting. He was almost certain it related to today's presidential election. On that subject the President had been in an increasing rage all fall, and the fact was that today's results weren't likely to bring forth anything very satisfying.

Without a doubt, just about everything the President had planned had gone wrong. It had started with James Harrington, the senior senator from Rhode Island and Democratic candidate for President.

As the President's second full term was drawing to a close,

8

his mind had increasingly turned to the subject of his successor. Harrington, who had long been close to the President, had been his choice. Even during the years the President had served in the Senate, he had taken Harrington under his wing, seeing to it that he received choice committee assignments and the best opportunities on key legislation. After he had assumed the Presidency he had made even greater use of Harrington, so that the phrase "clear it with Jimmy" had become a Washington by-word. Now, at fifty-five, after sixteen years in the Congress, the last ten as senator, Jimmy Harrington was an acknowledged protégé of the President. Harrington, in turn, had not forgotten the source of his power, and his loyalty never deviated.

Throughout this past winter and spring the President had openly put his imprimatur on Harrington, and such was the weight of the Presidency that Harrington hadn't entered a single primary and had made no appearances except for carefully staged occasions and selected speeches on the Senate floor. That was more than enough. Almost untested in national campaigning, he had been nominated on the first ballot at the Convention in August. As it happened, this was about the biggest mistake the President or the Democratic party had ever made. Jimmy Harrington had turned out to be an undependable political commodity. On some days he would be unable to make a judgment on his own, running to the President for guidance. On other occasions, when he would speak without his prepared text, he would unpredictably fly off in just about any direction.

Stu shuddered to think of the campaign. When, in September, teacher strikes had hit thirty cities, Harrington, who was a traditional union supporter, had let loose with the remark that, by God, if he were a teacher he would support his union all the way. This statement had alienated every parent, taxpayer and militant Negro in sight.

On the issue of Selective Service, Harrington had answered a reporter's informal question with the statement that a small, volunteer army was probably sufficient for the country. This remark had set off howls, not only from the super hawks, but from good middle-class folk as well.

The Republicans had gleefully jumped on each error, making the most of every chance, and the President had done his level best to rescue Harrington each time. Thirty-seven speeches in twenty days, Stu remembered with a grimace—almost as much campaigning down the stretch as the candidate. Then, there were all those private talks, cajolings and lectures, when the President tried to steady Harrington. But for every step forward they took, Harrington managed two backward. The truth was that the senator just did not react well to the excruciating pressures of the campaign.

It would have been down the drain for sure, except that the Republicans selected a candidate who was, if possible, worse: good, gray Maynard Nelson, the steady governor of Pennsylvania, having the great advantage of looking like everyone's father, had managed to come off with about as much charisma as a pet poodle. And that just didn't wash. Not today. Not with the country seething beneath the surface, the discontent an almost physical presence. The governor just wasn't with it, and the people knew it.

That left Jack Parker, the third-party candidate. A freshman senator from Florida, Parker had hit the country like a cyclone during the past two years. Tall and good-looking, absolutely uncanny on television, Parker had found an issue and he, and it, had caught fire. Standing behind the wall of senatorial immunity, he had said what others had only dared to hint.

Parker's opening blast had been a sensation. "I have locked in a vault," he had said, "safe from even the fearsome powers of Washington's bureaucrats, the proof that this country is being taken over by a conspiracy—not of Communists, my friends, but an insidious combination of black power and Jewish money. A conspiracy whose objective is to bring revolution, chaos and the complete destruction of our Christian culture. I have the proof. I have the names."

And he had linked such disparate people and groups as Mamba Z and the Black Guards on the West Coast, and Julie Cohen, chairman of the American Civil Liberties Union. To top it off, he had mentioned just about every Jewish appointee of this administration.

Parker had caught on, and he had wasted no time in capitalizing on his skyrocketing popularity. For the past year he had unceasingly criss-crossed the country, spreading his message and captivating audiences. He managed to get on the ballot in every state. He had pounded his issue home with a single-minded purpose that had driven most reporters up the wall. But they couldn't let him alone, and their fear of him only increased his visibility.

Parker might have been harmless except for two things. In the first place, to people everywhere it appeared that the whole safe, familiar social fabric of America was disintegrating: There was Negro violence, strikes by police, teachers and public employees everywhere, and student revolts. The United States was increasingly despised throughout the world, and, on top of that, when the country could afford it least, it now appeared that the two great political parties, on which so much depended, had both defaulted.

The scenes of these hectic months spun through his mind as Stu finally reached West Executive Avenue and pulled into his parking space close to the west basement White House entrance. As he walked toward the door he could not help feeling depressed over what this election day was going to bring. He briefly nodded to the guard on duty, took the steps to the main floor two at a time, and walked across the outside passage to the Mansion.

As he entered the Mansion, two secret service agents were, as usual, at the checkpoint across from the elevator. They stood up as he appeared. "You're the sixth," one of them said. "It must be some big deal to get all you guys out of bed and down here this time of day."

Stu pushed the elevator button and waited for its leisurely descent. "Who all is here?" he asked.

"Well, Alvin Morgan, of course, and Sam Baker, Haines Morrison, Mike Potofsky and Mark Brozman," the agent said,

11

referring to members of the President's staff. "John Kelly is on the list, but he's not here yet," the agent added, naming the chief of the President's congressional liaison team.

"Thanks, buddy. Now don't fall asleep," Stu smilingly called over his shoulder, as he stepped into the ancient piece of machinery, laughingly referred to as an automatic elevator. When Stu got off on the second floor, he saw the five other staff members standing in the hall just outside the bedroom door, talking in hushed voices. No one seemed especially cheerful.

"What's going on?" Stu asked of Alvin Morgan, the gray-haired, somewhat stooped-shouldered man for whom this early morning duty was routine.

"I'm sorry, Stu, but I haven't seen him yet, either."

Just then, Bill Norris, the President's valet, stuck his head out the bedroom door. "Is everyone here?" he asked.

"No," said Morgan, "Kelly is missing."

"The boss wants to start now, so go on into the Yellow Oval Room. He will be right with you."

They filed into the lovely, comfortably furnished second-floor room with its magnificent view across the south lawn toward the Washington Monument. It was a room the President dearly loved, and he used it often for off-the-record meetings and quiet get-togethers with old friends. Decorated in a soft yellow motif, its oval shape was accented by the "Truman" balcony upon which it opened.

The room could be entered from both the hall and the President's bedroom, and now the latter door swung open and the familiar tall and sharp-featured man strode into the room, still wearing his pajamas and bathrobe.

They all murmured "Good morning" to the President, but he merely scowled and motioned them to be seated.

It was then that Kelly came into the room, smiling his great Irish grin and, irreverent as always, opening with "Hi there, Mr. President, it was a hell of a short night."

The President ignored this and launched right into his subject.

"Today's election is not going to decide a damn thing," he

began. "Harrington is not going to pull it off, and neither is Nelson."

The staff members all nodded.

Stu looked around the room. They are all pros, he thought. No sign of emotion. They were ready for whatever the boss had in mind. Stu had always admired this quality of political professionalism and he was proud to be a part of it. These men were the President's loyal and devoted inside team. They had all been with him for years, and, although others in government had long since begun to return to private affairs during this last year of the administration's life, these men would stay on until the end. They had been there at the beginning and would not leave before noon on January twentieth.

"We are going to be ready," the President continued, "and each of you will have a job to do today."

"Brozman"—the President fixed his penetrating stare on the lawyer who was his Special Counsel—"I want you to get me all there is on the Electoral College and a House of Representatives election of a President. Work with the Attorney General, but I want it all, including everything that happened every other time an election went that route."

The Special Counsel took notes. He will get it all done, too, thought Stu. Although he was only thirty-five, Mark Brozman had a deserved reputation of being one of the finest legal talents in Washington. An honors graduate of the Harvard Law School, Brozman had been, successively, a clerk to the Chief Justice, an associate in a prestigious Wall Street law firm, special assistant and General Counsel to the Secretary of Defense, and for the past five years the chief legal advisor to the President of the United States. Although sometimes abrasive and not too well thought of by the Establishment at Justice, Brozman more than earned his way and, in Stu's opinion, was about as valuable a staff member as a President could have.

"Alvin, I want you to take the men in the Electoral College." For the first time the President smiled, as he warmly contemplated his old friend and now Special Assistant, Alvin Morgan. "I'll need every bit of background you can dredge up on each of them. Who they are, who they'll listen to, how they got to be electors, their weaknesses and strengths." The President was intense now. "We will need to know everything."

Morgan quietly smiled at the President. "I'll have it for you, Mr. President."

"And, Alvin, I'll want you close by me all day and tonight." Then, turning to the others, "I want all of you to coordinate with Alvin. He'll be in charge."

"Now, Kelly," the President scowled at his congressional liaison man, "You will need to get me a workup on the new House. I don't want you disappearing today. No boozing it up with your political buddies. And no celebrating tonight."

"I wouldn't think of it, Mr. President," said Kelly, smiling. "Those bastards will be too damn scared to pop in for any drinks anyway."

"What I really need to know, John, is how each of them will stand up if this election goes into the House. Who will vote with his party, who might make a deal, who might vote the way his state went, and so forth. I want the House counted, just like on any major bill."

"Will do," Kelly responded.

Stu contemplated the still-smiling Kelly. He's the essence of Irish politician, he thought. Hard drinking, hard living, but always there when needed. And he loved a good political fight like nothing else. Despite his devil-may-care exterior, Kelly was shrewd and damn good. He was well liked on the Hill and his vote predictions were accurate. For this the President forgave him all else.

"Potofsky, you will keep an eye on the country." The President stared gravely at his Special Assistant for Domestic Affairs. "I not only want a rundown on everything vital that is going on today, but I also want to know all the pressure points, all the weaknesses. Give me your best judgment on what's likely to happen between now and January if nothing is settled today. What will break out, who will do it, and what we will be able to do about it. Work with all of the key departments and make it complete."

14

The President paused, and stared at the floor a long time before continuing. Then he spoke to Haines Morrison. "Haines, I'll need the same sort of thing in the foreign field. Collect all the intelligence you can. Who will try to pull something off if we don't have a presidential winner, what they will try, and how we can block them off."

Stu looked at these two repositories of presidential trust. They are so different, and yet there is such similarity in what they do, he thought. Potofsky was the oldest thirty-eight-year-old Stu had ever known, perpetually on the run, harassed, and willing to work incredible hours, even by White House standards. And Morrison, the urbane and unflappable product of the very best the Eastern establishment had to offer. Stu wondered if the often printed accounts of Morrison's bitter disappointment over not being Secretary of State were accurate. You would never know by looking at him, Stu contemplated, and he is the President's utterly loyal servant in coordinating foreign operations from the White House.

"As for you, Sam, just keep the press from having a nervous breakdown," the President smiled ruefully at Sam Baker, his Press Secretary. "Get me everything you can on how they are playing it. Keep in close touch with the White House reporters and also the major publishers. I want to know the direction of their thinking. And, Sam, you work with the speech writers and get me a series of statements that I should make tonight and tomorrow."

"They'll have an orgy over this one, Mr. President," Baker responded.

"The country would probably be better off if we could just black out the news until this gets settled," the President murmured.

He's only half in jest, and Baker probably agrees with him, Stu thought, as he contemplated his immediate superior. Sam Baker, like the President, came out of the old school of politics, which believed in keeping reporters at arm's length, using them when you could but always being on guard, assuming that any reporter would screw you at the first opening.

Stu had never bought that philosophy, which had led to some bitter arguments with Baker and considerable hell from the boss. It was Stu's belief that if you leveled with reporters they would repay you by the use of discretion in what they wrote; and in the long run this was a better shield than silence and distrust. Stu tried his best to operate on this premise, but he was forever running up against a wall. Worst of all, there were some who whispered, and not so quietly, that he would leak a story. Around the White House, this was about the worst possible sin.

Stu had never been able to live down the fact that he had spent four years as a Washington reporter. Despite his recent years of service with the President, there was always the underlying thought that maybe he had kept a foot in both camps. It was not true, but there seemed nothing Stu could do to erase the feeling.

"Brady, now you be alert." The President looked at Stu, catching his far-away expression. "You are not here just to record this for posterity. There is work for you too." The President's stare was, as usual, utterly penetrating. It had taken Stu a long time to learn to return the President's gaze without a mental flinch.

"I want you to maintain contact with both of the major candidates," the President continued. "But leave out Parker."

The President stood and walked to the south windows and gazed at the still green White House lawn and the cloudless fall sky. His back was turned to them and he spoke in a voice so low they could hardly hear him. "Whatever happens, we will have nothing to do with that son of a bitch. Absolutely nothing." As the President turned around, his face was tightly set. "Everything that we do from now on will be for the purpose of denying him power. He will not be President, and he will not be a maker of Presidents."

Returning to his chair, the President stared at them all for a long moment before returning his attention to Stu. "Get with whoever has the ear of Nelson and Harrington. Find out their plans, all of them, in case there's no decision today. Feel them out on working with me in this. Most of all, establish a means of communication that can be maintained and activated instantly until this is over. I know I could do this myself, especially with Harrington, but I think more options will be open to me if I work through an intermediary. And, Stu"—the President's face broke into a big grin—"I don't want to read about it in Evans and Novak tomorrow morning."

Stu winced at this jab, but managed to smile while shaking his head. His mind was now racing over the possibilities in each camp. With Harrington it would be Sandy Corso, of course, Stu thought, as he pictured his old friend and much-harassed chief speech writer for the Democratic candidate.

But the Republicans posed a much more delicate problem. Stu's relations with the other party had never been particularly close. It was not so much mere partisanship on his part as simply the lack of opportunity. Although he had a number of Republican friends, he was hard put to single out one who was really inside with Governor Nelson.

The President stood, and they all jumped to their feet. "Now, gentlemen," he said, "I'll want you to be over here at, let's say, nine o'clock tonight and I'll want a report from each of you. Have a pleasant day." The President turned abruptly and walked to his bedroom.

Stu thought about his headache, which was getting worse. He thought about Sari and what she would say when he told her he wouldn't be home until very late that night. And he worried that he had absolutely no time to come up with a Republican contact.

CHAPTER TWO

It was drizzling when Charlie Jefferson stepped off the plane in San Francisco. All the way to the West Coast he had been thinking about today's election. He was deeply concerned about what was going to happen, what impact Senator Parker would have on the two major parties. Whatever that impact was, he thought, it certainly wouldn't be good for the blacks. But the Attorney General had managed to deny him his one vote by sending him to Oakland with instructions to quietly check on disturbing F.B.I. reports on that city. So here he was, spending election day as a gumshoe.

Charlie walked quickly toward the terminal, a tall and very dark-skinned, clean-shaven man with even features. He spotted his friend standing by the entrance, nervously puffing on a cigarette.

"How are you doing?" he asked, carefully scanning the features of Simon Pettigrew, a short Negro a few years younger than Charlie. Pettigrew was wearing a beard and a colorful African shirt.

"We'll talk in the car," Pettigrew replied. He grabbed Charlie's arm and led him briskly through the terminal.

Once in the car, Pettigrew headed directly toward the Bay Bridge and Oakland. It was not until they were almost there that Pettigrew seemed to relax. "We'll have to get you out of the Brooks Brothers suit," he remarked. "And I wish we could do something quick about your short hair. But if you can keep your mouth shut, maybe you'll pass."

Charlie smiled. He had known Pettigrew since they were kids on the streets of Cleveland's Hough ghetto. They had both made it out, Charlie going into law, while Simon had hooked onto a dozen different civil-rights groups. Simon had fought the good fight in Selma, registered voters in Mississippi, marched with King in Chicago and Abernathy in Washington. As a consequence, Pettigrew had spent about as much time in jail as if he had turned to crime.

He and Charlie had maintained their friendship through all the years, although Charlie suspected that Pettigrew had never quite approved of his playing the establishment game. Charles Jefferson began his career in the Cleveland prosecutor's office, then became United States Attorney for his northern Ohio district, and finally went to the Civil Rights Division at the Justice Department. Now Charlie broke the silence between them.

"Simon, give me a quick rundown on what is going on."

Pettigrew's hands seemed to tighten on the steering wheel. "It's the Black Guards—and Mamba Z. They've got something cooking, that's for sure."

"Mamba is always sounding off, so what's the big deal this time?" Charlie asked.

"Two things, Charlie. One, Oakland is being flooded with guys I never saw before. I figure maybe three thousand, maybe more. All black, all young and all militant as hell. Two, Mamba and his top boys suddenly dropped out of sight the last few days."

Charlie looked sharply at his friend. "Simon, this may all be bad news to a guy like me, but why you? Hell, the militancy and the secret moves, that's been your bag for years. Why tell me?"

Pettigrew stared straight ahead. It was a gut question, and he knew it. "You've got to understand what I've been trying to do, Charlie. I've been out here for over two years, and we've been building something good. I happen to believe that these cats are about to tear it all away."

"But you've always gotten along with the Guards," Charlie persisted.

"That's right. But they've changed. I think they're up to

something very big, and, if it is like what I think it is, I don't want it to happen."

Charlie thought about what he knew of the Black Guards. The Bureau had them down as subversive, or worse, but Charlie had never judged them quite so harshly. They had been just another youth gang, not much different from the Blackstone Rangers in Chicago or hundreds of others in every ghetto in the country—until Mamba Z had risen out of their midst.

Mamba was quite a phenomenon. He had been born and raised in the cozy, middle-class environs of Berkeley, the son of Moses Barnum, a professor of sociology at the University of California's Berkeley campus and one of the country's outstanding Negro leaders. Moses Barnum, Jr., had inherited his father's brilliance as well as his name, and his early life had been favored by every opportunity indulgent parents and a helpful environment could provide.

Then, at the age of seventeen, Barnum had discovered the ghetto, and with it he had discovered his own black heritage, black power, and the writings of Malcolm X. Barnum had started haunting the Oakland ghetto, and eventually he had joined the Black Guards. Three years later Mamba Z had emerged and Moses Barnum, Jr., was no more.

That was five years ago and Mamba was now twenty-five. During those years, he had caught on. A fluent public speaker, Mamba could turn on a crowd, inflame a rally, and, most importantly, lead his people. His message had been increasingly militant, and he had become a national figure and a very useful symbol for every bigot in sight.

Charlie didn't buy Mamba's brand of hell-fire but he could understand the man, as well as his appeal to so many people. The problem seemed to be to produce leaders who could say it like it is—as Mamba often did—and also be able to maneuver with whitey. Too often, the situation that black leaders were thrust into seemed to drive them to extremes and that, in turn, drove the whites to still more fear and hate. Charlie's sympathies were with Mamba and the people who followed him, but he felt that their tactics were self-defeating.

"Tell me about what you've been up to." Charlie asked.

"You know I've been doing the street work for O.I.C.," said Pettigrew.

Charlie nodded. He knew all about Reverend Leon Sullivan's Opportunities Industrial Centers, which had started in an old police station house in Philadelphia and now was finding, training and placing the really hard-core unemployed in almost a hundred cities. Street work was its most difficult phase, involving getting into the nitty gritty of the ghettos, working with the youth gangs, and attempting to guide them into some positive action.

"They trust me," Simon continued. "So they tell me things. There's this one gang, the East Bay Kings. They've managed to stay independent of the Black Guards, though there have been a few skirmishes. Anyway, there's some kind of a pow-wow between them tonight, and they've asked me to come. I want you there with me."

"How do you get me in?"

"I've already fixed that. I told them I've got this old buddy in town from Cleveland, and they said to bring him along."

"You're a damn fool, Simon. Somebody might recognize me."

"If I wasn't convinced that something pretty big was up, I'd agree with you. But I'm willing to chance it if you are."

"Okay, man. Lead away."

It was nine P.M. when they walked into the basement of an old Baptist church located in the Flatlands of Oakland, not far from the Bay. In Oakland, elevation determined your status. The Hills rose dramatically in the background of the city and on their slopes lived the affluent, the successful and the accepted. The Hills were shielded from the sights and sounds of the Flatlands along San Francisco Bay, which were populated by the blacks, the Mexicans, the unwanted, and the unloved. It was as much a ghetto as the teeming squalor of any Eastern metropolis.

The church Simon and Charlie now approached was a decrepit, brick-veneered structure that had seen better days. Its large basement meeting room was filled with folding chairs, and at the front was a long table set on a slightly raised platform. The poorly lit room was already filled with the cigarette smoke from about seventy-five men, all black and all apparently in their late teens or early twenties.

Four young men were seated at the head table and they, in turn, were flanked by two tough-looking giants who stood stoically, with folded arms, carefully eying the crowd. To Charlie, they seemed to give off the same violent impression as Jack Parker's goons. We all paint the same pictures, he thought, only we color ours black.

"All right, everyone come to order," shouted the man seated at the center of the table.

"That's Jimmy Tyler, the president of the Kings," whispered Simon.

The room slowly quieted. "Clinton Jones is with us tonight," Tyler continued. "He's a vice chairman of the Black Guards and he's here on friendly business."

Jones stood up. He was a tall, thin young man, dressed in a multicolored flowing robe and African skull cap. "Are the doors locked?" he asked. "And is everyone here okay?"

Charlie felt a twinge of nervousness, and though he was dressed much like everyone else in the room, he saw several sharp glances directed at him.

"Everyone here is fine," Tyler replied. "You can speak freely."

Jones continued. "First off, I want a solemn pledge from everyone that what he hears tonight goes no further than this room."

"That's understood," Jones replied. "Silence it is." With that Jones held his right arm high, fist clenched. Every man in the room, including Charlie, did likewise.

Jones was apparently satisfied. "We are going to liberate Oakland," he said dramatically. "I have come to ask all of you to join up." Everyone was listening now. "This is not going to be just another march, another rumble, another burning. We mean business. We are going to take over this city, and we are going to hold it."

Charlie shuddered as he realized the seriousness of what he had stumbled into and what would happen if those present ever realized that a Justice Department man was sitting in their midst.

"I can't tell you when or how." Jones was very intense. "But I can tell you that we've got thousands of good men. They are training now. And we've got the firepower to back us up. What I want to know tonight is, Are you with us?"

The room erupted into a bedlam of roaring approval.

After a long while Tyler succeeded in restoring order. The meeting then continued for well over an hour. There were many questions, but at the end there could be no doubt that, almost to a man, those present were ready for action. When the discussion finally ended, Tyler asked that all volunteers stand up and be counted. Not a man refused. Charlie, trapped and somewhat desperate, stood along with the rest.

"I'm proud of you," Jones went on. "Tomorrow night we will meet again, but with many others. Then we shall begin."

Charlie looked at the frenzied faces all around him. It was a frightening experience. Have we come to this? he thought. Is all our work going to end with rage and revolution?

"Tyler will contact you tomorrow afternoon and tell you where we will meet," Jones concluded. Then he stopped, and raising his clenched right fist, he shouted, "Power to the black man!"

"Power!" the audience yelled back.

Over coffee at a restaurant on the outskirts of downtown Oakland, Charlie and Pettigrew compared impressions.

"Now we know, Charlie."

"It sounds damned bad, but I wonder how much is wind and how much is real," Charlie responded.

"If you're up to staying with it for another night, maybe we'll find out."

"All right. We might as well dig our graves a little deeper." Charlie was not at all happy about his prospects but he felt that the information he had was too skimpy to bother the Department with yet. He would wait until tomorrow's meeting to fill in the details.

They sat for a long time, staring at the stark emptiness of the almost-deserted restaurant. Through the dingy windows Charlie and Simon could see small groups of young people loitering around, staring at anyone who walked by, shouting at passing cars. Charlie felt that the whole town was sitting on a bomb with a short fuse.

Simon interrupted his thoughts. "There is one more person I want us to see tonight. Nina Moran."

Charlie was startled into attention. "Where does she fit into all of this?"

Simon's face lighted up. "Only that Nina has been Mamba's girl, and now she isn't. She's an old friend of mine, and I think she'll talk to us."

"I know Nina," Charlie replied in a soft voice.

"You do?" said a surprised Simon. "How is that?"

"She lived in Washington for a while, and I used to see her quite a bit. I always thought she was something special, but she just dropped out of sight a couple of years ago, and I haven't seen her since."

"I guess she just dumped you for Mamba. She must have had a bellyful of that Establishment life of yours," Simon said with a grin.

"It wasn't that way at all. I just liked her, though I wouldn't have minded seeing more of her."

"Well, maybe we shouldn't see her now," Simon said, serious again. "If she knows who you are she might blow the whistle on us."

"I don't think she'd do that, Simon, and she may have a lot to tell us. If she is upset about my being here, she'll tell me to my face. I'm sure of that. No, let's go ahead and risk it."

"It's my neck too, man," Simon said resignedly as they started for the car.

A short time later they drove along the freeway toward neighboring Berkeley. Charlie was exhausted. It was almost two A.M., Washington time, and he had started his day almost twenty hours earlier. His body felt like it was about to collapse, but he guessed he could hold together for a while longer, and the thought of seeing Nina again was exhilarating. In the meantime, Simon had regained much of his own natural exuberance and was chattering away about the Oakland scene. Charlie only half listened.

They turned right and started the climb toward the Berkeley hills, swinging around the university campus and driving for another half mile before they stopped in front of a two-story house, well kept, in a quiet, middle-class neighborhood.

The door was opened by a medium-tall light-skinned girl who appeared to be in her mid-twenties. Her hair was worn in the natural style, short-cropped and curly. She was strikingly attractive, with deep, dark eyes, and a quick, sensitive mouth.

"Charlie Jefferson!" she exclaimed with a broad smile, giving him a quick hug and looking happily up at him. "What in the world brings you all the way out here?"

"I'm just visiting my old friend Pettigrew, and he told me you were in town. I'm happy to see you again, Nina. You're looking just fine."

"You too, Charlie," said Nina, taking his hand and leading him into the sparsely furnished living room. The walls were covered with paintings and posters, mostly dealing with black militancy. The only furniture, except for an ancient table piled high with pamphlets and a manuscript, was a worn sofa and two mismatched easy chairs. Nina sat beside Charlie on the sofa.

"I always said that Washington life agreed with you," she said. Then, clapping her hands together, she jumped to her feet. "It's great to see you guys. What do you say to having a drink to it."

"That would be good," said Pettigrew, who was still standing, looking nervous.

Nina left the room.

"Aren't you going to tell her what you're doing, Charlie?" whispered Pettigrew. "What's all this mickey mouse about just visiting me?"

"Take it easy, Simon," Charlie said with a grin. "We'll get to that, but let's just relax for a little while first."

"I sure hope you know what you're doing."

Nina returned with the drinks. "To old times sake," she said, lifting her glass.

"And a little luck for the future," muttered Simon.

"Sit down, Nina, and tell me what you've been doing with yourself," said Charlie, motioning for her to sit beside him. "To start with, why did you leave Washington without a word to anyone?"

"I couldn't take any more of that mealy-mouthed liberal talk, Charlie," she said. "All that fine talk about integration and civil rights. It just wasn't getting us there fast enough."

"But I thought you believed that was the way?" asked Charlie.

"I was hooked on that dialogue for a long time, that's true. But, finally, I began to see that a lot of it was just white cover talk for delay and for keeping us down indefinitely. Being in Washington was too close to everything that was holding us back. So one day I said to hell with it, and left."

"What brought you to Berkeley?"

"I went back to school. I've been a part-time graduate student here trying to make a little progress toward my doctorate in sociology."

"What about the rest of the time?"

"Well, I've had to earn my keep too. So I've been working on a number of poverty projects in the area, at least those I believe in. That government of yours pays me for it."

"Which ones are you in?" asked Charlie.

"Head Start, mostly, and trying to improve the Flatland schools. Right now they are just awful. They may talk integration here, but all the whites live in the Hills, and they've got their districts gerrymandered so that no blacks can get into any of the good schools. That's especially true in Oakland. Berkeley, at least, is experimenting with integration, but they've got a long way to go too."

"She should tell you that she's also shaking them up on the

Berkeley campus," interjected Simon. "Nina's a leader in the black student movement, and she has really raised a lot of hell with the regents."

"That's true, Charlie," she said. "I guess I've moved a long way from your peaceful, comfortable Washington world."

"I don't object to that, Nina," said Charlie. "We're all trying to do the same thing, only in different ways."

"How is Mamba these days?" Simon asked, finally broaching the subject.

Nina took the question in stride, answering without any hesitation. "You know I don't see him much any more."

"What's the hangup?" Simon continued.

"It's both him and the Black Guards. They've changed, and I guess I've just had enough of that scene too."

"Tell me about Mamba," Charlie asked. "I've never met him, though I've heard him speak a few times."

Nina sat back and seemed to stretch herself, almost catlike. "You should have known him a couple years back," she said. "He was magnificent. All that fire and talent, all that certainty in what he was doing."

She closed her eyes, looking very sad. "But in the last year Mamba's changed. You know, he always did talk wild, but we all knew it was just something that had to be done to keep the people with him, and enthusiastic. And he knew it more than anybody else. But then it changed, and Mamba started believing his own rhetoric. He got so he couldn't laugh at himself at all. Finally, I guess I just got frightened of him and what he had become. So I broke it off."

"What about the Black Guards?" Simon asked.

"They went the same way he did," Nina continued, in her low, soft voice. "All those happy, dedicated kids slowly got replaced by the tough guys, the ones with guns and knives. It got so they would give orders to everyone, and back it up with threats that they would cut you down if you didn't go along. And they weren't bluffing. They would do it, and enjoy it."

"So where does that leave you?" Charlie asked.

"I imagine I will leave town," she said. "Maybe I'll go to

New York. Perhaps I can find the beauty of the movement again and get away from all this violence."

"Is it really that bad?" Simon asked, obviously concerned.

"It's been very difficult, especially the last few weeks. Mamba has sent a couple of his boys around looking for me, checking on me, I guess. Then yesterday he sent a message that he wants to see me about something. I refused, and that sent him through the ceiling. I've had about a dozen phone calls today threatening me in no uncertain terms if I don't go to him. So I think I had better get away from here."

"But what about right now?" Charlie asked. "Are you safe tonight and tomorrow?"

"Oh, I don't think they'll actually do anything to me. After all, I've known them all for a long time, and I've never done them any harm." Her eyes suddenly narrowed, and she turned to look directly at Charlie. "Why all the questions about Mamba and the Black Guards? Does that have something to do with your being out here, Charlie?"

Charlie returned her gaze. Well, here it goes, he thought. "I'm afraid it does, Nina. We've heard some pretty disturbing things in Washington and I've been sent here to check them out."

"What have you heard?"

"Nothing too definite. Only that Mamba is up to no good and might be planning to start some trouble."

Nina continued to stare at him, her face impassive. Then she stood and walked to the table, absently fiddling with some of the papers. No one said a word. Finally she turned to them, leaning back, her hands grasping the table's edge. "I should tell them about you. You know that, don't you," she said in a tight voice.

"That's up to you, Nina," Charlie said, walking up to her. "You do what you think is right."

She stood motionless. "You really know how to put someone on the spot."

"I'm truly sorry to do this to you, but it just can't be helped," Charlie said. "You may not like what they do in Washington, but you know violence isn't the way either."

"I know that, Charlie," she said in a quiet voice. Then, pulling herself upright, she said, "All right. I won't cause you any trouble. I don't want Mamba to break loose any more than you do."

"Can you tell us anything about what he is planning?" Charlie asked.

"I'm sorry," she said. "I've told you that I haven't seen him for a long time, and I don't plan to."

As they left, Charlie asked if he could call her tomorrow, just to see if she were all right. "Suit yourself," she answered. "But I wouldn't get too involved with this if I were you. You could get hurt."

Charlie told her he would take his chances on that, and waved a more cheerful goodbye than he felt.

It was only much later, after they had returned to the Oakland rooming house where Simon lived that Charlie realized that through the whole evening he had not heard one radio broadcast; a new President of the United States probably had been elected, and he didn't even know who it was. He thought that, like Harry Truman, he would just have to read about it in the morning newspapers.

His last thought before falling asleep was that he had not reported to the Attorney General. And he hadn't called Stu Brady either.

CHAPTER THREE

It was almost midnight before the White House staff finally reassembled on the second floor of the Mansion. They had been moved down the hall from the Yellow Oval Room, where they had met that morning, and were now in the West Sitting Room. There, the usually comfortable setting of sofas and easy chairs had been rearranged to make room for extra television sets and a long table replete with adding machines, telephones and three of the President's secretaries.

Stu arrived late, but it was obvious he hadn't missed a thing. The President was sprawled in a corner chair, intently watching all three networks, nervously flicking the sound from one to another so that he could get the full flavor of all the commentary. The others present were also watching closely, not saying a word.

Stu thought that the President looked refreshed and well rested. He had managed his usual afternoon nap, and had just finished a leisurely two-hour dinner with his wife and several old friends from the Hill.

Stu, however, was exhausted from the pressures of the long day, which had not been made easier by his one conversation with Sari. Despite his best intentions, he had not remembered to telephone his wife until after eight P.M., and she had been furious when he told her that it looked like virtually an all-night session.

"When you get home," she had said, in an acid voice, "that is, *if* you get home, don't be upset if I'm not here."

"What's that supposed to mean?"

"Just what it sounds like. I've been invited to a swinging election party. I've decided to go, with or without you."

"Listen, Sari," Stu had pleaded, attempting to placate her, "you know I can't help having to stay here. After all, it's election night, and the President is going to need all the help he can get."

"To hell with the President. To hell with your job. And to hell with you," Sari snapped, hanging up.

The call had badly shaken Stu. It was only with great effort that he was able to pull his mind back to the report he had been trying to write for the President.

He had spent the day attempting to carry out his assigned task of making contact with the camps of both major candidates. As he had expected, the Democrats had been easy. His good friend Sandy Corso had been spending the day in Washington prior to joining Harrington in Providence that evening. Corso, of course, was the natural contact. He was not only the number-one speech writer for Harrington, but, more importantly, the candidate confided in him, and, on occasion, actually listened to him.

Stu had invited Corso to lunch in the staff dining room, located in the White House basement adjoining the Situation Room. It was about the only place Stu could have lunch, unless it was in his own office, where he could munch on the dry and singularly unappetizing sandwiches from the White House vending machines. The President had strong feelings about his staff's being immediately available to him while he was at work, and since his schedule kept him in his West Wing office until time for his own lunch and nap, around two-thirty P.M. or later, this meant that the staff could go nowhere during what passed for the normal lunch hour for the rest of the world.

On rare occasions Stu had taken his courage in hand and accepted an invitation to dine like a human being at one of the restaurants in the vicinity, usually as the guest of a member of the press corps. Part of his job, he always rationalized. And, of course, as luck would have it, there was that one time when he had been wanted by the boss.

He had been enjoying the prospect of a delightful lunch at

the Sans Souci with one of the more sympathetic Washington pundits, who represented a powerful New York newspaper. Stu had just finished the appetizer when the captain came hurrying to his table with the nervously whispered message that the White House was calling him.

It had been the President, and, of course, his first words were to sourly ask what in the hell Stu was doing out at a restaurant. Stu had received a pretty good chewing out, concluding with the order to get his "tail" back to the White House. As a result, Stu had been deprived of a good meal, and the reporter had lost the opportunity to ferret out a juicy nugget or two.

So on this day Stu and Corso sat at one of the small tables along the wall of the staff dining room. Their intense conversation was occasionally interrupted by a wave or a word from other staff members who would stop by to say hello. A rule of the dining room was that only the President's staff and certain others could use it, along with those guests who could be trusted to be discreet as to who was seen or what was heard. Under no circumstances was any member of the press to be invited. In this way, somewhat sensitive luncheons, such as Stu was now having with Corso, could be held with relative impunity.

The two of them had rehashed the campaign at length before Stu finally launched into what was on his mind.

"Sandy, it's our opinion that no one is going to win today," he started.

Corso looked incredulous.

Stu forged ahead. "Look, I'm not trying to get you to concede anything, but we want to know your plans in case of a deadlock." He paused, and then continued rapidly. "This is from the boss. He feels that, as President, he is responsible for holding the country together, and a no-decision contest could be a national disaster if plans are not made. So he's asking for the cooperation of your man, and he's directed me to work through you to get this done." Stu felt he could stretch the truth just a little on this score.

"What about the other candidates?" Corso had asked, somewhat bitterly. "Are we all being tapped by the Almighty?"

Stu couldn't blame his friend. It must hurt to put your soul into a campaign and then, even before the results are in, to be told that your old coach doesn't think you are going to pull it off. But he had no choice but to bull his way forward.

"I'm to make contact with the Republicans, but not with Parker," he said.

"Well, thanks for little favors. At least you haven't thrown us completely into the dirt." Corso had made no attempt to hide his feelings.

The dining room was almost empty by then, and the Filipino waiters, all regular navy men, were hovering in the background, waiting for the two of them to leave so that they could take off for the rest of the day. But Stu had taken his time in answering.

"I know how you feel, Sandy, but it's nothing personal. Nobody can say that all of us, from the President on down, didn't do everything possible for the senator. But the time has come to face reality. You've just got to understand that the boss is completely behind Harrington, and always has been, but besides being a good Democrat he is also President, and he is now forced to think in those terms."

"Okay, Stu, exactly what is it you want me to do?" Corso asked, still not mollified.

"When you see Harrington, tell him how we look at things. Tell him the President is praying that he wins tonight, for Jimmy's sake and for the country's. But tell him that we need to work with him, and closely, if it doesn't come out that way."

"All right, I'll do that. What else?"

"Just two things. Call me early tonight and give me his thinking, and set yourself up to work closely with me from now on."

Corso finally allowed himself a thin smile, and seemed to relax a little. "Okay, buddy, I guess you're the best of the lot. If I've got to talk to one of you ghouls, it might as well be a nitwit Irishman. When do I report in, your eminence?"

"I'll be here late, but I've got to write it up early for night reading. So I'd be grateful if you'd call before seven."

3 3

"Why I'm doing you favors, I'll never know, but I'll do it. And if you don't mind, I'll also call you around midnight with our victory statement."

The lunch had ended amicably enough, although Stu felt that his harsh predictions would not fade quickly from Sandy's mind, even if—and especially if—they proved to be accurate. There are costs and costs to this job, he had thought.

Not until late in the afternoon was Stu able to reach his Republican contact. He had really struggled deciding who it ought to be. By midmorning his secretary, Mary O'Brien, had conjured up a complete list of Governor Nelson's top campaign staff, along with brief biographies on each of them. He thanked her, wondering, as he often did, what an exquisite creature like Mary was doing working day and night in this prison. She had been in the press office even before Stu had come on board, brought to Washington from her Boston home by John Kelly, for whom she had worked since college. When Kelly had joined the White House staff, he had talked Sam Baker into hiring her, and no one had ever regretted the choice. Although she was only twenty-six, she was a wonder. She handled the front desk, which meant she was the first line of defense against the charged-up demands of the gentlemen of the White House press corps. But she never complained, and she was always willing to work late and to go anywhere at any time, as this crazy job often required. This morning, as usual, she had been quick to sense Stu's needs.

"I'd call Jerry Greenberg," she suggested, as she dropped the list on his desk. Greenberg was Governor Nelson's press secretary, and reputedly an able man.

"I barely know him," Stu replied.

"Well, I've known Jerry for a long time and I can tell you he can be trusted," Mary persisted. "Anyway, that's my two cents' worth of bright thought for the day." She smiled broadly, executed a slight curtsy, and softly shut the door as she left.

Stu had thought about the problem all morning, poring over each of the names, looking for someone to whom he could relate and who also had the trust of the candidate. Finally, almost in desperation, he decided that maybe Mary was right, and since he had no better idea, he would go with that.

Greenberg had not been easy to track down, and without the persistence of the White House telephone operators, he would have been impossible to reach. The press secretary had been playing golf at a club just outside of Philadelphia, close to Governor Nelson's Main Line home. He had given strict orders that he was out to everyone but the governor. However, the operators, by alternately using the White House name and other forms of quiet persuasion, had tracked him to the club and then persuaded the club pro to send out a cart and caddy with the message that the White House was urgently calling. The operators had duly reported their progress to Stu, who, with each succeeding step, had inwardly groaned as he realized that a difficult conversation was not about to be made any easier. But he had no choice. He had to speak to Greenberg.

Surprisingly enough, Greenberg had been in good humor when he finally called in around four P.M. "I imagine you're just putting your job application in early," he said. "Well, we have openings, but I'm afraid we would have to insist on some valid past experience, which probably lets you out."

Stu laughed. "To tell you the truth, after a few years in a soft spot like this it is difficult to contemplate a career with regular hours, weekends off, two-hour lunches and a drink or two now and then. I'm not sure I could take that kind of grind after being so spoiled around here."

"That's just what I thought. You tired old men do need a rest. So what else is new?" Greenberg asked.

Stu quickly came to the point. "Are you where you can talk freely?"

"I guess a phone booth in the men's locker room is about as secure as any place else," Greenberg replied.

Stu never particularly liked to use the telephone for anything difficult. He much preferred facing his man, and had learned through hard experience that it usually went much better that way. But there were times, such as now, when he had no choice but to use the instrument at hand.

"Jerry, I'd appreciate your keeping this conversation in the strictest confidence," Stu said.

"Of course, if that's what you want."

"Thank you." Stu took a deep breath and stood up, as he always did while on a tough telephone call. "The President has asked me to call. We are deeply concerned about an electoral deadlock tonight and what that might do to the country's stability. If the election does go that way, we want to work with both major candidates. We think that some type of cooperation will be essential."

There was a long silence on the other end of the line. "I'm not quite clear about what you're asking," Greenberg finally said. "You know we're vitally interested in the country's stability, but we are also interested in changing the country's direction. I'm not trying to give you a campaign speech, Brady, but it seems to me that if what you predict does happen, the campaign still continues, only the forum is changed from the people to the electors or to the House of Representatives."

"That's true," Stu replied. "And we're not asking you to stop your campaign. What we do ask is that, consistent with your own interests, you work with us as best you can."

"What do you propose to do about Parker?" Greenberg asked.

"Our third-party friend is one of the gut reasons why we think that some quiet cooperation between the major parties is imperative," Stu said. "Look, Jerry. All we are asking is that you and I establish some kind of liaison on this, and that you tell the governor our thinking and give me his reaction."

"I'd be less than candid if I didn't tell you that I've got some doubts about the wisdom of all this," Greenberg said. "But I will take it up with the governor, and I will get back to you as soon as I can."

"Fair enough, Jerry, now go back and break seventy on that fat cat golf course."

"There's no chance of that now. Your call has made me a working man again, which is typical Democratic hanky-panky. Believe me, when we get in, the first change will be to allow

3 6

exhausted staff people their little pleasures without interruption."

"I'll drink to that," Stu said as he hung up.

Stu felt he had done the best he could in establishing contacts. Corso, although somewhat disgruntled with Stu, had called back early with the report that he had passed the message to Harrington, who had taken it well enough but had no plans and was awaiting election or defeat tonight. Corso also said that he was now authorized to work with the White House in case of a deadlock. Stu had been satisfied enough with that.

Greenberg had never called back. Although Stu would have preferred some kind of report, this was not really surprising. It was an arm's length situation, to say the least, and Stu was content that he had at least made contact. In any event, he had dutifully put it all in his contribution to the President's night reading, on this occasion having no difficulty in keeping the memo down to the preferred one-page length.

Now, as he and the others sat in the Mansion, Stu's thoughts were interrupted by the President, who suddenly bounded to his feet and slammed his fist on the table. "That did it," the President said in a hard, tight voice. "There goes Pennsylvania. We're in for it now."

Brinkley on NBC then announced that their election desk predicted that California would also go to Governor Nelson, and within five minutes the other two networks did likewise.

"If the South all goes to Parker, that will put him up to a hundred and twenty-two electoral votes," the President said. "That will be enough to block both of the other candidates."

Stu knew that this was so. Although California and the other Western states had not yet swung decisively, it just didn't appear likely that Harrington could pull it off. Every poll had shown Harrington losing in the West, with the exception of Washington, Oregon and Hawaii, and these states were not enough, with only nineteen electoral votes among them.

As of the moment, Harrington had won most of the Northeast, with the notable exception of Nelson's home state of Pennsylvania, and he had also won the industrial Midwest of Ohio, Michigan and Illinois. However, it took 270 electoral votes to win, and if Parker carried the entire South, plus the border states of Kentucky and Maryland, there weren't enough votes left to give victory to anyone. Nelson was piling up all of the small Western states, but with the exception of California, with forty votes, and Pennsylvania, which had twenty-nine, the largest state in Nelson's whole bag was Indiana, with only thirteen votes.

The President returned to his chair and closed his eyes for a long time. His face seemed to sag and, for the first time all day, he looked tired. After a long while he sighed deeply and reached for the little electronic box, turning the sound down on the TV sets, with only the pictures to be seen.

"All right, let's go to work," the President said, in a voice once again purposeful. "Brozman, you were supposed to get the law together on what happens now. Give it to us, only I want it in language we can all understand, and keep it short. I can read the details in your report."

The President's Special Counsel was obviously eager to begin, and he stood up quickly, holding a few notes and a copy of a lengthy memo.

"As you know, Mr. President," Brozman began, "the Constitution provides for five hundred thirty-eight electoral votes, and a candidate must have an absolute majority of two hundred seventy in order to win. Each state elects its own slate of electors, on a winner-take-all basis, and the number of each state's electors equals the total number of its congressmen and senators. The District of Columbia is special, and has three electoral votes."

The President nodded impatiently and as he gestured, Brozman continued. "The first Tuesday after the first Monday in November, today, is election day for the electors in every state, and the first Monday after the second Wednesday in December, this year December sixteenth, is fixed as the date the electors vote for President and Vice-President. If someone receives a majority of their votes, then he will be President. If not, the election goes to the House of Representatives."

Alvin Morgan broke in with a question. "Are the electors bound to vote for their party's candidate?"

Brozman smiled as he warmed to his role as the Constitutional lawyer. "Alvin, that is a point of law which has never been clearly decided. There are some states, such as Oklahoma, that have made it a criminal offense if an elector doesn't vote for his party's candidate, and, in one way or another, the electors are usually pledged to support their party. But, in my mind, if an elector is determined to vote some other way, no court could stop him. He might be punished later, or ostracized by his party, but his vote would have to be counted exactly as he cast it. You see, the Constitution provides that these men vote by ballot, and the founding fathers made it quite clear that they were intended to be independent selectors of the President. So, in my judgment, they are free to vote their will."

The President leaned forward, quite alert to Brozman's last statement. "Mark, does that mean that anybody is free to negotiate with them?"

"Yes, sir," answered Brozman. "Any legitimate attempt can be made to persuade them to jump the traces."

The President turned to Morgan. "Alvin, you were supposed to check out the electors. What can you tell me about them?"

Morgan was slouched in a deep cushioned chair close to the President. He answered without standing, and in a soft drawl that was difficult for the others to hear. "Well, sir, they aren't the leading men of wisdom the founding fathers intended. They sure aren't that. Mostly, they are party hacks. Nobody pays much attention to them. Their names usually aren't even on the ballot. So the state party leaders normally give the honor to long-time party workers as a token of appreciation for loyal service."

Brozman broke in. "It's not even much of a token. The Constitution requires that each state's electors meet separately in their respective state capitals and mail their vote to the President of the Senate. So they don't even get a free trip to Washington for their efforts."

"Alvin," the President continued, "what does it mean in practical political terms?"

"I would say two things, Mr. President. First, as loyal party people they will be strongly motivated to vote for no one but their party's candidate. Second, the best way to get them to change, if there is to be any chance of that, will be through the regular party organization in their states."

"But what about Parker's electors? They aren't from an organized party in any traditional sense."

"That's true, Mr. President," Morgan continued. "And for them, it is an entirely different story. I would guess that they will be much more amenable to the wishes of their man, Parker, but they will also be much more vulnerable than regular party people to being picked off one by one."

"What's your best guess on what Parker's move will be?" the President continued, still looking at Morgan.

"Well, sir, Parker will have much more power to persuade his own electors than the members of the House of Representatives. Therefore, his maximum bargaining position should be prior to the December sixteenth voting of the electors. I would guess that Parker will make his move before that time. He could set his price and go shopping between the two other candidates. Or, he could throw his votes to one or the other without a deal and spend the next four years claiming that he elected the President. Of course, this presupposes that he will want to elect one of the others. He may not. He could decide to stay in it himself to the end."

The President turned back to Brozman. "All right, Mark, give me a quick rundown of what happens if the electors don't cast a majority for anybody."

"Then the new House would attempt to elect a President," answered Brozman. "They convene on January third and on January sixth start their balloting. The representatives vote by state, with each state casting only one vote, based on a majority of its House delegation. It's on a winner-take-all basis, and in case of a tie in the delegation, the state can't vote."

"Can they vote for anyone they wish?" Stu interjected.

"No," said Brozman. "They are required to choose among the top three electoral vote-getters. If no one can get a majority of the states, the House has until noon on January twentieth to resolve the deadlock. If they can't, then the Vice-President becomes Acting President until someone is able to get twenty-six state votes in the House. So, in any case, we would have someone to lead us."

"That is, if the country isn't so shattered after all those goings-on that there is nothing left worth leading," the President muttered.

The President then turned to John Kelly, his chief congressional liaison man. "What is the situation in the House?" the President asked.

Kelly, who had been talking intently on the telephone, ended his conversation and turned toward the President. His usual sardonic smile had been replaced by a look of complete concentration. "I've been trying to get a line on it, Mr. President, but it's a little too early. Everyone's attention has been so fixed on the big race that the House figures are slow coming in. All I can say at the moment is that it looks as if there is going to be little change across party lines in the House, but that's just an educated guess. I ought to have something more solid in an hour or so."

"Hurry it as quickly as you can. I need that information," the President said. "In the meantime, tell me what those Southern delegations will do if this election does go into the House."

Kelly paused and carefully phrased his answer. "That will be the whole game, Mr. President. In my judgment, the Southern and border boys will have all the leverage. They can deadlock the House, or throw it to either Harrington or Nelson. But they aren't going to feel completely free. No matter what their own party affiliation is, their states will have gone for Parker, so they are going to be very careful before voting against the will of the people who elect them. Also, most of them are conservatives, and they may have personal as well as political qualms about going for an all-out liberal like Harrington. On the other hand, they are Democrats, and many have chairmanships and other marks of seniority in the hierarchy of the House. I guess what I'm saying is that it is going to be a very complicated little game that will have to be played."

"Do you think we will be able to do business with them?" the President asked.

"Yes, sir, I think that we can. Of course, different members are going to react in different ways, but I'm sure that most of them will negotiate, either individually or in blocs."

"What about Parker?" asked the President.

"He will be in there pitching, no doubt about that, but it seems to me that his personal punch in the House will be nothing like what he has with the electors. After all, most of the House members are pros, and pretty well entrenched in their own right."

The President nodded briefly and turned his attention back to the election results. It was now well past one A.M. and the networks were reporting that California's forty votes had definitely gone to Nelson. It had, by this time, become clear to every commentator that the election would not be decided until the Electoral College met on December 16, and, if the electors voted as pledged, the President of the United States, for the first time since 1824, would be elected by the House of Representatives.

"I'm going to bed," the President said. "I'd suggest that all of you do likewise." He started for the bedroom, and then continued. "I'm sorry to do this, but I think we'd better meet here again at eight in the morning. We aren't going to have much time, and I'm afraid we are in for a good deal of trouble." He nodded to all of them and left.

The television sets were immediately turned off, and the staff quickly departed, hoping to get as much sleep as possible.

Stu ordered a White House car to take him home, too exhausted to drive himself. He wondered if Sari would be home and decided that she probably would not. He felt depressed, and he wasn't at all certain he was up to facing what the months ahead would bring, either in his personal life or on the political front.

CHAPTER FOUR

Charlie Jefferson awoke in his Oakland room feeling almost rested. The sunlight was streaming through the windows, and he could see that it was going to be one of those clear, splendid days that are unique to northern California. But it was the thought of Nina Moran that really affected Charlie's mood. He had always been too busy to slow down or feel lonely, but now he felt strangely delighted to meet this girl again.

He and Pettigrew were to leave in about an hour, but first he had to report in to his office in Washington. He dressed, waved a happy hello to the landlady, and walked briskly down the street. He spotted a street-corner pay phone, safer than his rooming house, and placed the collect call to Washington.

In a few moments the Attorney General came on the line. "Where in the hell have you been, Charlie?"

"I'm sorry, chief, but I've been running from the time I got here. It was after four A.M. your time before I could have called."

"Okay. What's up?"

"I think I'm on to something, but I can't tell you how real it is. I attended a meeting last night, incognito of course. The Black Guards were trying to recruit for some kind of action they're planning for Oakland. I heard that they have been pulling together a large group, maybe running into the thousands, and they're militant as hell."

"Have you any idea what it is they are going to do?"

"I'm going to another meeting tonight, and I hope to be able to piece it together after that," Charlie replied.

The Attorney General paused. "Don't take any unnecessary chances, Charlie. I don't want what you're doing to get out, and I surely don't want you to get hurt."

"I think I'm safe enough. Tell me what happened in the election?" Charlie asked.

"It's a deadlock. It looks like it will go to the House."

"Christ, that's terrible."

"The President has already been on TV this morning telling us all to cool it because the country has a system for resolving the deadlock. He said that he is still President and will be in complete charge until January twentieth."

"What are the candidates doing?" Charlie asked.

"Harrington and Nelson haven't said anything yet. But Parker is saying plenty. He promised—maybe threatened is more like it—that he is going to take a careful look at both candidates before he decides anything. He said that he considers the election a vindication of himself and his policies, namely that the country is sick and tired of pandering to the Negroes."

Charlie said nothing, thinking of what all of this would mean to the country. Parker was going to cause trouble, that was clear, and if he sounded off enough, there was apt to be a reaction from the blacks. Also, no decision on the Presidency and having to go through all the Electoral College drivel was bound to make everyone nervous.

"It's going to be very tough," he said aloud. "And it will be open season for every rabble-rouser in sight."

"I'm afraid you're right," said the Attorney General. "Just make sure you report back to me as soon as possible."

"I'll call you tonight or tomorrow."

Charlie dug out another dime and called Nina.

"Simon and I are going to spend the day touring the East Bay area," he said. "I'd sure like you to join us if you can."

"I'd be delighted to, Charlie. When do we start?"

"We'll be by in about an hour, and I want you to be ready to show me what it's really like out here," he said with a laugh.

"Listen, my friend," she answered softly, "when I'm done with you you'll never be the same."

44

It was mid-morning by the time Charlie and Pettigrew picked Nina up. She was waiting for them, and Charlie thought she looked lovely dressed in a fashionable pants suit with a silken white scarf tied around her hair. She gave him a quick, gay kiss and ran to the car.

"I'm the tour guide today," she said to Simon.

"My mom always said that her boy was meant to be a chauffeur."

They spent several hours touring Oakland and Richmond. Nina pointed out the new job training center and other anti-poverty facilities that had appeared during the past several years. She also showed Charlie the marks of the desperate poverty in the East Bay area, the broken-down, half-empty blocks of stores and apartments, the scores of aimless men standing around, the black areas of Richmond, almost encircled by railroad embankments and factories.

As they drove, Nina spoke of the recent history of the East Bay area. She explained that before World War II few blacks or Mexicans had lived in Oakland, but the industrial boom of that conflict had resulted in massive migration to the area from the South. Unfortunately, the migration, once started, could not be turned off. At the war's end, however, the jobs began to vanish. The industries moved to the suburbs, where blacks could not follow because of housing restrictions. Then, with automation, the demand was for highly skilled workers to fill a smaller number of jobs for which the untrained migrants could not hope to qualify.

"There's real bitterness around here," Nina explained when they stopped for lunch in Oakland.

"Is it any more than anywhere else?" Charlie asked.

"I would say yes. First of all, there's all that migration local industry promoted. The people who came here expected so much. They were led on by all those promises of jobs. Then when they got here they found that Oakland is almost like a Southern town in its attitude toward blacks. The whites here ignored the problems even more than in most Northern cities."

"But the blacks can vote here, can't they? They can generate much greater political pressure than in the South."

"That's easier said than done. The city council and school board have developed a neat little system here. Nobody serves out their full term when they plan to leave office. They simply resign before the nominations and election. Then, the remaining office holders fill the vacancy themselves by appointing one of their friends. When the election comes, the new man runs as an incumbent. That way, they manage to perpetuate themselves in office."

"I still say Negroes could organize and be heard," said Charlie.

"Well, we are trying, but there are plenty of problems. Except for Mamba there aren't any real black leaders around here, and he doesn't believe there's any point in going the straight political route. For instance, the new-left group from Berkeley had tried to form an alliance with him, but he'll have nothing to do with any white organization."

"Is it really all that grim?" asked Charlie.

"I'm telling you this place is seething. Even the statistics the whites put out show that twenty percent of all blacks are unemployed. It's even worse with the young men. With them the unemployment rate is seventy-five percent. Those are official figures. I think it's actually much worse than that. And, believe me, it means trouble."

"What about the job programs?"

"They are fine as far as they go. But there aren't enough of them around. And then when the men finish their training, they can't find work anyhow. They are taught skills, right? But when they look for jobs, the unions say 'No, sir, no blacks are going to work with us.' So the employers knuckle under, and the black man—what does he think? He says, 'To hell with it. Why go through all that schooling just to find myself squeezed off at the end of the line.' "

"It was like this in Cleveland, and I managed to get out," said Charlie.

"Charlie, you know you're the exception. Most black kids

46

are just trapped. The elementary schools are so bad that by the time the children get to high school they simply can't keep up. They quit, out of frustration. After that the boys can't find jobs and get into trouble."

"I know all that," said Charlie. "But we've got to keep trying to improve it. And I think we are moving forward."

"But it's taking too long, Charlie, and, around here, I'm not at all sure we've got that kind of time."

It was late afternoon when they returned to Nina's home. Simon waited in the car while Charlie took her to the door.

"I want to see you again," Charlie said.

Nina looked at him for a long time before answering. "I enjoyed it, Charlie," she finally said. "But we're in different worlds now, even though we're both black. I'm not sure we would fit."

"I am," he said.

"I'll think about it," she said, smiling and kissing his cheek. Then she turned and entered the house.

In the late afternoon Pettigrew called Jimmy Tyler, the leader of the East Bay Kings, whose meeting he and Charlie had attended the previous night. Tyler gave them directions to the place they were expected to assemble. He also told them not to come unless they were prepared to stay out of sight for quite a while. This came as something of a shock to Charlie, but he decided he had come too far to back off now, especially since he felt he needed more information before he could make a report to Washington.

Shortly after eight P.M. they arrived at the warehouse Tyler had described to them. There were several Black Guards standing at the entrance, and Charlie could see that security was tight. However, Tyler passed both of them through. They were given colored plastic identification cards and were told to wear them at all times.

Inside, the warehouse was swarming with activity. Over five hundred men had grouped themselves under large signs designating various teams, and Charlie and Pettigrew were directed to sit with the Kings. A platform had been set up at the front,

47

and behind it hung several large maps of the Oakland area. On either side of the platform were two flags of a dramatic black-and-red design that Charlie did not recognize.

A few minutes later ten men walked onto the platform. They wore black boots, combat fatigues, khaki shirts, and red-and-black arm bands like the flags. Clinton Jones, who Charlie recognized as Mamba's representative from the previous night, stepped forward to start the meeting.

"Every one of you is a volunteer," Jones said. "By coming here tonight you have become a part of a great movement, and you have put yourselves in the hands of a great leader. He is here to give you the word. Mamba!"

The room erupted. "Mamba! Mamba! Mamba!" reverberated through the hall.

The young man who was the object of the excitement slowly rose, walked forward, and stood in the center of the platform, alone, with both fists held high. Everyone in the huge room was on his feet, shouting and clapping, frenzied.

Charlie had seen photographs of Mamba, and once, several years before, he had been at the back of a Howard University auditorium where Mamba was speaking. This was the first time he had seen the black leader at close range.

Mamba was dressed like the others, except that he wore a red silk scarf around his neck. He had grown a beard since Charlie had last seen him and though he was not a large man, he looked well put together, and fit.

"We welcome you to the cause," Mamba began, in a low, melodious voice.

"We're with you!" someone shouted.

Mamba nodded, and continued. "Last night the country showed us what a real mess it is in. Whitey couldn't even elect himself a President!"

"That's right—that's the truth!"

"Let me tell you how it is. They got this idiot Harrington. They got this namby-pamby Nelson. And they got this son of a bitch Parker. Do you want any of them shoved down your throats?"

"No! No!" roared the crowd.

"Let me tell you something else. Over eleven million honkies voted for that racist bastard Parker. That's right, and he just might be President. And if that happens, a black man's life won't be worth shit in this country."

The room had become quiet, everyone intent on Mamba's every word.

"We are not going to take it lying down. We are men—brave, beautiful black men—and we are going to stand up and fight like men." Mamba paused dramatically. "Will you be men?" he demanded.

The room erupted, every man on his feet, shouting out his approval.

"You are men of destiny. You are the point of the spear." Mamba continued, slowly scanning the crowd. "We are done taking the white man's crumbs. We are done licking his boots. We are done doing his dirty work. We are done running his cities. We will not bow our heads again."

Charlie looked at the faces all around him. They were enraptured, completely entranced.

"This day begins your work for a great cause, for the freedom of black men everywhere," Mamba shouted. "We are here to make Oakland the black man's city. It belongs to us, and we will take it. We will take it with our hearts, with our souls, with our blood, and, if we must, with our lives! We do this so that our people can live. And be free. And walk in the sun as God intended us."

Mamba raised both of his fists, tightly clenched, and every man in the room was again on his feet, cheering and chanting "Mamba! Mamba! Mamba!" Mamba stood for almost five minutes, utterly still, not saying a word, merely standing and acknowledging the tribute. Then, abruptly, he turned and walked off the platform.

Despite himself, Charlie was deeply moved by Mamba's performance. He could feel the pull that Mamba's powerful presence exerted. Now, Charlie's deeply engrained pride in his own race and the bitterness that, always, was not far below the surface of his consciousness combined to the point where, at the end, and before he knew what he was doing, he found himself on his feet, cheering along with the rest. Only by an act of will was he able to bring himself back to the realization of who he was and why he was there.

Clinton Jones had stepped forward once more, attempting to bring the room to order. Finally, he was able to speak. "Now we must go to work!" he shouted. "Each of you has been assigned to a team. Each team has a mission which will be given to you. You will be trained for it and armed for it, but to succeed you must give your body and mind to your team leader. Are you prepared to make that sacrifice? Are you ready?"

The room again rang with approval.

Pettigrew turned to Charlie with a woeful, almost despairing look. It was obvious that they had come too far, gone into this too deeply—and that now they were trapped. Charlie gave a slight nod to Pettigrew, trying to reassure him, but he himself was not at all certain about what they should do. For the moment they had no choice but to go along with the action and hope for a way out.

The large meeting recessed, and each of the teams was directed to meet separately in various parts of the building. Tyler's group of fifty or so men met in a basement room filled with old crates and lined with pipes and wiring overhead. A single bare bulb swinging from the ceiling provided the only light.

"Our target is the Bay Bridge," Tyler said, after they had assembled. "Our mission is to block the approaches to it at this end of the Bay."

All the men murmured approvingly. Charlie saw that they appeared eager, but also very young. He wondered how Mamba hoped to pull anything off without a highly trained group, but, obviously, he was prepared to try.

Tyler continued with the briefing. "When we leave here tonight we will stay together, but in smaller groups. You will be living together in houses we've arranged for that purpose, and during the day you will be told where you are to be trained. We

50

won't be separated until the job is done. Is that understood?" Everyone nodded.

They were given more detail, mostly dealing with the geography of the bridge approaches, and the importance of the bridge as a key transportation and communication link. However, there was no conversation about the dates planned for the mission, or how the action at the bridge was meant to fit into the larger plan. Charlie did not dare ask any questions.

They filed out of the basement. Charlie noticed two of the burly guards standing by the door. He felt a moment of panic and turned to Pettigrew, intending to make a comment, but before he had a chance to do anything, the guards moved quickly toward them and blocked their passage. "You two will come with us," one of them said. Charlie started to reply but then thought better of it, and followed.

They were led up the stairs to the main floor and into a small room behind the platform. They were told to wait, and were locked in. After only a few minutes the door burst open and Nina Moran was roughly shoved inside. Mamba and the two guards followed her in.

"We know who you are," Mamba said without emotion. "And we know why you're here."

Charlie stared at Nina, who was standing impassively against the wall. She told, he thought.

"Don't look at your friend so accusingly," Mamba said with a tight smile. "We just picked her up and she hasn't had a chance to say a thing. Not yet, anyway." He walked over to her and, his smile still fixed, slapped her twice across the face. Nina did not utter a sound.

"We know you've been with him," Mamba said. "We've been following the three of you around all day. You've joined them, haven't you? Well, I'll tell you one thing, bitch. You and your friends are not going to screw this up. Do you understand that?" Mamba's voice rose in anger.

"You're out of your mind," Nina said, her voice surprisingly calm. "These are old friends of mine and that's all. I haven't done

5 1

a thing to bother your crazy schemes. How could I when I didn't know a damn thing anyway?"

"Don't give me any of that crap," said Mamba. "It won't do you any good now."

Mamba turned to Charlie. "We know your name is Charles Jefferson. You are employed in the Civil Rights Division of the Department of Justice. Now that's accurate, isn't it?"

"Why do you think that?" asked Charlie, stalling for time.

"Look, Jefferson," Mamba said. "We're not stupid. You were recognized almost as soon as you walked into town. A black man like you, so heavily in the pay of the white establishment, has a lot of notoriety among our people. You're famous, my friend, and you underrate your own visibility."

Charlie could see that there was no point now in denying his identity. As a matter of fact, his best bet probably lay in the power of his position.

"Okay, Mamba—although I won't agree that I'm spying on you. It's more like trying to keep the country in one piece."

"You're a fool, Jefferson, but at least you have the sense not to continue this charade. The problem now, however, is what we should do with you."

"What about Nina and Pettigrew?" Charlie asked, thinking that his friends were probably in even greater danger than himself. He could see Mamba's rage against Nina. And Pettigrew, being local and the instrument of his own infiltration, would undoubtedly be the object of Mamba's wrath. To make matters worse, neither Nina nor Pettigrew had the cloak of official Washington, which Charlie believed would, in the end, save his own skin.

"These two are our business," Mamba replied. "You better think of yourself instead of worrying about these Uncle Toms."

"I don't want them hurt," Charlie said in a tone far more authoritative than he felt. "I think you will want some cooperation from me, Mamba, and if you are going to get it, I'll want your assurance that they will be all right."

Mamba laughed heartily. "At least you've got balls, Jeffer-

5 2

son, I'll give you that. But you've got no bargaining power. We can cut you down, or not, as we see fit. But because it suits *me*, for the moment, at least, I'll postpone the treatment your friends so richly deserve."

Mamba looked at Pettigrew, who seemed very frightened, and then motioned the guards to take him and Nina from the room. He then waved everyone out. "Mr. Jefferson and I want to be by ourselves for a few minutes."

"Sit down, Jefferson, and let's talk," Mamba said after they were alone. "You can start by telling me exactly why you decided to come all the way to the West Coast to pay us a visit."

"We want to stop you from performing a tragic act," Charlie said.

"What's so tragic about demanding freedom?" Mamba shot back.

"You are going to lead all of these people to death and imprisonment and you know it," Charlie replied. "You can't take over Oakland, and if you do succeed in some momentary tactical surprise, you can't hold it. The authorities will crush you and everyone else who is with you."

"Perhaps, but maybe not. If we do our work well, in order to crush us, they would have to mount a major military action against an American city, and I'm not at all certain even your government will want to do that."

"They will have to do it, Mamba. The government can't allow you to succeed. No administration could survive politically if it did. They won't like to use force against you, but you can bet that they'll use whatever is necessary to get you out."

"That remains to be seen, but even if we're destroyed we will have made our point, and the whole world will know it."

Charlie saw that Mamba could not be reached, at least not on this level.

"I haven't time to waste on philosophy, Jefferson. I want to know how much you know of our plans, and what your people intend to do."

"They know enough to stop you long before you start,"

53

Charlie said, hoping to bluff his way through. "My presence should convince you of that. My job is simply to persuade you to stop before force becomes necessary."

Mamba stared at him for a moment, and then rose. "You may be telling the truth, and maybe not. Still, I think I'll continue to play this hand with the cards I've got."

"What do you mean by that?"

"Merely that I'm forced to keep you with us for a while, and then we'll see what happens." Mamba banged on the door, which promptly opened. "Perhaps we can continue our discussion at another time. In the meantime you'll be staying right here," he said, as he left the room.

Charlie could hardly believe his own stupidity. No one knew where he was, and it would be at least another day before the Attorney General would react to not having heard from him. Then, he would start some kind of search, which meant telling the F.B.I. director about what Charlie had been attempting to do. That disclosure would produce an explosion that doubtless would be heard all the way down Pennsylvania Avenue. In any event, Charlie wasn't at all sure how much the Bureau knew of what was going on. They probably had heard some generalized rumors, but they might or might not know any of the details. Letting his head sink to his arms, Charlie realized he was definitely not cut out for undercover work. This job he had totally botched, but good.

CHAPTER FIVE

The election had been over for two days, and Senator Jack Parker's feeling of well-being had improved with each passing hour. He was relaxing in his well-guarded suite at the Americana Hotel just north of Miami Beach.

"Janice, be a good girl and pour me a bourbon and water," he said to the tall, attractive young woman who was his private secretary. "And do the same for Billy Dan and Millard," he continued, indicating the two men sitting on the couch in the spacious living room. One of the men, Billy Dan Reeves, was Parker's campaign director. He was a florid-faced giant of a man, who appeared to be in his early fifties but was actually almost ten years younger. The other man, Millard Duval, was Parker's administrative assistant. Duval was in his late thirties, of medium height and quite thin, with quick, darting eyes set in a long, rather sad-looking face.

It was now one in the afternoon and the four of them had been working since mid-morning. Billy Dan and Millard had been on the telephones, continuing what they had been doing since election night, when it had become apparent that Parker held the balance of power in the Electoral College. They had personally spoken with each of the 122 electors pledged to Parker, rapidly dictating their impressions to Janice following each conversation. Parker, although he had not spoken to the electors himself, had been following the procedure with avid interest, now and then giving suggestions to his two assistants.

They had just completed the last call, and Janice Pruitt,

svelte and unhurried as always, moved to the well-appointed bar, mixing the drinks. She had been with Parker since shortly after he had come to the Senate almost two years earlier, and her long, brunette hair and smoldering features, together with her long-legged, large-breasted figure, belied her remarkable efficiency and quick intelligence, which had been so valuable to Parker in his rapid rise to national prominence since leaving the governorship of Florida.

"All right, Billy Dan, tell me how we're doing?" asked Parker after they had their drinks.

"It looks good. Every elector has given us a pledge. They'll do whatever you say."

"How solid are they?" Parker shot back.

"I think we can count on them. They all sounded firm as hell."

"Well, I'm not that confident," Millard Duval broke in. "I think we've got to do more."

"What would you suggest?" drawled Billy Dan, somewhat defensively.

"For one thing we have got to keep the pressure on. We can't afford to play games. We should get to the people who appointed each elector, and get all the muscle on them that we can possibly manage."

"I'll buy that," Parker said. "You get the boys working on it. What else do you suggest?"

"I think that in the next couple weeks we should call all of our electors together. Have a big public meeting and open it to the press and television."

"I don't know about that," said Parker.

"Why do we want to give those bastard reporters a field day with our people?" asked Billy Dan.

"There are a number of benefits," explained Duval patiently. "The very fact that the press will play it big will be good for us. The coverage will make the public completely aware of us and of our power, and that ought to drive the point home to both Harrington and Nelson. As I see it, a meeting would increase our bargaining position with both of them. Also, the meeting will

56

give the senator an excellent forum to speak to the entire nation. Finally, out of that meeting should come a public pledge by each of the electors. After that, it would be next to impossible for any of them to defect."

"I always said you were a bright boy," said Parker. "You go ahead and start turning the screws but let me think some on whether we want to have a public pow-wow. Billy Dan, you go with him to help get things started." As they stood sipping their drinks, he added, "You might as well begin now."

The two men put down their glasses, hardly touched, and left the suite. They nodded to the secret service agents, state troopers and Dade County detectives who were standing in the hallway guarding the suite. The senator, his staff and his campaign organization had taken over most of the eighteenth floor of the hotel. The remainder of the floor had been cleared of guests. No press was allowed on the floor. The fifty or so reporters who were covering Parker had been provided rooms elsewhere in the hotel, along with a press room on the second floor. Television cameras had been set up in the lobby, but thus far had been given little to show except for Parker's brief statement early on the morning following the election. Other than that, Parker and his chief lieutenants had remained in their quarters, with only a few scattered, surreptitious trips out of the building through a back way.

Millard and Billy Dan now entered another suite, only two doors from Parker's. It was almost a duplicate of the one they had just left, except that all of the living-room furniture had been moved out and replaced by desks, electric typewriters and a large bank of telephones. Perhaps as many as thirty people were busily at work, and the noise was deafening, with typewriters, telephones and conversations all going at once.

Billy Dan and Duval motioned to five of the men, Parker's regional coordinators, to come with them into the bedroom. Duval quickly sketched what they wanted from them. It had been decided that Duval and Billy Dan would make the necessary telephone contacts themselves, but the task of finding and applying pressure points was far too delicate for long-distance maneuvering. Consequently, the twelve states carried by Parker were to be personally visited by the coordinators.

"It's imperative that you work quietly," Duval concluded. "Absolutely no one is to know what you are doing."

"But these electors are our own people," commented one of the men.

"That's exactly why this is sensitive," snapped Billy Dan. "If they find out what you're up to before we are ready, it can hurt us, and I'll have your ass if that happens."

"I didn't mean I wouldn't do it, Billy Dan," the man replied plaintively. "And I can keep my mouth shut."

"See that you do," said Billy Dan, his voice hard. "Your job is to find which string makes each elector jump. Maybe he owes the bank, maybe he drinks, maybe he's got a girl shacked up somewhere, maybe he's queer. Whatever it is, you find it out, and then you tell it to us and we'll decide what to do with it."

While Billy Dan and Duval were continuing with the details of the political operation, Parker and Janice Pruitt were finishing a leisurely lunch. Parker was relaxing with his second bourbon.

"I know they say I'm a no good bigot," he was saying, "and maybe I do go too far sometimes. But you know what I say is true."

"We all know that, Jack," Janice replied. "And the country knows it too."

"Just look at what the niggers are doing," Parker continued. "Tearing up our cities. Killing, looting, not a god-damned bit of respect for the law. And the crime. Jesus Christ! Everyone knows you can't walk on any city street in the country without being mugged or raped."

"Yes, sir, I know," said Janice, listening carefully.

"It wasn't that way when I was growing up here in Florida. Or anywhere else for that matter. But now, even in Miami, they are raising hell all over the place. By God, if I'm given the chance I'll change all of that."

Parker walked to the bar and refilled his drink. "All those New York Jews," he went on. "They give the niggers money and God knows what else. It's like a cancer. It's spread to the colleges and now the government is crawling with niggers and Jews. I just don't think that's what this country was meant to become."

He walked over to the window and stared out at the magnificent coastal view. "They will try anything to stop me," he said in a soft voice. "But, by God, I am right, and the people know it. We've been given a good chance, Janice, and I mean to take it."

Janice walked over to him and lightly touched his arm, thinking how fortunate she had been to find a job with this man. Like thousands of other girls, she had come to Washington looking for the excitement of power and the men who exercised it. She had not immediately found what she wanted, but with her beauty, she had easily landed a job as a receptionist at a local television station. She had held that job for three years, but had never stopped looking for the right opportunity.

It was soon after Parker had been elected senator that she had first met him. He had come to the studio for an interview, and, as she watched him perform, she had immediately sensed his strength. What he had said during the program, his attacks on the militant Negroes and Jews, made no particular impression on her, and she couldn't have cared less whether he was right or wrong. But her instincts about Parker were strong. She knew that this man would go far.

The next day she had gone to his office in the New Senate Office Building dressed as attractively as she knew how. After demonstrating that her shorthand and typing were both rapid and accurate, she had the job, and within six months she was his private secretary. By that time she was also sleeping with him.

That situation had caused some problems, all of which were, with care, solvable. The first was his wife. However, Jean Parker, a home-loving and trusting soul, who never traveled with her husband, had an intense dislike of politics, was completely unaware of his infidelities, and never thought to question him.

The second problem of their private relationship—the senator's special and rather violent tastes in the bedroom—was something Janice had come to terms with, part of the price of their association. But lately his demands had become increasingly difficult, and Janice was worried that her own disgust might become too much for her to conceal.

Another obstacle was the press. This had become increasingly more irksome, especially as Parker had grown in national visibility. The always-cynical Washington reporters would naturally assume the worst; however, suspicion and knowledge were two separate matters, and the solution they worked out was never to be seen together alone, or in any social situation. The press had nothing to write about. Thus far they had managed it, but Janice had become worried that Parker might one day conclude that the risks were too great, especially if he felt that the Presidency was a real possibility. Then he might decide to put an end to their relationship and her job.

She had often thought about what she would do if Parker did come to that conclusion. Would she smile and quietly walk away, or would she stand and fight, using the same black-jack tools that Parker was so capable of employing on others? She didn't know and, fortunately thus far, the matter had not come up.

"What do you hear from Jean?" Parker now asked, interrupting his monologue to inquire about his wife. "Has she bothered to call today?"

"No," replied Janice. "All I know is that the morning papers in Washington reported she has been spending her time at home in Chevy Chase, apparently minding the children and her housework."

"Jesus Christ, but isn't she some woman. Here I might be President, or, at least, have the power to decide who will be President, and she couldn't care less. If she had her way I'd still be practicing law with that one-horse Miami law firm."

"She is important, Jack," Janice softly replied. "She gives you a very nice aura of domesticity, and balances that tough exterior of yours."

"You know I'm not so tough," he said, pulling her close. She moved against him, meaningfully, even though she knew it could lead to nothing at this moment, when Billy Dan or Millard might burst in at any time. But, as usual, she made it a point to be compliant, making him fully aware of the promise of her body.

"Still," he continued, as he nuzzled her long, soft hair, "I wish she'd care about what I do, at least sometimes."

He abruptly broke away, as a thought occurred to him. "I think it's about time I went on television again. I want to keep the pressure on both of the other candidates, put the fear of God in them. A little statement about the efforts of the Jews and black men to fix this election, and how they're denying the people what they want and need. I think that would be very much in order right now. You call Billy Dan and Millard and tell them to get back in here."

"Yes, sir," Janice said, once again the efficient secretary.

A few minutes later, Parker's two chief staff men reappeared. "Millard," began Parker. "I want you to set up a press conference this afternoon. Make it early enough to hit the evening television news and all the morning papers."

"All right," replied Duval. "What format do you want?"

"I want to make a short statement, and then answer questions, but very briefly. No more than about ten minutes. After you set it up, then I want you to write the statement. I want to lay it on the Jews and blackies for the mess the country is in, and particularly the election situation. I want it strong. Don't pull any punches, but keep it to about three hundred words. Billy Dan, you stay here with me."

After Duval left the suite, Parker turned to Billy Dan. "You get on that phone and start trying to get the President for me. But before you start, go get a tape recorder with one of those little attachments. I want a record of everything that is said from the first moment the operator answers."

"I don't think he'll talk to you," said Billy Dan.

"Well, now, you might just be right, but I guess as a citizen I've got the privilege of trying to talk to my President and give him my opinions on what he should do to get the country out of this mess. As a matter of fact, seeing that I've got a hundred and twenty-two electoral votes, maybe I've got just a little extra right to talk to him. Of course, if he refuses I might just feel obliged to mention that fact in my press conference."

Billy Dan returned in about five minutes with the recorder. He attached the listening device to the phone and Parker told him to place the call. It was now almost two P.M. and normally the President would be in his office. Billy Dan dialed the White House directly. When the operator came on, he identified himself and his position as Senator Parker's campaign manager. He said he was calling for the senator who wished to personally speak with the President. The White House operator politely thanked him, and asked him to hold on for a minute.

While Billy Dan was waiting, Parker whispered to him, "Be careful, and remember they are probably recording it at their end." Billy Dan nodded, as another operator came on the line and asked him to identify himself again, and the number from which he was calling.

In a moment, Alvin Morgan, the President's Special Assistant, came on the phone.

"How are you doing, Billy Dan?" Morgan began.

"Fine, just fine, Alvin. We've just been soaking up all of this beautiful Florida sun and wishing you folks back in Washington could come join us."

"There's nothing we'd like better than to lie around Miami Beach and just forget the cares of the world. And, of course, I would always enjoy seeing you again. But I guess we're stuck here for now."

"Well, maybe I'll get to gossip with you some when I get to Washington next time."

"Maybe. What can we do for you now, Billy Dan?"

"As a matter of fact, Senator Parker is sitting right here, and he would like to speak to the President."

There was a slight pause before Morgan answered smoothly. "I'm terribly sorry, but the President is tied up right now. Perhaps I can be of some help, that is if the senator wouldn't mind talking to me."

"Alvin, you know Senator Parker thinks the world of you,

but I'm afraid this is something he has to take up personally with the President."

"I don't have to tell you how busy the President is these days," Morgan replied, "and I'm certain that the senator can appreciate the demands upon the President's time, especially in these times of crisis."

"The senator is not only aware of the problems, Alvin, but he feels that a personal conversation with the President could go a long way to help matters out."

"Of course the President welcomes the views and the help of any member of the Senate," said Morgan. "Perhaps if you could tell me the nature of what Senator Parker has to say I could relay it to the President."

"I'm afraid that's impossible. This concerns the welfare of the nation and the senator feels quite strongly that he must take the matter up directly with the President. On the telephone, if necessary, but in person if that could be arranged."

"Let me see what I can do. I'll call you back," said Morgan.

"The senator feels that there should be no delay on this request, so if you could call back within an hour or two we would be grateful."

For the first time, Morgan's voice lost its tone of urbane politeness. "Now you just hold on, my friend. Nobody sets ultimatums for the President. We will consider your request, and we will respond to it, but neither you nor anyone else can tell us when to do anything, or how to do it. Your man is not President yet."

"Calm down, Alvin," drawled Billy Dan. "I meant no ultimatum. I'm just requesting a response in a reasonable time."

"You will get it," Morgan replied, and hung up.

Billy Dan turned to Parker, a big smile on his face. "What do you know. I got his goat. They must really be feeling tension up there, and I would say that it is mostly because of us."

Parker also looked pleased. "Good work, Billy Dan. He's stalling, that's for sure. If they were smarter they'd see me and then try to put me down. As it is, it's pretty clear the President is

63

really hungup about me and is reacting emotionally. I'd say that is good for us."

"What can we do about it?" asked Billy Dan.

"I think that if we don't hear from them we should mention it in the press conference. You write me a real good paragraph or two. And, Billy Dan, let's take a little gamble. I want to accuse the President of consorting with the other two candidates. I don't have anything concrete, but I'd be willing to bet some high stakes that it's going on. So you just go ahead and write me a little accusation."

"With pleasure, boss," said Billy Dan, as he left to join Millard Duval in the adjoining suite.

Two hours later the second-floor press room was packed and buzzing with anticipation. A platform had been constructed at the back of the room. On it were the reel cameras for the news services and television outlets. All three networks had decided to carry the conference live. This was to be done under an arrangement where NBC would furnish the camera and crew and the other two networks would take direct feeds from them. Thus, the center of the platform was monopolized by the large color television camera, which had muscled the grumbling reel men off to either side. The area immediately in front of the podium had been roped off for the still cameramen, and behind them seats had been provided for about a hundred newsmen, staff, and other hangers-on, although the audience was severely restricted by the tight security imposed by a very nervous secret service.

Because the conference was live, it had been agreed that Parker would start promptly at four P.M. so as not to interrupt in-progress network programs. The senator came down the elevator five minutes early and stood at the back of the room waiting for the signal to come forward. He appeared relaxed, and joked amiably with the reporters nearest him. This was not unusual. Despite the fact that the reporters themselves as well as their editors were almost as one in their abhorrence of Parker's philosophy, they nevertheless could not help responding to this man who was invariably friendly and, at least on the surface, could laugh at himself and the reactions he created. Often, when he had made a particularly vicious point, he would surreptitiously wink and smile at the press, as if saying, "Isn't this the biggest joke." It was difficult to respond with anger, and the press had always found this a most difficult dilemma in covering the man.

The TV director now motioned thirty seconds. Parker straightened himself and the smile vanished from his face. Then the director waved that they were on the air, and Parker strode down the center aisle, tall and purposeful, without a look to either side. He rapidly mounted the podium and, at once, began his statement.

"I address these remarks to true Americans everywhere.

"The United States has been brought to the brink of disaster.

"The policies of this administration, and of the administration that preceded it, have been soundly rejected by the people.

"The people have now spoken against the coddling of criminals; against the legalized lawlessness encouraged by the courts; against the billions of dollars thrown away to the shiftless, the uneducated, and the dregs of society; and particularly against those un-American types who have so insinuated themselves among us and who through money and violence have attempted to destroy the greatness of our Christian and Western heritage.

"The President of the United States, despite how obvious it is that he has been rejected by the people, persists in attempting to foist himself, his choices, and his machinations upon our society.

"I accuse the President of entering into a conspiracy with the other two candidates, with the objective of denying to the people their free choice of leaders and policies.

"I have attempted to contact the President in order to dissuade him from pursuing these un-American activities, and to offer him a last chance to govern impartially for the few remaining days of his administration. But he has refused to see me, or even to talk to me, despite the fact that I am the choice of the people of twelve states representing a hundred and twenty-two electoral votes.

"However, I will not be silenced. Despite all of the awesome power of the President and of his henchmen, I am without fear, and through me the people will be told the truth."

Parker, who had made the entire statement looking directly into the television camera and without once glancing at his written text, now paused, indicating that he would take questions. A half dozen reporters simultaneously were on their feet. Parker smilingly nodded to the U.P.I. man.

"Senator, you claim that the President is conspiring with the other candidates. That is a serious charge. Would you give us the evidence you have to back it up?"

Parker appeared completely at ease as he calmly responded to the question. "Of course it is a serious charge, and I would hope that the people of the United States are now awakened to exactly how dangerous these machinations are. As to the evidence, you will appreciate that my sources must, for the moment, remain private. To reveal names while these people are still in power would put them and their families in considerable danger. I would suggest, rather, that you put the question to the President, or either of the other candidates. If you press them as hard as you like to press me, I'll wager that they will admit the accuracy of my charge."

Parker nodded at the reporter for the *New York Times*, who asked the next question. "But what about this so-called Jewish and Negro conspiracy? What facts can you give us which support that charge?"

"Now, Mike, you must have been asleep during the entire campaign," Parker responded. "You've been covering me for two months, although I must say that your paper has not seen fit to print much of what I have been trying to say." Parker's voice now became hard as he peered intently at the reporter. "You must think that because you won't report the facts as I state them, therefore, those facts don't exist. Well, that isn't so, and as to the evidence, I would suggest you do a little work for a change, and go back and read my speeches. Perhaps if you report what I said, rather than what your editors think the public ought to hear, then the proof will become apparent."

Four or five reporters now rose at once, most of them attempting to continue the same line of questioning. However, one of the great advantages of the format of a press conference, especially one with severely limited time, was that the candidate could choose the questioner to be recognized, which, if shrewdly done, could result in a blameless change of subject. Parker now did this by nodding to the heavy set, middle-aged lady reporter, representing a chain of small Southwestern papers whose questions, although posed with sincerity, usually allowed a candidate the opportunity for a harmless response.

"Senator, why do your wife and children stay in Chevy Chase while you are here in Miami Beach? Isn't that a little unfair to them?"

Parker's face took on a look of benign patience, and he smiled pleasantly throughout his answer. "Now, Fanny, nothing would give Mrs. Parker and me greater pleasure than to be together. However, the children must continue with their schooling, and, as you no doubt have noticed, my enjoyment of beautiful Florida is somewhat diluted by the fact that the demands of my work have prevented me from ever leaving this hotel. However, my disappointment in missing the joys of the sun and sand is somewhat diminished by the knowledge that you ladies and gentlemen of the press have undoubtedly made up for what I have missed in sampling the pleasures of this lovely city."

Despite themselves, the reporters openly laughed at this inside reference to the fact that, of all the candidates, at least Parker had chosen a pleasant watering spot. It was an especially comfortable assignment compared to Harrington's Providence, Rhode Island, and Nelson's Philadelphia.

Parker gestured to a young reporter in the back of the room who had not previously clamored for attention.

"Have you decided whether you are going to instruct your electors to vote for you or for one of the other candidates? If so, would you tell us which one?"

"That is a fair question, son, but somewhat premature. You will understand, however, that I cannot direct the electors what to do, and would not be so presumptuous as to attempt to do so. They are all fine, upstanding men, every one of them, and I am

67

especially proud of those who are pledged to me. In due course I will give them the benefit of my thinking, and, I would hope, they will give me theirs. But for the moment, as I said the other night, we are all carefully studying the situation and the desires and needs of the United States."

As he completed his answer, Parker nodded almost imperceptibly to his aide, Millard Duval, who was seated in a front row chair. Duval instantly caught the cue, and yelled a strong voiced "Thank you, senator," whereupon Parker waved good-bye, and left the podium, terminating the press conference. Some reporters attempted to get close to him to ask further questions, but the secret service and police effectively blocked them off as he strode from the room, his face beaming with a confident smile.

A few minutes later Parker was back in his suite. He immediately turned on all three television networks and watched the commentaries and replays of his conference. As he expected, his accusations were creating a good deal of consternation, and he was reasonably certain that he had succeeded in grabbing the news lead for the morning papers.

He asked Janice to pour him a bourbon, lit a large cigar, and turned to Duval. "Millard, I've decided to go along with your suggestion about calling the electors together. Set it up for here in Miami Beach, and schedule it within the next two weeks."

"Shall we announce it?" asked Duval.

"Not yet. Let's keep the press guessing as much as we can. It will leak soon enough, and at the proper time, we will confirm it."

Parker looked at Billy Dan, who was hunched over a television receiver. As he watched a prominent commentator's calmly acidic analysis of Parker's performance, Billy Dan scowled and muttered, "That pinko son of a bitch ought to be locked up."

"Calm down," said Parker. "He can't hurt us. All those network reporters have been ganging up on me nonstop for two years, and look where we are now. You should applaud him for the service he's doing for us."

Parker affectionately patted Billy Dan on the shoulder, and

then continued. "I've got another little job for you. I want to personally meet with Governor Nelson, and I want to do it before we meet with the electors. I want it set up so absolutely nobody knows about the meeting, or even that we are attempting to meet."

"Are you going to make a deal with him?" asked Duval.

"If I wanted you to know what I'm going to do I would have told you," snapped Parker. "For now, you work on the electors and Billy Dan will set it up with our Republican friend."

"Yes sir," said Duval, his voice betraying his hurt feelings.

"I'd think I'd best not try contacting Nelson directly," broke in Billy Dan. "I'm too well known. I'll get one of our best people, somebody the press doesn't recognize, to go to Philadelphia and make the contact. I'll get it started today."

"I don't care how you do it," said Parker. "Just get it done right."

After Billy Dan and Duval left the room, Parker, now alone with Janice, sat sipping his drink, quietly puffing his cigar. "That old biddy had to ask about my beloved spouse," he said. "I'm surprised that she didn't come right out and ask if I was sleeping with you."

"They wouldn't dare do that," said Janice.

"Well," said Parker reflectively, "they just might get to that. Yes, sir, they just might."

He got up abruptly and walked quickly toward the bedroom, motioning to her over his shoulder. "Get in here quick, kid. I might as well give them something hot to talk about."

CHAPTER SIX

All right, who leaked it?" demanded the President, looking livid, and staring straight at Stu. "I want to know how Parker found out you contacted the other two candidates."

They were sitting in the President's small office adjoining his main working quarters in the West Wing. It was an hour after Parker's press conference and the President had summoned Stu, Alvin Morgan and Sam Baker to join him.

"I have no idea, Mr. President," Stu replied, feeling more than a little defensive. "I talked to no one except Sandy Corso, who is Harrington's speech writer, and Jerry Greenberg, Nelson's press secretary. They both understood that our talks were confidential, and I can't imagine that they would have leaked it."

"Well, someone sure as hell did," growled the President. "I want to know who did it."

"Maybe no one leaked it," Alvin Morgan said in a quiet voice. "It could be that Parker was just shooting in the dark. After all, it's not entirely unreasonable that we would be in touch with both major candidates."

Stu looked at Alvin with a feeling of gratitude. Ever since Stu had come to the White House, Alvin had protected him. Although much of the press had depicted Alvin as something of an ogre and an unfeeling and autocratic whip of the White House staff, nothing could be further from the truth. He was as loyal to the President as any man could possibly be, and executed presidential wishes with unfailing precision. Nevertheless—and sometimes under the most difficult of circumstances—he was invariably helpful and considerate to every man around him. He could be just as tough as the situation demanded, but his actions were always tempered with intelligence and sensitivity. On many occasions Alvin had interposed himself between Stu and the President, taking blame for Stu's errors, and catching the President's wrath when he himself had been blameless. In addition, Alvin always saw to it that the President was made aware of any good work Stu turned out. That's how it was now, as Alvin stepped into the middle of the President's displeasure.

"Damn it, Alvin, can't we do anything around here that isn't either leaked or figured out!" the President said, momentarily forgetting that the contact with the candidates had been his own idea.

"I've already received several inquiries," broke in Sam Baker, the President's Press Secretary. "They'll surely ask me about it at tomorrow morning's press briefing. Shall I deny the charge?"

The President's anger now faded, and he paused for a moment before calmly answering, "No, Sam, I don't believe we should take that tack. They'd catch us at it for sure, and, in any event, I don't want to be on the defensive about this. I think I've got a better approach."

The staff relaxed, instantly responding to the President's change of mood, relieved that the inquisition was at an end.

The President continued. "Sam, you put off answering those questions until morning." He turned to Alvin Morgan. "How does my schedule look for the next few days?"

"It's awfully tight, Mr. President. This is Thursday, and tomorrow you have a National Security Council meeting in the morning, a speech to the Labor Council at the Hilton in the afternoon, and a long get together with the people from the Treasury and Council of Economic Advisers in the evening. On Saturday you promised the First Lady you would go with her to Camp David. You've postponed that twice before, and she is insisting that you get some rest. Sunday you are free, of course, but Monday is bad all day and ends with a Veteran's Day speech before the American Legion at the Waldorf in New York."

71

"All right," said the President. "Stu, I want you to call those closed-mouthed friends of yours, Corso and Greenberg did you say? Set up a meeting with both Harrington and Nelson. We'll do it after the Legion speech Monday night in New York. Make sure they accept tonight. Tell them that the President feels such a meeting is essential."

"Yes sir," said Stu, feeling mixed emotions about the request. He was delighted that the President still considered him a reliable member of the team. On the other hand, it was a tall order, and the President expected it to be fulfilled. It obviously was going to take time to run down his contacts, and then wait a long night at his desk for replies. Then, on the home front, Sari undoubtedly would have some comment, particularly since the two of them had been invited out to dinner tonight.

"Let me know as soon as you have it arranged," the President continued. "Then give the information to Sam, and Sam, you announce it at the press briefing tomorrow morning. Don't elaborate on it. Just let the meeting speak for itself. If things work out, we'll have something to say about it afterward."

The President indicated that he had finished, and the staff immediately left his office. Stu, however, lingered for a moment with Alvin in the corridor outside.

"I want to thank you for standing up for me," Stu said.

"Don't you worry about it, Brady. Obviously the President is taking the initiative, and it is probably all working out for the best. Now you get to work. Let me know if you get stuck. I'll be here late."

Stu returned to his office and instructed the operators to place the calls to Corso and Greenberg. While he was waiting, he decided that now was as good a time as any to call Sari. As he did, he thought that this kind of bad news seemed to be a constant state of affairs between them.

"I know what you are going to say," Sari said. "My fine non-husband finks out again. Right?"

"Damn it, Sari, why can't you ever understand?"

"I've been 'understanding' for two years, and I've had enough."

72

"What are you trying to do?"

"For one thing, I'm going to the dinner tonight, alone as usual. For another thing, you had better start thinking about how life is going to be without me around. Just think about that while you are serving that master of yours." She was in tears as she hung up on him.

Stu sat cradling his head, feeling utterly frustrated. He knew only too well how she felt, and yet he did believe that other wives adjusted to this kind of existence. But Sari seemingly would not make that kind of effort. He thought that perhaps it was the lack of children, or maybe she just felt inadequate to cope with things by herself. Whatever it was, she obviously was reaching the breaking point, and Stu felt helpless to prevent it. He just couldn't bring himself to leave the President during this time of crisis. He shook his head, thinking that if he could just find some way to hold his marriage together for the next few months, perhaps he could find a more humane job. But he could do nothing until January twentieth, and he wasn't at all certain that Sari was going to give him that much time.

Stu was on the phone for the next four hours. First he told Corso and Greenberg of the President's desire for a meeting with the candidates. Then they consulted with their bosses, and called back with more questions. What did the President have in mind? Stu couldn't say. Was it to be public? Yes and no. The President would like to announce it tomorrow, but the meeting itself would be strictly private. Doesn't this play into Parker's hands and admit the conspiracy that he charged? No, just the opposite. It takes the initiative away from him, and isolates him. Stu gave what answers he could with the little information he had.

It was eleven P.M. when Corso called once again, reporting that Harrington was agreeable, although reluctant.

A half hour later Greenberg called.

"Stu, I'm sorry, but Governor Nelson just won't do it. He says to tell the President that such a meeting would compromise him with his party and his electors."

"Christ, Jerry, he's wrong. It will be an open meeting of three leaders. There will be nothing in it but good publicity for

73

the governor, and nobody is asking him to agree to anything in advance."

"I tried my best. Frankly, I tend to agree with you, but the governor is adamant, and his answer is no."

"Okay. Thanks for trying, but don't get where I can't reach you. I may have to talk to you again."

"It won't do any good," Greenberg said, sounding sympathetic to Stu's plight, "but I'll be right here if you need me."

"Thank you, my friend." Stu slowly replaced the receiver, thinking that there was nothing to do but give the bad news to the President. He quickly typed a short note on plain white paper, which was what the President preferred on sensitive political matters of this kind. He explained that Harrington was willing and Nelson was not, and he put down what he had done toward attempting to persuade the governor.

Stu walked across the West Wing press lobby and into Alvin Morgan's office. It was getting close to midnight and the place was deserted except for two uniformed guards. Alvin, however, was still at his desk.

"I struck out on Governor Nelson," Stu began, handing his memo to Alvin. "Should I put this into night reading?"

"I think you had better give it to him in person. I'm sorry about throwing you at him like this, but when he left his office a while back he said to send you over whenever you were ready to report."

Morgan picked up the phone and asked for the President. Within seconds he had him on the line, and he asked if Stu was to come over. He listened to the brief answer and then hung up. "Good luck, Brady," he said with a smile, as he motioned Stu to go.

Stu walked along the darkened passageway to the Mansion, barely able to see where he was going, muttering about White House practice of turning off "unneeded" lights. In the basement of the Mansion a secret service agent sat at the checkpoint. Stu glumly nodded to him as he waited for the elevator, and with considerable trepidation, he proceeded to the second floor.

The President was in bed, but not sleeping. A foot-high pile of reading material was stacked beside him, and it looked as if he had just started to go through it. He waved Stu to a chair as he completed the document in his hand.

The amount of the President's required reading was a constant sore point. A surprisingly large number of people, including staff, cabinet, sub-officials and friends, were permitted access to the President with whatever writings they might choose to submit. The cumulative effect was to inundate the President, who conscientiously and exhaustively read it all, and constantly complained about the quantity. The reading often kept him up until two A.M. or later, and, though various programs were set up to limit the flow of documents, the incredible variety of the nation's problems created an irreducible minimum which would have sunk a man of lesser energy.

After a few minutes the President motioned Stu to hand him his memo, and rapidly read it. Stu nervously watched, waiting for the explosion he was certain would be coming. However, the President laid the paper down and looked at Stu with a wan smile.

"You did a good job, Brady. Don't feel badly that old Nelson wouldn't come through right away. I really didn't expect that he would. You did get Harrington, and Nelson is at least considering it."

"His press secretary was fairly certain that Nelson had closed his mind," said Stu, feeling vastly relieved.

"That may be true, but maybe we can still get him," said the President, picking up the phone by his bed. He instructed the operator to get Governor Nelson and then asked Stu to join him in a drink while they were waiting. "I didn't want to talk to the old goat myself," the President continued, "but I suspected that it would eventually come to that."

In a few moments the valet appeared with their drinks, and the President put down his reading and looked at Stu.

"How have you been getting along, Stuart, and how is that lovely wife of yours?" he asked.

"Just fine, sir," said Stu, briefly tempted to unburden his problems to the President, but thinking better of it as he realized that the last thing the President needed to hear about was his messed-up home life.

"I know what you fellows have been going through, especially since the election. I am deeply grateful, I hope you know that, and somehow I want to make it up to you."

"Thank you, Mr. President."

"I know how loyal you have been, Stu. You've been very helpful to me. It's satisfying to know that I have people like you on my staff."

Stu felt like a puppy dog who had just been patted on the head. He knew he shouldn't react so joyfully to appreciation from the President, but he couldn't help it. Moments like these, so rare in the harassed existence at the White House, almost made up for all the hell that went with working for the man. The President was one of the most intensely human persons Stu had ever known. He was overdemanding, expecting perfection from those around him, and fully capable of berating his staff in private or in public. And yet, with all of that, he was loyal to those who gave him loyalty, and generous as well.

The bedside phone quietly buzzed, and the President picked it up. He nodded at Stu, indicating that it was Governor Nelson.

"Maynard, please forgive me for disturbing you at this time of night. How have you been getting along?" The President listened for a moment, and then continued. "I need to see you, and I would very much like it to be Monday night in New York." The President frowned as Nelson replied, and then broke in again. "I know the problems, Governor. I'm fully aware of what Parker has been saying, but the country is in deep trouble and it is my judgment that the two major candidates should meet with their President. There is absolutely nothing partisan in this. As your President, I am requesting you to meet with Senator Harrington and myself."

The President frowned as he listened to Nelson's answer, and then he went on in a firm voice. "This is a difficult and novel situation, and I believe we are in need of some bold approaches to it." There was another pause. "I propose that the fact of our meeting be public, but, quite obviously, the meeting itself will be private."

The President listened again, and then he turned toward Stu with a big wink. "That's right, Maynard. My suite at the Waldorf at nine P.M. Monday. I'll look forward to seeing you, and I deeply appreciate your patriotism in agreeing to this."

He bade the governor a friendly goodnight, and then looked at Stu. "I guess a lame duck President still has a little persuasive power. Nelson is reluctant, but he will do it. Now you call Sam Baker and give him the details, and tell him to announce it at the morning press briefing."

"Yes, sir," Stu responded. He stood and quietly departed, as the President returned once again to his reading.

Promptly at six P.M. the following Monday, the presidential party departed from the south lawn of the White House by marine helicopter. In less than ten minutes they were deposited at Andrews Air Force Base, where Air Force One was waiting. Because this was to be an overnight stay in New York, a larger contingent of staff and support personnel was required than a normal quick trip to a speaking engagement. The trip's manifest included forty-five people—men from the secret service and signal corps, two valets, three secretaries, two presidential photographers, the doctor, the military aide, and a dozen members of the staff. In addition, the President had invited a number of administration officials who came from New York, and top people from the Veterans Administration. The President was especially conscious of cost when the trip had to be classified as political, and thus paid for by the Democratic party. For those occasions he preferred taking the smaller and less expensive Convair on the short hop to New York. However, this speech was quite legitimately a non-political presidential appearance celebrating a national holiday, notwithstanding the meeting with the candidates scheduled for later in the evening. The President considered that meeting too much a part of the nation's, rather than the party's, business.

As usual, the hour's flight to New York was chaotic. The

President was not satisfied with his speech, even though he had himself approved a final draft earlier in the day. Thus, the two speech writers and all of the secretaries were rewriting just as rapidly as they could, running suggestions to the President and then putting the results on the five by seven yellow speech cards the President would use at the dinner.

In the meantime, Alvin Morgan was on the plane's radio talking to his advance man in New York, trying to obtain a final and firm list of the dignitaries who should be recognized by the President in his introductory remarks, a task made almost impossible because of the fact that no one at the dinner could yet say for sure precisely which members of the large New York congressional delegation would be attending. This information was, in turn, typed on the speech cards with the fervent hope that there would be no glaring omissions.

To all of the working staff it seemed as if they had landed at Kennedy airport only minutes after taking off. The big plane pulled into a parking area well away from the commercial facilities. There they quickly loaded into buses, while the President, Alvin Morgan, Stu and a secret service agent rode in the presidential car, which had been driven from Washington to New York earlier in the day. As they sped into the city, escorted all the way by a full contingent of New York police cars and motorcycles, the President, quite oblivious to the massive parting of the waters for his passage, read over his speech cards and made several last minute changes in his big, scrawling handwriting.

The motorcade turned up 50th Street, completely blocked from Park to Lexington, and into the hotel's basement garage. The President was met there by several high Legion officials and the hotel manager, and was immediately escorted to the main ballroom. The press, and most of the White House staff, followed after him but Stu and Alvin Morgan went directly to the suite to see that everything was in order for the coming meeting with Harrington and Nelson.

The large and beautifully furnished quarters the President used each time he was in New York were in perfect order, with drinks and hors d'oeuvres arranged for their arrival. Security had been set up in the hallway, and the rooms in the immediate vicinity of the President had been assigned to his staff. Alvin gave orders to the guards that both Senator Harrington and Governor Nelson were to be immediately cleared through to the President's rooms, along with whomever of their staffs they desired.

Over four hundred newsmen had jammed the hotel to cover the meeting. The press had responded to the White House announcement of the previous Friday by inundating the public with views, comments and speculation concerning the purpose and impact of this conference. Throughout the weekend endless stories had been filed and the television networks ran several specials on the "Waldorf Summit Conference," as it had come to be called. The entire affair was made even more fascinating by the exclusion of Parker, particularly in view of his charge of conspiracy.

All three networks were planning live coverage, not only of the President's speech, which they hoped might bring some enlightenment, but of the subsequent events of the evening—as late into the night as developments warranted.

There was no press or television anywhere near the presidential quarters, however. The meeting was to be held in complete privacy, and the press was confined to the lobby and lower floors of the hotel.

After satisfying themselves that everything was in readiness, Alvin and Stu watched the President's speech on television while they waited for the candidates. It was more or less a standard Veterans Day appeal for national unity in foreign affairs, containing no mention of the country's political impasse. Although some of the staff had urged the President to take advantage of the live coverage to strike out on the political situation, the President had vetoed any mention of it on the ground that the meeting with the candidates was far more important, and if he said anything on the subject just before that meeting, the candidates might feel entrapped, thus lessening whatever chances might exist for an agreement.

A few minutes before nine, Senator Harrington arrived at the suite, accompanied by Sandy Corso. He had barely stepped

79

inside when Governor Nelson and Jerry Greenberg were escorted in by the agent on duty at the door. Alvin Morgan, pointing to the TV screen, explained that the President's speech was still in progress. The room was tense as they all sat waiting, and the small talk proceeded in a strained manner.

Twenty minutes later the door opened and the President walked briskly into the room. "Stu, you fix me a scotch and soda, and make sure that everyone is refilled," he said as he greeted both candidates and their associates with strong, friendly handshakes. "We might as well relax for a moment before we get to work," he said, taking off his tuxedo jacket and loosening his tie. "I'd like to take off these damned tight shoes, but I suppose that's going a little too far, considering how the press has labeled our little 'summit conference.' "

For the next few minutes the President chatted amicably with Harrington and Nelson, recalling old times and regaling them with anecdotes of past experiences they had shared. Stu marveled at how the President gave the appearance of not having a care in the world, and if one didn't know better, it would seem as if the President was involved with nothing more than having a late night drink with two old friends. Finally, however, he came to the point, and Stu noticed that when he set down his glass the drink had been barely touched.

"As you know," the President began, "today is November eleventh and on December sixteenth, now less than five weeks away, the electors are going to meet. Between now and then, and between then and a January decision in the House of Representatives, if it comes to that, this country is going to be under a strain the likes of which it hasn't experienced since 1824, the last time this sort of thing happened. Only our world is nothing like 1824. Everything is more complex, fast moving and, as I don't have to tell you gentlemen, incredibly more hazardous."

The two candidates listened intently, but they were expressionless except for a slight nodding of heads at this last observation.

The President continued. "I asked for this meeting to see what we all could do to lessen those risks. I do this without any

thought of partisanship. I have no political ambitions and no political interest. That is all behind me. I happen to be the only
President this country has, and I am President of all the people.
It is my sworn obligation to hold the country together, and I am
determined to do so." The President looked deeply into the eyes
of the two candidates. "Can we, at least, start from that
premise?"

"Of course, Mr. President," Senator Harrington promptly
replied.

Governor Nelson, however, hesitated before answering in a
slow and careful voice. "You have spent a lifetime in the Democratic party, Mr. President, and you campaigned against me
with great vigor, I must say. I grant the sincerity of your intentions, but it is difficult for me to conceive that your clear personal
preference could be so quickly buried. I only say this because I
know it would be difficult for me to do so if our positions were
reversed."

"If you were President, Maynard, and you may very well be
President one day soon, then you would understand that partisanship is a luxury and that there are times when the President
simply cannot afford it, not if he is to uphold his oath to support
the Constitution. This is certainly one of those times. You have
my word on that."

"I don't want to belabor my point, Mr. President, and I
don't for a minute doubt your word. I am perfectly willing to
accept your statement of impartiality as being made in good
faith and go forward from there. I assure you that I too am concerned about the nation's stability in these trying times, and I
want to do all that I reasonably can to cooperate with you."

"That's fair enough," the President answered. "As I see the
situation, the least divisive course the country could follow during this period of uncertainty is to permit the mechanics of the
Electoral College and the House of Representatives to work their
natural course, without hysterics or undue tampering. In practical terms, this means that the campaigning should be done quietly and it should be tempered at every turn with expressions of
unity of purpose. It is just that basic unity that I think both of

you gentlemen represent. You are both part of the great, historic center of American politics. In other words, the country needs a joint statement now, and others later, on your areas of agreement, rather than continuing to hear about how you differ."

Senator Harrington broke in at this point. "It is damned hard for me to see many issues where the governor and I have taken the same stand. He spent the campaign knocking about every important vote I cast in the Senate."

"I'm not talking about specific programs, Jimmy," the President interrupted with a frown. "I'm only concerned with broad objectives, and I do believe we could draft something that we could all buy."

"Well, I'm willing to look at it, but I'm not at all confident about reaching an agreement," said a skeptical-sounding Harrington.

"There is one other thing," continued the President. "In my judgment Jack Parker poses the greatest danger to the country. The drivel he preaches, his appeal to the worst in our natures, can only lead to trouble. He riles up the whites, and he could cause a revolution of the blacks. Now I know that neither of you agrees with a thing he says. So what I am asking is very simple. I would like the two of you to reaffirm publicly your opposition to his policies, and pledge that you will make no deals with him."

The room was silent as the President scanned the faces of his two guests. "A statement of unity in our high national purposes, and a further statement that will isolate Parker," the President summed up. "Is it agreeable that our bright staff boys here start drafting something while we relax over some good scotch and this delicious food? They can bring us their product and then we can see if we can get together. Shall we tell them to get to work and leave us alone for a while?"

The President rose with a smile, and started to motion the assistants out of the room.

"I'm sorry, Mr. President, but I'm afraid that is out of the question." It was Nelson who spoke, as he too rose to his feet. "I cannot agree to the issuance of any joint statement with Senator

Harrington, so there is no point in wasting the time in drafting one."

"That's not an insurmountable obstacle, Maynard," the President persisted. "If you agree with the general outlines of what I propose, perhaps separate statements might be worked out."

"Perhaps," Nelson responded, "but not tonight. I am perfectly willing to give serious consideration to your suggestions, but I insist on captaining my own ship. If I say anything, then it must be at a time and place of my choosing."

The President's face drained of color as he stood face to face with the Republican governor. Stu was momentarily concerned that the President's famous temper would break loose, but he quickly saw that there was no chance of that. The President was in complete control, and only his blanching betrayed his reaction.

"I'm disappointed, Governor, but I do hope you'll see the wisdom of what I am saying. There is no doubt but that it is the only course the nation can safely follow. I'd prefer you to say something along these lines when you are cornered by the press after this meeting. If you cannot, then may I ask that you at least not say anything that will make it difficult for you to go along at a later date."

"I'll agree with that, Mr. President," said Nelson.

"That's fine with me," answered Harrington.

A short time later the candidates and their assistants departed, leaving the President alone with Stu and Alvin. The President sat for a long time, staring at the fireplace. He looked very sad and the lines in his face seemed deeper and more harsh. "Maybe Nelson will come around later," he murmured in a tired voice. "At least I gave him something to think about."

On Wednesday, November 13, there was a black-tie dinner at the White House in honor of the Prime Minister of Canada, who was in Washington on a state visit. Although the guest list was the usual conglomeration of high government officials, big party

83

donors, old presidential friends and a sprinkling of people from the arts, there were also a few members of the staff invited, along with their wives, as bona-fide guests of the President's. On this evening, Stu and Sari had made the invitation list and Sari was delighted.

In the two days since the Monday meeting at the Waldorf there had been no statement from Nelson. On his departure that evening, Nelson, true to his word, had been noncommittal with the press, saying only that there had been a full and frank discussion of the situation. Since then he had been unavailable for comment. As for Harrington, he too had been discreetly silent, waiting to see what position might be taken by his opponent. This period of silence necessarily resulted in tying the President's hands. It was his feeling, as he expressed it to Stu the next day, that he must remain quiescent, giving Nelson every opportunity to come through.

The most surprising element of all, however, was the complete absence of comment from Parker. They had all braced themselves, after the New York meeting, for a blast from the third-party candidate and had been amazed when it had not come. As expected, the press had a field day speculating on the lack of action, and the White House press office had been bombarded with constant questions.

On this Wednesday Stu had taken a White House car to work so that Sari could drive down and meet him in his office, where he was to change into black tie for the eight o'clock affair. Sari came in wearing a long white gown, which flowed over her lovely, trim figure. Her black hair was accentuated by the tiara her mother had given her, its sparkle matching the glow in Sari's eyes. She looked radiant as she told Stu that this was what she dreamed her life as the wife of a presidential aide would be like.

They walked together over to the Mansion, where they were met by a social military aide, who escorted them into the East Room. There Sari and Stu stood among the other staff people, sipping drinks, awaiting the arrival of the President and his honored guests.

Shortly after eight-thirty, the presidential group descended the grand staircase, formed a receiving line, and the party officially began. Each of the guests was formally greeted by the President, who, when Stu and Sari came through the line, made a point of stopping Sari, giving her an affectionate hug, and telling her what a grand job Stu had been doing for him. Stu beamed and Sari looked content.

Stu was just beginning dessert when an usher came over to him and whispered that he was wanted on the phone. Stu noted that it was almost ten P.M. With a look toward Sari, who appeared to be in animated conversation at her table across the room, he excused himself and went into the usher's office, located only a few steps from the formal dining room.

It was Jerry Greenberg, Nelson's press secretary.

"Stu, I've got to see you tonight."

"Can't it wait until later? We're just finishing dinner here," Stu answered, somewhat querulously.

"I'm awfully sorry, I really am, but it's urgent or I wouldn't bother you. If I don't see you now I'm not sure I will be able to later."

"I don't suppose you can give it to me on the phone?"

"No, I don't want to do that."

"Okay. Where do you want to meet?"

"Drive over to the Jefferson Memorial. I'll meet you there. I have a cream colored Ford. Is half an hour all right?"

"I'll be there," said Stu, hanging up.

He considered returning to the dining room to tell Sari, but he simply didn't have the heart for it. So he wrote her a short note explaining that he had been called away on an urgent matter, that he was taking their car and expected to return before the party ended. If not, he wrote, Sari was to call for a White House car to take her home. He gave the note to a social aide and asked him to hand it to Sari after dinner. Then he returned to the office, shrugged into his topcoat, and departed.

It was a crisp fall night with just a touch of winter in the air. The traffic was light and it took only fifteen minutes to reach the place Greenberg had suggested. The memorial was deserted when he arrived and he waited impatiently, hoping he could get back to the party before Sari left.

It was not too long before a Ford pulled up beside him. Greenberg was in it and moved quickly to Stu's car.

"I don't have much time," Greenberg said, sounding tense.

"All right. What is it?"

"Before I begin I've got to have your word that what I tell you goes only to the President. You can tell him your source, but I must have your assurance, and his, that I'll be completely protected. Whatever you do, I don't want it known that I was the one who told you this."

"I guess I've had the world's best teacher for keeping my mouth shut," said Stu. "As for the President, all I can do is give him your request. I'm sure he'll honor it, but you know I can't give you any guarantee."

"That's good enough," Greenberg replied in a clipped voice. He paused for a long moment before going on. "Nelson is going to meet with Parker. It's going to be Sunday night, and no one is supposed to know."

"How are they going to manage that?"

"Parker is going to be in New York Sunday. He'll take a private plane to a small airport outside of Philadelphia. The governor is going to drive out there to meet him."

"What's going to happen?" Stu asked.

"I have no idea. I wasn't invited, but I was there when the meeting was set up."

"I appreciate your telling me this, Jerry, but frankly I don't understand why you are doing it."

"That is very simple. Parker is a no good son of a bitch. He attacks my people. He attacks everything I believe in, and he is a disaster for the country. If Governor Nelson is doing business with him, then that is more than I can bear."

"I can understand that," said Stu sympathetically.

"I'm not sure you can. I'm torn apart. I've been with Nelson for a long time, and what I'm doing here tonight is completely disloyal, there is no question about that. But if he is making an alliance with Parker, that is the last straw. I feel the President should know about it. I don't know if there is anything he can do, but I'm convinced he ought to know. So here I am."

"What will you do after tonight?" asked Stu.

"I guess I'll stay with him as long as I can, but if I think that there is something else the President should know, I'll be in touch."

They sat quietly, both immersed in their thoughts. Then Greenberg, looking as if he were in great pain, abruptly left Stu's car and drove off. Stu remained for a few minutes, mulling over how he should tell the President.

CHAPTER SEVEN

For a week Charlie Jefferson, together with Nina Moran and Simon Pettigrew, had been held captive in the church basement in Oakland. They had been kept under constant guard, with food and water brought to them twice a day. So far, they had heard nothing from Mamba, and had endlessly speculated on what was going to happen to them.

Pettigrew became increasingly despondent, and during the last few days mentioned more and more that they were all going to be killed. Charlie and Nina did their best to keep up his spirits, but to no avail. Nina, in Charlie's view, had been magnificent. Not once had she lost her calm control.

They would sit and talk for hours on end. She told him about her affair with Mamba, how he had been so attractive to her at first, but how, as she came to know him better, he changed, becoming more irrational, more violent.

"He tried to get me to come with him in this," she explained. "He talked to me for months. He seemed to want me by his side when he started his great revolution. I tried to tell him how I feel, how sick I am of violence and his way. Mostly, I told him I could no longer be part of his movement, or of him."

"I'll bet he loved that," Charlie said.

"He's simply incredible, Charlie. He's really gone off the deep end. He just couldn't believe that any black person wouldn't follow him, and he couldn't accept the fact that I just didn't care for him any more."

Charlie could not help feeling a twinge of jealousy about all of that, though he knew that Nina's involvement with Mamba was long over and that he himself had no claim on her. But he felt close to her now. Sometimes they would just sit against the wall holding hands, not talking at all. Or they would try to cheer up Simon. At times, as they talked long into the night, they would almost forget where they were or what might become of them.

Charlie was lying on his cot, morosely staring at the door, when it suddenly opened and one of the guards walked in. "You two come with me," the man ordered, pointing at Charlie and Nina. "The other one stays here." Charlie noticed that the guard carried a pistol stuck loosely in his belt. "Don't get any smart ideas," the guard snapped, noticing Charlie's gaze. "We'd just as soon shoot you."

Charlie shrugged and nodded at Simon, who was standing quietly by the wall. He and Nina followed the guard up the stairs to a closed door, where two men stood at attention. The guard knocked politely and ushered them inside.

Mamba was seated at a desk, alone in the room. He smiled at Charlie. "I trust you've not been too uncomfortable, Jefferson. It's not exactly the Waldorf, I know, but it's the best we could do."

"Exactly what do you think you are doing with us?" Charlie snapped. "We've been kidnapped, held prisoner, and barely fed. You know damn well you can't keep this up forever. They are bound to find us."

"They may, Mr. Jefferson, but I am not concerned about that."

"How long do you expect to keep us like this?"

"You will find that out in due course. If it makes you feel more secure, I assure you that you will not be harmed. You have noticed, I trust, that despite the provocative nature of your little spying game no one has laid a hand on you."

Charlie turned away, realizing that there was no point in arguing further. He looked around the large room. It was spotlessly clean but sparsely furnished, with two portable cots, an old desk, a long table and several rickety chairs. The walls were covered with maps and large blown-up photographs, all of the Oakland area. He recognized the toll station on the Oakland side of the Bay Bridge and various shots of what looked like government buildings.

Mamba broke into Charlie's inspection of the room. "I've decided to invite you and Miss Moran on a small tour. There are a few things I want you to see."

They left Mamba's office and went into the same large meeting room where Charlie had heard Mamba's speech a week ago. It was bustling with activity. There appeared to be about a hundred young blacks in the room, divided into five groups, each engaged in a separate meeting.

Mamba led them close to one of these groups. The men sat on the floor, and an instructor stood before them, lecturing from an enlarged map of a section of Oakland. He would also point from time to time to a series of large photographs of the exterior and interior of what looked like a public building.

"These are the leaders of the team that is to take and hold the police station," Mamba said to Charlie. "They've been training for months on this sole objective."

Charlie listened to the instructor. He was explaining various internal functions of the Oakland police operation, while flipping over several large charts of the police headquarters. He explained where each police operation was located and delivered rapid instructions to the group. The men responded with complete attention.

"You will see that there are four other teams in this room," Mamba said, with a sweeping gesture of his arm. "Each team has a separate objective, and they are all being carefully trained."

"You expect to take over Oakland with this small group?" asked Charlie increduously.

"You underestimate us, Jefferson. You are seeing only a small part of our army. I will show you more, but not all of it by any means. Suffice it to say that there are a great many groups, just like the ones in this room, scattered throughout the city."

"Why are you showing me all of this?"

"I think it is important for you to know the seriousness of

90

what we are doing. Quite frankly, I want to impress you with our strength and our will to succeed in this venture."

"But what purpose does that serve?"

"At the proper time you may be of some use to me. I have decided to prepare you for that moment."

"You can't honestly think I will ever join with you."

"No, I am afraid you have become too much the lackey of the white establishment. Nevertheless, I am confident you will willingly serve me in the capacity I have in mind. However, that is not our problem today, so if you will follow me, we will see some more."

Mamba took them on a tour of the rest of the old church building and it was a startling experience. Each room was filled with groups of men being briefed for military action. Charlie was impressed with the size and thoroughness of the preparations. There was no doubt at all that Mamba intended to go through with his plans.

Finally, Mamba took them to the basement. He walked up to three heavily armed men standing guard before a bolted door.

"Open it up," he ordered.

He was instantly obeyed.

The door swung open and Mamba switched on the light. "I especially want you to see this," he said, motioning Charlie and Nina inside.

Charlie gasped with shock. The room was large, and from floor to ceiling was crammed with arms and ammunition—enough to supply a small army.

"Where did you get all of this?" demanded Charlie.

"That's no big problem," Mamba said with a smile. "In this country anyone can freely buy almost any kind of weapon, just so long as he can pay for it."

"But where did you get the money?"

"We have friends, both in the United States and elsewhere," answered Mamba. "They have been quite generous, and we have been accumulating our supply for over a year."

Mamba walked over to a box and opened it. He picked up an army light machine gun and showed it to Charlie. "We have

91

heavier weapons even than this, including hand grenades and mortars," Mamba explained with pride.

"You can't just buy those things," Charlie murmured.

"You're wrong, Jefferson. You are undoubtedly familiar with the white vigilante group, the Minutemen. Well, they have done it, not only here in California but throughout the country. So why should it surprise you that black men can accomplish the same thing? Doesn't it occur to you that when we see white bastards like that arming themselves we know who they're planning to aim those guns at? And that we're going to do likewise?"

"How can you get away with storing all of this in a church?" asked Charlie.

"It's been done before," said Mamba. "We control this church and there is no danger of anyone talking around here. The people in this neighborhood aren't about to tell on us to the same honkie cops who've been beating up on them all their long black lives."

They returned to Mamba's office and he motioned them to be seated. "You have only seen a part of what we are doing. What is going on here is happening all over this ghetto," he said.

"The police must know about it. How could you possibly keep such a thing quiet?" asked Charlie.

"I am reasonably certain that they don't know," said Mamba. "We started well over a year ago, and there hasn't been any sign that whitey knows."

"But how do you do it?"

"You would be amazed at how many covers we have been able to develop for our training program. You saw how we use this church. There are others just like this, some of them small street-front operations that no one pays any attention to. We have made use of karate schools, a trick I borrowed from my friends in New York. And gyms, meeting halls, house basements, any place at all. We have also been taking small groups into the mountains at night. It has worked out very well."

"Where do you get the men?" asked Charlie.

"There are members of the Black Guards to begin with, but we have also recruited brothers from all over the country. There

92

has been no problem securing volunteers. Black men have been suffering in silence for too many years. They know the only way they're going to get anything at all, for themselves or their kids, is to take it. We don't have to do much convincing to get people. At the moment we have more than five thousand men in training right here in Oakland. That, Mr. Jefferson, will be more than enough to succeed."

"I just can't believe you can hide all those people," said Charlie incredulously.

"You don't know Oakland, my friend," said Mamba. "Nobody pays any attention to who comes or goes from the Flatlands, and, of course, we are never seen in any large groups. We disperse at the end of each day. To whitey, all black men look alike, and even if they do notice more young blacks on the streets, I'm sure they think only that here are more shiftless niggers, too lazy to work."

"You must know that you will eventually be discovered," said Charlie.

"I am aware of that risk," said Mamba. "But we are almost ready to be discovered, Mr. Charlie."

When they got back to his office, Mamba offered them water from a thermos jug on the table. Lifting his glass he said, "I give you a toast, Jefferson. To the beautiful black man. May he right the wrongs that have been done to him."

"I have no objection to that toast," Charlie said. "But how in the hell can you justify the killing and destruction you are about to start? Of black people as well as white? How can that right anything at all?"

"A fair enough question, but your premises are wholly in error," Mamba replied. "What we are going to do is not wrong. We are going to take our own city, Oakland, not by a riot, but by the ancient American custom of force of arms. Then we'll hold Oakland, and you will be surprised at how long we can hold it. While Oakland is ours, we'll be the focal point of the world, and the world will hear about the injustices done to our people. This will not be anything evil, but an expression of our spirit, our racial pride and our strength."

"You are out of your mind, Mamba," Nina said quietly. "You are going to set back the black cause, not help it."

"What set back, woman?" Mamba shot back, his voice full of bitterness. "All we've ever got was tokenism, a little sop from whitey to hold off the devil nigger, a bone to placate the wild dog. We have gained nothing we haven't forced. The whites respond only to fear and that is what we are going to create."

"You are so wrong, Mamba," Charlie said. "We have made progress. The blacks don't need your violence, and when the moment of truth arrives, you won't be supported by the majority of our people."

"You will, I suppose," sneered Mamba. "You nibble at the edges of their power, Jefferson. They give you a peek in their doors, a look at their mansions and their women, and you're hypnotized into believing you're one of them. Well, you are not, and you never will be. So you are a dupe and a fool."

"I don't deny we have been wronged, that I have been wronged and used, and that all of this continues," Charlie said. "But there is hope now where there was none before. There are chances now, for all of us. Education, jobs, a decent home, a chance at pride. It is all possible. Times are changing, Mamba, and I am not ashamed to be a part of it. What happened to me can happen to others. I want to create those opportunities, not destroy them."

Mamba looked at Charlie incredulously. "Are you buying that 'go slow, nigger,' shit? Try telling that to one of our brothers. They're not sitting around waiting for the white establishment to tell them when they're ready to accept them. You are a small man, Jefferson, and you have forsaken your race."

"Just the opposite," Charlie answered, as he pushed back his chair and rose. "However, I will give you a toast. To equality and to peace."

Mamba glared at Charlie, and then slammed his glass on the table. "I've had enough of this crap. You are in a fog, man, and not in this world at all." He motioned to the guard as he glared at Charlie. "Take them back to Pettigrew," he ordered.

They were brought back to their room and again locked in. Charlie looked around. "My God," he exclaimed.

Simon lay doubled over on the floor. They both ran to him. Simon was retching and holding his head with both hands. He was bleeding and badly bruised, and his shirt had been partially torn from his back.

"Oh, baby, what have they done to you?" Nina asked, her voice rising. She tried to cradle his head, but he shook her off and vomited again. He was incoherent and could only mumble something they couldn't understand.

Charlie ran to the door and pounded on it with both fists. "Come in here!" he shouted.

The door opened and the guard shoved Charlie away. "What do you want now?" he demanded.

"What in the hell have you done to Pettigrew?" Charlie asked angrily.

The guard laughed. "He gave us a little trouble, so we quieted him down."

"You sons of bitches," yelled Charlie, starting for the guard.

Two more men entered the room, one of them pointing a pistol directly at Charlie's stomach. "Just cool it, man," the first guard warned, "or you are going to get some of the same."

Charlie stopped and tried to get himself under control. "Put that gun away," he said, struggling to stay calm. "What are you going to do about Pettigrew. You bastards beat him up and God knows how badly he's hurt."

"That's your problem, boy," said the guard.

"Won't you even get us some water and bandages?" Nina asked.

"You just do the best you can," the guard snapped, slamming the door as they left the room.

Charlie and Nina helped Simon to his cot and tried to clean him a bit. Finally, he appeared to fall asleep, though his breathing continued to be labored.

"Those sadistic sons of bitches," muttered Charlie. "All that high and mighty talk from Mamba about racial pride. This is what he really means."

"That's what I've been telling you about him," said Nina. "He's perverted the whole idea. He's sick, but they listen to him. That's the tragedy of it."

"How could you ever have been with him?" Charlie bitterly asked.

"I believe in black power," Nina replied, holding Simon's head in her lap. "I believe in militancy and pushing our race forward in every way we know how. But I know there's a limit and that Mamba has gone way beyond it."

"There has got to be another way," Charlie said. "Black people don't want this kind of solution. They have too much heart to accept this way."

"I've been looking for another way for years," Nina said. "I've seen your way and I've seen Mamba's. Neither of them seems right to me. They both lead nowhere. But I'm going to keep on looking."

"I wish it could be with me," Charlie said.

Nina looked up at him and smiled softly. "I do too," she said. Then she turned back to Simon and gently tried to comfort him.

O n Sunday, November 17, twelve days after the election, Senator Jack Parker, Janice Pruitt and Millard Duval were having an early dinner in Parker's suite in New York's Americana Hotel.

It had been drizzling all day, and a low cloud cover obscured the view from their top-floor room. Out on the street a heavy police contingent had thrown up barricades at both Seventh Avenue corners of the hotel. A large crowd had gathered, as sullen as the weather, heavily pressed against the wooden barriers, waiting for a chance to see Parker and shout their derision. They had not been given that chance. Parker had flown in from Florida the previous night and had been whisked to the hotel, where he remained in seclusion. He had no delusions about his popularity in this ethnically mixed city.

The announced purpose of his trip was to conduct private conferences with several of his Northern leaders. To give that story credence, his state chairmen from New York, New Jersey, New England and Pennsylvania had been dutifully brought to him. Except for the talk with his Pennsylvania man, the meetings had been devoid of real purpose, consisting only of short reports on Parker's strength and enough political gossip to fill a reasonable amount of time.

With his Pennsylvania chairman, Parker had wasted no time on trivia and had come straight to the point.

"Is Governor Nelson still set to meet me?" Parker asked.

"I spoke to his man again this morning, and he said that the governor definitely will be at the airport at ten P.M."

"What about his mood? Did you get any reading on his thinking?"

"Not really. They were completely noncommittal with me, but my guess is that his willingness to meet shows he is so eager he can taste it."

"If I wanted your guess, I'd ask for it," Parker shot back. "Just give me what you know."

"Only that they will see us," said the chairman.

"All right. You be somewhere around that airport in case we need you," Parker said, concluding the conversation.

Sometime later Parker was alone with Janice Pruitt and Millard Duval. He had barely touched his dinner and now nervously lit a cigar and walked to the window to peer out at the rainy darkness.

"Is there any chance we will be weathered in?" he asked Duval.

"I just spoke to the pilot at the Westchester airport. He says that it is still well above the minimum up there, although there is a chance it will close in."

"We can't take that chance, Duval. You get me a firm forecast. If we can't fly, then we'll have to drive." He looked at his watch and saw that it was a few minutes past six. If we drive, we will have to leave very soon."

"I'll check it again," said Duval, feeling the tension. He left the room.

Janice Pruitt, who was the only one enjoying her dinner, gave Parker a slow smile. "It's going to be just fine, Jack. I think you have Nelson. All you've got to do is dangle the bait. He has nibbled and I know he'll take the whole hook."

"That's easy for you to say," said Parker, still irritated. "It's my future we're negotiating."

"You will do it, honey." She walked around the table and stood behind him, softly rubbing his forehead.

He abruptly moved away from her. "I've got no time for that," he said. "Just be ready when we leave. You're coming with us, and I don't want to wait around for you."

"Yes, Senator," she said, pulling back.

98

Duval returned to the room, reporting that he had spoken to both the weather bureau and the pilot. Both sources were almost certain they would be able to fly at their scheduled eight-thirty P.M. takeoff time. Parker reluctantly accepted the advice, and the three of them silently waited.

It was close to seven when Billy Dan Reeves, Parker's chief political operative, came to the room. He appeared flushed and slightly out of breath.

"I just got back from Washington, boss," he began. "There was such a stackup over LaGuardia I wasn't sure I would make it in time. Anyway, it's all set. It was tough, but the secret service has agreed."

"Can we trust them?" Parker asked.

"We have no choice, Senator. You know they have an agent right outside your door at all times, and there is no way you can walk out of here without him and others tagging along, especially with that crowd of rabble rousers waiting on the street. The secret service is bound by law to give you constant protection, and they would raise all sorts of hell if they lost track of you even for a short while."

"I know that. That's why I let you talk to them. Just tell me what they've agreed to do."

"I spoke to the chief of the secret service at his home in Washington. I told him we wanted to make a short trip, and we wanted no one to know about it. I made it very clear that this meant everyone, including the President. He gave me a hard time about that, but I told him his department never dreamed of the kind of trouble you would cause in the Senate if he leaked this meeting."

"I'll have his ass if he talks, you can bet on that," muttered Parker.

"He knows that. I also pointed out that the candidate protection law was not intended as a vehicle for revealing everything we wanted to do. In any event, he finally agreed."

"Does that mean they will call off their agents?" asked Parker.

"They can't do that. The law won't permit it. He did agree

to remove all his agents except for one man who will be at the door when we leave. He will come with us."

"Will he keep his mouth shut?"

"The chief personally spoke to him, and it's all set. He's out there now and I talked to him before I came in. He understands, and I'm convinced he won't talk."

"You had better be right," snapped Parker. "I still think there is a way to do this without their knowing, and, believe me, it will be on your head if it screws up."

"It will work," said Billy Dan.

Shortly before seven-thirty, Billy Dan left to get the car. A few minutes later the rest of them—Parker, Millard Duval, Janice and the secret service agent—left the suite. Parker had donned a raincoat, which he wore with the collar turned high, and a hat pulled low over his eyes. The agent led them through the hall to a waiting service elevator. They descended to the basement, went out a delivery door, and quickly walked to Sixth Avenue, where Billy Dan was waiting in his car.

No one saw them leave Manhattan.

Governor Maynard Nelson was, if anything, more nervous than Parker as he sat in the living room of his Philadelphia home, waiting to drive to the small suburban airport where he was to meet with Parker. His press secretary, Jerry Greenberg, was with him, and Nelson was pacing the floor. Nelson was a man who perspired easily, and the cool temperature of the room did nothing to prevent the moisture from forming on his forehead and around the tight collar of his shirt.

"Do you think the President is going to do anything?" he asked Greenberg.

"That's hard to say, Governor."

"Well, I imagine I will have to take the risk," said Nelson, sounding somewhat less than firm.

"You know how I feel about that, sir. I think it is a very bad mistake to do any business with Parker."

"I know your thoughts, Jerry, but I feel I must see this through." Nelson peered at his press secretary. Ever since the

President had called earlier in the week there had been a distance, an undefined defensiveness about his assistant.

The President's call had come as a complete surprise to Nelson. No one was supposed to know of his planned meeting with Parker, and yet the President, somehow, knew all about it. He had known both the date and the place of the rendezvous. The President had, by turns, sounded indignant and hurt, as he had attempted to dissuade Nelson from going through with it. Nelson had denied the accusation, but without much conviction. At the end, the President had attempted to invoke patriotism, but Nelson continued to profess his innocence, and the conversation had ended on that note.

Governor Nelson had waited through these intervening days, watching to see when the other shoe would drop. He had expected the President, or Harrington, to make some kind of charge, but nothing had been said. So now, on Sunday, he was faced with the dilemma of either going through with the meeting on the almost certain assumption that the public would eventually know of it, or calling it off, either with or without telling Parker that the President had wind of what was going on.

The problem was, Maynard Nelson wanted to be President, and he had no doubt that he would make a good President, offering the type of constructive conservatism the country so badly needed in these trying times. Of course, there was personal ambition mixed in with his attitude—he was honest enough with himself to admit that—but there was also an overriding sense of public duty. He was convinced that the country needed him, and that he would serve the country well. But he had not been elected on November 5th. He had carried twenty-one states, more than either Harrington or Parker, but he had only 183 electoral votes, compared with Harrington's 233 and Parker's 122. This meant that, without Parker, there was no way for him to be President except by a House of Representatives vote, and that route was so fraught with unknowns he was unable to see his way.

Consequently, when Parker had sent word he wanted to meet, Governor Nelson had not hesitated for a moment. He was prepared to do business, providing the price was not too high. He had decided that, despite the almost certain exposure of the meeting, he would have his entire four-year term to demonstrate by actions that he was a good President.

He had also concluded there was no point in telling Parker that the President knew, at least not just yet. This might scare Parker off. Nevertheless, Governor Nelson was disturbed by how the President had come by this information. It could have leaked from Parker's end, or from the secret service, who were, of necessity, aware of the meeting. It also could have come from any of the half dozen of his own people who knew of the rendezvous, and it was this possibility which most upset Nelson. That would mean the worst kind of disloyalty and a weakness in his own organization which might be exceedingly dangerous to him.

As the time to leave neared, the telephone rang. Greenberg answered it, and with a somewhat stricken look cupped his hand over the receiver.

"It's the White House. The President wants to talk to you."

Governor Nelson cursed and briefly considered not taking the call. Then he said, "I'll take it."

There was a brief delay while the operators got the President on the line. "Governor, have you decided what you are going to do about meeting with Parker?" the President asked without preliminary.

"I believe I have," Nelson responded, deciding neither to admit nor to deny the planned meeting.

"I am delighted that, at least, you are no longer playing games with me. However, you are making a terrible mistake if you make a deal with Parker."

"I'm afraid I'll have to be the judge of that, Mr. President."

"Be that as it may, you know that I am completely aware of what you are going to do. I've only held it close this long because I thought you might still change your mind and call it off. You must realize that I cannot continue to remain quiet."

"Just what are you planning to do?" Nelson asked.

"You can be assured that I will have something to say at the appropriate moment. The manner and timing of that statement,

I'm afraid, will have to remain undisclosed, at least for now."

"That is your prerogative, of course."

"Governor, my call is simply to give you fair warning. Your meeting with Parker will become public knowledge. If you make any arrangement with that man, you can be certain it will become known, and I do not think that will do your cause any good."

Nelson frowned deeply as he again realized that, somehow, the President had a source of information about his activities. He had to assume that the President was not merely bluffing but would indeed know of any bargain that might be struck. However, he was determined to go forward. "I'm sorry, Mr. President, but my plans are made," he said.

"If you must see him, I can only ask that you consider all the consequences before you agree to anything."

"I shall, as always, think most carefully before I act," Nelson replied coldly.

"You be certain to do that," the President said, matching Nelson's icy tone and concluding the conversation.

Governor Nelson looked at Greenberg, who was morosely shuffling some papers, and then walked to the bar and poured himself a drink. He glanced at his watch, saw that it was time to go, and said to Greenberg, "Tell them to bring the car around. Let's get this over with."

"Yes, sir," said Greenberg, still looking glum.

"You'll be staying here, you know. Somebody has to mind the store," Nelson said, attempting a lightness he did not feel. Jerry Greenberg was valuable to him, and normally he preferred having him around at important moments. Greenberg's unflappable nature and his cool judgment were invariably helpful. However, Nelson had decided that there was no sense in unduly antagonizing Parker. In view of the senator's highly publicized anti-Semitism, the presence of Governor Nelson's well-known Jewish staff member could conceivably add an unnecessary divisive note.

Nelson, accompanied by a secret service agent and a member of his own staff, arrived at the airport at ten P.M. The misting rain, which had been falling all weekend, showed no sign of letting up and the temperature had dropped.

The airfield was deserted except for the maintenance shack, where one man was on duty to handle the radio and field lights. There was one other car parked at the field in which a lone man was sitting. Nelson directed that their car be parked well away from both the shack and the other automobile, and there they waited.

They heard the plane before they saw it. It circled the field once and then landed, taxiing to the grass a short distance from Nelson's car. Parker and four others alighted from the twin Beechcraft. As the governor and his two escorts started toward the plane they saw that the man from the other car was also approaching and they stopped.

"He's okay," shouted Parker, as he walked toward Nelson. "He's my Pennsylvania chairman, and I asked him to be here."

Nelson nodded and walked up to Parker. The two of them perfunctorily shook hands.

"Your car or my plane?" asked Parker.

"Let's use the car, and I think it should only be the two of us," said the governor.

"Of course. Our people can wait in the plane," Parker said, gesturing to the others to move away as he and Nelson walked to the car. They sat in the back with the doors and windows tightly closed.

"What can I do for you, Senator?" asked Nelson rather abruptly. "You will recall that you asked for this meeting."

"I am aware of that, Governor," Parker answered, and then paused to light a cigar before continuing. "You and I find ourselves in an interesting position. Neither of us can be President without the other, and unless we come to some understanding neither of us will be President."

"You could make the same statement concerning Senator Harrington," Nelson said dryly.

"Naturally. However, for me to make an arrangement with Harrington would be too destructive to my ideas, and, more importantly, my people would not accept a coalition with a woolly-minded liberal. On the other hand, for you to make a deal with Harrington would be equally unacceptable. Your party's concept of the two-party system would never bear up under such a strain. Isn't that true?"

"Go on."

"So the only position that makes any sense is for you and me to explore what might be done. From my point of view, your conservatism is not too distant from my own views, although I am disappointed that you do not share my concern over the growing black-Jewish conspiracy. However, I have noted that you have never directly attacked me on these points."

"Senator, I must tell you that I emphatically do not agree with those charges you have been making. My silence has only been because I don't wish to dignify your position by responding to it. I feel constrained to tell you that."

Parker shrugged, and then continued. "Actually, that doesn't surprise me. Of course, that's what is wrong with your party. You claim to represent the traditional elements of the country, but you are forever temporizing, attempting to play to the left while protecting the right. It is an impossible stance, and the reason why I felt obliged to give the people a third and, if I may say so, more honest choice."

"Then, why are you here tonight?" Nelson asked.

"I want to make you President."

"But I cannot, I will not, give voice to your prejudices." Nelson's tone was firm.

"I do not expect you to."

"Then why are you willing to back me?"

"I do not think that I can get enough electoral votes to win myself, and I'm sure that neither you nor Harrington would throw your votes to me. If I thought that such a result were possible, believe me, I would not have asked for this meeting. As I said, I also happen to believe that your Presidency would more closely approach what I believe in than would Harrington's. Consequently, I am willing to compromise and offer you my electoral votes."

"Just like that?" Nelson asked, somewhat incredulously.

"Not quite," Parker said, his smile broadening. "I would expect the same willingness to compromise from you."

"Just what is your price, Senator?" snapped Nelson, becoming irritated with Parker's supercilious tone.

"You have put it rather harshly, Governor," Parker responded. "I would rather call it a show of reasonableness on your part."

"All right," said Nelson with increasing impatience. "What is it you are asking of me?"

"My administrative assistant, Millard Duval, is a highly trained attorney. He graduated from the Harvard Law School, served a brief period in the F.B.I., and has been an Assistant Attorney General in Florida. He is thirty-seven years old, and I will vouch for his character and ability. I want you to appoint him Attorney General of the United States."

Nelson was shocked. "I've never even heard of the man," he exploded. "Nobody knows who he is. How can you possibly expect me to do such a thing?"

Parker continued in his slow, careful drawl. "Duval is here with me tonight and I am perfectly willing for you to meet him. I am sure you will have the same good impression of him as I do."

"That has nothing to do with it, Senator. You know as well as I that the Attorney General appointment is extremely sensitive. His responsibilities are so vast these days that it takes a man of great depth and experience to adequately do the job. The public will accept nothing less, not to speak of the Senate, which must confirm him."

"I'm completely aware of the latter problem," responded Parker. "I'm willing to take my chances with the Senate. There will be difficulties with confirmation, I am sure of that, but I think we could get him through. The fact that I am a member of that illustrious body, plus the traditional willingness of the Senate to permit a President to choose his own Cabinet, should be sufficient."

Governor Nelson had been listening with great concentration to Parker's discourse, but now another objection entered his mind. "Senator, I simply cannot permit a situation to develop where another man, be it you or anybody else, would control a member of my Cabinet."

"Of course, Governor, and I would not ask that of you," answered Parker smoothly. "I demand no strings on the appointment. Duval will be your Attorney General, not mine. He will be responsible only to you. It is sufficient for my purposes that he hold the office. I will take my chances on how he will perform under your direction."

Governor Nelson stared out the car window at the rain which by now had begun to come down much harder. He was being offered the chance to be President of the United States, and the package was being wrapped as attractively as possible. Parker may not have been sincere when he said he did not intend to control Duval but it would prove almost impossible in any event, since, once elected, Nelson could fire the man at any time. Parker would be content with the mere fact of an appointment of his administrative assistant as Attorney General, an event that the national press would unquestionably interpret as a great and significant showing of Parker's strength. The fact that Duval was unknown only added to the prestige the appointment would bring to Parker.

"Do I have to give you an answer tonight?" he asked Parker.

"No, I don't expect that. You think it over, but I must know before Saturday. I'm meeting with my electors in Miami Beach this weekend, and it is essential that I have an answer before then."

"All right. Now why don't you bring Duval over here and let me have a look at him."

Parker nodded, got out of the car, and walked to the plane where the others had been waiting.

"He wants to see you, Millard," he said to his assistant. Duval, who had first been told of Parker's proposal when he had been taken aside by the senator just before they boarded the plane to Philadelphia, was still stunned by the news. He had no previous inkling that the senator had such a thing in mind, and he hadn't for a moment believed that Governor Nelson would consider naming him to the Cabinet. Yet here was Parker saying that the governor wanted to see him.

They returned to Nelson's car, and Parker motioned Duval to get in back with the governor while Parker took the front seat. They conversed for a long time, with the governor asking questions of Duval concerning his background, his philosophy and his views on law enforcement. Finally, Nelson came to the main points of his concern.

"If I were to name you Attorney General, where would your loyalties lead you if I ordered you in a direction different from that advocated by Senator Parker?"

"I would follow the President," said Duval, who had been warned by Parker on this aspect of Nelson's possible interest.

"You have no hesitancy on that matter?" persisted Nelson.

"You know that I have deep feelings about Senator Parker and what he stands for, but I quite clearly understand that I would have to submerge these feelings if I were to remain in your Cabinet. Of course, if your policies diverged too much from my views, then I would have to resign."

"You say you believe in what Senator Parker has been saying. Does that mean that you would feel obliged to speak out along those lines?"

"No. You have my assurance that I would not say anything to cause you embarrassment. As I see it, there have been Attorneys General who have spoken out on issues, and there have been those who have not, who have been content to enforce the laws and to administer the department as best they could. I would take the latter course, and I think I would do it well."

They continued the conversation for a while longer, and then Governor Nelson asked that Duval excuse himself.

"He sounded very good, don't you agree?" Parker asked after Duval left the car.

"I admit he gave the right answers, but I certainly want to give more thought to your proposal."

"Very well," answered Parker. "I'll wait for your answer. Is there anything else we need discuss?"

"Yes, there is one other matter." Nelson paused briefly before continuing. "The President knows of our meeting tonight and he may break it publicly at any moment."

"What?" said Parker, his face becoming suddenly flushed. "How in the hell did he find out?"

"I don't know his source, but he obviously had been correctly informed. He was quite accurate on the details. It could have come from my people, or from yours, or perhaps from the secret service. I have no idea who did it."

"Well, goddamn it, how long has he known?"

"He called me tonight," Nelson answered, deliberately omitting the President's call earlier in the week. "I don't know when he found out. He didn't volunteer that information."

"Why in the hell didn't you tell me before this?" said Parker.

"Now look here, Senator, the fact that there is a leak is potentially more damaging to me than to you. I trust you can see that. Obviously I have nothing to gain from a disclosure and an attack from the President. However, I am willing to accept that cost in order to fully consider whatever you have to say. That is my position. If it is not yours, then we might as well terminate our discussion now."

Parker stared hard at the governor, whose voice had risen during his last statement. Then, with some difficulty he forced himself to regain control. "What will the President do?" Parker asked, somewhat calmer.

"I do not know. I would only suggest that you and I should operate from the premise that the President's source remains and that he will soon know of the substance of our conversations."

"That may be, Governor, but let's not make it any easier for him than we must. As of the moment only you, Duval and I are privy to what I am asking. If we agree not to allow anyone else to have that information, and I mean anyone, then perhaps we can cut off the leak."

"That is fine with me."

"Good. Then my offer will remain open, and I trust that I will hear from you by Saturday."

On Saturday, November 23, six days after his conversation with Governor Nelson, Senator Jack Parker convened the meeting of the 122 electors pledged to him. The schedule called for a banquet on Saturday night, and a formal meeting of the electors on Sunday afternoon. However, the public show was only a small part of what was going on, the culmination of weeks of intense effort.

Three weeks had passed since the election, and Billy Dan Reeves and his state chairmen had contacted each of Parker's electors. Reeves and his assistants were aided by bankers, politicians, publishers, industrialists and other backers of Senator Parker who were willing to work with those who would be voting on December 16. The message was simple: vote for Senator Parker or anyone else he may recommend.

Now the results were all in, carefully carded and indexed by Billy Dan—who had personally verified the accuracy of the information. Thus he reported that the senator could exercise effective control over each of the electors. They were his to vote as he alone saw fit. He was free to negotiate from a base of solid strength.

Parker was also aware of two other developments: on Monday the President had held a nationally televised press conference at which he had revealed that Parker and Governor Nelson had met secretly. The President furiously attacked both of them for attempting to subvert the free vote of the electors and for striking a secret bargain to deliver the Presidency to one or the other of them.

Parker had watched the President's performance with grudging admiration. There was no doubt that the old man was effective. However, the President had not revealed the substance of the alleged "deal" between the candidates, even though he had been hard pressed on this point. He had candidly admitted that he did not know the details, but he warned that such an agreement, whatever it was, could only harm the office of the Presidency and the country. Senator Parker took considerable comfort from the fact that the President's incomplete knowledge meant that they had apparently isolated the source of the leak.

Nevertheless, the President's charge had raised a storm of publicity, almost all of it unfavorable to Parker. The newspapers and the network commentators were virtually unanimous in their condemnation of any arrangement between Nelson and Parker, and Parker did not for a moment doubt that if a poll were taken today his and Nelson's stock would have fallen by a considerable margin. More importantly, Parker was willing to grant that if the general election were being held on this day, Harrington would probably be able to win it.

None of this bothered Parker, for from here on out only the electors counted, and he was confident that he could maintain the necessary control over his own people. The Democrats and Republicans would continue to vote their party, and this, of course, gave Senator Parker precisely the leverage he desired.

This brought Parker to the second development. The public outcry following the President's attack had not panicked Governor Nelson. On Friday evening Nelson had telephoned to inform Parker that he had decided to accept the offer; that nothing the President had said changed his mind; and that in return for Parker's 122 electoral votes he would, if elected President, appoint Millard Duval as his Attorney General.

On this Saturday night the Miami Beach banquet hall was packed with the electors and several thousand other carefully selected supporters. As Senator Parker entered the room, there were frenzied cheers from the crowd. He stood before them hearing, feeling, tasting, their approval. As he approached the podium, the cheering increased and Parker raised both arms above his head, hands clasped together in the victory gesture that he had made familiar during the campaign. Finally the shouting subsided and he took his seat, secure in the power he was about to wield.

His speech revealed nothing new, not a hint about his arrangement with Governor Nelson. Instead, it was a wildly swinging reprise of most of his familiar themes, concluding with an attack on both the Democratic and Republican parties. To the assembled press, however, it was significant that Parker made no denial of the President's charge of a deal, and their stories that night carried as their headlines, "Parker fails to deny deal with Nelson."

It was after eleven P.M. when Parker and Billy Dan returned to his suite. Janice was already there, and she reported that Millard Duval, whom Parker had ordered to stay out of sight while they were in Miami, had left to go to bed.

Parker took off his coat and tie and casually tossed them over a chair. "All right, Billy Dan," he said. "Give me a rundown on what happens tomorrow."

"It's all set, boss. I've got the pledge drafted and I can just about guarantee that all of your electors will execute it."

"Read it to me."

"Yes, sir," answered Billy Dan, pulling a neatly typed sheet of paper from his coat. He read: "I solemnly pledge and agree, in consideration of similar pledges from one or more of my fellow Presidential Electors, that I shall cast my vote as a Presidential Elector on December 16 of this year for Senator Jack Parker of Florida for President of the United States, unless prior to the time of such voting, Senator Jack Parker shall notify me in writing not to so cast my votes, in which event I shall cast my Presidential Electoral vote for such person as Senator Jack Parker shall designate in said written notification."

Billy Dan explained that each elector would sign an individual instrument, and that each signature would be acknowledged before a notary public.

"Why did you put in that 'consideration' business? Do you think that makes it legally binding?" asked Parker.

"No, not really, but our lawyers said that there is nothing in the law to say it isn't binding. So we stuck it in. Actually, these pledges are nothing more than a public affirmation. The real muscle is the personal pressure we have put on all of them, and, naturally, their loyalty to you."

"Fine. Now you and your boys start tonight and get all

112

those fine electors on the dotted line before we convene tomorrow. I want to have those papers before I speak to them."

"There will be no difficulty with that," said Billy Dan. He paused, and then asked, "Now can you tell me what you've decided to do?"

"No, I cannot. No offense, Billy Dan, but you will just have to wait to learn along with everyone else. Just accept that I have good reasons for the way I am doing this."

"Of course," said Billy Dan, feeling somewhat hurt that the senator wouldn't confide in his own political manager. He managed a smile and a wave to Janice Pruitt, and left the room.

Senator Parker and Janice were now alone. She sat quietly looking at him, not sure of his mood and of what he wanted of her. He caught her stare, and grinned at her from the deep cushioned chair where he sat, feet stretched before him and arms flung loosely over the sides.

"Get out of your clothes, and come here," he said in a cold, even voice.

Janice shuddered and rose to her feet. Fighting to keep her face expressionless, she slowly removed her blouse and skirt. Parker said nothing, but his eyes narrowed and he impatiently motioned her to continue. She hesitated, then unsnapped her bra and stepped out of her slip, panties and shoes. They faced each other for a long moment.

"Pick up the phone and call my wife," he said, his mouth suddenly going slack as he slouched in his chair. "Tell her I'm busy but I wanted to find out how she is getting along. Don't forget to give her my deepest love."

Janice could not control her trembling. She started to object, but she was conditioned to accept his directions without question and could not bring herself to defy him. Feeling sick, she reached for the telephone and continued to stare at Parker while she dialed directly to the Parker home in Chevy Chase.

"Mrs. Parker, this is Janice Pruitt," she said. "The senator asked me to call. He apologizes for being so busy, but he wants you to know that everything is all right. He sends his love," she added, almost inaudibly. She listened as Jean Parker in her high, nervous voice said that she was fine, that she had spent the afternoon with her garden club, and that she "just knew" the senator was going to have a successful meeting tomorrow. Through it all, Janice stood, naked and ashamed.

Parker's eyes had begun to glaze. "Now ask her about the kids," he whispered.

Janice violently shook her head, suddenly unable to go on. She quickly said goodbye. Then she dropped her arms to her sides and stood very still as Parker slowly rose from the chair and walked to her, his big body towering over her. Without a word he slapped her sharply across the face.

"You filthy bitch," he said, slapping her again. "Get the hell out of here."

Tears streaming down her face, Janice awkwardly gathered her clothes, pulled on her dress, and ran from the room, while the senator, laughing sharply, poured himself a tall, straight bourbon and walked into the bedroom. Within minutes he was sleeping, fitfully and alone.

Sunday morning dawned brilliantly in Miami. Senator Parker awoke early, feeling groggy and unrested. He dressed and called Billy Dan Reeves, who reported that he had obtained all but twenty-five of the pledges, and that there would be no problem with the rest, which he expected to have by noon. Parker then called Millard Duval.

"I hope you've remained out of sight and have kept your mouth shut," he said.

"I haven't breathed a word, Senator, but I am sure getting sick of looking at these four walls."

"Well, you just stay there for a while longer. We'll be leaving here later today, after I've had my little say downstairs."

"Is everything still all right?"

"It couldn't be better," answered Parker. "Nelson's in the bag, and so are our electors."

"I'll be right here, sir."

Parker hung up and called Janice Pruitt, telling her to

come to his suite right away. In a few minutes she arrived, her beautiful features looking uncertain and haggard. Parker asked her to join him for breakfast. Although she had no appetite, she sat with him while he spoke expansively of his plans. No mention was made of the previous night; Janice, however, felt numb inside, wondering what she was becoming and where it all would lead.

Promptly at two P.M. Senator Parker entered the hotel's small ballroom for the elector's meeting. He was carrying a briefcase and was surrounded by his usual entourage of staff and security people. The back of the room was filled with press and camera equipment, while the front chairs were reserved for the electors, all of whom were present, the V.I.P.'s of the moment. They all stood and cheered their candidate as he mounted the rostrum and stood before them. Parker extracted an inch-thick sheaf of papers, carefully placing them before him.

"You men and women represent the true hopes, the true history, and the true beliefs of the nation," he said. "This magnificent country of ours is in a state of crisis, a crisis which is becoming worse with every day. The blacks and Jews and liberals are chipping away at everything you believe in. They want your jobs, they want your homes, and they have taken away even your God-given birthright to walk safely on your own streets. The only hope lies in you and the millions like you throughout the land. And your time has now come. I only ask that you stand up and be counted. Will you do that?"

The response was deafening.

Parker continued. "I know it is said that you are only from twelve states and number but one hundred twenty-two votes, but in unity you have the power to change the course of events. And you shall!

"The Constitution has cloaked you with a precious mantle of freedom. It has given you the unfettered responsibility to select the President of the United States. There is no earthly power which can diminish or restrain your right to choose as only you see fit. No one, not the conspirators of International Jewry and black madness, not their handmaidens in the press and on television, not the politicians who fear them and whom they control, none of them can touch you or what you are about to do."

He now picked up the pack of papers and held them high, tightly clutched in both hands. His eyes were wide and bright as he continued.

"These papers are our covenant to go forward together. I announce to the world that we are now united. We are of one mind. We are of a single purpose, dedicated and together.

"In sovereign exercise of your powers you have agreed to vote for me or for whomever I shall designate at your December sixteenth election. Thus, these documents constitute a solemn pact between us. They are a tool of strength, not for me, but for all of us and for that in which we so fervently believe.

"I am humbled by your faith in me, and I pledge before God that I shall not lightly exercise the judgment which you have directed me to make.

"I shall not shirk the task which you have laid before me. I shall decide, and that decision, with your help, shall reshape the United States into that Christian nation which it was originally intended to be and which, before Almighty God, it shall be again."

The roar was overwhelming, and he stood before them, the pledges in his hands, exultation welling up within him. These were his people, he thought, and his time had come.

CHAPTER NINE

On November 30th, a Saturday night, Stu Brady and Sari went to a party in Georgetown. It was six days after Senator Jack Parker had made his emotional announcement that he was in solid control of his 122 electoral votes and would deliver them to whomever he saw fit. The intervening week had been hectic, even by White House standards, and Stu, feeling unusually tired, welcomed the diversion of the party. Sari seemed delighted that Stu was available on this night, and she had sparkled with anticipation as they prepared to go.

Stu was relieved that the week had finally ended. The pressure had started on Monday when the President, enraged at what Senator Parker was attempting to pull off and certain that he had come to some kind of understanding with Governor Nelson, had called in the Attorney General and ordered him to use every legal means at his disposal to stop Parker. The Attorney General had stubbornly argued that such a move was hopeless, that the Constitution permitted electors to vote as they pleased, and that, although Parker could in no way enforce his written pledges, there was nothing that could be done to prevent the electors from voluntarily following Parker's wishes, if that was their desire. The President, however, would have none of this carefully reasoned legal opinion.

"Are you telling me that there is nothing we can even try in order to stop this?" he asked.

"No, Mr. President, we could attempt to enjoin them in the courts. I'm only saying that in my opinion we won't get the injunctions."

"Are you afraid to give the courts a chance at it?" the President snapped.

"No, sir, I will do whatever you say."

"Then do it. Now what are the procedures?"

"We can start proceedings in each of the judicial districts where Parker's electors live, and attempt to get a court order preventing them from voting in accordance with anyone's will but their own."

"I want you to put your heart into this case," the President said. The Attorney General had assured the President that he would do his best, and had then departed.

Before he left the White House, the Attorney General had briefly stopped by Stu's office.

"You are a friend of Charlie Jefferson's, aren't you?" he asked.

"That's right," Stu said. "As a matter of fact, he called me on election day about a trip he was making for you, something about some trouble in Oakland. I expected to hear from him again, but I guess you just keep him too busy to bother with his old friends."

"I wish that were the situation, Stu. The fact is that Charlie did go to Oakland, but he has completely disappeared."

Stu had been taken aback. He had been so engrossed in his own problems that he had completely forgotten about Charlie's strange call. "Do you have any idea what happened?" he asked.

"He called me the day after he arrived out there. He said he was on to something, but he didn't give any details. I waited a few days, and when I didn't hear from him again I had our District Attorney's office out there start looking for him."

"What about the F.B.I.?" Stu asked.

"They are in it now. I suppose I made a mistake in not alerting them sooner, but since Charlie's mission was intended to verify the accuracy of some F.B.I. reports, I was hesitant about telling the Director. When Charlie had not been found by the weekend I leveled with the Bureau. The Director was upset, but I must say they have really pitched in. Unfortunately, no one has come up with anything except a lot of unsubstantiated reports that there may be some trouble brewing. And Charlie is still missing."

Stu was upset about the Attorney General's delay in getting the F.B.I. involved, and told him so. Now, there seemed nothing further to be done but to wait and hope.

All in all, it had not been a good week for the Justice Department. They had started a series of actions in all the appropriate District Courts, just as the Attorney General had promised. They had asked for injunctions and, so far, there had been a half dozen preliminary hearings. The government had not prevailed in a single one. Justice was starting appeal procedures and was hopeful of getting a quick Circuit Court opinion and then moving, if necessary, into the Supreme Court for a decision prior to the December 16 deadline. Nobody involved held out much hope, and even the President had privately admitted to Stu that he considered the entire effort a desperation move.

The President had also attempted to contact Governor Nelson, but the governor would not take any White House phone calls. Finally, on this Saturday morning, the President had asked Stu to call his Nelson contact, Jerry Greenberg. Stu had fervently argued that this would be extremely unfair to Greenberg and that even a telephone call from the White House might prove dangerous to him. But the President had not backed down, and Stu had reluctantly agreed to try.

So far there had been no success in this effort either, and Stu had instructed the operators to keep trying and to call him if they made contact. He warned them not to identify themselves or Stu under any circumstances, in order to give Greenberg at least this much protection.

The Georgetown party was in full swing when Stu and Sari arrived. The town house, located on a quiet, tree-lined street, was a three-story red brick structure, beautifully renovated and expensively immaculate, quite in contrast to the Bradys' slightly run-down apartment only a dozen blocks away. Tonight the host, a wealthy and politically active attorney, had turned over his entire home to the party. Posters of the past campaign were pinned on every wall, a small combo was loudly playing on the first floor, tables of food were on the second floor, and one of the larger third-floor bedrooms, now stripped of furniture, was softly lighted and filled with the sounds of soft music from a record player. There was a well-stocked bar on every floor, and waiters and some very pretty, briefly clad girls circulated among the guests, seeing that glasses remained full.

Perhaps a hundred people were there when the Bradys arrived. They knew many of them, not surprising considering the intimate, ingrown world of Washington politics, government and press. Both major political parties were represented, and Stu recognized a good many old friends, and a few enemies.

He went to get drinks for himself and Sari, and when he returned he saw that Sari had already been taken up by a tall and very good-looking fellow in formal military uniform. The two of them were engaged in an uninhibited Watusi. Stu motioned to her that he was setting her drink on the piano, and then he wandered off. He was quickly caught up in a conversation concerning Senator Parker's machinations. The participants, two of Washington's better-known pundits, attempted to draw Stu into offering some views, but he remained noncommittal, having learned early in the game, and the hard way, that information dropped at Washington cocktail parties, where the atmosphere and the drinks created a sense of intimacy and confidentiality, was the press's best source of leaks. The carelessly stated fact or rumor almost always managed to appear in print. So Stu smiled, and kept his mouth shut.

He had been circulating like this for almost two hours, moving from conversation to conversation, slowly sipping his drink and munching food, when a waiter told him he was wanted on the phone. He looked around for Sari, but she was nowhere in sight. In fact, he hadn't seen her since they had first arrived.

He asked the waiter if there was a private phone where he could talk. He was told there wasn't, that every room in the house was being used for the party. Stu took the call in the kitchen. He recognized the White House operator's voice when she told him she had his call ready. He asked her if she could hold the party on the line for about ten minutes, and when she said that she could, he said he would call her back.

Stu quietly left the house and started walking toward Wisconsin Avenue, Georgetown's main street, where he hoped to find a pay phone. When he reached Wisconsin he spotted a drug store a couple blocks up the street. He ran up the street, and he was puffing hard when he reached the store. He paused to catch his breath, berating himself for never getting any exercise. He then walked into a phone booth and dialed the White House. The operator instantly connected him with Jerry Greenberg.

"Jerry, are you where you can talk freely?" Stu asked.

"It's all right," Greenberg answered. "When the operator reached me I guessed who it was, so I drove to this shopping center and returned the call. I'm at a pay phone now."

"Same here."

"This is some way to transact our earth-shaking business," said Greenberg with a somewhat nervous laugh.

"Well, you can put it in your memoirs, unless you think that no one will believe what's happening these days."

"I'm not sure I'm going to have much of a future to write about."

"Does the governor know about our last conversation?" asked Stu, now very much concerned.

"No, he doesn't *know*, but he hasn't plugged me in since the President broke the story about his meeting with Parker. So he must have some suspicions."

"Forgive me for bothering you again, Jerry, but the President can't get through to the governor, and we wondered if you could help, or maybe give us some idea of what's going on."

"I'm afraid it's a negative on both counts," said Greenberg. "The governor is adamant about not talking to the President. Guilty conscience, I suppose. And if I had known anything more I would have told you, just as I said I would," he added testily.

"I know that, but we wanted to be doubly sure. Do you have any guesses?"

"Well, I'm convinced he has made a deal with Parker. They did meet right on schedule, and the governor has been very relaxed ever since. His refusal to talk to the President would fit in with that. But I have no idea of what the deal is. He hasn't given a hint."

Stu thanked him and, although feeling somewhat sheepish about saying so, told him that, in Stu's opinion, Greenberg had done a courageous thing in informing the President of Governor Nelson's deal with Parker. Greenberg scoffed, but Stu meant every word of it.

After saying goodbye, Stu flashed the White House operator. Seeing that it was past midnight, he asked for the Center Hall in the Mansion. In a moment the President's valet picked up the phone. Stu asked if the President was in bed and was told that, no, the President was in the West Sitting Room with the First Lady and some friends. Stu told the valet to pass a message to the President that he had completed his call, and to ask the President if he wanted a report. Stu held the line. In a few moments the valet came back and said that the President wanted Stu to come directly to the Mansion. Stu said that he would be right there.

He swore softly to himself as he hung up. Now he would have to leave Sari at the party, and he had no idea when he would be returning. He didn't relish the thought of her reaction when he did get back, although, he realized, she hadn't paid much attention to him while he was there.

He hailed a cab, and in a few minutes was at the southwest gate of the White House. Flashing his pass, Stu hurried through the darkened West Wing to the Mansion and went directly to the second floor. He discreetly stood at the entrance to the Sitting Room, where he saw the President and the First Lady chatting with three senior members of the House of Representatives and their wives.

"Come in here, Stuart," called the President.

Stu walked in, greeting the First Lady and shaking hands with the guests. The President placed his large hand on Stu's elbow and drew him to his side.

"I want all of you to remember this young man," the President said. "He is one of the brightest, most hard working, and loyal people that I have."

Stu inwardly groaned at this typical example of presidential over-praise. Although he was certain that the President meant every word while saying it, Stu had learned through the years that the President's enthusiastic encomiums could be balanced on occasion by equally scathing and sincerely meant criticism. Stu's adjustment to it all was to adopt the perspective that the truth, and the President's most enduring opinions of his staff, probably lay somewhere between the highs and the abyss of his colorful comments.

"I want you all to know," the President went on, still tightly clutching Stu's elbow, "that when this member of my staff speaks to you, he speaks for me. He has my ear and my trust. So if you ever have anything you want me to know, even in the strictest confidence, you can feel free to tell it to Stuart."

Of course, what the President was doing, Stu realized, was engaging in some long-range lobbying with the Hill. From the President's praise tonight the word would spread in the Congress that Stu Brady was "inside" on the White House staff. This, in turn, would permit Stu to be more effective when he would be calling on members for their votes on the new Presidency.

The President invited Stu to join them for a drink, and while he stood chatting with the guests Stu could not help surreptitiously glancing at his watch and worrying about Sari. Finally, after over an hour had passed, the guests bade the President a lingering goodnight, and left. The First Lady excused herself, and to Stu's relief he and the President were finally alone.

The President's attitude immediately changed to one of intense seriousness as he asked Stu to tell him what had happened. Stu briefly sketched his essentially negative conversation with Greenberg, and the President nodded.

"It appears as if we can't stop this alliance," he said, as much to himself as to Stu. "Parker is shrewd and Nelson is ambitious and also a little weak, I think. It looks like they've put something together, and I don't see a thing I can do to prevent it. The country is the loser and all I can do is stay locked up in this prison and watch it happen."

Stu could think of no adequate response. He had no ideas on what more could be done. There was simply nothing he could say to lighten the President's painful burden.

"Thank you for coming up here tonight," the President said, after a long pause. "You can go now, and please give my apologies to your lovely wife for pulling you away like this."

"That's all right, Mr. President. She will understand," Stu lied.

He stopped briefly at his office on the way out, saw that there were no pressing messages on his desk, and called for a White House car. It was, by then, past two o'clock, but he thought he might as well go back to the party on the chance that it was still going on and Sari was still there. Perhaps, if he were lucky, she'd still be having a good time and not have minded his absence.

A short while later, the black White House Mercury came and returned him to Georgetown. As he got out of the car he saw that the lights were still on downstairs. Since the front door was not locked, he walked in. The living room was deserted except for the host and a girl Stu did not know. They were slowly dancing to music from the radio, the band having long since departed. Engrossed in each other, neither of them paid any attention to Stu, although the host did give him a desultory wave. The room was a shambles of spilled drinks, empty glasses, cigarette butts, and half-eaten food. Glancing around, Stu asked about Sari but received no answer.

Stu waved goodnight and went home. Sari was not there. It was almost three o'clock in the morning and Stu had no idea where she was. He briefly considered calling the police, but concluded that would be ridiculous. She could take care of herself. His eyes were burning from fatigue, as he slowly slipped out of his clothes and climbed into bed. The loneliness of the quiet apartment surrounded him as he fitfully struggled for sleep. Finally, he gave up and walked into the kitchen to fix some hot chocolate. He was sitting at the breakfast table when he heard the front door open and, in a moment, Sari walked in. She looked slightly disheveled.

"Hello, Stu," she said laconically, seating herself across from him.

"Where have you been?" he asked, suddenly afraid of her answer.

"I don't really think, after your performance this evening, that's any of your business."

Stu rubbed his aching head. "Tell me, Sari."

She stared at him, then walked to the stove and started fixing herself some coffee. She lit a cigarette and searched in the refrigerator for something to eat. "Why don't you go to bed? There's no point in your just sitting here."

"Where were you?" he asked again.

"It won't do any good to talk about it," she said, not looking at him. "It isn't going to get us anywhere, and I don't want to hurt you."

"I've got a right to know," he insisted, completely unable to stop himself. "I've been waiting here worried about you for hours. Then you walk in and say it's none of my business."

"That's how I feel."

"Well, damn it, we're still married and you've got some obligations to me whether you like it or not."

"Do I, Stu?" she asked with a small, bitter laugh. "Your marriage is to that President of yours. Maybe he's the one who has the obligation to you. Why don't you ask *him* what's wrong."

"You know I hate that job as much as you do."

"If you hated it so much you'd quit."

"With only two months to go? I can't do that now. You know that."

"Well, then, I can't do anything else either."

Stu stood up and walked over to where she was buttering some toast, her back turned to him. He saw that her hands were trembling.

125

"Tell me, Sari," he said.

She leaned against the counter, still not looking at him. "Go to bed," she murmured.

"I want to know what's going on and you've got to tell me," he insisted. "God damn it, turn around and look at me," he said, grabbing her arm.

She yanked herself away from him. "Get your hands off me and please get out of here, will you?" Her voice was shrill and tears were streaming down her face.

"Not until you give me some answers," he demanded, stepping back from her.

"You really have to know, don't you," she said bitterly.

"That's right."

"All right." Her voice was quiet as she looked right at him. "I've found someone else."

Stu walked back to the table and tried to pick up his cup, but his hands were shaking so much he couldn't do it. He clasped them tightly together and tried to control his voice. "Who is he?" he finally managed, his voice sounding hoarse.

"No, I'm not going to tell you that," she said. Her face was drawn, remote.

"Have you slept with him?"

"Yes."

"Was it good?" he asked, compelled to go on.

"Yes," she answered, very softly.

He couldn't stop the shaking. He could feel tears welling in his eyes and he struggled for some kind of control.

"What do you want to do about us?" he finally asked.

"I guess that's up to you," she said, sounding closed in.

"Do you want to separate?"

"I don't know. I guess I do. I don't have you now anyway, so what's the point of it?"

Anger suddenly flooded over him. "God damn it, Sari. I'm working my ass off down there and then you go and do this. Jesus Christ," he muttered. "How in the hell could you?"

"Look what you've done to me," she said, her voice matching his. "For two years you've left me alone. I'm a human being

126

too, Stu, not some nice decoration you can admire whenever you have some time for it. I need somebody and you've deserted me the same as if you'd moved out. I've been lonely and empty, and I'm sick and tired of it. You can do what you damn well please, but I'm going to live my own life."

Stu shuddered with indecision. Then, unable to say anything more, he abruptly turned away and left the room. He threw some clothes into a suitcase and walked out of the apartment.

A half hour later he checked into the Hay Adams Hotel on 16th Street. He dutifully called the White House operator and gave his number. Then he lay on the bed, still clothed, staring at the ceiling, his thoughts wildly tumbling as he waited for the morning to come.

CHAPTER TEN

On that same night, at two A.M., Pacific Coast time, the door to Charlie Jefferson's room was suddenly opened and a strong flashlight beam was directed on his face, abruptly awakening him.

"Get up," said the guard. "You and the Moran girl are coming with us."

They pulled Charlie out of his cot and tossed some clothes at him. He dressed without a word, noticing that Nina was already up.

Outside their room, they could see that the church was bustling with activity, filled with khaki-clad men. They were immediately taken to Mamba's office where a number of men stood around him. Mamba looked up from his desk. "You two are going to stay here with me," he said.

"What do you want with us?" asked Charlie.

Mamba smiled. "You are going to see for yourselves exactly what we are going to do. All you have to do is be quiet and not cause any trouble. Jefferson, if you perform satisfactorily, then I may have a little task for you. As for you, Nina, you will soon have the proof of how right I have been."

"What about Simon?" Charlie asked. Pettigrew was far from fully recovered from his beating although he had been slowly regaining his strength.

"He's no concern of yours," Mamba snapped.

"Like hell he isn't," Charlie said. "Now you just listen to me for a change. You'll get nothing, absolutely nothing, out of me unless you agree to leave Simon alone. If you do, then maybe I'll play your little game. Otherwise, no deal, and that you had better believe."

Mamba started to say something, then glanced at his watch and shrugged his shoulders. "I don't have to do this, Jefferson, but to humor you, I will. No one will touch Pettigrew."

"All right," said Charlie. "What are we supposed to do now?"

"Just sit over there and watch. Operation Liberation is about to begin."

The attack began at five A.M., Pacific time, on Sunday, December 1. Several thousand men participated in the initial operation, which was marked by split-second timing and careful coordination. The attack was mounted simultaneously on a number of Oakland's vital centers. By dawn, Oakland had been sealed off from the rest of the Bay area, and its government and police forces deprived of effectiveness.

One team, totaling approximately a hundred men, blocked the Bay Bridge, Oakland's main link to San Francisco, by capturing the toll station plaza on the Oakland side of the Bay, easily subduing its night attendants, then moving outward several hundred yards toward the bridge. There they set up a road block of old trucks, driven across the highway and turned on their sides. Automatic weapons were mounted behind these vehicles. The attack team then moved a half mile back toward Oakland, where the interstate highway interchange led from Oakland and Berkeley to the Bay Bridge. By blocking this access point, they stopped traffic from the south as well. Every artery into Oakland was simultaneously sealed, with the heaviest concentration of forces placed at the main thoroughfares.

This operation effectively closed off an area comprising approximately six square miles, and containing almost all of downtown Oakland and its Negro residential areas.

Oakland's police headquarters, located in a new multi-storied structure adjoining the Nimitz Freeway, was well within the boundary of Mamba's area of control. The building occupied a full square block and housed the command post for the city's police operations, as well as the police arsenal, communications center and vehicles.

Using five hundred of his carefully trained men, Mamba overran the entire building in less than half an hour. His attack commenced just before dawn, and the minimal police force then on duty was far from alert. They offered surprisingly light resistance and, except for several bruised skulls, there were few casualties as the police capitulated to overwhelming force.

Mamba's men efficiently exploited their surprisingly easy victory. The police arsenal provided additional arms, and the captured police vehicles provided mobility. The police radio system was usefully employed. It was in this building, on the chief's top-floor office, that Mamba established his headquarters.

A half dozen blocks from the police station, just off Oakland's picturesque Jack London Square, was the structure housing Station KTVU, Oakland's Television Channel 2. A small force of men captured this facility and immediately commenced broadcasting.

Mamba's forces also took the power station, the telephone building and other key structures. They set up mobile command posts at strategic points within the downtown and inner city area. In addition, Mamba had over a thousand armed men in reserve, now all mobile and provided with communications.

By sunup the city was firmly in his hands.

Oakland's ghetto was the first place to react. The word spread swiftly, and long before dawn the streets were filled with people. At first they merely milled around, but then a carnival atmosphere began to fill the air. The youngsters began to yell and march. Exhilaration was the dominant mood. Then a few windows were broken and, within moments, looting began and a few scattered fires were started.

Mamba's troops stood by impassively. Their orders had been two-fold: first, they were to let the people of the ghetto have their head. Mamba had expected that they would loot and burn, but he correctly surmised that they would not interfere with his operations and would respect the orders of his men. He also calculated that chaos within the city would be to his advantage,

130

making it extremely difficult for outsiders to judge the extent of his forces, with the likely result that his power would be considerably overestimated. Additionally, rampant violence within the city's core would make an all-out attack against him exceedingly difficult to mount.

Mamba's second order to his men had been to set up recruiting posts throughout the ghetto to exploit the opportunity. They were to attract to his forces as many young men as possible. These recruits were instantly integrated into existing units. There they would be given the Black Guard arm band and, if possible, provided with weapons. The recruiting efforts were also successful.

At dawn the governor of California was awakened with news of a reported riot in Oakland. The chief of the state police had received an emergency flash from San Francisco that the Bay Bridge was blocked and that contact had been lost with the Oakland police.

By the time the governor had been up thirty minutes he knew that this was no ordinary riot. Continuous telephone reports were coming in, and the pattern of the massive takeover had begun to emerge. The San Francisco police reported that an attempt by them to run the bridge blockade had been turned back by heavy gunfire. Similar reports came in over police radios from Berkeley, Hayward, and San Leandro. Then, when Mamba's forces began broadcasts announcing their "Operation Liberation" to the outside world, the full extent of the capture of Oakland became known.

Within an hour the governor flew from Sacramento to San Francisco. There he boarded a helicopter and flew across the Bay. He was told that it was too dangerous to fly directly over Oakland's occupied downtown and ghetto area. Previous attempts at low overflights had drawn gunfire and it was considered too hazardous for him to make such an attempt. The governor reluctantly acquiesced, and the helicopter, flying high and outside the occupied perimeter, hovered over an incredible scene. Fires were raging throughout the ghetto area. They appeared to be spreading with no attempt at control. With strong field glasses the governor could see mobs of people freely roaming the streets. He could pick out carloads of armed men driving among the rioters. Downtown appeared to be free of fires and relatively peaceful, although the police escort informed the governor that there were large groups of Mamba's troops concentrated in Lakeside Park along the north edge of Lake Merritt. To the governor, Oakland looked much like a war-torn, occupied city, which, he wryly concluded, was exactly what it was.

When he landed, the governor's fist act was to order a complete mobilization of the California National Guard. He was told that this would take at least twenty-four hours. He was also informed that until such mobilization was complete, there were insufficient police forces available in the state to re-take the city; that the police were neither trained nor equipped for such an operation; and that even after mobilization it was doubtful if the Guard could do the job without a fearful cost in lives and property.

Thus, at ten A.M. the governor of California decided to call the President of the United States.

CHAPTER ELEVEN

The lovely, old and comfortably furnished Hay Adams Hotel, where Stu had spent the night he left Sari, had given him little comfort. He had chosen this hotel both for its quiet elegance and its proximity to the White House directly across Lafayette Park. He had thought that perhaps these surroundings would bring some peace to his troubled mind, but he had not slept, and when the sunlight had finally filtered through the curtains, he felt exhausted.

He was lying in bed, his mind blindly circling his problems with Sari, when the phone at his ear gave a harsh ring. He grabbed the instrument, thinking that it might be Sari, then realizing she had no idea where he was.

It was the White House operator. She told him that the President was calling a meeting in the Situation Room for eleven A.M., and that Stu was expected to attend. Stu was too distraught to ask any questions, and it was only as he stood under a hot shower a few minutes later that he was struck by the unusual nature of a Sunday morning meeting.

He gulped a quick breakfast in the hotel dining room, and then trudged across the park, cold and barren on this December morning, to the northwest gate of the White House. He walked down the curving driveway leading to the main entrance of the Mansion and to the White House West Wing, where the Situation Room was located.

Stu quickly ran down the steps, and entered the door behind the guard post just inside the West Basement entrance. He walked by the offices of Haines Morrison, the President's Special

Assistant for Foreign Affairs, and through the quarters occupied by his staff. Descending a short flight of stairs, he passed the desk of the ex-C.I.A. man who, under Morrison's general direction, efficiently ran the Situation Room. Just past his office were the worldwide communication and information facilities, constantly operated and watched to provide the President with instantaneous intelligence. As always, the teletype machines were noisily clattering their endless stream of news.

Stu walked past the duty officers and into the conference room. The President was already there, and he briefly waved Stu to a chair at the long table. Stu nodded at the others who were present: the Attorney General; Michael Potofsky, the President's Special Assistant for Domestic Affairs; Mark Brozman, the President's Special Counsel; and, as always in any emergency, Alvin Morgan.

When Stu arrived, the Attorney General was in the midst of giving a report. He was standing before large maps of Oakland, California, set up along one wall. Stu rapidly picked up the gist of the crisis: there had been some kind of black uprising and, presumably, the blacks had gained control over most of downtown Oakland.

"They seem to have done a thorough job of blocking access to the city," the Attorney General was saying as Stu took his seat. "As far as we can tell, the police facilities have been captured and the Oakland police force is unable to function."

"Who is behind this?" the President angrily asked.

"We think it is a militant leader who calls himself Mamba Z. I believe the F.B.I. has been sending you reports on him, Mr. President. He's been something of a troublemaker for several years. His real name is Moses Barnum, Jr., and he's originally from Berkeley. His father is a professor at the University of California."

"You *think* it's Barnum," the President snapped with biting sarcasm, as he strode over to the Oakland map. "You are supposed to know those things," the President said.

"We did have some vague information, Mr. President," the

134

Attorney General said. "But nothing definite enough to bother you with. As a matter of fact, I sent one of my assistants out there several weeks ago. His job was to check on these rumors, but he seems to have dropped out of sight. The F.B.I. has been searching for him, but we haven't had any luck."

The President abruptly turned from his intense study of the map. "God damn it!" he roared. "Why in the hell didn't you tell me that? I'm still President, not you, and you are supposed to work for me, not keep me in the dark."

The Attorney General briefly glanced at Stu, who, with a sinking feeling, realized that the Attorney General had indeed told Stu about Charlie Jefferson's disappearance. Stu, in the frantic pace of the election machinations, had simply forgotten to pass the information on to the President.

"I knew about it, Mr. President," Stu admitted. "The Attorney General is talking about Charlie Jefferson. Charlie is an old friend of mine and called me just before he left for Oakland, and, a week or so later, the Attorney General told me he was missing." The President was now glowering at Stu, who quickly added, "I'm sorry. I should have told you."

The President's voice was ice cold. "My Cabinet and my staff think that they are running this country. That's why we're in this mess, and now I'm expected to get us out of it."

Stu wished that he could just disappear, but all he could do was murmur again that he was sorry for the slip-up.

"Tell us what you do know," Alvin Morgan said quietly to the Attorney General.

The Attorney General appeared relieved, and he quickly responded. "Mamba heads an extremely militant group called the Black Guards. They started out as just another youth gang, but when Mamba got hold of them they suddenly took on a much more cohesive purpose. Mamba is quite a natural leader, and he is dedicated. In any event, he has been preaching violence and separatism all over the country. It's the same kind of talk that's now being broadcast from Oakland."

"Why didn't you nip him in the bud?" the President asked, still angry.

"We couldn't do that, Mr. President," the Attorney General answered patiently. "He was well within his rights."

"You mean to tell me that a man has a right to organize for violent revolution?" the President exploded.

"Of course not, sir. But we had no firm evidence, only rumors. We were trying to watch him and would have moved in on him when we had something solid."

"Well, you've got your evidence now," the President growled. "Only it's too damned late."

The conversation was interrupted by some further reports brought to the President by the Situation Room duty officer, as well as several telephone calls for the Attorney General. They worked in this manner for another hour while sandwiches and coffee were brought in. Shortly afterward the President placed a call to the Secretary of Defense and asked him to come to the White House.

The Secretary had been working at his Pentagon office for several hours in anticipation of the President's call, and was able to get to the Situation Room within minutes of the President's summons.

"What can you tell me about what's going on in Oakland?" the President asked him when he arrived.

The Secretary was, as usual, quick to answer in his clipped and efficient voice. "The governor has ordered mobilization of the California National Guard, but they won't be ready until tomorrow." He paused briefly and then continued. "I have, however, set several things in motion so that you might have all possible options open to you. I have ordered that the personnel at our military bases in the immediate vicinity of the disturbances take no action except to secure their areas of responsibility. This includes the Oakland Army Terminal, which adjoins the point where they've roadblocked the Bay Bridge, the Naval Reservation on Treasure Island, which is halfway across the bridge, and the Naval Supply Center and the Naval Air Station at Alameda, both of which are on the Bay quite close to the scene. This has all been done. I've also placed the Second Airborne Division on complete

136

alert. They've been training in civil control techniques ever since the Detroit riots the summer before last. By tonight the Second will be ready, on your orders of course, to move by air to the Alameda Air Station."

"That is excellent work," said the President, not missing a chance to peer meaningfully at Stu and the Attorney General. "I want to wait a little before deciding whether to move the troops out there, but you keep them set to go on an instant's notice.

"We are doing that, Mr. President," said the Secretary. "We've assembled the necessary transports and the division will be ready to go any time after late afternoon."

The group continued watching the worsening situation for another hour. Then, at about one P.M., the duty officer reported that the governor of California was on the telephone, asking to speak with the President.

The President took the call. After some brief amenities, the President said that he was in the Situation Room with the Secretary of Defense, the Attorney General, and several members of his staff. He asked if the governor had any objections to conducting their conversation on a speaker arrangement so that all present could participate. The governor agreed, the President pressed a button, and the room was filled with the Californian's voice.

"Go ahead, Governor. Give us the facts," the President said.

"It is very bad," said the governor. "They are obviously well armed and well trained. They have captured Oakland, that's all there is to it. Our police forces have not been able to penetrate the center of the city, and I have refused to order the police to attempt any sort of direct assault on their roadblocks. It would be a massacre."

"What about your National Guard?" asked the President. "I understand that you've ordered them mobilized."

"That's true, but it will be tomorrow before we can get them down here in anything approaching adequate numbers."

"What can I do to help?"

"My military adjutant advises me that even when the

137

Guard is mobilized they are not sufficiently trained or equipped to re-take the city. He strongly recommends that the task be taken over by federal troops."

"Are you prepared to make the necessary certification that California is in a state of insurrection and that you are completely unable to deal with it?" asked the President, referring to the constitutional and statutory prerequisites for using federal forces.

The governor did not hesitate to reply. "Yes, Mr. President, I'm prepared to so certify immediately."

The President blanched a little, and after a brief pause said, "Well, we will have to study the situation."

Informing the governor that he would get back to him, the President stood up and restlessly paced the room. "I don't like it," he said to no one in particular. "Why would he be so anxious to get our troops in there? It doesn't make sense for him not to first try with his police and National Guard."

The President turned to his Secretary of Defense. "How quickly can you get a good military man on the scene and have him report in to me?"

"I've already dispatched General Slocum," answered the Secretary. "He is in San Francisco now, and I've ordered him to establish immediate liaison as my personal representative. We should be hearing from him within the hour."

"Good." The President then turned to Michael Potofsky. "Mike, I want you to get out there as quickly as possible. You can use my Jetstar if you can't do any better. As soon as you arrive call me, and I'll let you know what you are to do."

Potofsky departed immediately, and the vigil continued.

A short time later, the call from General Slocum came in for the Secretary of Defense. The President put the general onto the speaker phone so that they could all hear his report.

"Go ahead, General," said the President. "Tell us what is happening."

"First off, Mr. President, you should know that I am at a military installation not a quarter of a mile from their Bay Bridge command post. However, this base is secure and they

138

have made no overt moves against us, although they have posted quite a number of observers. I got here by chopper, and they did not fire on me."

"What's the situation?" said the President impatiently.

"I've spoken to the governor and to the commander of the California National Guard. I've also met with the police chiefs in the area, including the Oakland chief, who is now working out of Berkeley police headquarters. In addition, I overflew the area and drove as close to some of those roadblocks as I could get without drawing fire."

"What is your assessment?" the President curtly broke in.

"I would guess that they have upward of five thousand men, most of them armed. I have no way of judging how well trained they may be, except that I would guess it to be minimal. Their firepower is also a question mark. We have observed some automatic weapons, but we doubt if they have anything heavier. On the other hand, they are obviously determined, and I expect that they will have to be rooted out."

"Exactly what will it take to do that?" the President asked.

"If this were a foreign city we would bomb them first and soften them with artillery, followed by some kind of multiple assault on their strong points."

"Well, this is Oakland, California. So what do you suggest that we do?" the President asked, his tone now exasperated.

The general paused for a moment, and then continued in his flat, professional voice. "I'm afraid we would have to march directly at them. Perhaps some mortar support might be in order. In all events, we will need a large number of troops, and it will cost lives. On both sides," the general added.

"How soon can we assemble the necessary forces?" asked the President.

The Secretary of Defense interrupted. "That's a little out of the general's sphere," he said. "We can get the men out there tonight, but preparations for an assault may take several days. However, if you okay it, I'll start the process now, including plans and logistics. This would not commit us to anything, Mr. President, either publicly or privately."

"All right. Go ahead with that part," the President said. Then he turned back to the speaker phone. "General Slocum, I'm sending one of my staff out there. Mike Potofsky. He's on his way now. When he arrives I want you to plug him in on every phase of what is going on. Is that understood?"

"Yes, sir."

"Until he gets there I want you to report directly to me every time there is any development. Don't be bashful about calling too often."

"I won't, Mr. President," the general said.

The President turned to the men in the Situation Room, his face gray and fatigued. "There's not much good in that report."

"At least, Mr. President, I think we can now see what the governor has in his mind," said Alvin Morgan.

"What is that?"

"It strikes me that the governor sees that Oakland can't be recaptured except by an overt military attack which will inevitably kill a lot of people and destroy a good part of the city if it is resisted. If that is what it is going to take, I don't think the governor wants to be held responsible for it. So he is passing the buck right to you."

"Well, here is where it stops," said the President, recalling one of Harry Truman's favorite expressions.

"I'm not sure it has to this time," the Attorney General answered quickly, anger rising in his voice. "We are not bound to accept the governor's assessment that he is incapable of handling his insurrection. If the fact is that his National Guard forces *are* sufficient to do the job, then we can push the ball right back to him and make him do it himself."

"I am aware of that possibility," the President said with a touch of sadness. "But the question is whether I would be doing my duty if I played this little game with the governor."

The room fell quiet, and the President stared morosely at the wall, his elbows on the table and his big hands clasped before him.

"I need time. I also need some room to maneuver, and I am

not being given very much of either." He then turned to his Secretary of Defense. "All right. You move your troops and equipment to the Alameda Air Station, but I don't want anything done, and I mean exactly that, unless I personally give you that order."

The Secretary nodded and picked up the phone at his side.

The President now turned to Stu. "I want you to contact Senator Harrington and Governor Nelson and brief them on what is going on." He stopped as another thought struck him. "Better yet, see if you can get them to come down here this evening. I want them both in on this takeoff, because one or the other of them is certainly going to be in on the landing."

Stu left the Situation Room and walked upstairs toward his office, glad to be let out, if only for a short while. He thought briefly about Sari, but quickly shoved that thought to the back of his mind.

Then he began his telephoning, making a determined effort to give his complete concentration to the problem at hand. He called Jerry Greenberg first, thinking that he had first better get Governor Nelson pinned to a time, and then go to work on Harrington. When Greenberg came on the line Stu briefly related the situation in Oakland. Greenberg, of course, had been closely following the news broadcasts. As to whether Governor Nelson would meet with the President, Greenberg would not hazard a guess, but he would take it up with him and report back as soon as possible.

For thirty minutes Stu sat at his desk, idly thumbing through several old newspapers. After a while he stopped pretending that he could work, and, swiveling in his chair, stared out the window toward Pennsylvania Avenue, thinking about his marriage.

His sleepless night's thoughts had convinced him of several things. He could never go back to Sari. What she had done was unforgivable. Besides, she had said she was in love with someone else, so that apparently was the end of it. He decided to stay another night or two at the hotel and then start hunting for an apartment.

Thinking that it was all so damnably bleak, he picked up the phone and dialed his home. Sari answered on the second ring.

"I wanted you to know that I've moved into the Hay Adams Hotel, at least until I can find an apartment," Stu began.

"That's your business. Why tell me?" Sari said in a dry voice.

"Only in case anyone wants to find me."

"Your precious White House would always know that anyway."

"I think we had both better find lawyers," he said, feeling the hopelessness of it all.

"Of course," she said. "Anything else?"

"I guess not. Goodbye, Sari."

"Goodbye."

For a long time he sat with his head in his hands. Then he walked to Sam Baker's bathroom, just off the office next to his, and gulped down two aspirins. His head was throbbing.

A short time later Jerry Greenberg called back.

"The governor will be there," he said. "But he wants a commitment that there will be no politics. I know that it is somewhat impertinent," Greenberg quickly added, "but he insists."

"Can you hold for a couple of minutes, and I'll get you an answer," said Stu.

"I'll wait."

Stu flashed the operator and asked for the Situation Room. The President came on right away, and Stu repeated Governor Nelson's condition for attending.

"Nelson should forget politics himself for a while," the President acidly replied. "There is a first-class crisis going on. He ought to know that, as a candidate, he has a duty to be briefed."

Stu listened, and then asked, "What shall I tell him, Mr. President?"

"You should tell him to go to hell," the President said, "but I suppose I had better agree to his idiotic request. Tell him whatever you have to in order to get him down here."

Stu hung up and got Greenberg back on the line, telling him that there would be no politics discussed at the briefing. Greenberg, sounding relieved, promised to have the governor at the White House on time.

Stu then called Sandy Corso, who, within five minutes, reported back that Senator Harrington would certainly attend the briefing.

It was past mid-afternoon when Stu returned to the Situation Room and reported his success to the President. The President merely nodded, though Alvin Morgan did smile and congratulate Stu on his good work. Everyone else was deeply engrossed in following the events in Oakland. Three television sets had been moved into the room. All networks had interrupted their regular Sunday programming to carry continuous live reports from the scene.

There had been no essential change in the situation. The crowds were still rampaging through the ghetto, and the looting and burning had not diminished. The downtown area remained relatively quiet. The radio and television station from Oakland blared out a constant stream of propaganda, and the city remained firmly sealed under Mamba's control.

During the late afternoon the Oakland television station announced that Mamba would make his first public speech at five P.M. Pacific time. Shortly after that announcement, the President left the Situation Room for the first time that day. He said that he wanted to be alone for a while and that he would return prior to the meeting with the candidates. He asked the others to stay and be prepared to give him a full report prior to the briefing of Harrington and Nelson by the Secretary of Defense and the Attorney General.

The tension level in the room remained high as they alternately watched developments and made telephone calls attempting to obtain all possible backup information. The Attorney General assembled a team at Justice to prepare a thorough memo on the legal implications of the Oakland situation. The Secretary of Defense called the Joint Chiefs of Staff into extraordinary session. They set up operations in the Pentagon and were feeding information and judgments to the Secretary just as fast as anything was available.

At six, the President returned. He was told that everything remained about the same in Oakland, but that preparations were proceeding at an accelerating pace, most especially that the airlift of the 2nd Airborne Division was now in progress and would be completed before midnight. He was also told that when the first troop plane had landed at Alameda, Mamba had immediately begun building roadblocks and fortifying positions facing the base.

The President, looking somewhat more rested than when he had left earlier, listened intently. Then he turned to Mark Brozman and said, "I want you to get together with the speech writers. Get all of them over here to help. What I want are drafts of three different speeches to the country."

Brozman was leaning forward, busily taking notes, as the President continued. "One speech should be based on the premise that we are going in with federal troops, using all necessary force to quell the rebellion. Another speech should be more conciliatory, giving Mamba a stern warning but leaving my options open. The third speech should throw the whole business back on the governor of California. Force him to use his National Guard before we intervene. Talk about the traditional reluctance of the federal government to involve itself in domestic police affairs."

"Can you tell me which way you are leaning now?" asked Brozman.

"No, I have no idea as yet. I just want you to be prepared for any eventuality."

"When do you want these?"

"See if you can get me some kind of drafts in about two hours, right after Mamba speaks. By that time we will have heard him and sounded out the candidates, and I hope to have a better idea of what should be done."

Brozman left, and the others returned to their preparations for the briefing, while the President made notes on the points he wished to emphasize.

144

Promptly at seven Governor Nelson and Senator Harrington arrived with Jerry Greenberg and Sandy Corso. Harrington, normally a delightfully outgoing man, was quite subdued and greeted both the President and Governor Nelson with a sober handshake. Nelson looked ill at ease and barely acknowledged the greeting as he immediately took his seat at the table. Stu cordially said hello to Greenberg and Corso, feeling sharp pain when Corso innocently asked him how Sari was getting along.

The briefing started with the President generally describing the situation in Oakland, the call from the California governor, and his dispatching of troops to the Alameda Naval Air Station. He said that he had not yet decided whether to use the troops, either alone or in conjunction with the California National Guard, and that the purpose of this briefing was to help him make this painful decision.

The President then introduced the Attorney General, who gave a rundown of the legal options open to the President.

The Secretary of Defense was next. "You can best understand the military situation by viewing Oakland as a city occupied by hostile forces," he began. "They are well armed and apparently determined. Obviously we can develop the necessary force to drive them out. However, to mount a traditional attack would require air strikes and artillery, which would destroy a good part of the city as well as killing countless innocent people. On the other hand, to attack without that kind of support would cost the lives of a great number of our own troops."

"When will your men be in a position to move?" asked Senator Harrington.

"They will be in place by tomorrow, but it may take several days to adequately stage an attack," answered the Secretary.

"What are the risks of delaying such an attack?" Harrington asked.

"Obviously, each day of delay will give Mamba that much more time to consolidate his position. Also, we understand he is busily recruiting throughout the ghetto. Assuming that he has sufficient arms, delay definitely enables him to add to his capability."

"Aren't there compensating advantages to us which are gained by waiting?" asked Harrington, striving to turn the conversation to other less violent, more hopeful possibilities. "It occurs to me that there may be something to be said for giving us time to build up an overwhelming force. Perhaps by then we can get Mamba and his people to listen to reason."

"Yes," said the Secretary. "There would be some psychological advantage if we did that. I might point out that we have been planning the movement of additional forces into the area even after the Second Airborne is in place."

"I think that any delay is damned foolishness," said Governor Nelson. "Mamba and those people of his are fanatics. They will not listen to any reason except greater force. We've got that force available now and I say use it. Maybe they will resist and maybe they won't. But we can't let them get away with capturing an American city while we just sit back and twiddle our thumbs."

"But what about all the killing that would result?" asked Harrington.

"There is killing going on now," Nelson snapped back.

"We don't know that there is, but even so, it's nothing compared to what would result if we went in there with an army," argued Harrington.

"They are looting and burning," Nelson went on. "They have taken the law into their own hands. We cannot permit it to continue. The country won't stand still for anything but an immediate response with everything we have to get them out of there."

"Sometimes it is the duty of leaders to be wiser than the people," said Harrington in a surprisingly mild voice. "The President has the responsibility and the power. He cannot afford to respond emotionally. He has got to think out all the alternatives, and then do what is the best thing for the country. We have got to give the President all the help we can."

Nelson's face had become red during this exchange, and he slammed his fist on the table. "Sometimes the people are right,

Senator, and it would do us all good if this government would start paying some attention to them."

The President had been sitting quietly, impassively watching. Now he interrupted.

"Please, gentlemen," he said. "There is nothing to be gained from becoming emotional." Although the remark was addressed to both candidates, the President stared levelly at Governor Nelson as he said it. "We all have the interests of the country at heart," he continued. "We ought to be able to start from that premise."

The President stood, clasped his hands behind his back, and then went on. "You both have all the information that is available to me. I'm sorry there isn't more, but I have to act or not act on the basis of what we know now. What I need to know from you is whether I can count on your support for whatever action I take."

"You mean you are asking for a blank check of approval without knowing what it is you are going to do?" asked Governor Nelson incredulously.

"Naturally, I plan to tell you just as soon as I reach any decision, and I am instructing my staff to keep you both completely informed. Right now I am merely asking you either to stay here and help participate in the decision or to give me your assurance as a matter of general principle that you will be behind me if it is at all possible for you to do so."

Senator Harrington blanched, and looked as if he were about to object, but then decided not to, as the President gave him a stern look. Harrington merely gave a slight nod of his head toward the President, then looked steadily at Governor Nelson.

The governor cleared his throat and cast a slightly nervous glance around the room. "I appreciate your keeping me informed, but I must make it crystal clear that, inasmuch as I am not President, I cannot give any manner of assurance that I will support your actions. I feel quite strongly that it would be improper for me to do so in advance. All I can say is that if what you do is, in my view, correct, then I will not hesitate to say so. Naturally, if I think otherwise, I will have a similar duty to speak out."

"Will you stay here with us and help in making that decision?" the President asked, gazing steadily at the governor.

"That will be impossible," Nelson replied without elaboration.

The President rose, indicating that the conference was at an end. "Thank you for taking the time to come down here, Governor," he said, making no effort to disguise the sarcasm in his voice. "We will keep you up to date on any developments."

Nelson and Greenberg departed, and the President and the others stayed behind.

"I don't understand that man," said Senator Harrington. "At a time like this he wants to squeeze every last drop of political blood out of us. He is going to sit back and watch, and then attack with the unbeatable wisdom of twenty-twenty hindsight."

"Don't be too harsh on him," said the President. "The Presidency is a real possibility for him, especially with his deal with Parker. He isn't about to risk it and I can understand that. Men have done much worse to gain much less."

"I would have hoped for more from him, Mr. President," said Harrington.

"Yes, I did also," said the President. His voice was heavy with sadness as he continued. "It's this damned election that is going to break our hearts. It's obvious that my own ability to bring the country with me is diminishing and there is no one yet chosen to pick up the reins. The country might be able to survive it if everything remained on an even keel. But we aren't going to be that lucky. This Oakland mess is a match on gasoline. My hope was that you and Governor Nelson would rise above ambition and form a united approach with me. I wasn't really sure it would happen, but I felt bound to try."

"What will you do now, Mr. President?" Senator Harrington quietly asked.

"I honestly don't know, Jimmy, I honestly don't know."

The room fell silent, as each man was deeply engrossed in his own thoughts. After a while Alvin Morgan got up and walked to the television receivers. "Mamba is supposed to go on the air any minute now, Mr. President. Do you want to hear him?"

The President nodded.

The networks had posted their cameras and reporters in various strategic positions circling the Oakland area. They were reporting the chaos with varying degrees of emotionalism. Then, simultaneously, all three sets suddenly flickered and after a short pause the image of Mamba, replete with uniform, pistol at his side, filled each of the screens. Stu was struck by the unreality of what he was seeing. In the midst of armed conflict, from the heart of a captured city, the electronic genius of the nation was still capable of functioning.

Mamba stood before his cameras and spoke without visible notes for nearly an hour, meticulously listing the centuries' old oppression and subjugation that had been wrought upon his people. He spoke of the beauty of his race. He spoke lyrically and threateningly, but always with deep feeling.

Then, finally, he came to the end, his strong voice rising with emotion and his face set in controlled anger, as he said, "to the whites of America I say that Oakland is your symbol of decadence, and, like Pompeii of old, it will be swallowed up by an angry upheaval. You have created the tragedy of Oakland, not us. You have created thousands of Oaklands throughout the land in which black people suffer. From this day onward none of your Oaklands are safe.

"It matters not whether we here live or die, for what we have started this day will not soon end. We are, at last, free men, and we shall exact the full price of men long wronged.

"To the blacks I say, rise up! Throw off the yoke of your oppression! Follow us in a thousand cities! We have opened the door of freedom and it shall not be closed again."

The screen went dead. Then, after a moment, the network commentators reappeared, summarizing and theorizing on what had just occurred.

The President sat quietly, staring at the screens, his eyes almost closed and his hands tightly gripping the arms of his chair. "He is good," he said thoughtfully. "And he is very dangerous."

"I don't think we can afford to wait to get him out of there," said the Secretary of Defense. "If you will pardon my saying so, Mr. President, I believe there is a great deal of truth in what Governor Nelson said. They will only listen to greater force, and time only gives them a better chance to prepare themselves. In addition, God knows what his speech and his actions are going to cause in other cities."

"Has anything like that developed?" the President asked the Attorney General.

"Not yet, Mr. President," the Attorney General said. "There have been a few scattered incidents, but nothing serious."

"That may be," interrupted the Defense Secretary. "But what is going to happen in a day or two if we don't root them out?"

"I understand what you are saying," the President said. "However, the question needn't be decided tonight. We won't be ready ourselves until at least sometime tomorrow, and I will decide by then."

The President rose, intending to return to the Mansion. As he gathered his notes, the duty officer came into the room.

"There is a telephone call for Mr. Brady," he announced.

"Who is it?" asked Stu.

"A man who says his name is Charles Jefferson. He says he is calling from Mamba's headquarters inside Oakland."

CHAPTER TWELVE

Charlie Jefferson hung up the phone. "It's done," he said. "He will be here."

Mamba smiled and stretched his legs out on the chief of police's desk, puffing on a big black cigar. They were in Mamba's commandeered headquarters in Oakland's police building, and Charlie had just completed his call to Stu Brady at the White House.

This was the end of a remarkable day. As Mamba had wanted it, Charlie had constantly been at his side. Mamba had been like a man possessed, shouting orders, inspecting strong points and troops. Always at a run, he held constant staccato conferences with his leaders and at the end of that long day had smoothly delivered his speech to the outside world over the captured television station.

Charlie's view of the city had been a kaleidoscope of sights and sounds. He had seen the eager young men, armed with a motley assortment of weapons, dug in behind their roadblocks of old automobiles, loose lumber, and anything else that provided shelter. These men had been shouting and singing, as if this were a crusade for freedom. He watched them as they were joined by new volunteers from the ghetto, all of them untrained and many unarmed. Each group had greeted Mamba like a savior, cheering him and listening to his every word with ferocious intensity.

Charlie had also seen the looting and fires. Mamba had driven down the ghetto streets, packed with people who were both milling around and surging toward any likely target: a store front, an old building, anything on which to vent their anger. He and Mamba had come upon one incident just as a mob had caught a carload of young white men who had somehow wandered into the ghetto area. The men's car had been surrounded, the windows smashed, and the occupants dragged into the street and beaten senseless. Mamba watched passively for several minutes and finally ordered his guards to pull the whites away from the crowd, give them first aid, and get them out of the area.

Even at that moment, when Mamba had thwarted the crowd, Charlie saw that the throng stopped and held silent when Mamba appeared. They had fallen away from him in awe, and as he walked among them they had surged forward to touch him and voice their support. It had been a deeply disturbing experience for Charlie.

When Mamba returned to his headquarters, he was exultant from the adulation. Then, shortly before the time he was scheduled to deliver his televised speech, he had dismissed everyone from the room except Charlie.

"You are well known at the White House, aren't you?" Mamba had begun.

"They know me," said Charlie.

"I am sure they know you well and admire you for all the cooperation you have given them."

"What are you driving at?" Charlie demanded.

"Ah, patience, Jefferson. I am coming to that. You have noted the strength of my forces and the thoroughness of our control. I trust that you have been adequately impressed."

"The only thing I'm impressed with is the tragedy of what you have brought about." Anger had risen in Charlie's voice as he said this. "They are going to attack you, Mamba, and there's going to be more killing."

"Yes, they may do that," Mamba said. "Of course, that is another reason why you may wish to perform this little task. You see, I wish to confer with the White House. I want to be reasonable. I have certain demands in mind, which I intend to present from a position of strength."

"What do you want from me?" Charlie asked.

"I would like to meet here with a personal representative of the President. I want him to see what we have done, and the extent of our power. I want to present my thinking to him. Would you be willing to arrange such a meeting?"

Charlie had not hesitated before replying. It was obvious to him that any talk, regardless of how ridiculous Mamba's demands might prove to be, would be infinitely preferable to armed conflict. Also, it would be his first chance to get word to the Attorney General that he was at least alive.

"Yes," Charlie had agreed, "I will do that."

"Fine. We will make the call just as soon as I return from my telecast."

Mamba had then left, leaving Charlie alone with his ever-present guard. Charlie had been surprised when a short while later he was brought a tray containing the first hot meal he had seen since his capture. He gulped it down with relish while he watched the television set in Mamba's office. The San Francisco station carried uninterrupted reports of the Oakland occupation, the newscasts revealing the frustration of the California authorities, and also the rising anger of the nation at large. Various political leaders had begun to speak out, crying for an immediate crushing of the uprising; and in some cities violence had broken out among both blacks and whites. The inexorable pressures were building, Charlie had thought, and they might well be irreversible.

At five o'clock, the guard had switched the set to Channel 2, and Charlie watched with horrified fascination as Mamba made his emotion-packed speech. He thought that it was pure demagoguery, whatever the justification, and that it could only result in inflaming the country. That was probably Mamba's purpose, he ruefully concluded, and whatever the outcome of this immediate problem, they would be repairing the damage for years to come.

Mamba had been back in his headquarters within minutes after the speech was over, and the call was immediately placed to Stuart Brady at the White House. Brady was on the phone almost at once.

"Where in the hell have you been, Charlie?" Brady had asked. "We've been looking for you for weeks."

Charlie looked at Mamba and cupped his hand over the phone. "They want to know what has happened to me. I assume you have no objection if I tell them the truth."

"Say whatever you wish," said Mamba.

Charlie again spoke to Brady. "I've been held prisoner by Mamba almost since I arrived out here. I was attending one of their organization meetings and I got caught. They've had me locked up while they were getting ready for this. Otherwise, I'm in pretty good shape."

"What is going on out there?" Brady asked.

"I'm sitting in what was the Oakland police headquarters, and Mamba has had me with him most of the day. From what I've been able to see it appears as if he has this area pretty much under his control, except that there is hell to pay out on the streets."

"We know that," Brady said.

"Mamba is here with me and, as you might guess, he instructed me to make this call. Although, believe me, it's sure good to hear a friendly voice and to let someone know where I am."

"What does Mamba want?" Brady asked abruptly.

"He wants the President to send someone out here to meet with him. He apparently wants to negotiate."

"What is he asking for?"

Charlie had turned to Mamba and repeated Brady's question.

"We will discuss that when they get here," said Mamba. "You just tell them to send their man as soon as possible. Time is running out."

"He won't say," Charlie repeated to Brady.

"Can you hold on for a while?" Brady asked.

"Of course."

The line had clicked off, and for fifteen minutes Charlie held the phone, irrelevantly wondering who eventually was going to pay for this call. Mamba sat silently, also waiting. Finally, the line clicked again and Brady was back on.

"We will do it," Brady said. "However, there will be two of us. Michael Potofsky, who is a Special Assistant, and myself. Is that agreeable?"

Charlie turned to Mamba and repeated the answer.

"How soon will they be here?" he asked, and was told that the White House aides would arrive before morning.

"How about if we set the meeting for eight A.M.? That will give us a chance to get briefed. By the way, how do we get in?" Brady asked.

Mamba told Charlie, "Tell them to come across the Bay Bridge. Just the two of them in a car. I'll arrange it so they can drive up to the roadblock. We will take it from there."

Stu spent the two hours between Charlie's call and his departure for California sitting with the President and the others, who by then had been in the Situation Room for well over twelve hours. They discussed incoming reports and speculated on what Mamba would demand and what the government would offer. Although the 2nd Airborne Division by that time had been well on its way to the coast, and was expected to be in place long before dawn, the President had not as yet given any indication of his final decision about whether and how the division was to be used.

When Charlie Jefferson's call came in there had been a short, intense argument over whether a meeting with Mamba should be held at all. The Defense Secretary had urged vehemently that it would be a terrible mistake; that the country at large would never understand such a conference; that for the President to send anyone to Mamba would inevitably give the appearance of legitimacy to that wild man and would constitute a loss of prestige for the President, something he could ill afford to squander. The Attorney General had also been against the meeting, but not quite so vigorously. The President had respectfully listened to the discussions, but finally said that he was going to agree to the encounter.

"It's a slim reed," the President said, "and I understand the risks. However, I am willing to take it on the chance it may result in some kind of opening. I don't want those deaths on my hands and, believe me, we will have them if we have to go in there by force."

"I don't like it, Mr. President," the Defense Secretary had emotionally insisted. "For one thing I'm not at all sure that they will resist us if we attack with sufficient force. For another, I'm afraid Mamba will try to turn any recognition we give him into a sign of our weakness."

"That may be," the President had answered. "But we will try to keep the meeting quiet. Something good just might come of it."

Stu left the White House and arrived at the San Francisco airport at two-thirty the next morning. He had flown in one of the President's fast Jetstars, a four-podded aircraft comfortably seating about a dozen persons.

As he alighted from the plane, which had been pulled up at an out-of-the-way ramp, Stu saw Mike Potofsky and an army general walking toward him. After Potofsky introduced General Slocum, the three of them boarded a marine helicopter, parked with its roters already in motion, just a few feet from the plane.

The chopper took off immediately, heading out over the Bay toward Treasure Island, the small piece of land between San Francisco and Oakland, bisecting the Bay Bridge. The naval base that occupied Treasure Island had now been converted into a central command post for all the local police, National Guard and federal forces.

The noise inside the helicopter was so deafening that there could be no conversation beyond a few perfunctory shouts. General Slocum yelled a question at Stu, which, after it was repeated, he understood to be whether Stu was interested in detouring close to the occupied area. Stu shook his head, thinking that they would be able to see very little on this moonless night and that they would be better off spending the time being briefed, making their inspection at dawn.

After landing at Treasure Island they went directly to the commandant's office. Although it was almost three, the building was alive with activity. Police officers in several kinds of uniforms, along with a large number of military personnel, were busily scurrying in and out of the crowded building. Radios blared messages on several frequencies, picking up police reports as well as military radio traffic.

Stu was taken into an office now littered with empty coffee cups and half-eaten sandwiches. There, sitting behind the desk, was the governor of California. Appearing fit and tanned, the governor rose and gave Stu his best professional grin. Then he sobered quickly and said, "So you are going to meet with that son of a bitch."

Stu was taken aback and he cast a quick look at Mike Potofsky. Stu had been under the impression that the meeting with Mamba was to be kept a secret. Then he realized that, since the governor had apparently made his headquarters at the military installation, Potofsky had probably felt obliged to reveal the information to him.

"That is correct, Governor," Stu replied.

"I think it is a very bad idea," said the governor.

"The President wants to explore every possibility of settling this without unnecessary bloodshed," said Stu. "Of course, we are aware of the risks."

"Well, I think you are making a terrible mistake, but for the moment I will go along with you."

"We appreciate that, Governor."

"What I really want to know is when the President will answer my request to use federal forces out here. You are aware that I called him yesterday morning. He said he would consider it, but I haven't heard a word from him."

"He is moving the Second Airborne Division, and they should be in place very soon," said Stu.

"That is a good step, but it is no commitment. When is that commitment going to be made?"

"I can't say that, sir."

"You tell the President that I can't wait much longer. The people of this state won't sit still for it, and neither will I."

Potofsky now spoke up for the first time. "Governor, you told me earlier you would wait until after our meeting with Mamba before doing anything. I trust that still stands." Potofsky cast a glance at Stu, who now understood why the governor had been informed of the planned meeting.

"Yes, I will hold off long enough for that, but not much longer. I really cannot tolerate any further delay," said the governor.

For the next few hours Stu was brought up to date on the situation in Oakland and the preparations being made to launch an attack against Mamba. The California National Guard was now assembling at the Oakland airport, south of the occupied portion of the city, but it would be late in the day before they would be ready to proceed. Meanwhile, the 2nd Airborne was almost completely transported to the Alameda Naval Air Station.

Throughout all of this, the various police forces, under explicit orders from the governor not to make any attempt to enter the center of Oakland, had ringed the city, keeping all persons out of the area and maintaining order on the fringes. Nevertheless, there had been some sporadic gunfire from Mamba's roadblocks. On occasion, it had been returned by the police. Thus far, however, there had been no known casualties on either side.

Some telephone reports had been received from within Mamba's perimeter. These included a great many cries for help. Some of the local people were on the edge of panic and pleaded for assistance. It could not be given. From what could be pieced together, the crowds were still marauding, burning and assaulting any whites unfortunate enough to be found on the streets. Most people, black and white, were locking themselves in their homes, but the whites were becoming increasingly frightened of being discovered and attacked. Officials who had received such calls for help had reacted with anger and frustration, and this mood had been communicated to those who were working at the Treasure Island headquarters.

Just before dawn Stu boarded another helicopter. He was joined by Potofsky and the general. They first flew to the Alameda Air Station. The edge of the airstrip had been turned into an army camp. Men and equipment were everywhere, including, Stu noted with a shudder, automatic weapons, mortars and even some light pieces of artillery. As Stu stepped off the chopper he saw that one mammoth jet transport, its tail gaping open, was discharging what appeared to be a motorized weapons carrier.

They walked past endless rows of hastily erected tents, in and around which were soldiers in full battle gear. The air station's main terminal had been taken over by the 2nd Airborne as its command post and General Slocum introduced the two White House men to Major General Henry Broadwell, commander of the division. The general and several other officers with him were dressed in informal khakis and polished boots. Although busily preoccupied with the logistics of the division's sudden movement to the West Coast, all of the officers gave a friendly welcome to Stu and Potofsky.

"Give these men a quick rundown on how it looks to you, will you, Hank?" General Slocum asked.

"We will be ready with sufficient equipment by midday, maybe sooner," General Broadwell answered. "Of course, how we deploy and use our forces is out of our hands. But we will be available for whatever mission is assigned to us. Those are good men out there."

"We think so, too," said Stu.

"How strong do Mamba's forces appear to be?" Potofsky asked.

"That's hard to say," said Broadwell. "We've had very little reconnaissance as yet, although we are going to start some overflights and photography within an hour, just as soon as there is sufficient light. That should give us a better notion of what we are facing. However, if you have an extra few minutes I can show you something of interest."

Stu glanced at his watch, noting that it was a little past six-thirty A.M. Their meeting with Mamba was scheduled for eight. "That's fine, if we can be back on board our chopper by seven-thirty," he said.

They then boarded two jeeps. With General Broadwell, Stu and Potofsky in the lead vehicle, they drove to the edge of the airfield facing Oakland. As they reached the end of the field, they stopped and the general hopped up on the hood of the jeep and motioned Stu and Potofsky to join him. He handed each of them a pair of high-powered binoculars and told them to look straight ahead. There, not more than a few hundred yards in front of him, Stu saw lines of overturned and partially destroyed cars and trucks. Behind these vehicles, in slit trenches, he could see hundreds of men. Stu saw the glint of their weapons in the early morning light.

"As far as we can make out, what you are looking at is only the advance line," General Broadwell explained. "We could bust through them with very little effort, and I imagine they know that. So I figure that they are out there only as a psychological show of strength. I imagine their main resistance will be in the built-up portions of the downtown area. There they would have a much more defensible position against us. At least, that's what I would do if I were running their show."

They drove back to the helicopter, soberly reflecting on their closeup view of Mamba's determination. They thanked the general for his cooperation, wished him well, and took off.

The sun was well up as they flew out toward Oakland. Stu and Potofsky decided to take the risk of drawing fire, and with General Slocum's concurrence they flew directly over the occupied area, although they maintained an altitude of over two thousand feet, out of the range of rifle fire.

The city appeared deserted, with only a few isolated vehicles moving on the streets. There were some scattered fires, and some burned-out hulks of buildings. Here and there they noticed pockets of men, apparently groups of Mamba's troops.

Shortly before eight A.M. they returned to Treasure Island. There Stu and Potofsky were given one of the naval commandant's cars, and Stu drove across the Bay Bridge toward Oakland.

A half mile before reaching Mamba's roadblock, immediately in front of the toll station on the Oakland side of the bridge, they came upon a police checkpoint. Over a dozen police cars were parked on the roadway, and a large number of police officers and National Guardsmen stood in view, all carrying arms. The police did not know who they were but had been alerted to expect "two federal representatives," so they rapidly passed them through.

The area between the police checkpoint and Mamba's blockaded access to the city was deserted. "Kind of like no-man's land," Potofsky observed to Stu, who nodded his agreement.

They approached Mamba's barriers slowly. As they came closer they saw that, just as at the air station, the highway had been strewn with overturned vehicles, many of which had been deliberately burned out. It was difficult to count the number of men behind the barricades, but Stu noted that everyone was armed with some type of automatic weapon. He was also shocked to see the gray-barreled snouts of machine guns sticking out from several points along the roadblock.

They drove up to the line of overturned cars and stopped. Two khaki-clad men came toward them, rifles slung over their shoulders. They were motioned out of the car and then led around the barricades. Stu took a quick glance at the large number of armed men positioned there.

"You come to see how we're going to slice you up, white boy?" one man taunted.

"You'll never get out of here in one piece," yelled another.

The two White House men ignored the jibes and, following the lead of their escorts, marched steadily ahead.

They were taken to a waiting police car, which started with a roar, the siren blaring full blast. Their route took them past many groups of similarly uniformed and armed men, and a short while later they screeched to a halt before the glass-encased front entrance to Oakland's new police building.

Mamba and Charlie Jefferson were waiting in the chief's office when Stu and Potofsky arrived. Stu was surprised at Mamba's slight size. Somehow, from his television appearances, he had thought Mamba would be a much larger man. However,

Mamba's eyes, penetrating and intense, exuded the force of his personality.

As Mamba picked up the phone to give an order, Stu turned to Charlie and vigorously shook his hand. "It's good to see you," he said. "We had almost given up on you."

"I can't say I've enjoyed this experience," Charlie replied sourly.

"Now, Mr. Jefferson," said Mamba, turning from the telephone. "We've been delighted to have you as our guest."

"You have dug yourself in pretty deep," Potofsky said to Mamba. "You've committed one hell of a list of crimes. Kidnapping a federal officer in itself is a damned serious offense."

Mamba waved the remark aside. "I'm afraid that is not our concern this morning. You gentlemen have neither the authority nor the strength to threaten me at this moment. Let's move on to more productive matters."

"I believe our power to act is quite material," continued Potofsky. "I am sure you know the extent of the forces which are now being brought to bear against you. You've seen what is being done at the Alameda Naval Air Station and you also know that the California National Guard has been fully mobilized. We will be ready to move in a very short time."

"Perhaps that will occur, if—and it's a big *if* in my mind— you are also prepared to destroy Oakland and a good portion of its civilian population. Understand also that my men are completely capable of forcing you into a very costly house-to-house operation before you can retake this city."

"If that occurs, it will be on your conscience," answered Potofsky, his rising voice betraying the emotion he felt.

Mamba remained calm as he answered. "It would seem that both sides have a few cards to play in this game. Under such circumstances it might be in order to explore the possibilities of a negotiated settlement. Agreed?"

"We are willing to hear you out. That's why we're here," said Stu. "What is it you propose?"

Mamba stood and leaned forward, both hands flat on the desk. His voice was low as he spoke. "I want a part of Oakland established as a separate black city with its own government, its own schools, and its own police. I want my people to have the same rights to self-determination and self-government that your founding fathers talked about in the Declaration of Independence. For this purpose, I want only the part of Oakland you call the ghetto. Since that area of the Flatlands is already the home of black people, the only home the whites have permitted us, I suggest that by every natural right, it is truly our land. All I ask is that we be legally recognized so that we can determine our own destiny."

"Are you suggesting that this new city be permitted to secede from the United States?" asked Potofsky.

"Not at all," answered Mamba. "We will live under your government as a full-fledged—and equal, I might add—participant."

"Is there anything else?" asked Stu.

"Politically, that is all I ask for. I consider it a reasonable request and the President has the power to negotiate its acceptance."

"You say 'politically.' Is there some other kind of demand you are making?"

"Only that my men and I be given assurances of immunity from prosecution for our actions." Mamba smiled. "That is most definitely part of the package."

"I am afraid you are asking quite a lot from the government," Potofsky said.

"Possibly, but those are my terms, and I would suggest that you seriously consider them. The alternative is not very pleasant. I believe we can all agree to that."

"All I can say is that we will present your request to the President. There is no way we can speak for him at this time," Potofsky said.

"I understand that. You'll get safe passage out of here but bear in mind that time is running out. The whole thing has to be settled as quickly as possible."

"I agree," said Stu, as they prepared to depart. "Are you going to allow Jefferson to leave here with us?" he asked.

"That's impossible," answered Mamba. "He stays here, but you have my assurance that he will be treated well."

"He is holding two other prisoners," Jefferson interjected heatedly. "Nina Moran, a young woman who has defected from him and who tried to help me, and Simon Pettigrew, the man who was my contact out here."

"What about them?" Stu demanded of Mamba.

"They, too, will remain with us," said Mamba. "But they'll be all right."

"I suggest you reconsider holding these people," said Potofsky, his temper rising again. "Perhaps if you released them it would be a sign of your good faith."

"Maybe I can do that at a later stage in our discussions," said Mamba. "For now, I can't do it."

A few minutes later, after giving Charlie Jefferson their assurances that he and his friends would not be forgotten, the two White House men departed.

It was just past ten in the morning when they were escorted past the Bay Bridge barricades. They were again greeted by shouted threats as they drove off in their car. Within ten minutes they were back on Treasure Island and in the commandant's office, were General Slocum and the California governor were anxiously waiting. They explained to the governor that they could not discuss their meeting with Mamba before informing the President. The governor was unhappy, but he agreed to step out of the room and seemed somewhat mollified when they also asked General Slocum to leave. Then, alone in the office, they placed their call to the President.

CHAPTER THIRTEEN

When Senator Jack Parker awoke on Monday morning, the second day of the Oakland insurrection, he thought he knew what had to be done. By the time he finished watching the morning news, entirely devoted to the Oakland situation and its developing repercussions throughout the country, he was certain.

On the previous Saturday night he had worked late with Billy Dan Reeves drafting the announcement endorsing Governor Maynard Nelson for President. Parker had decided to issue the statement on this Monday morning, simultaneously sending written notification to each of his electors, timing it exactly two weeks before the Electoral College was to meet. This would give his endorsement adequate time to be assimilated. However, Oakland changed everything.

Without awakening his wife, he walked to the kitchen and dialed Billy Dan's apartment.

"You didn't send out those notices to my electors yet?" Parker asked when Billy Dan came on the phone.

"No, sir. I was going to go over the statement one final time with you this morning."

"Good. Don't do a thing, and meet me in the office in an hour. Have Millard there with you."

"Yes, sir."

During the drive from Chevy Chase, Senator Parker considered the turn of events in Oakland. He was amazed that the President was doing nothing about the uprising and that the California authorities were apparently either helpless or unwilling to act. The silence from both major candidates was also incredible.

Parker was certain that public opinion would demand strong action and was incredulous that other politicians, supposedly tuned to the public's thinking, could not see that just as clearly as he did.

Billy Dan and Millard Duval were waiting for him when he arrived, at just past eight A.M.

"I am flying to San Francisco," Parker announced. "Notify the press, and charter us a jet. Set the departure time for three hours from now."

"What are you going to do out there?" asked Duval.

"I'm going to show the country just what a leader does in a crisis," Parker answered with a smile.

"What about the endorsement of Nelson?" asked Billy Dan.

"I'm not endorsing anybody right now," snapped Parker, and then continued, "Millard, you will go with me. Billy Dan, you are going to stay in Washington. I'm going to have another little job for you. In the meantime, the two of you start fixing up the trip, while I think about what I want to say when I get there."

"Where will you give the speech?" asked Duval.

"Right where it should be given. In Oakland."

Parker motioned Billy Dan to stay behind as Duval left the office. "I want to get rid of Janice," he said.

"Are you serious?" Billy Dan exclaimed before he could stop himself.

Parker's face darkened. "You're goddamned right I am. She knows too much and I'm beginning to have doubts about her stability. So we dump her, do you understand?"

"Yes, sir. How are you planning to do it?"

"That's why you're staying here. I want it done smoothly and I don't want her running to my enemies. So you are going to handle it just right, tonight after I leave."

"Yes, sir," Billy Dan said. "But what should I tell her? She's going to be mighty shocked."

"Jesus Christ, do I have to tell you everything. You're supposed to have some brains. That's what I'm supposed to be paying you for."

166

"I just thought you might have some ideas," Billy Dan said.

Parker stood up and glared down at his assistant. "What a horse's ass you are," he said. "All you have to do is take her aside tonight and fire her on the spot, but sugar-coat it so she doesn't get hysterical. Don't give her any notice because I don't want her to get a chance at the files. Offer her a couple of months' pay, or maybe more, just to ease the blow."

"Yes, sir."

"On second thought, give her six months' pay. Pay it to her monthly. That way we continue to have a hold on her. Also, you tell her we will help her find a job."

"Okay. I'll do it that way."

"Don't you screw this up. It's your fucking ass if you do."

"I'll do it right," murmured Billy Dan.

While Senator Parker and his entourage were flying westward, the President was deeply engrossed in a crisis meeting of his Cabinet called for two P.M. on this Monday afternoon. The Cabinet Room was filled, each member seated at his traditional place around the long wooden table. The President sat in his highbacked chair, facing the Vice-President. Some twenty other people were seated around the room. They included the members of the President's staff, several heads of major government departments, and representatives of the Joint Chiefs of Staff. Also present were the directors of the Federal Bureau of Investigation and the Central Intelligence Agency.

The President had opened the meeting by briefing those present on the gravity of the Oakland occupation. He had pointed out that Mamba's control was apparently complete and that it would take a full-scale military movement to dislodge him, at an incalculable cost in lives and property. The President had then turned the meeting over to the F.B.I. Director, who had reported on the rapidly deteriorating situation and unrest in several other cities. Chicago in particular had experienced considerable rioting on the west side, and similar outbreaks had occurred in Baltimore, Philadelphia and Detroit. The Director was unable to say whether these had been isolated incidents or whether they were part of some master plan. He was also unable to give assurances that the situation would not continue to worsen.

The President had then told of Mamba's meeting with two members of his staff, a meeting that had concluded only a little over an hour ago. Then the President had thrown the meeting open for comment.

"Speak frankly," he said. "I want honest reactions from all of you."

What followed had been as vehement a debate as the room had witnessed in many a year.

"Mamba's demands are absolutely insane," the Defense Secretary said. "We cannot give him anything. The entire country will rise up if we reward him for what he has done." This viewpoint was loudly seconded by several other Cabinet officials, all of whom spoke passionately and at length.

"There is no way we can guarantee them immunity from prosecution without completely destroying our entire legal fabric," said the Attorney General. "The repercussions from such an act would be unendurable. God knows the eventual price we would have to pay."

"I agree with you," said the President. "But let's assume that these are only Mamba's opening demands. Of course, there is no possibility of assuring them they will go unpunished. They will have to take their chances on that. What I want to know is, Can we negotiate any part of their offer? Should we bargain, and, if so, what can we give?"

"If you can't give them their immunity, why go any further with them?" demanded the F.B.I. Director. "They want to save their own skins first, that is for sure, and if we won't do that for them, then the rest would seem to be pointless."

"I don't see it that way," answered the President. "If there is some way we can negotiate their substantive demands, then I think they will be forced to take their chances with the courts. I think their own people would force them to do that."

"Why in the hell don't we just go in and smash them!" growled the C.I.A. Director.

"Let me try to explain what I think would happen," answered the President. "Putting aside the loss of innocent lives on both sides, there is the matter of what reactions such a military move would create in cities all over the country. I think it would result in the greatest outpouring of racial war this country has ever seen. When you put all of that together you can begin to see why I want to bargain with them if it is at all possible to do so."

"We are already in a race war, and more riots are popping out all over the place," persisted the Defense Secretary.

"Yes, we do have some reaction, but I don't think it is anything like what we will see if we start a war out there," answered the President.

The Defense Secretary leaned forward in his chair, and said, "With all due respect, Mr. President, I think you would be making the gravest of errors if you do not immediately move against these people. I cannot state too strongly how I feel about that."

The President showed no apparent reaction to this outburst, although there was a perceptible stirring in the room. The President stared down at his hands, clasped before him on the table. Finally he spoke.

"I will only be President for another six weeks or so, and then this burden is going to be cast upon someone else, though God knows who it will be. In the meantime, I will not have it said that I started a race war in this country by invading an American city with an army. Now, it may come to that, but it is going to be only after I have explored every other possibility."

"How long will you wait before using the army?" asked the Defense Secretary.

For the first time the President showed anger, as he sharply answered, "I do not have to make that kind of a decision now, Mr. Secretary. I am not bound by a timetable, and I will constantly re-examine my options every hour if I have to."

The Attorney General quietly spoke up. "The question is, as I understand, what are we willing to offer Mamba, is that right?"

"That's part of it," answered the President, traces of anger still evident in his voice. "Another part would be what we might do to dissuade him from pursuing his folly."

"I would suggest as a starter that we send Brady and Potofsky back to Mamba and try to set up a private line so that we may conduct continuous negotiations," suggested the Attorney General.

"If they talk to us from Mamba's phones there is too great a risk of our conversations being bugged," said the F.B.I. Director. "It would be no trick at all to tap the line."

"I will take that risk," said the President. "I agree that we should send them back. Now, what kind of guidance should we give to them?"

The Secretary of State, always a quietly thoughtful man, now spoke up for the first time. "I have been making some notes here on various possibilities. Let me read them to you for whatever they might be worth."

"Please go ahead, Mr. Secretary," the President said respectfully.

"For one thing," the Secretary of State continued, "it occurs to me that we might offer to bring Mamba, and whoever else he wishes to have along, to the White House for a personal conference with the President. That way he could express his grievances directly. Another possibility is that the President might set up a special Presidential Commission, perhaps of the stature of the Warren Commission, to explore the demands. The commission might start by holding its public hearings in Oakland. A third thought, which is probably somewhat radical, is that the President might agree to actively explore and give sympathetic consideration to the possibility of using some appropriate federal lands to form a new city. Perhaps funds might be found to aid in its formation. Of course, Congress would have to act on anything like that, and I suppose that is not a very hopeful prospect under the circumstances."

"I like your first two suggestions," said the President. "The third one I would want to think about some more."

"I am sure you are aware of the extent of adverse public

reaction your bringing those criminals to the White House would arouse," said the Defense Secretary.

"Yes, Mr. Secretary, I am," the President impatiently replied. "But these days I am not too concerned about public opinion. If we can shut this tragedy off without further bloodshed then I have no doubt but that we will be fairly judged by the people, and, eventually, by history."

There was further discussion, but the ideas of the Secretary of State were accepted by the President. Thus, at four P.M., the meeting was adjourned and the President called Potofsky and Brady. He directed them to return to Oakland and gave them the guidelines for negotiations with Mamba.

A few hours later, Senator Parker arrived in San Francisco. The news of his trip had preceded him, and as he stepped from his plane, several thousand people were jammed inside the terminal. They had come to see Parker and to cheer him on. They surged forward, breaking past the few airport police attempting to hold them back, and surrounded him with screaming, almost hysterical, shouts of approval. They reached to touch him, to get a glimpse of him. "You get them, Senator." "We'll back you all the way." "God bless you," they shouted. The senator nodded and smiled, responding with murmured "thank you's" as he shook as many hands as possible. His secret service guards were pushed back against him, struggling to move him through the mass of people. The going was slow, but the senator was in no hurry as he reached, touched, and inched ahead.

It took over thirty minutes to get to the waiting car at the terminal's main entrance. Parker's northern California manager had arranged for that, and also for a motorcade of several additional cars and a large bus for the press. Still, as it turned out, there was not enough transportation, for, when the news of Parker's appearance had hit the area, fifty additional representatives of local newspapers and television stations had shown up at the airport, demanding the right to accompany the senator. The manager did his best, and with frantic scurrying obtained a half

171

dozen more automobiles, barely sufficient to handle the overflow.

Senator Parker had asked to travel over the Bay Bridge as far as the police checkpoint on the Oakland side, but the bridge had been closed to all civilian traffic since early Sunday morning and the police were adamantly against allowing a political entourage to get that close to Mamba's armed troops. They strenuously argued that it could be exceedingly dangerous and provocative. Finally, Parker's manager contacted the governor of California at the Treasure Island command post. The governor agreed that a presidential candidate had a right to make such an inspection, and, to the manager's surprise, orders were quickly given to this effect.

Thus, with a large police escort leading the way, Senator Parker and more than one hundred press people headed toward the Oakland side of the Bay. It was now late Monday afternoon, and the motorcade sped rapidly across the deserted bridge. They arrived at the police checkpoint, and Senator Parker got out of his car, walking toward the line of police cars blocking the highway. The governor of California was waiting for him.

"We are glad to have you here, Senator," the governor said, giving Parker a hearty handshake in full view of the cameras. The reporters crowded closely around, and the entire conversation was recorded.

"I'm sorry that no other national figure has seen fit to come out and see this terrible thing for himself," Parker responded in a resonant voice.

"It is inexcusable," answered the governor.

"What is being done to help you out?" asked Parker.

"Nothing but procrastinating talk. I have asked the President for help, but so far he has done nothing."

"That's typical of the wishy-washy coddling of black rioters that has been going on for years," said Parker.

"I am beginning to agree with you," answered the governor.

Several members of the press, listening to the stilted conversation, obviously intended for public consumption, cast amused glances at one another. Others, however, were struck by the significance of the governor's presence at this time as well as his sympathetic responses to Parker's views. The governor was a Republican, a leader of the conservative wing of his party, and his state had voted for the Republican candidate, Governor Nelson. With the Electoral College meeting only two weeks away, the political implications of the governor's actions could not be overlooked.

The governor and Senator Parker continued to view Mamba's forces, stepping in front of the police cars and looking at the toll station barricades through field glasses. Then, the two of them got into the governor's limousine and headed back toward the San Francisco airport, alone, except for the driver and a secret service agent. The press could do nothing but follow, now no longer able to overhear their conversation.

At the airport they boarded a police helicopter and for the next hour flew high over the Oakland area, looking at the occupied city.

It was nearly dark when they landed. By this time, the crowd at the airport had multiplied and the police were estimating its size at over ten thousand. A small platform and microphone had been placed in the parking lot just outside the terminal and Senator Parker and the governor pushed their way through the mass of people and headed toward it. The governor stepped to the microphone and spoke first.

"I have reported to Senator Parker, and I will now tell all of you exactly what the President of the United States has been doing these last two days to undermine the safety and security of us all. The riot started early yesterday morning. It was soon clear that neither the police nor our National Guard forces would be sufficient to control the situation. I immediately called the President and requested that he send in federal forces. The President did not give me an answer, although he did start moving some troops out here. He still has not responded to my request and the troops are sitting over at the Alameda Naval Air Station doing nothing, while Oakland burns.

"The occupation of Oakland continues, people are being killed and driven out of their own city, yet the President has sent two of his staff men into Oakland to *negotiate* with Mamba. They are with him now, dealing with that criminal, offering him concessions, and putting their stamp of approval on an insurrection against the people of California and the laws of this land. I begged the President's representatives not to take this fearful step and to urge the President to uphold the Constitution and his oath of office by doing his sworn duty and sending in the troops now. So far, he has failed to do so, and the occupation continues."

The governor now looked at Senator Parker, who was standing beside him, and put his hand on the senator's arm as he continued. "Only Senator Parker has had the courage to come here and view this dastardly act for himself. Although the senator is not of my political party, I say that patriotism knows no party lines, and I am, therefore, compelled to give him the full credit he so richly deserves. For years he has been speaking out and warning us of just such an event as we are now witnessing. He has been a true prophet, and I salute him."

The governor stepped back from the microphone and motioned Parker to come forward. As he did so, the crowds erupted with a deafening roar. It lasted for a full five minutes, gradually changing into a chant of "We want Parker!" swelling with intensity and accompanied by stamping feet and angrily raised fists. The reporters, looking over this mass of people, were stunned by the immensity of the emotional outpouring.

Finally Parker raised both hands over his head, and the crowd slowly quieted. Then he spoke.

"Oakland belongs to you, not to these black hoodlums!" he shouted.

A roar of approval washed over the crowd.

"I demand the impeachment of the President of the United States," Parker intoned, his voice rising.

A surging scream came back at him from the crowd. "Yes, yes!" they cried.

Parker continued, his voice strong. "The governor of California has told you the facts. They are unbelievably true. These facts tell us what we have suspected all along. We are being led by the handmaidens of a conspiracy that intends to destroy our

174

country. A revolution has started, and our so-called leaders are a part of it. They are the allies of monsters. They are their dupes. If this is not the work of traitors, then I have never seen it."

Parker stood still until the cheer subsided. "Thank God that there are fearless men such as your governor," he continued. "Your governor has done his best. Now it is up to the rest of us to carry on."

Then, in slow and measured tones, the now silent crowd hanging on his every word, the senator concluded. "I will not shirk my duty to you. God willing, I will lead you out of this wilderness. Give me your support, and we will triumph over these evil men."

Stu Brady and Mike Potofsky had spent this same afternoon engaged in frustrating negotiations with Mamba. Wholly unaware of Senator Parker's charges against the President, they had been attempting to carry out the President's directions to work out a settlement. An hour or so prior to Parker's arrival in San Francisco they had driven, for the second time, across the Bay Bridge and were escorted into Mamba's command post. Then, with Charlie Jefferson present, they again commenced their conversations with Mamba.

"We have a proposal which we believe will be attractive to you," Potofsky said. "The President is agreeable to taking several actions. First, he will see you at the White House and spend as much time as is necessary for you to present your grievances and discuss them thoroughly. Second, he will establish a Presidential Commission to investigate and report on these grievances. Third, the Commission will hold public hearings in Oakland and in all other places where it may be indicated."

"What about what I asked for—the independent government here and assurances of safety for my men?" Mamba asked.

"We cannot agree to that," Stu said.

"Then, there is no point in continuing this discussion," Mamba replied, although he made no move to stand up.

"I believe there is," Potofsky said. "Look at it from our point of view for a moment. As for setting up a separate government, the President has absolutely no power to do that. It is a matter of state law, and there is a whole series of legal procedures involved before a new city can be formed. As regards immunity from prosecution, again it is a question of state law. Perhaps we could do something about federal crimes, but we just cannot control state prosecutions. More importantly, we don't feel the country would stand for that kind of a deal, and in the long run that would hurt your cause a great deal."

"What would happen to my 'cause,' as you put it, is my concern, not yours," Mamba replied. "Concerning the so-called impossibility of the rest of what I ask, I have found that what the government finds impossible to do is a somewhat variable concept depending on the circumstances. If the screw is turned tightly enough, ways and means can often be found. Perhaps you had better take another look at the price of reaching no agreement with me before turning me down quite so cavalierly."

"I don't think you appreciate how far the President has already gone to be conciliatory," Stu persisted. "This is not an easy step for him. He is under great pressure to come in here with maximum force, and he has got the troops in place to do just that. He wants to avoid that kind of step, but he can go just so far, and he can't indefinitely postpone what the rest of the country is demanding."

"That remains to be seen," Mamba commented.

The discussion continued in this vein, neither side giving anything from their original position. To Stu, the only encouraging sign was that Mamba continued to talk, though he remained adamant in his demands. Then, in the late afternoon the telephone rang on Mamba's desk. He listened for a moment, hung up and turned to them.

"You gentlemen may be interested in knowing that Senator Jack Parker and the California governor are together," Mamba said with no visible change of expression. "They are on our side of the Bay Bridge, along with a large number of press. They are apparently looking us over."

Stu glanced at Potofsky, but neither one made any comment to this startling news. Nonetheless, Stu was deeply concerned. The governor knew all about their negotiations with Mamba, and they had been relying on his word to keep it quiet. Though the governor had been upset when they were directed to go back to Mamba for a second time, he had made no further threat to take any kind of action. But it certainly seemed as if the fat was in the fire now.

"I had thought that the good governor was a solid Republican," Mamba said, voicing Stu's exact thoughts. "His coming together with friend Parker is an interesting turn, would you not agree?"

"It is what we've been warning you about all day," said Potofsky. "You must see that the political pressure for action is building just as we've been trying to tell you it would. When a political animal like the California governor is willing to act in this way, it can only mean he thinks that the wind is blowing damn strong."

"We shall see," said Mamba, as he turned and went out of the room.

As soon as Mamba left, Potofsky said, "We ought to call in and be brought up to date."

"Let's wait awhile," suggested Stu. "I think this has made some impression on him, and if we leave now we may miss our chance."

They sat for another hour, talking in a desultory way, feeling cut off from the world, and worried. The sun was going down, and Stu felt exhaustion closing in on him. It was now Monday night and he had not had a good night's sleep since Friday.

Finally Mamba returned. This time his face betrayed his consternation. "Senator Parker and the governor have just made a joint appearance at the San Francisco airport," he said in a tight voice. "The governor revealed your presence here and attacked the President for sending you to me. Parker was much stronger. He demanded the impeachment of the President."

Stu shook his head in amazement. "Now you can see the

way it is going," he said. "Perhaps you will now believe that the President is under terrible pressure, and if anything is to be done, it will have to be soon."

Charlie Jefferson, who had been sitting quietly in a corner chair throughout the afternoon's negotiations, now spoke up for the first time. "It is going to be too late for you, Mamba," he said. "You are just too damn pig-headed to see your opportunity when it waltzes by."

"You don't know a damn thing, Jefferson," said Mamba, showing emotion for the first time. "Why don't you just shut up and let me think."

"He's right, Mamba," said Potofsky. "If you have any reason left in you, now is the time to show it. There's no time left."

Mamba sat quietly for a long time, staring out over their heads at the city below. When he did speak, it was in a voice strangely subdued from his earlier strident manner. "Perhaps there is some middle ground," he said. "You go back to San Francisco now. I will think it over. We will meet again at eight tomorrow morning."

"I'm not sure we have that kind of time," said Potofsky.

"Then so be it," said Mamba. "However, I will not be rushed. We will just have to take our chances, I'm afraid. If you wish to do so, you are welcome to return tomorrow." Then he stood and abruptly left the room.

Stu and Potofsky said goodbye to Charlie and then started their now familiar route back across the Bay Bridge to Treasure Island.

"Well, he appears to be moving," said Potofsky as they drove toward the command post.

"Yes, but we don't know how far, or how fast."

While Parker was heading back to Washington after his tumultuous reception, Billy Dan Reeves sat alone with Janice Pruitt at a back table at The Monocle, a small, intimate restaurant a few blocks from the New Senate Office Building in Washington. It was almost ten o'clock at night, but they had not been able to get away from the office until long after Parker's impeachment demand. The telephones had rung incessantly. Most of the calls were from the public, generally expressing praise for the senator. There had also been many calls from the press. Since the staff had received no advance warning of what the senator had planned to do they had quite truthfully answered the press inquiries with the statement that they had no comment; that the senator would be back in Washington late tonight; and that, undoubtedly, he would have something further to say tomorrow. Finally, after more than an hour of fielding the telephones, they had given up and left.

Janice had been feeling rather left out and vaguely disturbed because she had not gone with the senator to California, and so she had gratefully accepted Billy Dan's dinner invitation. Yet, he had been subdued during the meal and, completely unlike himself, had barely touched his food.

Now, as they were drinking coffee, he looked at her and nervously cleared his throat. "Have you thought much of your future, Janice?" he began. "I mean, have you decided what you would like to do with yourself?"

"I'm not sure what you are driving at," she replied warily. "I'm happy with my job if that's what you're asking."

Billy Dan looked down at his coffee and rearranged the silverware. "Well, the Hill is not a lifetime career for most people," he said. "It seems that attractive girls like you often move on to bigger and better things after a few years around this place, and I was wondering if you might have started thinking along those lines."

"No, I haven't," she said sharply. "I'm satisfied. The senator's been good to me and I think I've worked well for him. I've had no thoughts at all about doing anything else."

"Maybe you ought to start thinking along those lines," Billy Dan said, not looking at her.

"Exactly what are you trying to say, Billy Dan?" she asked, suddenly feeling very tired.

"The senator thinks you should find another job."

179

Janice sat quietly and stared blankly at him. Then shock and anger washed over her. She tried to control her voice but she could not stop the tremor. "Why?"

"He thinks it would be better for you to leave."

"But that doesn't make any sense," she continued, knowing it was hopeless to argue, that Billy Dan was just carrying out his orders.

"I'm afraid he has made up his mind. Of course, we will pay you until you find something. He's willing to keep you on the payroll for six months."

"That's sweet of him."

"You won't have any trouble. We will help you find a good job."

"When am I supposed to leave?"

"Now," he said, finally looking up at her. "You won't have to come in tomorrow, though you will stay on the payroll until you get settled somewhere."

Janice sat sipping her coffee, unable to understand. There had been no hint of dissatisfaction from the senator. She had been performing well at the office and their personal relationship seemingly had been good. She was good in bed, he would tell her, and he always seemed to be satisfied, even at his strangest moments. Thinking about it, though, it did seem that when they had made love recently his cruelty had become more frequent and she had found herself struggling to hide her disgust. Still, except for that awful call to his wife which she just couldn't finish, she had never refused him anything nor questioned any of his demands. She had paid her price, she bitterly concluded, and this was to be her reward.

"Please tell me what it is, Billy Dan," she implored.

"I honestly don't know," he answered. "He only told me that he wants you to leave. He didn't give any reasons."

Tears were now running down her cheeks. It was all she could do to keep from openly sobbing. Parker, for all the trouble, had been what she wanted, and she had been willing to do anything to stay with him. And now, with no warning, without his even having the humanity to tell her himself, she was being booted out, and for good.

Janice could hold her anger and shock no longer. A racking sob broke from her throat and, stumbling from the table, she ran from the restaurant. She was crying uncontrollably as she half walked and half ran to Constitution Avenue.

When she got to her apartment it was close to midnight. Janice threw herself on the bed, shaking with sobs. Finally she got up, walked to the window of the darkened room and looked out over the lovely city. Then she reached a decision. She fumbled in her desk drawer for her address book, found what she was looking for and walked to the phone. She paused for a moment and, taking a deep breath, resolutely dialed.

I don't like it one bit," said Governor Maynard Nelson. He was sitting at his desk in the Capitol at Harrisburg, Pennsylvania, alone with his press secretary, Jerry Greenberg. The Tuesday morning newspapers were spread before him, filled with stories about Oakland, Senator Parker's call for the President's impeachment, and speculation regarding Parker's possible alliance with the California governor. Nelson looked haggard and upset.

"Perhaps you should make some statement," offered Greenberg.

"No, I can't do that yet," said Nelson. "What time is it in California?"

"Seven A.M."

"That's late enough." The governor picked up the telephone and said, "Get me the governor of California." Turning to Greenberg, he added, "It's time to find out exactly what is going on."

It took about thirty minutes to locate the California governor. He was no longer using the Treasure Island command post but the operator finally found him at the St. Francis Hotel in San Francisco, his temporary headquarters until the Oakland situation was resolved.

"Maynard, how in the world are you?" asked the Californian in his hearty voice.

"I am doing just fine. I trust I didn't get you out of bed," Nelson said.

"I've been up for quite a while. It's been a long time since we've talked, Maynard. I haven't seen you since your last swing through California just before the election. That was a good trip, and our state certainly did come through for you."

"Yes, Governor, and I'm sorry I haven't thanked you sooner for all you did for me. We couldn't have carried the state without your efforts."

"I was delighted to do it," said the Californian. "I'm disappointed I couldn't have done more outside the state and helped avoid this damnable deadlock."

"I want to tell you how terribly distressed I am about what's happening in Oakland. I wish there were something that I could do to help on that," said Nelson.

The Californian's friendly tone abruptly changed, his voice becoming hard. "Frankly, I am more than a little upset that you have remained silent. I hoped you would have seen fit to strike out on this problem. It's a terrible thing that has happened out here. They've got Oakland and the President of the United States is not only not helping us, he is actively consorting with those bastards, and you haven't said one damn thing." The anger rose in the Californian's voice as he continued.

"I think you are being a bit hasty," said Nelson, attempting to placate him. "The incident only occurred on Sunday. After all, it's not unreasonable to allow me some time to judge the problem."

"It didn't take Senator Parker any time to come to California and respond. You may be interested in knowing that his reception out here was fantastic."

"So I read," said Nelson somewhat querulously.

"You read correctly," said the California governor. "Parker did exactly what you should have done. I need help out here and he came through with it. His statement was exactly right."

"I want to speak to you about Parker," said Nelson. "The morning papers are hinting that there is some kind of a deal between the two of you. I know that is ridiculous, but I wanted to ask you to scotch the rumor as soon as you can so that the electors don't get upset."

There was a long pause and Governor Nelson nervously

183

drummed his fingers on the table as he waited for the Californian to respond. When the answer finally came, the California governor said, in a flat voice, "I'm afraid I cannot do that, Maynard."

"What do you mean by that?"

"I am going to reconsider what I must do. The Oakland business has opened my eyes to what the country needs. Perhaps the time has come for just the kind of tough leadership Senator Parker can offer us."

Nelson rubbed his hand over his forehead. He felt the beginnings of discomfort in his stomach, a sure sign that his ulcer was about to act up again. Forty electoral votes, he thought, straight down the drain if California defected, since the California governor could undoubtedly deliver his state to whomever he chose. Worse than that, a breakaway in California could start a stampede among the remaining Republican states. Where that would lead Maynard Nelson could not begin to imagine. There was no precedent, no experience for this kind of electoral situation, and he was unable to see his way through it. What he did believe, however, was that he had been trapped by his deal with Parker. It had tied his hands, and it looked now as if there was a good possibility that Parker was about to break his commitment.

"I would be grateful if you wouldn't do anything precipitous," Governor Nelson continued. "After all, we are all Republicans, and I am the nominee of our party. I think we still have a chance of pulling it off, and I beg you to consider carefully before taking any step that would destroy our chances."

"I do not intend to act irresponsibly," the California governor said, his voice again becoming hard. "However, I will make my own judgments as to what is best for the state of California and the country."

Meaning, what is best for yourself, Nelson thought bitterly. Then he said, "I gather that your mind is not fixed as yet, and that you have made no definite commitment to Parker."

"I have made no deals. But I will make up my own mind."

"I hope that we can talk again," said Nelson.

"Any time, Maynard," said the Californian, his tone once again pleasant. "I always enjoy talking to you."

After hanging up, Governor Nelson turned to Jerry Greenberg, who had been standing by his desk throughout this conversation. "I think I had better talk to Senator Parker," he said, his face betraying his deep concern. "Try to find him for me."

Nelson absent-mindedly leafed through the papers on his desk while he waited for the call to be completed. He was in a quandary about what to do. If Parker stayed with his agreement, the election was certainly his, and he did not want to rock the boat. But if Parker was about to jump the traces, then he should be taking action to solidify his own party's support. He would ask Parker straight out about his plans.

Greenberg was trying Parker's office phone. After a long wait, he was connected with Parker's assistant, Billy Dan Reeves. He told Reeves that Governor Nelson wanted to talk to the senator. Reeves went off the line but very quickly came back.

"The senator is getting ready to leave town. He is awfully sorry, but he cannot talk now. Can you give me the message?" Reeves asked.

Greenberg reported the request to Nelson, who scowled and sharply shook his head. "No," said Greenberg. "He wants to speak to the senator personally."

"Well," Reeves drawled, "I will tell him and he will try to get back to the governor as soon as he has some time."

"Please do that," said Greenberg, unable to keep the sarcasm out of his voice.

Governor Nelson angrily pushed away from his desk and walked to the pot of coffee across the room. He poured a cup for himself, spilling some in his trembling hand.

"You shouldn't be dealing with that man," Greenberg said in a quiet voice. "You can't depend on him, I don't care what he has said to you."

Nelson turned around and walked up to Greenberg. "I know how you feel about Parker," he said bitterly. "I've never been quite sure of what you might have been trying to do about it."

Greenberg quailed inwardly but tried to keep all emotion

out of his voice as he answered. "I want only the best for you, Governor, that's all I've ever had in mind," he said, avoiding a direct answer.

Nelson walked over to the window and sipped his coffee. "I'm sorry, Jerry," he said. "Bear with me. These are difficult days."

"I'll be with you as long as you want me," said Greenberg, "but you have to understand how I feel about Parker. You just can't depend on that man."

Nelson paced the room. He was probably being too anxious, he thought, and reading a lot of nonsense into what was going on. There was no sense in doing anything foolish. He would just wait to talk to Parker. Then he would know what to do.

CHAPTER FIFTEEN

Nina Moran spent the first part of Tuesday morning in her jail cell in the Oakland police station, her home since Sunday morning. Charlie and Simon were being kept elsewhere in the jail. During her month-long captivity, Nina had become increasingly disconsolate, wondering when, if ever, they were going to be released. Her bitterness against Mamba, compounded daily by the incredible acts for which he was responsible, had grown to a point where she could remain civil to the man only with the greatest effort. Nina felt that they personally, as well as the country, had been brought to the brink of disaster: federal troops, armed and ready, only a few miles away; Parker violently threatening; the President himself, trying desperately to find a solution; and Mamba, the man who had caused it all, who might well ignore all chances to extricate himself. As she turned on her bunk to face the cell's blank wall, Nina felt a hopeless despair about the world.

It was close to eleven in the morning when a guard entered Nina's cell and, in a surly tone, ordered her to follow him. She was taken up the elevator and put into a room near Mamba's office. She silently waited, staring out the window at the quiet city, on this morning bathed in bright sunlight from an unusually cloudless sky. The door behind her opened and Charlie Jefferson walked into the room. As soon as he entered, the door was locked behind him.

They ran to each other, kissing, holding each other in a tight embrace.

"How is Simon?" Nina asked.

"He's not doing very well. I think they must have broken a rib when they beat him and there's something wrong inside him. He can't seem to straighten up without a lot of pain. He needs a doctor, but they won't do a damn thing to help him."

"Oh, God, how terrible," said Nina, clutching his hand.

Charlie then told her about the meetings with the White House representatives, and added, "Maybe it will all be over soon. At least Mamba is still talking to them. If he's got any sense left at all he'll agree to their proposal."

"But he's not normal, Charlie. He's just as sick as that man Parker."

"I'm not so sure you're right," said Charlie. "It could be that he's wavering."

"I hope so, but what will they do about us?"

"I don't think there's anything to worry about. I know Stu Brady very well, and he will make sure we get out of here safely. That's one thing I'm certain of," he said with a smile.

At this moment the door opened and Mamba walked in. He went directly to a chair and sat down. "I want to ask you what you think the President will do," he said. "You have both been involved with the white establishment, and I want your judgment on what is going to happen."

"I think you had better take their offer," said Charlie. "I think it's more than you deserve, and you won't be able to better it."

"Nina?" Mamba asked, gesturing toward her.

"You've got yourself in pretty deep, Mamba, and you'd better get out of this any way you can," she said.

"I'm not as unreasonable as you might believe," Mamba said. "I think I have done something meaningful here. I've shown that the black man can and will take direct action to right whitey's wrongs. I've focused the world's attention on us, and I've caused other cities to stir into action. They are rioting now in Detroit and Chicago, and there is going to be a mass rally of support for me on the Berkeley campus today. What I've done is the only way to get meaningful changes for our people."

"But at what price?" Nina asked. "Even if what you say is

188

so, the cost is going to be terrible. You have done an awful thing, and all I can say to you is undo it as quickly as you can."

"When do you think they will move against us?" Mamba asked Charlie.

"I'm amazed they haven't done it by now, and I can't believe they will wait much longer. You are lucky to even talk to them, and you had better take advantage of it," Charlie said.

"I've been talking to my people," Mamba said quietly, half to himself. "They don't want me to give an inch. They are willing to die if necessary. You see, under any circumstances, I will have difficulty in convincing them to surrender."

"You created this situation, Mamba," said Charlie. "I only hope that you can assert some leadership in getting yourself out of it."

Mamba rose abruptly. "You two stay here. I am going to meet with the White House people. I may want to talk to you again."

Stu Brady and Mike Potofsky had been kept waiting for over three hours in a downstairs room at Mamba's headquarters building, without any explanation for the delay, yet there seemed nothing for them to do but bide their time.

Earlier in the morning, before they had left Treasure Island for their eight o'clock meeting with Mamba, they had received a disturbing briefing from General Slocum.

He had breathlessly burst into the room shortly before they were scheduled to leave, saying "I'm glad I caught you. My driver had to break every speed limit in the book to get me here."

"What is it, General?" Potofsky had asked, motioning him to a seat in the small office that had been assigned to them.

"I've just heard from the Pentagon, and have talked to General Broadwell of the Second Airborne. They now have a plan of action and are fully in position to strike just as soon as they get the order from the President."

"What is the plan?" asked Stu.

"The army is strongly recommending that they start the attack with a pinpoint air strike on each of their strong points.

They feel they can bomb precisely enough to keep civilian damage down to an acceptable minimum. They will follow that with a mortar attack, and then move in with armored vehicles. They are convinced they can complete the breakthrough in less than a day."

"What about re-taking the downtown area?" asked Stu.

"They will use whatever force needed to take the area building by building if necessary. The division has had good experience in city street fighting. They have no hesitancy in performing that kind of mop-up operation."

"Do they really feel that the air and artillery part is essential?" asked Potofsky.

"Absolutely," General Slocum had said. "They have examined the other alternatives and are convinced that the manpower cost to the division would be considerably higher if they don't. In the army's view this is a military occupation and it must be dislodged with all the force at our disposal. We cannot allow our hands to be partially tied, and the President should not permit a halfway action. It would be disastrous. We are recommending this plan in the strongest possible terms. The Joint Chiefs are unanimous and the Defense Secretary has concurred. It is being transmitted to the President now."

General Slocum's report was uppermost in Stu's mind as he and Potofsky waited out Mamba's unexplained delay. Out of fear that the room was bugged, they could not now discuss the situation, but during their short drive to Oakland, they had reviewed the army's strong recommendation, Parker's demand for the President's impeachment, and the rising emotion throughout the country. They did not see how the President could hold out against such pressure much longer.

It was almost noon when the two White House aides were summoned to Mamba's office. Mamba was alone and appeared to be somewhat more tense than on Monday.

"Please forgive the delay, gentlemen," Mamba began. "There were a number of people with whom I had to consult before I could see you, and the process took more time than I thought it would."

"We don't mind," said Potofsky, "but, as we told you yesterday, we don't think that there is much time left to talk."

"Well, I shall come directly to the point," Mamba said. "I have decided to accept your offer of a White House invitation and a Presidential Commission. However, my people and I still must be assured of immunity against any retaliation for our actions here."

"Do you mean a promise you won't be prosecuted?" asked Potofsky.

"Exactly," said Mamba.

"We told you yesterday it is impossible for the President to promise you that," said Stu. "He couldn't do it even if he wanted to."

Mamba sighed and leaned toward them across the big desk. "I will be perfectly frank with you, and you must believe me," he said. "I cannot sell this deal to my people without that condition. I have been arguing with my leaders all morning, and if you could have been there you would know that 'argue' is far too mild a word. I had the greatest difficulty in convincing them even of this much. But without immunity it will do no good to reach an agreement with me because no one would follow me and you would have to attack Oakland in any event."

"That's hard to believe," said Stu. "You are their hero, and they'll listen to whatever you recommend."

Mamba permitted himself a slight smile. "There are those such as our friend Charlie Jefferson who think that my ego is so immense that I could believe such a thing. However, I am a realist and I am telling you they will not go along with any deal unless there is some assurance of their own safety. You can believe me or not, but that is a fact."

"You have nothing further to offer?" asked Potofsky.

"That's it," said Mamba. "That condition is not negotiable."

"We'll have to call in from here," Potofsky said. "I don't want to take the time to return to Oakland."

"Just a minute, Mike," said Stu, turning to Mamba. "Do we have your assurance that our call will not be tapped?"

"Of course, gentlemen," said Mamba. "I will leave you right here and you may use any telephone line on this desk." With that Mamba rose and walked toward the door. "I'll be back when you are ready to talk some more."

Stu dialed the White House directly, with no confidence that this call would not be overheard, but with no choice but to take the chance. He asked for Alvin Morgan, who came on the line almost immediately. Morgan listened without comment while Stu repeated Mamba's words and then Morgan asked Stu to wait for a few minutes.

There was a long wait. For almost half an hour Stu sat holding the silent receiver against his ear. Finally, Morgan came back on the line. "We want you two to come back to Washington right away," he said.

"Do we have that kind of time?" Stu asked.

"You let us worry about that," Morgan said in a sharp voice that implied this was an order. "You just get out to the San Francisco airport and on the Jetstar. It will be ready to go by the time you get there. Call me when you arrive at Andrews, and I'll let you know what you are to do."

"What do we tell Mamba?" Stu asked.

"Tell him we must personally consult with you, and that we will do the best we can. You can't make him any promises, so make sure that you don't."

Stu hung up, and looked forlornly at Potofsky.

"I gather we are to come home," Potofsky said.

"Right away," answered Stu. "I have no idea whether they are breaking off negotiations or just want to talk about Mamba's conditions."

Stu walked to the door and banged on it. A few moments later Mamba strode back into the room. They explained that they had been ordered back to the White House and that they were to leave immediately.

"Does this mean that the federal troops will not attack me until I hear from you one way or another?" Mamba asked.

Stu shook his head. "I wish I could give you that kind of assurance, but I can't. All I can tell you is that we will report directly to the President and will do our best to work this out."

"That's nothing at all," said Mamba.

"That's all there is," said Potofsky, "We can't even promise that you'll be hearing from us again."

"Then I, too, am free to act as I please," said Mamba.

"Of course," Potofsky said.

They drove directly to the San Francisco airport, not taking time to stop at Treasure Island. Before boarding the waiting airplane, they instructed the air force sergeant who was in charge of the ground crew to call General Slocum to inform him that they were returning to Washington. Within minutes they were airborne and on their way east.

It was after nine in the evening when they landed at Andrews in Washington. Stu went directly into the Flight Operations Building and, reaching across the counter near the entrance picked up the black phone marked "White House," and asked the signal corps operator to connect him with Alvin Morgan.

"Well, we're here," said Stu when Morgan answered. "Do you want us to come down there?"

"That's right," said Morgan, "and don't waste any time."

Stu and Potofsky got into the waiting White House car and reached the White House in about a half hour. Almost giddy from exhaustion, Stu, with Potofsky right behind him, trudged up the steps from the basement entrance to Morgan's first-floor office.

Morgan, who also looked like he was under considerable pressure, was in the midst of dictating to the secretary who shared his office with him. It was close to ten P.M., yet it looked as if he still had a long way to go before his day would end. Obviously he had no time for civilities with his colleagues, but merely glanced up as they entered his office.

"The President's waiting for you in the Mansion," Morgan said. "Go right on over." With that he waved them off and continued his work, scarcely missing a step.

As they walked to the Mansion, Stu realized that he had been going non-stop since he had made this same trek the previous Saturday night. He was almost at the end of his endurance, and he knew it.

And there was Sari. He had no idea what she had done since he last talked to her on Sunday morning. He was exhausted and depressed, he had hardly had a moment to think about his personal life, and he had no idea where he would get the energy to continue with whatever the President might have in mind.

When they reached the second floor of the Mansion they were ushered directly into the President's bedroom. He was sitting at a small table having dinner alone.

"Come right in, boys," he said, motioning to them with a wave of his hand. "Why don't you join me for dinner? The First Lady is off to New York doing some shopping, and probably spending me into bankruptcy, so I have been left here by myself."

The two staff men had eaten the usual fare of small dry sandwiches on the Jetstar. But, knowing the President and how he detested eating by himself, they readily accepted.

"I called you back here because I wanted to get personally your reactions to what is going on out there. Now, tell me about what he wants," the President said.

"He will go for the meeting with you here and the Commission, but he insists on legal immunity for his men," Potofsky said.

"He insists?" the President asked.

"Yes, sir," said Stu. "He says that he can't do anything without that kind of assurance, that his people won't follow him unless he gets it for them. He met with his leaders for a long time while we were waiting this morning, and he came back saying that is what they must have."

"How do you size him up?" asked the President.

"I believe he means it," said Potofsky.

"And you?" the President asked Stu.

"Well, he says he can't negotiate his need for some kind of immunity. Apparently he's got himself in a box with his own

194

people and there is no getting out of it. I agree with Mike. I think we will have to fight if we can't give him that."

"We explained as strongly as we could how impossible it is for you to grant him freedom from prosecution," Potofsky broke in, "but we can't budge him."

"I see," said the President, as he continued to eat in silence, while Stu and Potofsky picked at their dinners. The room was quiet and Stu had the feeling, here in this great house at the center of power, that they were somehow isolated from the world around them. A lovely illusion, he thought.

"I wish I knew more about Mamba," the President said in a low voice. "It is so difficult to size him up without ever having looked him in the eye."

"Yes, sir, I know," said Stu, feeling a surge of sympathy for this man and the remoteness that was necessarily forced upon him. "We've been with him for two days and all we can say is we believe he's not bluffing. I guess the fact he has gone as far as he has, pulled all of it together and carried it off, goes a long way to show that he means what he says."

"The way I see him," said Potofsky, "is that he has to make certain moves to satisfy his people and continue to lead. But, underneath that, I think he has a streak of the practical politician. He postures a lot, but he does seem to have at least some common sense."

"You fellows are all I've got," said the President in a soft voice. "You must be my eyes and ears in this." The President paused, and then asked, "How long have you been on this mission?"

"Since Sunday morning," Stu answered.

"Then why don't you both go on home and meet me here at eight tomorrow morning. I'll sleep on it and you do the same," said the President.

Stu could only feel intense relief at this short reprieve. He had dreaded the thought that they might be sent back to Oakland tonight. Now, at least, he could get some rest.

They said goodnight to the President. Stu then walked alone across Lafayette Park to the Hay Adams, hoping that his room had been held for him. When he checked at the desk he found that the room was still available and, leaving a six-thirty morning call, Stu undressed, threw himself on the bed and, within minutes, was sound asleep.

CHAPTER SIXTEEN

Stu Brady awoke on Wednesday morning feeling refreshed. It was still dark outside, but he had slept for almost six hours, his longest sleep in over four days. He supposed the accumulated tension would affect him before the day was out, but for now, despite the pressures of his assignment and his devastated home life, he felt reasonably good. He stepped into the shower and stood luxuriating in the hot water pouring over his head.

There had been no messages from Sari, but he had not expected any. He imagined that she had not done anything as yet about the divorce proceedings, not because she thought that the marriage had any hope but because she was habitually unwilling to move ahead on anything without being pushed. Most likely she would leave it to him to start the domestic surgery.

He vigorously toweled himself dry, putting off the thought of his wife and their marriage. Dressing rapidly, Stu threw some clean clothes into a small suitcase and left the hotel, walking back across the park to the White House.

In the West Wing basement, he greeted the Filipino mess boys and sat down at the large round table where the staff normally ate. Despite the early hour, three people were seated at the table: one of the President's secretaries, a pretty and talkative girl whom he had wooed away from a major New York advertising agency; the pleasant ex-C.I.A. man who ran the day shift in the Situation Room; and a young lawyer, the newest member of the President's staff, who had what Stu felt was the worst task in the White House—reading the Congressional Record, marking and summarizing it, and then delivering it to the President in his bedroom by eight each morning.

These staff people seemed delighted to have Stu join them. His mission had been revealed publicly on Monday night by the California governor and by Senator Parker, and his colleagues ribbed him about his inability to avoid the public spotlight. Behind the light talk, Stu realized, was their decided curiosity about what he had been doing, but he parried their questions with easy banter.

"I think every last one of them should be locked up and the key thrown away," the ex-C.I.A. man said. "Can you at least tell us whether you agree with that?"

Stu thought for a moment before replying. "I think they ought to be prosecuted, yes. But maybe some of us ought to try to understand why all of this has happened. The blacks have been beaten down for centuries in this country. Even today, almost everything is second class for them. Schools, housing, jobs, the works. They know there's a better life. They see it every day on television. It's all around them. I just don't think you can cage a whole group of people and expect them to take it lying down. At least not today."

"But does that justify what they've done out there?"

"Of course not," answered Stu. "But it doesn't hurt to understand why it happened and to accept a good deal of the blame ourselves."

"Is that how the President feels?"

"That's how I feel. You've been around here long enough to know I can't speak for him," Stu answered irritably. "Why don't we just drop the subject."

Stu continued to eat his breakfast, and at a few minutes before eight he excused himself and walked over to the Mansion. He waited in the long hall outside of the President's bedroom. Potofsky had not yet arrived, and Bill Norris, the President's valet, told him the President had slept later than usual and was just now getting up.

In a few moments Mike Potofsky came in. He looked exhausted. His normally deep-set, dark eyes appeared even more shadowed, and his shoulders were slumped as he sat down heavily in a chair. "Jesus," he said, "I couldn't sleep at all. I kept thinking of Mamba and Oakland and the boss. It just kept going in circles."

"I know, Mike," said Stu, his own depression returning as the reality of the crisis again washed over him.

"It is a tough business," Potofsky mumbled. "I just don't see any way out."

"At least it won't be our problem much longer," Stu said grimly.

"That's right," said Potofsky. "God, I dream of January twentieth and turning all of this over to some other poor devils."

Bill Norris came out of the bedroom. "He will see you now," he said.

The President was having breakfast and, without pausing, came right to the point. "I've decided what I am going to do," he said. "It is extremely delicate, as you will see, and absolutely no one is to know about it. Not your wives, not the staff, not the Cabinet, and not the generals. Do you understand that?" The President fixed them both with a penetrating gaze.

"Yes, Mr. President," they both answered.

"Mamba has got to be made to understand that this is absolutely all that I can do," the President continued. "He must see that he either accepts this proposal or I must order the troops in."

They nodded.

"All right," said the President. "I will see him at the White House and I will set up a commission to hold the hearings in Oakland and elsewhere. Mamba has got to submit himself to arrest after he leaves here. I cannot have it any other way. He will just have to take his chances with the courts."

The President paused, and they waited for the rest of his thinking.

"As to his men," the President went on, "I will give them a chance to slip out of Oakland. How they do it is their problem, and whether they can then elude the police is also something I cannot guarantee. However, I will withhold sending in the troops for twenty-four hours after he gives himself up. During that time they must disperse as best they can."

"If we tell him that how can we hope to keep this quiet?" asked Stu. "It will be certain to leak out."

The President looked very tired. His long face was drawn and the lines were deeply etched around his mouth as he answered. "That would be true *if* you told him what I have just said to you," the President replied. "But you are not going to do that. All you are to say to him is that I will not surround the city for twenty-four hours. I shall order an immediate attack after that, however. He will have to make his own assumptions, but you cannot admit them. As a matter of fact, if he asks, you are to deny any such intentions on our part."

"How can we be sure he will understand what we are trying to tell him?" asked Potofsky.

"He will understand," said the President. "I am not concerned about that."

"How can we get Mamba out of there without having him picked up by the California authorities?" Stu asked.

"I'll have a helicopter standing by at the Naval Air Station, which, by the way, is where you will be landing this time. The chopper will come right into Oakland to pick the three of you up."

"There is one other thing, Mr. President," said Stu.

"What?" asked the President impatiently.

"Mamba is holding three hostages," Stu went on. "Charlie Jefferson, the Assistant Attorney General, and a girl and man who helped him. They've been held captive for over a month. I think we should insist that they be released."

"You mean, tell Mamba it's no deal unless he lets them go? Is that what you are suggesting?" asked the President incredulously.

"Yes, sir," replied Stu hopelessly.

"That's ridiculous," snapped the President. "I want them released as badly as you, but I can't let this whole thing fall apart just on account of that."

"If you leave them there you might be accused of abandoning them just because they're Negroes," Potofsky said quietly.

"Now you look here, Potofsky," the President shot back, suddenly angry. "Their race hasn't got a damn thing to do with it. My judgment would be the same if they were white. We're talking about saving hundreds, maybe thousands, of lives, and you ought to know that."

"Yes, sir," said Potofsky.

"Can I at least ask that they be let free?" implored Stu.

"Yes, but that is all. If he says no, then drop it. Do you understand that?"

"Yes," said Stu flatly.

"When are we to leave?" asked Potofsky.

"Now," said the President. "Call me after you have seen Mamba, and before you leave there."

They left the President, summoned a car, and drove out to Andrews Air Force Base. Though the streets were jammed with morning rush-hour traffic, it was all coming toward the city, and they made very good time. It was another beautiful day. Washington was beginning its normal routine, the people struggling to get to work, seemingly oblivious to the crisis now boiling up in the country. But the great majority of them were undoubtedly painfully aware of what was going on.

They could hardly miss it. The morning papers were full of Oakland and the nation's reaction to it. Yesterday's session in Congress had accomplished little, with one member after another deploring the events, attacking the President and, in general, demanding an immediate and violent response to Mamba. Most significantly, no one had spoken for moderation nor defended the President's efforts to seek a peaceful solution. Even the usually vocal liberals had been strangely intimidated by the turn of events. Only Senator Harrington, true to his promise of loyalty, had issued a statement praising the President's efforts at conciliation, but the only effect of this effort was to draw fire upon himself.

The angry cry for revenge was being taken up throughout the land. The mayor of Chicago had issued a statement the day before demanding that the President act immediately. His city was in its second day of Negro rioting, and segments of the white population were reacting with armed excursions into the ghettos. Unlike previous flareups, the situation gave every evidence of turning into a pitched battle between the races, and the mayor was incensed with the President, whom he generally supported, for not removing "the cancerous cause of it all," as he put it.

Chicago was not alone. At least a dozen other cities were experiencing similar outbreaks, and in all of them the political leaders, now joined by most of the newspapers, were calling on the federal government to move. Even in Washington, D.C., fires had been set along 14th Street, and the mayor, himself a Negro appointed by the President, had issued a statement saying that the situation could not be quieted until Oakland was re-taken.

Stu could only hope that the President was doing the right thing, that his gambit would work, and that his implicit deal with Mamba would never be revealed.

At seven A.M., on this same Wednesday morning, Senator Parker telephoned Governor Nelson. He had no difficulty getting the governor on the line.

"Please forgive me for not getting back to you sooner," Parker blandly began. "Yesterday was just too much and I didn't get a moment alone."

"That is all right, Senator," said Nelson. "Can you talk freely now?"

"Of course. What can I do for you?"

"I want to know if our understanding is still on or not," Nelson said, coming right to the point.

"These are difficult times, Governor, and I really haven't given the matter any further thought," said Parker.

"What is that supposed to mean?"

"Now, Maynard, it's too early in the day for you to get excited. I merely mean I want to carefully consider the situation and, then, perhaps you and I should talk again."

"Senator, you and I had a deal. Is it on or off? You should be able to answer that." Nelson's voice betrayed his tension.

"We will talk about it, Governor, but I would suggest you relax. There is nothing for you to worry about."

"How can I not worry?" asked Nelson. "You are making speeches, and holding hands with the governor of California. I can't conclude anything else but that you are campaigning. Now, what is the point of that if you are going to throw your electoral votes to me?"

"I must go now, Governor," said Parker, his voice soothing. "Please do not become concerned."

"Will you give me an answer?" Nelson demanded.

"We will talk again, so don't do anything rash," said Parker.

Governor Nelson sputtered a reply, and Parker quickly said goodbye. The Florida senator smiled to himself as he slipped on his coat and walked out the door to his car. His driver and the ever-present secret service agent were waiting to drive him to the airport so that he could begin a nationwide speaking tour.

Senator Parker had spent all day Tuesday making the necessary arrangements, and shortly after nine o'clock he and his entourage of staff and press boarded the chartered jet to begin their journey. Their itinerary was to take them to New York, Boston, Chicago, Des Moines and St. Louis before the day was over. In each city his plan was simple. He would travel by motorcade to the busiest downtown intersection. There he would speak to what he was confident would be large and enthusiastic crowds. Only in St. Louis would the plan be different. Here he had scheduled a night rally at the ballpark.

The cities and states had been carefully selected. Each of them was beset with varying degrees of Negro unrest. Most importantly, they were areas of electoral support for either Senator Harrington or Governor Nelson. Parker was storming their bastions of strength, only a week before the Electoral College meetings, in the midst of an extremely volatile crisis.

The first stop was the Wall Street area of New York City. Parker spoke from a hurriedly constructed platform in front of Trinity Church. The people crowded the street as he spoke movingly about the threat posed to them by the lawlessness in Bed-ford-Stuyvesant and Harlem. He was given a surprisingly warm reception from the all-white audience which had flocked to hear him from their jobs at the great banking houses, law firms and corporations in the area.

Boston turned out to be better than Parker's most optimistic expectations. His motorcade arrived at Courthouse Square during the noon hour, and he spoke from a platform bedecked with flags to a great mass of pushing, shouting people. When the crowd finally quieted, Parker told them that Negroes had taken their homes in Roxbury. He repeated his demand for the President's impeachment and cried out for new leadership in the land. In all that he said he was enthusiastically cheered in the traditionally Democratic city.

The size and emotional pitch of the crowds increased as he traveled westward. The Democratic mayor of Chicago personally greeted Parker and stood at his side as he spoke. In Des Moines the entire non-partisan city council turned out for him, and the narrow downtown streets were jammed with people for blocks in all directions from the intersection where he spoke.

The tour was climaxed by a night rally at the new sports stadium in St. Louis. Word of the growing crowds, and their frenzied enthusiasm, had preceded Parker, and by the time he arrived, thirty thousand people filled the stadium to hear him give voice to their rage.

"They have moved into the north and west sides of your city!" Parker shouted. "Those streets were once populated by law-abiding whites. Now they are black, and you are no longer safe. Is that what you want?"

A roaring "No!" came from the crowd.

Pulling out all the stops, in a voice ringing with emotion, Parker attacked Negroes and Jews without restraint, and whipped himself and the mass of people before him into a burning anger.

As he left the stadium, his way was blocked by a thousand marching Negroes, together with some whites, carrying signs of protest, shouting their disapproval. The police attempted to clear a way, but the demonstrators would not be moved. Parker was delayed at the gate, and for a moment the hatred of the protestors washed over him. Then, almost simultaneously, the audience leaving the stadium rushed toward the marchers. For a few minutes they exchanged angry shouts. Then a few blows were struck and, before the inadequate police forces could do anything, the two groups clashed in a bloody melee, swinging anything at hand: sticks, rocks, boards. A gun went off somewhere, and then another. The police seemed helpless, merely falling back and allowing the riot to run its course.

It did not last long. The demonstrators were soon overwhelmed as more whites poured out of the stadium and joined the battle, chasing those who tried to break and run. Soon, black people were lying on the street, bloody and beaten. There was no respite, even for the injured whom enraged whites continued to kick and beat.

Senator Parker was finally led away to another car, and with some of his scattered press following behind, he was rushed to the airport.

"This is what the country has been brought to by those nigger rioters," Parker told Billy Dan Reeves as they headed toward the airport.

"That's why the country needs you," Billy Dan responded fervently.

"They listened to me today, didn't they?"

"It was tremendous, Senator. I've never seen anything like it."

"Yes. I think things are beginning to come my way," Parker said, smiling contentedly.

It was early in the afternoon of that same day when Stu and Mike Potofsky arrived at the Alameda Air Station in California. They immediately transferred to a helicopter and returned to Treasure Island, where General Slocum was waiting for them.

"I am supposed to be liaison for the Secretary of Defense, and yet you two left last night without telling me a damn thing about what was happening, or even that you were leaving the area," the General said angrily.

"I'm really sorry, but we had orders to depart immediately and there was to time to tell anyone. We left a message for you, though," said Mike Potofsky, attempting to soothe the general, and struggling to control his own temper.

"I would be grateful if you would tell me what you are up to now," the general said, unable to keep the bitterness from his voice.

"I'm afraid we can't do that," Stu said.

"You *can*not or will not?" the general asked.

"I am sorry, but those are our orders," said Potofsky. "We have no choice."

The general turned abruptly and walked briskly into the headquarters building, not saying another word. Stu sympathized with the general's reaction, but the President's orders had been clear. Absolutely no one was to know their plan. Stu was certain that General Slocum would immediately call the Secretary of Defense, who would have no knowledge of their orders either and would also feel slighted. It was certainly a mess, Stu thought, which would considerably strain the President's relations with his own Cabinet, though perhaps it was too late for that to matter, anyhow.

They left for Oakland, driving with extreme care as they approached the Bay Bridge toll station. No specific time had been set for their return and Mamba's troops probably had no orders that they were coming. It was a hazardous half mile and they could only hope that their car would be recognized and that no trigger-happy guard would fire upon them before they could identify themselves.

As they approached the roadblock they could see several men bringing their weapons into a ready position, training their sights upon them.

However, they were not fired upon, but were permitted to drive up to the toll station. A man approached them, an automatic weapon loosely slung over his shoulder and an unholstered pistol in his belt. He was the same guard who had been on duty on their last trip into the city and, luckily, he recognized them. As they waited for permission to proceed, Stu noticed that, unlike the experience of their previous trips, there were no catcalls or threats from the men manning this post. To Stu, they appeared to be considerably more subdued than they had been on either Monday or Tuesday. The tension on all of us is increasing, he thought; they are beginning to realize this is no game and that the fuse is getting short.

The guard returned and told them that Mamba was waiting for them. He shouted an order and a commandeered police car was driven up. They jumped in and were taken directly to the police headquarters building. The streets were much more deserted than they had been, and this time the driver did not use his siren and lights as he passed through the downtown area.

Mamba was in his office. Charlie Jefferson and Nina Moran were with him. It was just past two in the afternoon.

"I'm happy to see you two back here," said Mamba. "I trust it means you're willing to meet my terms."

"Not exactly," said Stu.

Mamba peered at him intently from across his desk. For the moment the room was very still.

"Perhaps I didn't make myself clear," Mamba said at last. "I cannot negotiate further regarding the safety of my men. I told you not to return unless you were prepared to give me that assurance."

"Let me tell it to you very straight, Mamba," said Potofsky. "Unless you can comprehend and accept what we are about to say, then it will be all-out war against you. There will be no more offers and no further conversations."

"Comprehend?" asked Mamba, puzzling over the word.

"That is right," said Potofsky.

"Go on," said Mamba.

"We have a helicopter standing by to come in here and pick us up," said Stu. "You will go with us directly to one of the President's jets at the Naval Air Station and fly straight to Washington and the White House. You will meet with the President and after that he will announce the formation of a Presidential commission, along with whatever else may be appropriate as a result of your meeting. You are to surrender yourself to the federal authorities in Washington, and from then on you will have to take your chances with the courts."

Stu paused for a moment and then continued slowly. "For twenty-four hours after we leave here by chopper . . . the federal forces will continue their preparations at the Air Station. They will neither attack nor surround the city until they are made ready, which will take *precisely* that amount of time. After that, however, they will be deployed and will immediately move against this city with all the power that is necessary."

Mamba stood up and walked to the window. "That's it?" he asked.

"Yes," said Potofsky.

"How am I to interpret what you've just said?" Mamba asked.

"We can't assist you in that," said Stu.

"And what in hell is that supposed to mean?" Mamba asked, his voice beginning to rise.

"Simply that we have nothing further to say on the subject," said Potofsky. "The ball is in your court."

Mamba, looking very tired, turned to Charlie Jefferson. "You know Washington. You are a part of them. What am I supposed to make of this?"

"I think I understand, Mamba," said Charlie, "But I don't believe it is appropriate for me to comment either."

"What about you, Nina?" Mamba asked. "Have you also gone so far over to them that you refuse to talk?"

Nina's gaze at Mamba was level and calm. "I believe they are giving your people a chance to escape," she said, "but that they can't say it in so many words."

"I see," said Mamba thoughtfully, his voice once again calm. "I gather you will not give me anything explicit to report to my people."

"I'm afraid not," answered Stu.

Mamba started for the door. "Wait here," he said, and he walked out of the room.

"What do you propose to do with us?" Charlie asked Stu when Mamba had gone.

"We will try to take you out of here, Charlie," said Stu. "That is, if he buys the rest of it. But we can't insist on it. We have no power to let this fall apart if he refuses to let you go."

Charlie was holding tightly to Nina's hand, and he glared at Stu. "I suppose that some might consider that a reasonable attitude, but I think it is damned unfair to us. We've gone through hell this past month, and God knows what they will do to us once they have nothing to lose and start running from here. I guess there is no such thing as compassion when it comes to the big issues," Charlie said, bitterly sarcastic.

"God, Charlie, I have all the compassion in the world for you two," said Stu. "But what can I do? If we have a chance to stop a massacre, we have got to take it. Can't you see that?"

"Two lives in exchange for thousands, is that what you are saying?" Charlie replied.

"Charlie, I will do everything I can to get you two out of here. We will keep on trying. Maybe Mamba will come through, or maybe the President will change his mind."

"It looks like we are just a couple of black pawns, Charlie," Nina said.

"You know that isn't true," said Stu.

They lapsed into silence and waited. It was a long wait, and it was beginning to get dark outside. No one brought them any lunch, and no one disturbed them. After a while, Stu and Potofsky stretched out in their chairs and fell asleep. Charlie Jefferson absent-mindedly fiddled with the television receiver, disconsolately watching the news reports of the country's worsening racial situation. He saw a live report on Senator Parker's reception in Chicago, which so upset him that he snapped off the set. Nina Moran sat quietly on the couch, her eyes never leaving him. She tried to comfort him, but Charlie shrugged her off, and she returned to the sofa and silently waited.

It was almost six in the evening before Mamba returned. His face looked haggard, and his expression was grim.

He took his seat behind the desk and said, "I will accept your offer. When do we leave?"

"I must make a call first," said Stu. "However, before that, there is one other matter I want to take up with you."

"You made a deal," growled Mamba. "There can be no other conditions."

"Just hold on for a moment," said Stu in exasperation. "All I want to know is whether you will permit Jefferson, Miss Moran and Simon Pettigrew to come with us."

"No," said Mamba.

"Why not?" asked Potofsky. "Of what possible use can they be to you now?"

"My people want to keep them. They may be of some value as hostages. Who knows? In any event, it is out of the question."

Stu looked over at Charlie, who shrugged resignedly. "All right," Stu said. "Leave us alone for a while and we will make the arrangements."

Mamba left them, and Stu picked up the phone and dialed the White House. "I will try again with the President," he said, as he was waiting. "You could see there was no point in pressing the matter with Mamba."

"Naturally," said Jefferson.

Stu waited for Alvin Morgan to come on the line. It was nearing nine o'clock in Washington, but Stu had no doubt that Alvin would still be at his desk.

When Morgan answered the phone, Stu said, "Mamba has agreed, but he won't release his three prisoners. Will you ask the President if we can insist on their release? I think it is a terrible mistake to leave them here."

"Hold on for a moment," said Morgan, who then left the line. In a few minutes he was back. "There is no way you can get back here in time to meet tonight," he said. "For that and other reasons we want you to leave there with Mamba at dawn tomorrow. That should put you here in the early afternoon. You set up a good landing point for the chopper and call me back. Then I'll arrange it. Is that clear?"

"What about the prisoners?" Stu asked, his voice harsh.

"No dice," said Morgan. "They'll have to remain there. In

210

our judgment they'll be safe enough. There would be no point in harming them now."

"That's a hell of a risk to take with three lives."

"That's the decision, Brady. Now you just do as you're told."

Stu paused, feeling sick inside. "I take it the twenty-four hours runs from dawn tomorrow?" he finally asked.

"That's right," said Morgan, and hung up.

Stu could not look at Charlie and Nina. "Call Mamba back here," he said.

When Mamba returned they told him the White House instructions. "The helicopter should land on the Nimitz Freeway just outside this building," Mamba said. "It will be easily accessible that way and, at dawn, the pilot should be able to pick out the area with no difficulty."

Stu placed another call to the White House and informed Morgan. "Do you want us to go back to Treasure Island tonight?" Stu asked.

"No," answered Morgan. "You'll just have to answer a lot of questions. Stay where you are until we come for you."

"Thanks a lot," said Stu, and hung up.

Charlie Jefferson and Nina Moran were then taken from the room. Nothing more was said to them as they left.

Mamba turned to Potofsky and asked, "Am I correct that the twenty-four hours begins when I board that helicopter?"

"Our forces will move in at dawn on Friday," said Potofsky.

"Good," said Mamba. "I need to be very clear on that. You should know that we have already started our preparations."

Stu and Mike Potofsky were then escorted to another office, which had been fitted out with two hard bunks. Cold sandwiches and beer were brought and then they were left alone.

"It's a lousy thing we've done to them," said Stu.

"There was nothing else to do," said Potofsky.

"I know that, but it isn't right. It's too much like justifying a stinking means to get to some political end. There should have been another way."

"There wasn't."

"We should keep on trying," said Stu.

"Of course."

"Like you said, just another month at this lousy job," Stu groaned, as he flopped on the mattress.

"Amen to that."

They lay there quietly, both unable to sleep. The night seemed to drag on endlessly. Although Stu dozed a bit, he could not stop thinking about abandoning Nina and Charlie.

At six o'clock the next morning, there was a knock on the door and a voice called out that they should be ready to go in fifteen minutes.

Mamba was waiting for them, and they left the police station with a small escort and drove up a ramp to the elevated freeway adjoining the headquarters building. They waited on the deserted highway, watching the sun rise over the city. Shortly after first light, they heard the popping sound of helicopter rotors, growing to a roar as the chopper came into sight. It hovered over them and slowly settled to earth. Mamba solemnly shook hands with the two associates who had accompanied him. Then they boarded the helicopter and took off on the short flight to the Air Station and the waiting Jetstar.

The trip to Washington was uneventful. For the most part, Stu and Potofsky slept and Mamba sat by a window, staring out at the sky and the ground far below. At one point Stu again brought up the matter of Nina and Charlie, but Mamba would not talk about it, so Stu finally gave up the attempt.

Two secret service men met them at Andrews and drove them to the White House. They entered the southeast gate, the most private access to the Mansion, the entrance the President used when utmost secrecy was required. Stu could recall the use of that gate when, prior to submitting a controversial nomination to the Supreme Court, the President held conversations with off-the-record advisors in such matters. Then, this gate had regularly been used for the President's hush-hush meetings with the Republican Senate leader. The good senator would slip into the White House to present his "shopping list," as he called it, those executive favors the senator would invite in exchange for his support on key legislation.

It was nearing three P.M. when Stu, Potofsky and Mamba ascended the elevator to the President's quarters on the second floor of the Mansion. They were escorted to the Yellow Oval Room, which was brightly lit by the sunlight streaming in from the windows overlooking the south lawn. Mamba appeared composed as they silently awaited the President's arrival.

A short time later, the President entered the room. Though they were not usually present during most meetings held on the Mansion's second floor, this time the secret service agents did not leave, but stood against the walls of the room throughout the meeting. The President did not bother to shake hands or say hello. He merely gave a short nod of his head and sat in a chair facing the black leader, who was still dressed in his khaki uniform.

"You have been the cause of a good deal of misery for the country," the President began in a hard voice. "There is no calculating the harm you have generated, and we will all—black people and white—be paying for it for a long time to come. You are a young man, well educated and from a good family, I understand. It is utterly beyond me how you could carry this nation into such an impasse and still be able to live with your conscience."

"I thought we were going to discuss the issues, not chew over the past," Mamba said.

"I am talking about the present. That is my concern, and it should be yours. Now what is it you want to say to me?"

Mamba returned the President's level gaze, his face expressionless. "The first thing I want to tell you," he said, "is what I have given up to be here. I am willing to go to prison. I have set in motion the evacuation of the city I control. I have convinced my people to go along with all of this on my assurance that you are a reasonable man who will hear me out on our grievances. None of this has been easy. There are, believe me, a large number of my people who would rather die than surrender or retreat. I fought with them, and I think I convinced them. It has cost me a great deal, and no doubt I will now be quite a target for all the racists

213

in this country since I will be in captivity. Give me some credit for courage and integrity, Mr. President."

"What you did in Oakland was totally unnecessary," the President responded. "This administration has done more for your people than all previous administrations put together. I have appointed more Negroes to high office than any of my predecessors ever dreamed of doing."

The President extracted a well-worn blue index card from his inside coat pocket and Stu inwardly groaned when it became apparent that the President was about to recite his accomplishments, a technique he had used on dozens of previous occasions.

"In the past eight years we have given the Negroes more jobs, more job training, more housing, more business loans, more education and more health care than in all of the preceding hundred and seventy-five years," the President said. Then he cited numbers, statistics, laws and programs to illustrate his point. He continued without pause for fifteen minutes, reviewing the list of which he was obviously proud.

"And besides all of that," the President went on, "I have sent my personal staff out to live in the ghettos many times during the past three years. They have not stayed in the nice hotels but have lived in the same housing conditions available to the residents of the ghetto. They have reported directly to me, telling me exactly how it is. These fellows didn't pull any punches and their reports weren't sanitized by any bureaucrats. I don't say we have found all the answers or that there isn't a lot left to be done. What I do tell you is that we are on the right road. We are discovering what works and we are doing something about it. We are also discarding what doesn't work. We aren't afraid to do that. We could have used all the help we could get, including yours, if you hadn't gone on the road you did. The wisest man I ever knew in Congress once told me that anybody can tear down a barn, but it takes skill and patience to build it. We want builders not destroyers, and, I am sorry to say, what you have done is nothing but pure destruction. It has hurt everyone, but mostly your own people."

It had been a long monologue, forcefully presented as always, Stu thought. The President was invariably at his best when he was face to face with his target, although, Stu realized, he did have the sometimes exasperating habit of talking more than he listened. But that was part of his technique, and more often than not it was effective. He could not have come as far as he had, or gained his reputation for getting things done, if this were not so. But Stu thought that this was neither the time nor the place for this approach. It was obvious that it had not worked at all.

Mamba had listened intently, not once attempting to interrupt. Now, however, as the President paused, Mamba said in a subdued voice, "I am mindful of all of the things you have tried to accomplish, Mr. President. As I said, that is why I have agreed to come here. But there are a great many things you do not understand, and even your bright staff have not seen or reported it all to you, I am sure."

"Go on," said the President.

"The entire history of my people's persecution in this country has been that unless we push you, nothing gets done. It is a sad truth that if we don't educate the country about how strongly we demand our rights, then nobody pays any attention. Stokely Carmichael, Malcolm X, even Martin Luther King, all of them, knew that. I also know it. Now, by educating I mean making our presence known. By marches, by strikes, by economic pressure, by political organization, and, of necessity, by direct action, which means violence, if it comes to that. Up until Kennedy's time we didn't know all of this, and your country slept on its obligations to us. But once we started, things started getting done. And we don't mean to stop now. What we have accomplished in Oakland is merely a part of the total picture. It is both a result of the past and a forecast of the future."

"Now just stop there for a moment," the President said, holding up his hand. "Neither I nor any other President is going to sit back and reward anybody for breaking the laws. And, my friend, your actions have gone further toward destroying the social fabric than any single event I can think of."

"You may not intend to react to what I've done," said

Mamba, "and, in your own moral code, you may not agree that it is right, but the country inevitably will take positive action. The response should be, if recent history is any guide at all, to scout around for ways and means of preventing such insurrections from recurring. The government will come up with something, I am sure of that."

"What are you asking for?" the President demanded.

"First, you need to know that what happened in Oakland did not take place in a vacuum. It occurred because blacks refuse to be stepped on any longer. We will not wait around for our liberty, our education, our jobs and our homes. Second, it will happen again, with or without me, you can be assured of that."

The President's head jerked up. "Are you making some kind of threat?"

"I'm telling you the hard truth," Mamba replied.

"What is it you want?" the President asked impatiently, pointedly glancing at his watch.

"We want every one of those programs you mentioned, but we want them doubled in size. Appropriate twice the money you are now asking for. Then we want your Commission to talk to the people, the black community, not just those so-called experts, black and white. I want them to get the right information for a change, not just double-talk."

The President stood up abruptly. "All right. I've listened to your demands." He started for the door, and then turned around. "Mamba, you are a naive young man," he said softly. "I would gladly double the appropriations if it were in my power to do that. Besides the fact that I am going out of office in a month, there is the Congress to consider. They must do the appropriating, and to have extracted as much out of them as I have been able to do has taken all of the skill I possess. It has been a small miracle to have come even this far, and I do not believe any President could have done more. But you will never understand that or appreciate what I have tried to do."

The President walked to the door, and then turned to Mamba one final time. "The Commission will do their job as you suggest. I only pray they do it well." He then motioned to Stu and Mike Potofsky to come with him, leaving Mamba alone with the secret service agents.

"What will happen to him now?" Stu asked, as they rode down the elevator.

"He will be taken out of here and placed under arrest," said the President.

They walked briskly over to the West Wing and into the President's Oval Office, where Alvin Morgan joined them.

"Are they ready?" the President asked.

"They want five more minutes," said Morgan.

"They've had all afternoon. What in the hell is the matter with them?" the President barked.

Morgan nodded, walked quickly out the door and returned almost immediately with Sam Baker, the President's Press Secretary.

"I will give you a one-minute warning, Mr. President," said Baker, nervously fingering his stopwatch.

Baker stepped back into the hall and the President fidgeted at his desk, then walked over to the two teletype machines in his office, leaning over to peer at the clattering A.P. and U.P.I. tapes.

"What's going on?" Stu whispered to Morgan.

"He's going on television," Morgan answered.

Baker came back into the room. "One minute, Mr. President," he said, holding the door open. The President pulled several yellow speech cards from his pocket and walked to the hall. He stopped while a secret service agent cracked open the door to the Fish Room, directly across the hall from the President's office. Then Baker signaled that it was time, and the President, looking solemn and intense, walked in.

The room was crowded with reporters and contained one large color-television camera. The press had been notified earlier that something big was coming up and reporters had flocked to the White House in such numbers that barely half of them could be accommodated in the medium-sized room. The rest overflowed into the adjoining press lobby, where loudspeakers and television receivers had been set up.

217

The President looked directly into the television camera as he spoke to the American people. "My fellow Americans," he began. "This has been a bitter week for our nation. Racial strife, violence and death have been brought to us. Voices of hatred have been heard on every side. I say to you that it must stop. It is wrong. Hatred breeds only hatred, and violence only more of the same. The time has come for us to put down our guns and to stop shouting at one another.

"I have been working around the clock since the lawlessness began in Oakland last Sunday morning. I have expended all of the strength God has given to me so that I might undo that terrible event. I have had only two things in mind throughout it all: to bring the rule of law back to that stricken city, and to save the lives of Americans. I have tried to prevent a holocaust while doing justice.

"It has not been easy. I have been attacked by many, my impeachment has been demanded, and I have been beseeched on all sides to act in this way or that. Through it all I have had but one guide: What is best for the American people? No threat to your President can or will change that goal."

The President paused and removed his glasses. His voice was slow and strong as he continued.

"This afternoon Mamba Z, the leader of the Oakland rebellion, surrendered to me. He is now under arrest and in the custody of federal authorities here in Washington. He will be prosecuted to the full extent of the law.

"I am, later today, appointing a Presidential Commission to investigate the Oakland situation as well as racial strife throughout the land.

"At dawn tomorrow federal troops will move into Oakland."

The President finished, and, stuffing his speech cards into his pocket, he strode from the room.

CHAPTER SEVENTEEN

On Monday, December 16, amid close national attention, members of the Electoral College met in their fifty state capitals, and in the District of Columbia, to cast their votes for the President and Vice-President of the United States.

Much had occurred in the eleven days since the President had announced Mamba's surrender to the nation. The country had anxiously waited throughout that night and the next day while the federal troops deployed and then moved into Oakland. However, Mamba's men had slipped out of the city on the preceding night and there was no resistance. Except for a few scattered instances of individual resistance and a lot of shouting at the troops, the city had been re-taken without notable incident.

The President had gone on national television to report that Oakland was secure, that this feat had been accomplished by federal forces, and that not a life had been lost.

However, Mamba's surrender and Oakland's recapture did not stop Senator Jack Parker, who had accused the President of making a deal with Mamba, and of conspiring to sneak him out of California and away from the state authorities. Parker had also pointedly asked what the connection might be between Mamba's surrender in Washington and the fact that his men had been permitted to successfully elude arrest.

"Those revolutionaries and murderers are still at large," Parker had charged. "They are free to attack any other city, or any citizen, and the President has permitted this to occur. I would ask these questions: Why did the President meet with Mamba in the White House? What was said? What deals were made between these two men, at least one of whom would lead this country into revolution?"

After Parker's appearance on television the networks had been swamped with calls and telegrams overwhelmingly supporting him. The White House also received a massive outpouring of sentiment, and though counts of this mail were never released, there was no doubt in anyone's mind that the country was reacting in favor of Parker's charges.

On the Monday prior to the meeting of the electors, Parker had again sallied forth into the country, this time going out for three days and traveling to key cities in the South, Southwest, and West. His reception had been as good as on his previous trip. Apparently, the President's solution of the Oakland problem had done nothing to dampen the people's enthusiasm for Parker and the senator attacked without letup, to full nationwide press and television coverage.

By the Tuesday prior to the electors' meeting, Governor Maynard Nelson had, at last, concluded that Parker was not going to carry through with their understanding, that Parker was definitely in the presidential race himself, and that he probably intended to stay in until the end. Nelson swung into vigorous action to attempt to stop whatever panic might threaten to develop among the Republican electors, and to re-establish his own image as a leader of the conservative elements in the country. To forestall the mass switching of votes which the likely defection of the California governor might cause, he personally telephoned every Republican state chairman. Through the Republican National Chairman, he caused the Republican National Committee to be thrown into high gear.

Nelson then scheduled a press conference in Washington on Wednesday night. In a packed meeting room at the Shoreham Hotel, during prime evening television time, he freely answered all questions for thirty minutes. By the end of his presentation he had made all of the points he intended: though he did not approve of Senator Parker's appeals to prejudice, nevertheless, he was harshly critical of the President's vacillation in handling Oakland; the troops should have moved into that city immediately;

all of the lawbreakers should have been subjected to full prosecution; the dignity of the Presidency should not have been com-
promised by any meeting with a man like Mamba; and law and
order, without racial hatred, would be the hallmark of his administration. The national reaction to Nelson's presentation was
approving but not enthusiastic. By this time the initiative was all
Parker's. However, the governor's performance did serve to establish his position and allowed Republican party workers to
start their ground work.

For Senator James Harrington, the Democratic presidential
candidate, the weeks since Oakland's takeover had been a period
of great anguish. Except for the first Sunday White House meeting, when the crisis had begun, he had not been consulted by the
President. Harrington clearly perceived the developing mood of
the nation, and he could not help being instructed by the tremendous reaction to Parker's hard-line attacks. However, he felt
trapped. Although he had a plurality of the electors, his 233
votes were short of the 270 needed for election. And even in the
Electoral College, any understanding between Parker and Nelson would mean his defeat. Thus, his only chance was through
an electoral deadlock, after which he could hope to put together a
majority of twenty-six states in the House of Representatives.
But, in such a contest, he needed the full support of the President, who controlled the party apparatus, and, of even greater
importance, controlled the White House congressional liaison
staff and the massive congressional relations operations. This
last, with its significant influence over federal projects and patronage, was the best tool to influence the House of Representatives. As a consequence, Senator Harrington had decided to say
nothing more, either in approval or criticism of the President's
actions. He waited out the crisis, fervently hoping that the President's solutions would ultimately be accepted by the people and
by the political leaders in his party.

Thus, on December 16, the Electoral College met as the
nation looked on in fascinated anticipation.

The pressures from each of the three political camps was
effective. Except for California, the final results certified by the

electoral meetings to the President of the Senate were precisely as pledged in the November election. In California, however, the state law requiring the electors to vote as pledged was ruled unenforceable by the state's attorney general. Five California electors had followed their governor's recommendation and had cast their ballots for Senator Parker, though the rest of the states' electors, as well as the remaining Republican electors in the nation, had not stampeded. Responding to the intense party pressure generated by Governor Nelson they had remained firmly behind their candidate.

Thus, the final Electoral College vote was cast as follows:

Harrington: 233 votes (17 states plus the District of Columbia)

Nelson: 178 votes (21 states including most of California)

Parker: 127 votes (12 states plus part of California)

No one had been elected President of the United States. The election was therefore thrown into the House of Representatives of the new Congress. The House and Senate were to meet jointly at noon on Monday, January 6, when the electoral votes would be officially counted, and since no candidate had a majority of the electoral votes, the House would then ballot immediately to choose a President.

In the House elections each state would have one vote, according to a majority of its delegation, and the votes of twenty-six states would be necessary to elect. Under this division the Democrats would control a majority of twenty-six state delegations. In five state delegations the representatives would be evenly divided between Democrats and Republicans.

If every member of the House voted for his party's candidate, Senator Harrington, the Democrat, would receive the votes of twenty-six states, precisely the minimum number to elect him President. But there was a significant lack of correlation between the political division in the Congress and how the people in the respective states had voted. For example, of the twenty-six states controlled by the Democrats in the House, ten Southern States had been carried by Senator Parker in November, and in eight of those states, Senator Harrington had run third behind both Parker and Governor Nelson. In addition, although the Democrats controlled the House delegations of California, Colorado, Missouri, Oklahoma, and Pennsylvania, each of these states had cast its popular vote for Governor Nelson. But the nineteen-state House count for Governor Nelson was also in conflict with the popular vote inasmuch as the Republican-controlled delegations from Alaska, Michigan, Minnesota and Ohio each represented states that had cast a majority for Senator Harrington in the fall election.

CHAPTER EIGHTEEN

At ten o'clock, Tuesday, December 17, the morning following the meetings of the Electoral College, the President met with
Alvin Morgan, Sam Baker, John Kelly and Stu Brady.

Though Stu greeted his fellow staff members cheerfully,
and though he had recovered from the sleeplessness of the Oakland crisis, he still felt enormous tension. Public events seemed
unbearably oppressive. He had heard nothing about Charlie
Jefferson or Nina Moran, and he was worried. His marriage
seemed to have quietly gone out of existence, with no contact
between him and Sari for weeks.

The President asked the staff to sit down, indicating the two
small sofas flanking his rocking chair. He went to take one last
look at the news tickers, then stood with his hands on the back of
his chair and peered down at the four of them.

"How do you size it up, Kelly?" he asked of his chief of
congressional relations.

"I think it's awfully shaky," Kelly replied, making no attempt at the flippancy that normally accompanied his observa-
tions. "To say that Harrington will have the twenty-six Democratic state delegations is a pipe dream, in my opinion. He could
conceivably lose up to half of those states."

"That's the way I see it too," commented the President.

"Some of those delegations could be had by Parker easier
than a round-heeled broad," Kelly observed, reverting to form.

The President smiled. He appeared to be relaxed this morning despite the controversy directed at him as a result of Oak-

land. "I imagine that there are several things we can do to make it difficult for them to leave the fold," he said.

"You will need everything you can get your hands on and even then, I'm not sure it will be enough to do the job," said Kelly.

"That may be," mused the President, "But we are going to do everything we can for Senator Harrington."

Alvin Morgan suddenly looked up, his face flushing. "Are you sure you want to do that, Mr. President?" he asked. "After all, Harrington hasn't said one word to support you since Mamba was in here. He just sat back and let you take all the heat."

"I know that, Alvin," the President said in a soft drawl. "But the other two candidates are infinitely worse than he is. One of them demands that I be impeached, and the other all but says the same thing. I'm sorry that Jimmy didn't see fit to stand on his hind legs and be a man about what we have been going through, but he didn't and that is that."

"And you want to help him just as if he had stood up for you all the way?" argued Morgan.

"That's right. We are talking about who is going to be President within a month, and I'm afraid that I couldn't live with myself if I did nothing while the country goes through this convulsion. Harrington is the best man. At least, he is the best we've got. So we are all going to pitch in and do the things that John Kelly is saying we have to do to get him elected."

Morgan dropped the argument and sat back. He had made his point and, from now on, he would follow the President's wishes with as much fervor as if he had been in favor of the decision from the beginning.

The President turned to Kelly again. "Where are the weakest points?" he demanded.

"Those twelve Southern states that went for Parker," Kelly answered without hesitation. "I would worry about all of them, even though most have pretty solid Democratic delegations. Then I would worry about Pennsylvania, because that is Nelson's home state and the Democrats only have a one-vote edge in the delegation. Add California because that is where Oakland is, and, of course, the state did go for Nelson. There are other problem delegations, but those are the main ones to begin with."

The President, who had now seated himself in the rocking chair, leaned forward. "I want every Democratic House member assigned to someone on my staff," he said, tapping a pencil on the table for emphasis. "Kelly, you make those assignments, and then I want everyone to start polling their members. I want that started right away. Don't let anyone tell you he has something else to do. Nothing is more important than this. I want a written report from everyone by the end of each day until the job is done."

"Okay," said Kelly. "Only what are we to offer the congressmen in return for their votes?"

"Nothing for the moment," said the President. "We'll get to that later. Right now I am primarily interested in getting an accurate count of the new House. These reports should tell me exactly how each member is thinking and what might be bothering him. If he has complaints, I want to know them. If he wants something done, I want to know that too. Later on, we will move on them, but right now I just want intelligence."

"There is one other thing," the President went on, still looking at Kelly. "Call a meeting of your congressional liaison people from the departments for eight-thirty tomorrow morning. I will come, but don't you tell them that," the President quickly added.

The President stood up and the staff members each left, except for the Press Secretary, Sam Baker, who stayed behind, motioning for Stu to remain with them.

"Mr. President," Baker began, "I had an unusual telephone call last night, and I thought you should know about it."

The President had returned to his massive desk, and was beginning to start through the stack of mail left there for him to read and sign. He gestured impatiently at Baker. "All right. What is it?" he asked.

"Jeff Taylor called to give me a tip," Baker said.

"What are you doing talking to that son of a bitch?" the President interrupted, exploding. "All he has been doing for the past three years is lying about me and my people. That bastard is no good, I've told you often enough. He's been trying to build his goddamned reputation by chopping us down."

"I know that, Mr. President," said Baker, "and I usually wouldn't talk to him at all. But he insisted that he had something big and he wanted to help us. So I took his call."

Stu looked at Baker, admiring his courage in bringing up Taylor's name. If there was one subject which was an automatic trigger to the President's wrath, this was it. Taylor, who was only in his late thirties, wrote a nationally syndicated column specializing in inside political news, most often pointedly directed at the President and his staff. His column was relatively new, but it had caught on and was now considered "must" reading for anyone remotely interested in politics. Stu liked Taylor, considering him hard working and honest, but there was no doubt the man did sometimes turn over some pretty embarrassing stones, most of which were related to the White House. In any event, Stu would never dare admit to a conversation with Taylor, because the President would undoubtedly thereafter suspect him as the source of every bit of leaked information that Taylor might print.

"Well, what did Taylor want to tell you?" the President asked.

"He thought we ought to know that Parker's ex-secretary and ex-mistress has called him and spilled everything she knows," Baker said.

"Why doesn't he print it?" snapped the President.

"Apparently he is afraid of a libel suit," said Baker.

"That concern never seems to slow him down when he writes about us," the President said, his temper again beginning to rise.

"Taylor says we might see some way to use the stuff, and he wants to go over it with someone from our office. He says he wants to stop this surge for Parker and is willing to do just about anything to accomplish that result. I believe him."

"I wouldn't buy that theory if you talked all day," the President shot back. "However, I see nothing wrong with taking a

227

peek at his cards if he is willing to show them to us." The President paused, and then turned to Stu. "Why don't you give Taylor a call and get together with him. You can use your own judgment about what to do after hearing him out. Just be certain you don't make any mistakes." The President was not smiling as he made this last remark.

The two staff men left the President and walked back to Sam Baker's office.

"Have you any idea what this girl said to Taylor?" Stu asked.

"No, I'm afraid I've told you everything I know," said Baker.

"How about a little guidance on how I should proceed?"

"If I were you I'd call Jeff Taylor, and then I might go talk to the girl myself. After that, you'll have to play it on your own."

"This has sure been some month for strange missions." Stu sighed.

"You've got nothing better to do with yourself." Baker laughed as he waved Stu off and turned to the telephone calls waiting for him.

Stu walked into his own office and arranged to meet Taylor for lunch at the Jockey Club. He then settled down to catch up on the out-of-town newspapers that had accumulated over the past several days. It felt good to get back to his normal work and away from acting as a part-time detective, racial arbitrator, political muckraker and congressional lobbyist. Before he knew it, Mary O'Brien stuck her head in the door to tell him that it was time to meet Taylor. He reluctantly put down the report he was reading and walked out the basement door of the White House to the car that Mary, thoughtfully, had ordered for him.

Jeff Taylor was already seated at a back table when Stu arrived at the dimly lit restaurant. Taylor was a fairly tall man who looked like he was fighting a losing battle with his expanding waistline. He jumped up when Stu approached and his face broke into a broad smile as he shook Stu's hand.

"I can't tell you how long it's been since someone from the

White House has openly sat down to have lunch with me," Taylor said.

"That's only because you know everything we're doing even before we think of it ourselves," Stu said.

"Or maybe I'm the only reporter in town who is devious enough to follow your machinations."

"I gather this time the tables are somewhat turned," Stu said. "I understand you are sitting on a hot piece of information you would like to give to us."

"That is right, my friend. Janice Pruitt, a very good-looking young lady, by the way, who happens to be the 'ex' of Jack Parker—in every way—gave me a call a couple of weeks ago. I was a little hesitant, but I finally got together with her last week, and she sure as hell did have a few things to say. It seems as if Miss Pruitt has been summarily canned by Parker for no other reason than she might prove to be an embarrassment to him just when things are looking up. Since his future was just what the young lady was counting on, the whole maneuver has sent her into orbit. So she calls me and spills it all."

"Go on," Stu said impatiently.

"It boils down to three things," said Taylor. He held up his fingers as he ticked them off. "First, Parker, who holds himself out as the epitome of American morality, has been bedding down with Miss Pruitt, and not just straight sex, but with quite a little sadism thrown in on the side. She has got dates, places, etcetera, and her own willingness to admit it, though no pictures or anything like that. Second, the senator made a deal with Nelson, which he didn't keep, obviously, to throw his electors to the governor in exchange for making Parker's assistant, Duval I think his name is, the new Attorney General. She has got nothing to back that up other than her say-so. But I believe her. Third, the senator has apparently been receiving significant chunks of financial support from some odd places, such as Argentina and Swiss banks. She has got copies of letters which she happened to keep at home for just this kind of rainy day, she said. She isn't sure what the letters might mean, but she thinks that somebody with

229

the wherewithal for investigation might unravel some interesting facts."

Taylor paused, a satisfied smile on his face. "How about all of that?" he asked.

"Sam Baker tells me you are afraid of a libel suit and that's why you aren't printing this," Stu probed.

"That is only partly it. The political deal with Nelson is printable enough as it is, but I'm not sure about the sex bit. That kind of goes against the unwritten rule of us political scribes that our zeal for the truth stops at the bedroom door. What I really want is to stop Parker, and I want to ally myself with you guys in order to do that. I figure you've got the resources to do a quick and thorough investigation on those financial matters, something I could never get done in time on my own. Also, your man has got the political savvy. I've always given him credit for that. I figure he can judge how to use all of this better than the rest of us. I guess what I'm saying is that I want to play on your team for a while."

Stu sat back in his chair and looked at Taylor. He didn't know how much to trust him. There was probably a good deal of truth in what he said about his motives, but there was also the considerable risk that Taylor was just using them and might turn on them when it suited his purposes. "Maybe we can do business," Stu said quietly, "but I'm afraid there is no way we can involve the President in this. I'm willing to do what I can to help, including putting the government into gear, but it will have to be understood that the President will have no knowledge of what we are up to."

"Whatever you say, pal," said Taylor, a cynical grin playing around the corners of his mouth.

Stu returned to the White House and immediately placed a call to Stan Brightwell, the F.B.I. Deputy Director, who, among his other duties, functioned as liaison between the White House and the Bureau.

"I've got a ticklish job for you," Stu began.

"That is what we are here for," said Brightwell.

"There is a girl named Janice Pruitt we want you to talk to," Stu said. "She used to work for Senator Parker and has now been fired. She claims to have some hot stuff, particularly along the lines of campaign contributions from foreign sources. We want it checked out, and as quickly as you can."

Brightwell hesitated before answering. "Well," he said, "you know we don't get involved in politics."

Stu felt there was no time for niceties, and so he pushed hard and with no finesse. "This is legitimate," he said harshly. "First of all, there may be a violation of the Federal Corrupt Practices Act involved here. Secondly, this is an order from the boss."

"All right, we will do it," said Brightwell, sounding uneasy at the prospect of taking on a powerful senator.

Stu gave him the remaining details and re-emphasized the need for swift action. He felt that he had done all that he could for the moment and that, with the F.B.I. now into it, there was no point in seeing the Pruitt girl himself.

By mid-afternoon he had received his congressional assignments from John Kelly. Stu had been given responsibility for the Democratic delegations from Arkansas, Louisiana, Missouri, and Washington, a mixed bag of four out of the twenty-six states the Democrats controlled. He assumed that a dozen other members of the staff had been given similar assignments and that all the Democrats in the new House would thus be covered by the White House. He stared at his list of congressmen for a long while, trying to crank himself up to starting the necessary telephone calls.

That evening Janice Pruitt, alone in her southeast Washington apartment, was visited by two clean-cut-looking men. One of them handed her an F.B.I. identification card and, deciding they were legitimate, she let them in.

The F.B.I. agents questioned Janice for two hours. They were thorough. She told them everything she knew and gave them all of the documents she had been so carefully hiding. It

231

was midnight by the time they left. Then, with a broad smile, Janice poured herself a straight scotch and went to bed feeling content for the first time since her dinner with Billy Dan Reeves.

At eight-thirty the following morning fifty men assembled in the Fish Room of the White House. The conference table and soft-cushioned chairs normally in the room had been taken away. In their place were enough mismatched chairs to accommodate the assembled group. A table had been placed at the front of the room, behind which John Kelly now sat. Beside him were two empty chairs.

The fifty men who had been summoned late the previous day constituted the congressional liaison officers of each of the various departments and agencies of the executive branch of the government. By and large, they were friendly and pleasant men, politically experienced and adept at working with elected officials. Most of them had been hand-picked by the President and were intensely loyal to him. The President, in turn, regarded these toilers on Capitol Hill with a great deal of affection. A product of the Congress himself, he placed great store on the importance of good relations with the legislative branch and gave credit to those whose job it was to smooth his way.

Kelly called the group to order, after asking Stu Brady to send word to the Mansion that they were starting. They had barely embarked on the meeting when the President strode in. At his side was Senator James Harrington.

Everyone in the room jumped to his feet, and the applause was loud and prolonged. The President smiled broadly, his arm affectionately around Harrington's shoulders.

"Since Jimmy Harrington couldn't win it in November, and couldn't win it Monday in the Electoral College, I've asked him to come over here to get a little free advice," the President said, still cheerful. "He says he is open to all suggestions, and I must admit that I did have a few thoughts to pass his way."

Everyone laughed, feeling a lessening of tension at this clear demonstration that the President was unreservedly backing

Harrington's candidacy. Washington had been flooded with rumors that the President had decided to let Harrington sink on his own, especially after the senator had been so conspicuously silent about the Oakland crisis. Now it was clear that these stories were unfounded.

"The election is now in the House," the President went on. "That is why I've called you gentlemen together. No one in Washington knows the Congress better than you do, and if Senator Harrington is going to be President, then it is going to have to be as a result of your efforts."

The President stopped for a moment, the smile now gone from his face. His gaze swept over the attentive faces before him. "I have one immediate job for each of you to do. Go back to your departments this morning and find out exactly what can be done, or can be stopped, which might be of any interest to any congressman. I want you to take your departments, turn them upside down, and shake them until every last morsel has been disclosed to you. Don't let any bureaucrat stop you. Don't take any excuses for delay. Get everything. I want a complete report in my hands by tomorrow night. Is that all clear?"

Everyone nodded.

"When you finish this job there will be more for you to do. So tell your wives and sweethearts you won't be seeing them much for a while." The President smiled and left the room, motioning Senator Harrington, John Kelly and Stu to come with him. The four of them proceeded to the President's Oval Office.

"Kelly, get the Democratic House leadership in here sometime tomorrow. Check with Alvin to get a time for the meeting, but bring them in here from wherever you find them."

"Can I have transportation if I need it?" asked Kelly.

"Yes," said the President. "Tell Alvin to let you have whatever planes you need."

Kelly left and the President turned to Stu. "Tell Jimmy what you found out from Parker's girl friend," he said.

Stu couldn't suppress a surprised look, since he had thought that the President wanted to be kept out of that business. However, he quickly related his meeting with Jeff Taylor and the fact that he had ordered the F.B.I. to check out the political contributions.

"What do you think of that?" the President asked Harrington, a satisfied look on his face.

"There may be something useful in it," Harrington replied cautiously. "However, you already broke the story on the deal between Nelson and Parker, Mr. President. His having an affair might hurt him some if it surfaces, but I'd hate to get at him in that way. Of course, the money business might prove to be interesting; that is, if the Bureau can turn up something solid."

"You are too damned conservative," the President growled.

"How soon will the F.B.I. have some answers?" Harrington asked of Stu.

"I don't know, Senator," said Stu. "I've told them to give this top priority, and they have already started on it."

"As you can see, we are working hard for your election," the President said to Harrington.

"I've always been grateful for your support, you know that," Harrington responded.

"That may be, Jimmy," the President went on. "However, I want to get a couple of things crystal clear with you. In the first place, I am goddamned unhappy you didn't help me out with the Mamba business." The President was peering intently at Harrington, his mouth a hard line.

"I just didn't know what to do," Harrington replied lamely.

"There will be no more of that if I am going to help you," the President shot back. "I'm going to put it to you straight. You can't get elected without my help. You need my muscle. There is no other way."

"I know that," Harrington answered.

"I am willing to give it to you," the President continued, "but I insist on two things. One, I want your undeviating support. No more sitting on the sidelines. Two, I want to be in charge of the election in the House."

"You know I've always listened to you," offered Harrington.

"That's right," snapped the President, "and if I am to put everything into gear for you now, I have got to know that you will give me a free rein. Is that understood?"

Harrington, looking very glum, nodded his agreement.

At almost this same time, on Capitol Hill, Billy Dan Reeves suddenly burst into Senator Jack Parker's office. Parker, who was engrossed in outlining several speeches, looked up in annoyance at his red-faced assistant.

"What in the hell do you want?" Parker growled.

"I'm sorry, boss, but I just learned something I thought you ought to know right away," said Billy Dan.

"Well, what is it?" asked Parker.

"A friend of ours at the F.B.I. just called. He says that Janice has talked to Jeff Taylor, the columnist, and to the White House. He says that the President has ordered the F.B.I. to investigate what she said."

"Jesus Christ!" bellowed Parker. "What did she tell them?"

"This guy couldn't give me that, but he is going to try to find out for us," said Billy Dan. "He did say she had some files that she took from here, and that she's turned those over to the Bureau."

"You sure screwed that one up. You were supposed to ease her out of here, not shove her into the arms of the White House."

Billy Dan leaned back against the door, his hand tightly clutching the knob, as he held it shut behind him. "Do you want me to send somebody over to her?" he asked.

"If you mean threaten her, then you are an idiot," Parker fired back. "That's all we would need now."

"Maybe you could call her yourself," offered Billy Dan, desperately casting for ideas.

"That's what I should have done in the beginning instead of leaving it to you, but now I can't talk to her under any circumstances. For all I know they've bugged her phone and her apartment."

"What should we do?" asked Billy Dan, looking miserable.

Parker swiveled in his chair and gazed out the window toward the Capitol dome two blocks away. Finally, with his back still turned to Billy Dan, he said, "We will do nothing. The way the country is coming to me these days, I don't think the rantings of one frustrated bitch are going to stop me. Just keep in contact with your source and let me know everything he tells you." Parker then turned back to Billy Dan. "One thing," he said. "Keep that F.B.I. fellow's name handy. He's a good man and he might be useful in other matters. Also, make sure he understands that I always reward loyalty."

Billy Dan, feeling relieved, started out the door, but Parker stood up and motioned him to stay. "Now don't be in such a hurry to get away from me. There are some other matters I want you to take care of."

"Yes, sir," said Billy Dan, pulling out a note pad and waiting expectantly.

"I want to make two more trips. First, schedule me into every one of those twelve states I carried in November. I'll leave on Friday and take four days, straight through Monday, for this trip. What I want is to spend mornings in one state, afternoons in a second, and evenings in a third, so I can cover three states each day. At each stop I want to make a public speech and then meet privately with as many leaders of that state as you can lay your hands on. I also want to meet with the congressmen. I want to use force—and I mean force—to turn the screws all the way so that all they can see is their political funerals if they ignore the people and vote against me."

"Will do," said Billy Dan.

"Then, just as soon as we complete that trip, I want to go west. I want to cover all the Mountain and Southwestern states. They may be small, but in this election each of them carries as much weight as New York or California. By the way," Parker added, "you may be interested in knowing that the governor of California has agreed to accompany me on the western swing."

"That's fantastic," said Billy Dan enthusiastically.

"Yes, I would say things are going my way," Parker said. "But we must stop Harrington first. That will deadlock the Congress. Then we can move. The way I see it, with the people behind me, nothing can stop me."

CHAPTER NINETEEN

Approximately one hundred men, those who would have been most subject to prosecution, the elite of the Black Guards, had been traveling south along the coastal mountain ranges, staying off the main highways and moving only by night and in groups of four or five men. Although the bulk of Mamba's forces had dispersed after slipping out of Oakland or had melted back into the population, the commanders of his small army had decided to stay together under the direction of Clinton Jones, Mamba's designated heir. They planned to go into hiding, and to ready themselves for a later action. Their objective was to reach the Mexican border, but the dangers they faced made the trip painfully slow.

Now, in this week of the Electoral College voting, they finally passed through the Mojave Desert, and, filtering in a few at a time, had reached the Joshua Tree National Monument. In the scenic but virtually uninhabited wilderness only thirty miles from the heavily populated Palm Springs resort area, these remnants of Mamba's army came together to make camp for the night. Charlie Jefferson and Nina Moran were with them.

Charlie and Nina had been kept together, locked in the back of a pickup truck, throughout the long journey south. Thus far, they had not been harmed but had been permitted to leave their cramped prison only for brief periods of guarded exercise. It had been an uncomfortable and disheartening journey. Nina, particularly, resented their captivity, expressing great bitterness toward the government for bowing to expediency and abandoning them.

Late that night a cold wind blew off the desert and through the drafty interior of the truck. Nina and Charlie had been locked in for the night and were lying on the thin bedrolls provided for them. They were huddled together for warmth. Charlie pulled Nina close. Even under these terrible conditions, he enjoyed the way she fit warmly into the crook of his shoulder.

He wasn't tired as he stared toward the dark roof of the truck. His mind whirled with alternative plans. It had been over six weeks since he had arrived in Oakland. He had had enough and he was determined to get out, and soon. But how to do it? He didn't mind risking his own skin. He was sick enough of the whole business not to care what they might do to him. But what about Nina? Could he take chances with her safety?

"Are you awake?" he whispered to her.

"Of course, Charlie. What is it?" she asked.

"How badly do you want to get out of here?"

"Very much," she sighed.

"It will be dangerous. Does that frighten you?"

"Not if you are with me."

Charlie fell silent once again. They would try it, he decided, and it might as well be tonight. He had been thinking about it for days, and he believed he saw a way. They had been captives for so long now, making no attempt to escape, that their guards had begun to relax, to take them for granted.

"I have an idea that might work," Charlie said.

"I've been waiting for you to think of something, baby," she answered softly.

"I've noticed that the two guys who are guarding us also drive this truck. I figure they must be sleeping just outside of here and that they probably have the truck keys with them." Charlie reached into his shirt front and pulled out a foot-long length of iron pipe. "I picked this up today when they let us out to exercise," he said. "It will make a pretty good weapon." He fingered its length. "It will have to do."

"What do you want me to do?" Nina asked, sitting up now, her voice low.

"I have no idea where we are or what the layout is around

here. We are going to have to be lucky, but if you are willing to take the chance, so am I."

Holding her face gently between his hands, he said, "This is what I need from you. I want you to start crying. Begin softly and then gradually build it up. Take all the time you want, but at the end I want you to be hysterical. That should get them in here. If you've done it right they should be thinking of nothing but trying to quiet you down."

"Then what?" she asked.

"Then I'll take them. We'll get the keys and drive out of here."

She nodded, sat quietly for a moment, and then began to sob softly. For a moment Charlie thought she was really crying, reacting to their captivity and to his desperate idea of escape. Then he realized that she had merely started to carry out his plan. Her crying soon became audible, and so he moved to the back corner of the truck. He crouched low, facing the rear door, and clutched the iron pipe tightly in his hand.

By now Nina was sobbing with harsh, racking sounds. Her moans filled the inside of the truck, gradually turning into shrill, hysterical screams. Charlie had no idea how long she had been at this when suddenly there was a banging on the door of the truck. "Shut up in there," someone yelled, but Nina continued her uncontrolled hysteria.

Charlie could hear nothing outside the truck, and he had to shift his weight to keep his legs from going to sleep. He tried to remain coiled and ready to react instantly, but it was becoming very difficult to stay in this cramped position. Nina was now shaking with sobs. She had crawled toward the front of the truck and was huddled against the wall.

Someone pounded on the locked, rear door. "I told you to shut up. Get that woman to quiet down, do you hear," someone harshly yelled.

"I can't control her," said Charlie. "She's wild."

There was another moment of silence from outside; then, amid muttered cursing, Charlie heard a key inserted in the door, and the handle started to turn. He did not hesitate. With the first crack in the doorway he shoved against it with all his weight. He felt some resistance as it hit against someone, and then it gave way and swung wide open. Charlie jumped to the ground and saw the guard lying on his back in front of him, struggling to get to his feet. Charlie leaped on him, simultaneously swinging the iron pipe against the man's head. He heard a crunch, felt blood spurt against his hand, and then the man was quiet. He had not had a chance to yell. Charlie wildly looked around for the other guard, but could see no one. He started through the man's pockets, silently praying for luck. There were no keys, and Charlie cursed. Then he remembered and leaped for the back door of the truck, removing the keys from where they still dangled in the lock. He yanked them out and scrambled for the front of the truck.

He jumped in the cab and was fumbling with the keys when he heard a yell. "What in the hell is going on over there?" Charlie ignored the shout, and turned the ignition. The motor started instantly. Charlie gunned the motor and turned on the headlights. He had no idea where he was and he had to see. The door to his left was pulled open as Charlie simultaneously started the truck forward. The jerking acceleration threw the man off the door, but now Charlie could see other men running toward him. Some were reaching for guns.

Charlie saw that he was on a narrow dirt roadway. He had no idea where it led. There was no choice but to hope that it would enter upon a main highway. He moved the vehicle straight on, holding on to the jerking steering wheel, and then, in front of him on the road, a posted lookout, shotgun in hand, shouted to him to stop.

Charlie desperately pumped the accelerator, trying to pick up speed on the rough road. Then he heard the first shots smack against the truck body, and the windshield shattered in front of him. He threw his arm over his eyes to protect them from the flying glass.

It was at that instant that the bullet hit him. He felt a terrible pain sear through him, and he was knocked sideways from the force of the blow. He fought to stay conscious and struggled

241

to sit up as the truck careened wildly on the narrow path. He could barely see through the smashed windshield, and fought back nausea and pain as he kept the truck moving forward.

He was swearing at the top of his voice and a terrible anger rushed through him as he clutched at the steering wheel. Then he saw a wide highway ahead, and with a roar he swung the truck out of the woods and onto the road. Charlie drove like a madman for almost ten miles, weaving across both sides of the deserted highway. He kept the accelerator down to the floor and cursed the pain.

The lights of a town loomed up. With a feeling of triumph he drove to it. He fought off the blackness welling up within him, and with tears streaming down his face he brought the truck to a lurching stop at an all-night gas station. He sighed once and slowly slumped over the steering wheel, his head cocked to one side, his eyes open and staring. He saw a startled attendant begin to run toward the truck. He heard Nina's voice asking something of him. He felt her hand touch his face. Then there was no more.

Charlie Jefferson was dead.

"Oh, my God," cried Stu Brady. It was nine o'clock on Friday morning, December 20, and he had just begun reading the overnight news summaries. "Sweet Jesus," he muttered, and grabbed the telephone, asking for the Attorney General.

"What do you know about Charlie Jefferson?" Stu demanded of the Cabinet official when he came on the phone.

"They shot him when he tried to escape," said the Attorney General. "Mamba's group was heading toward Mexico and they camped in the hills not far from Palm Springs. Jefferson and the girl made a run for it late last night, and they got away. Charlie apparently drove the truck, though with the wound he had it was a miracle he was able to get as far as he did."

"Where is the girl?" Stu asked.

"The F.B.I. is questioning her in Palm Springs. She is not hurt."

"Are you bringing her to Washington?"

"Not necessarily," answered the Attorney General. "We

don't need her here, and obviously we can't force her to come."

"I'll call you back," Stu said abruptly, and hung up.

Holding the wire service tear sheet tightly in his fist he walked directly to the President's bedroom in the Mansion. When Stu got there he asked Bill Norris to ask Alvin Morgan to step out, that it was urgent.

"I've got to see the President now," Stu said, when Morgan came out of the bedroom.

"Now calm down, my friend," said Morgan. "What do you want?"

Stu made an effort to control his boiling emotions. "Charlie Jefferson was killed this morning."

"We already know that," said Morgan.

"The woman who escaped with Jefferson, Nina Moran, I want to bring her to Washington and I would like the President to see her," said Stu.

"Why?" asked Morgan.

"We owe it to Charlie," said Stu, his voice choking with anguish. "She was with him through all of it. They were both at our last meeting with Mamba. We left them out there. We should have insisted that they be released and brought out with Mamba. But we didn't, and now Charlie is dead. He was doing his best for his country and we left him to die. We owe him plenty, and I think the President should see her." Stu had spoken this in a rush, the words tumbling over one another.

"Did Jefferson have any family?" asked Morgan.

"I don't think so," said Stu. "He was a bachelor and I don't believe he had any people left in Cleveland."

"Wait here," Morgan said, and walked back into the President's bedroom. In about ten minutes he returned.

"The President won't be able to see her," Morgan said.

"Goddamn it, why not?" Stu asked, his voice shaking.

"I'm sorry, Stu, but we just can't do it. Now why don't you get hold of yourself and get back to work."

"Just tell me why?" Stu implored.

"The President just doesn't have the time to see her, and there is no reason why he should become more deeply involved in the Oakland business. He's had nothing but trouble from it. The F.B.I. can handle this, and should."

"You're wrong," Stu shot back. "This is a debt we owe to Charlie, all of us. And there is one other thing," Stu added. "We never expected Charlie to be murdered and we were goddamn wrong about that. If she talks, she could cause a hell of a lot of trouble. Does the President understand that?"

"I just told you the President won't see her. I'm not going to take it up with him again. I would suggest that you drop the subject," said Morgan, patiently.

"I can't drop it," Stu replied. "Do you see anything wrong if I bring her out here and see her myself?"

"Don't you do that," warned Morgan. "It would amount to the same thing. You would be getting the White House involved in something the President wants to stay away from."

"What if it doesn't surface?" asked Stu.

"I'm afraid we can't take that risk," said Morgan, turning away and going back into the President's bedroom.

Stu was livid. He returned to his office and slammed the door behind him. He stared out toward Pennsylvania Avenue, thinking that he should resign right now, that he owed that much to Charlie. It had been a terrible wrong to have left him with Mamba, and now there was no undoing it. The simplest measure of compassion cried out for the President to see Nina, but the President had his mind on other matters and wasn't willing to spend time on anything else. His ear was tuned only to the hard political reality that the election of a new Chief Executive was the prime issue. Stu could well understand that kind of reasoning. He had been around long enough to have seen hundreds of instances of similar decisions. A President simply could not concern himself with every problem. He had to concentrate his energies. Still, Stu thought, we are personally responsible for this tragedy, and the President also owed a terrible debt to Charlie Jefferson.

He slammed his fist on the desk and picked up the phone. There were some things a man must do. He asked for the Attorney General and got him on the direct White House line almost instantly.

"If I go to Palm Springs today, will I be able to see Nina Moran?" Stu asked.

"I have no objection, but as I told you earlier, I can't guarantee that she will be there," said the Attorney General.

"All I ask is that you tell her I am on my way, and that I would like very much to talk to her. Just pass that message, please."

Stu asked Mary to come to his office. "If anyone asks," he told her, "and you feel you must give them the truth, tell them that I've gone to Palm Springs, California, on an off-the-record trip, and that I will be reachable only through the F.B.I. out there."

"I hope you know what you are doing," she said, looking concerned. "I heard that the President turned you down on getting more involved in that problem."

"How in the hell is anything ever kept quiet around here?" Stu asked in exasperation.

"Don't jump on me," said Mary, reaching out and lightly touching his hand. "I'm a friend, remember?"

"I'm sorry," said Stu, "but seeing Nina Moran is something I've got to do."

Stu caught the noon flight from Dulles to Los Angeles, buying his own ticket and flying commercially for the first time in years. When he arrived at mid-afternoon he rented a car and drove directly to Palm Springs. He pulled up in front of the United States Courthouse and trotted up the steps to the second floor, looking for the room number he had been given by the Attorney General. It was at the end of a long, drab corridor. He knocked on the door, identified himself to the F.B.I. agent who opened it, and asked if he could talk to Nina Moran. They were expecting him and the agent asked him to wait in the room next door.

After a few moments Nina Moran entered. She was alone, dressed in the same old army fatigues Stu remembered her wear-

245

ing in Oakland. She looked very tired, but there was a determined look about her, and she held her head erect.

"Hello, Nina," said Stu after she closed the door.

"I've told the F.B.I. everything I know, so why don't you just talk to them," she said in a flat voice.

"I didn't come here for that," said Stu.

"Then what do you want? Isn't Charlie's death enough for you?"

"I came to ask forgiveness for what I did," Stu said. "Charlie was my friend." Stu faltered, and then went on. "He was your friend, too. All I can do is ask you to forgive me."

"It is too late, Mr. Brady," she said, her voice icy. "There is nothing I can do to make life easier for you."

Stu forged ahead. "Somebody needs to talk about what Charlie accomplished for his country, what a courageous man he was, and the debt that we owe him."

"To hell with your country," Nina exploded, losing all composure. "It left a black man to die because of a white man's politics. If Charlie had been white you would have saved him, but one black man more or less was expendable. I say to hell with that." Tears were now running down her cheeks and her gaze was fierce.

"That's just not true," Stu replied. "I did everything I could to get you out. You saw that."

"I saw you ask, but what good did it do? Your white leader abandoned us, and that is all that matters."

Stu shook his head and looked down at his hands. "Is there anything I can do to help you?"

"Just get out of here," she said harshly. "I've learned my lesson. I'm sick to death of you and your Washington ways. You arrest a militant like Mamba and you let a friend like Charlie Jefferson die. Well, if those are the rules, then I choose to go Mamba's way. I say that you and your President can go straight to hell."

Stu held out both hands to her, silently pleading, but she turned and left the room.

By the time Stu returned to Washington, it was late Saturday afternoon, December 21. By then the newspapers were in full cry about Charlie's death. The story of his long captivity, his dramatic attempt at escape, and his murder, was being told and elaborated in endless detail. The public was particularly fascinated by Nina Moran. The press played up her past relationship with Mamba, which, together with her photogenic beauty, created intense national interest in her.

On that Saturday evening Stu made one last attempt to have the President see Nina, deciding that he would take his chances on the President's reaction to his unauthorized trip to the coast. Alvin Morgan listened stoically to Stu's warning and plea. Then, without comment, he typed a note containing Stu's request and took it into the President's office. Within minutes Morgan returned and silently handed the note to Stu, who saw the emphatically scrawled "No" slashed across the bottom. Stu said nothing, handed the paper back to Morgan, and returned to his office.

He slipped a piece of note paper into his typewriter and slowly wrote out his resignation. He stared at his handiwork for a long time. Then, angry tears forming in his eyes, he ripped it from the machine and tore it up. He had come this far, he thought, and he would stick it out until the end.

On that same Saturday evening Nina Moran flew to Washington. She had been invited to appear on "Meet the Press" on Sunday afternoon and had accepted. There were several hundred representatives of various Negro organizations at Dulles Airport when she arrived and they gave her an emotional, tearful welcome. There were also some newsmen present, but Nina curtly told them she had nothing to say at that time.

She accepted the offer of the local chairman of the N.A.A.C.P. to meet with a number of the city's Negro leaders, and was driven directly to the chairman's house. There a dozen people had already assembled in the basement. Some she knew from her previous years in Washington, and she was introduced to the others. These people represented the old line, traditional battlers in the black man's struggle for equality.

"You can't imagine what an impact Charlie Jefferson's death has had on the country, and especially on the black community," the chairman began after they had been seated. "Jefferson was a man with a great future. He was a natural leader, and he could communicate with blacks and whites. It was a terrible thing," the chairman went on, shaking his head. "He was killed by our own people."

Nina stared at him out of deep, tired eyes. "You have got it all wrong," she said in her level voice.

The chairman looked surprised. "He was killed by Mamba's people, wasn't he?" he asked.

"Only technically," said Nina. "The real cause of his death was whitey, and whitey's leader, the so-called President."

The people in the room reacted in shock. "How can you say that after Mamba held you captive all that time?" the chairman asked in wonderment.

"I will tell you what I am going to tell the whole country tomorrow," Nina said. "Charles Jefferson was in Oakland to do a mission for the President, and he did that job well. When the time came to bring about the peace that Charlie Jefferson negotiated, then the white man said to Charlie, 'All right, boy, you have finished your work for us, and now we will throw you to the dogs.' That is what the President did to Charlie Jefferson and to me. We were black, and therefore our lives were expendable so that the white leader could get the credit. To me, the hand on the trigger of the gun that shot Charlie belonged to whitey. It was whitey who killed Charlie Jefferson."

"What are you proposing to do about it?" asked the chairman.

"Avenge him," Nina said, her voice remaining calm. "I am calling on black people to right this terrible wrong. We have now learned our lesson. Charlie Jefferson tried to help the honkies. He was taken into their camp, and he did their work for them. For that, they killed him."

The chairman stood and walked over to her, looking down at her set features. "You should think very carefully before you do this thing," he said in a gentle voice. "You are distraught. If I may say so, you are quite irrational about what has happened. If you do what you threaten, you could cause immense harm."

"You are an old fool," Nina said, rising and brushing past him. "Your philosophy has gotten us nowhere, and black people no longer listen to the likes of you." She looked scornfully around the room. "If someone will be good enough to let me out of here," she said, "I am ready to leave."

Nina was taken to the Mayflower Hotel, and checked into her room. It was now one o'clock Sunday morning, but she was not tired. She still wore the wrinkled khakis she had on at the time of her escape. She had decided to continue to wear them through the telecast on Sunday afternoon. She lay down on the bed, staring at the ceiling, and thinking. An hour later the telephone rang. It was Mamba.

"I hear you've come around to my way," Mamba began.

"I thought you were in jail," Nina said, amazement, shock and anger tumbling through her mind.

"Not for the moment," he said with a laugh. "I have a good lawyer. I'm fighting their attempt to extradite me to California, and he says that can be delayed for maybe a year. In the meantime, I'm out on bail, free as a bird just as long as I don't leave Washington."

"What do you want with me?" Nina asked in a hard voice.

"To talk," Mamba replied. "Could I come up to your room? I'm only a few minutes away."

"Suit yourself," she said, and hung up.

Nina took a long, hot shower, thinking that if she washed off all that accumulated grime, maybe it would clear her mind. She would see Mamba, and perhaps something would begin to make sense. She lit a cigarette, and waited only a few minutes before he arrived.

"You and I have come a long way," Mamba said, after he had casually seated himself.

"I'm listening," she said, her voice flat.

"I want you with me again," said Mamba. "Join the Black Guards. I'll put you on the governing board. We can really shake this country up."

"All right," she said. "I'm willing to meet with your people. Now what else do you want?"

"You," Mamba said, suddenly rising and coming over to where she sat on the bed. As he started to reach toward her, Nina froze for a moment. Then, with all her strength, she hit him in the face. Mamba stepped back in shock, attempting to fend her off. He tried to push her back as she continued to hit at him, not uttering a word, tears flowing down her face.

Finally, she stopped. "Never, as long as I live, do I want you to touch me," she said, her breathing heavy. "We may or may not be doing the same thing, but I will kill you if you ever come near me again."

Mamba shrugged and started for the door. "Is it agreeable if I set up a joint press conference tomorrow for the two of us?" he asked, as if nothing had happened.

"You have my permission," she said, calm again.

At one o'clock, on Sunday afternoon, Nina Moran appeared on "Meet the Press." She gave an extraordinary performance. She was dressed, as she had planned, in army fatigues, but even that did not detract from her compelling presence. She was emotionless, certain of herself and persuasive, as she smoothly handled the probing questions. She did as she intended.

"I am a black woman," she said in her intense, throaty voice. "I have tried to live in the white man's world, and it is no good. All black men and women learn this. They know what it is like to walk and not be seen. That is all over now. We no longer ask; we demand. We no longer whimper; we shout out our rage. And you are going to listen."

"Are you saying you approve of violence?" she was asked.

Her eyes flashed as she answered. "I approve of anything that will tear away your smugness and hypocrisy. Anything that will teach you shame. If I have to destroy you to do it, then so be it. The guilt is on you, not on me."

She spun a web of blame around the President and the white establishment. She called on the black communities to rise up. She argued that cooperation had failed and that vengeance had to be sought. No amount of reasoned questioning from the reporters deterred her from the points she was determined to make.

The show's producers watched in amazement as Nina proceeded to voice her incitement to violence. If they could have done so, they would have cut her off the air, but this show was broadcast live, and there was nothing they could do but suffer it through. At the end of the telecast, Nina announced that she and Mamba would hold a joint press briefing at the Mayflower Hotel later that day.

By evening the nation's attention had been caught. The networks, instinctively responding to fast-breaking news, arranged live coverage of the press conference. They did this despite the arguments of some public officials that such publicity would needlessly inflame an already dangerous situation.

The news conference was held in a large ground-floor ballroom of the hotel. The room was packed. In addition to the reporters, the black community of Washington had come out in great numbers to see Mamba and Nina Moran. They overflowed into the long corridor that ran from Connecticut Avenue to 17th Street, and they filled the sidewalks adjoining the hotel. It was almost impossible for the newsmen, ostensibly the invited guests for this appearance, to get close to the principals. Only the television cameras and crews, set on their raised stands at the back of the ballroom, were in their proper place as the meeting began, and even they had to fend off the shoving crowd.

Mamba started the conference with a long, impassioned speech about the wrongs that had been done to him. He spoke about Oakland and about the oppression that had caused the insurrection. He told of the magnificent response of the black people of that city and said that their courage should be an example to black men everywhere. Mamba spoke for about half an hour, and he concluded by saying, "I am here to testify that I was a fool. We could have held Oakland forever. They would never have taken it from us. But I listened to the President. I believed his assurances that something would be done for our people if we gave them back the city. It was a lie. I came to Washington to talk to the President, but all he did was throw me in jail. That is a lesson for all of us. We cannot surrender. We must burn them to the ground."

When it was Nina's turn, she spoke quietly. There was not another sound in the room as she told her story of the President's betrayal of Charlie Jefferson. Her voice rose in emotion as she demanded retribution for his murder. She spoke for only ten minutes, but it was enough. "Charlie Jefferson and I tried to play their game," she said at the end. "But like Mamba, we too were betrayed by the white man and the white man's President. Co-opting with them will not work. They will only listen to the sound of guns. They can only feel their own pain. They can only see the red of their own blood. And that is what we must give them."

There were no questions asked of the two speakers because the reporters, despite their desperate efforts to shove forward, had been unable to get near them. But Nina and Mamba had been heard. Television receivers throughout the nation had captured their vehemence. The grumblings in the staid, middle-class black homes became curses in the crowded ghetto apartments. And among the young adults and teenagers, out of school or out of work during this Christmas season, a cry went up for action.

The appearance of these two apostles of revenge in a prepared setting during prime time had given legitimacy to the demand for violence. This was all that was needed for a spontaneous outpouring of emotion. In a dozen cities the black ghettos suddenly erupted on this Sunday night.

The sudden turning of individual emotions into frenzied mob action was nowhere more apparent than in Washington. In the nation's capital the black population, realizing that Nina Moran and Mamba were physically in their midst, reacted with bursting empathy. It started with the people jammed into the ballroom and corridors of the Mayflower. The combination of overcrowding inside, and the people outside pressing to get in, sparked panic. There was a sudden surge. Then, without warning, the crowd began to smash at the hotel's interior. Furniture was tipped and hurled against the walls. Three men behind the front desk were pulled over the counter and beaten. A large group shoved into the bar just off the main lobby, and when the bartender tried to get them out, he too was hit and the liquor bottles behind the bar smashed and stolen.

The havoc inside quickly spread to those standing on the streets outside the hotel. Someone screamed that the police were trying to get Mamba and Nina Moran. Another yelled that they should march on the White House and seek a confrontation with the President. The mob instantly responded, and within minutes the people began to move down Connecticut Avenue toward the White House just a few blocks away.

At almost the same time Nina and Mamba were speaking in Washington, Senator Jack Parker was convening a very private meeting in his suite at the Americana Hotel in Miami Beach. The meeting was similar to the off-the-record get-togethers Parker had been holding in each of the eight Southern states he had thus far visited since leaving Washington early on the previous Friday morning. This meeting, however, was slightly different. It was in his home state and the twenty-five powerful men who were present—including seven of Florida's Democratic congressmen—had known him longer and more intimately than any others.

The room was heavy with cigarette and cigar smoke, and those present were coatless as they relaxed with their old friend. The liquor was good and plentiful. Senator Parker was in an expansive mood, cordially greeting everyone and spending some time in private conversation with each. The public speech he had made earlier in the evening at the jammed auditorium in downtown Miami had been as well received as any he had given since the Oakland insurrection. The crowd reaction here, and throughout the country, was one of unreserved approval. His home state had eagerly anticipated his arrival and the crowd greeted him like a returning hero. His forays throughout the nation, his unstinting attacks on the rioters and the President, and the way his message had caught on, all built to a tumultuous reception in Florida. Parker had been lifted up by their approval. He had no doubts about where he stood in the affections of the people. He felt as if he were being carried forward on a vast wave, and he was prepared to ride it all the way.

Now, he stood in the center of this hotel suite, at ease among these men who had been backing him since his first venture into statewide politics. They and their followers constituted the mainstream of Florida's economic power. Among them were the bankers, publishers and industrialists who controlled the bulk of the money that flowed into Florida's expensive political machinery. These men had the power and they had never been reluctant to use it.

"Gentlemen," Parker began as he seated himself, "I've asked you all here tonight because at this moment in our history we have a unique opportunity to shape the destiny of our country."

He paused and looked slowly around the room. "I happen to believe I can be elected President of the United States," he continued, "but I cannot do it without your help."

"How do you think you are going to win?" asked one of the men, thoughtfully sipping a bourbon. "You don't control a single congressman outside of this state, outside this room, really, and the Democrats control twenty-five other states. Harrington looks like he has it almost locked up, but even if he doesn't, you don't appear to have the votes."

"I'm telling you we can do the job," answered Parker calmly. "I may not have the votes now, but I will before we're finished. Have you been following what I've been doing these past weeks? Do you have any idea the reception I've been getting from the people? Believe me, there has never been anything like it in this country."

Parker stopped. The men were nodding in agreement. "That kind of support will not be ignored by the House of Representatives," Parker went on. "I know that in my bones. You have got to take my word I know what I am doing."

"Just tell us what you want done and we'll do it," another man offered.

"Thank you for that," Parker said gratefully. "What I need is to make absolutely certain that you gentlemen of the Florida congressional delegation vote the way the people of this state demanded last November. In other words, you cannot vote for the Democratic or Republican candidates. I am the choice of Florida and you congressmen cannot take that away from me."

"What will that do to the Democratic party in this state?" one man asked. "Won't it destroy their organization?"

"Do you really believe that is important?" Parker said sarcastically, his eyes glinting. "We will re-make the party. If I am President, we can build it to our own specifications."

At that moment Billy Dan Reeves came bursting into the room. Parker looked up in annoyance, but Billy Dan, somewhat breathless, waved his arms and interrupted. "I just got a call from Washington," he said. "Mamba and some woman just made speeches urging revenge against the President, and, by God, the blackies just tried to storm the White House. The riot police were called and there was gunfire and killing right there on Pennsylvania Avenue. It's still going on and it's a mess."

"There you have it," said Parker, his voice rising in hard emotion. "That is what we have got to stop. I tell you the country has had enough of this." He slammed his hands on the table as he continued. "Now they try to take over the White House itself! Are we going to do something about it or not? Are you with me in this or aren't you?"

Parker's voice was barely controlled as his gaze swept the room. "The country is ours for the taking."

CHAPTER TWENTY

Stu Brady was in his room at the Hay Adams Hotel, intently watching the television speeches of Mamba and Nina Moran. He felt sick with shame as Nina made her slashing attack on the President, and he continued to stare at the screen after the conference was over, deeply engrossed in his own thoughts.

It was several moments before the words of the announcer penetrated. Something was said about difficulty in the halls outside the ballroom; then there was confused shouting, and the announcer excitedly reported that there was a riot in the hotel and on the streets outside. There was more confusion, and then a report that the Negroes on the street had begun an angry march to the White House.

Stu quickly pulled on his sweater and rushed downstairs, intending to hurry across Lafayette Park to the White House. He was too late. He reached the park at the same time as the first of the marchers.

Pushing his way toward Pennsylvania Avenue and the White House gate, Stu was caught up in the angry mob. The night was dark, and the shouting, shoving and confused surging was nightmarish. For some inexplicable reason the White House police and secret service had not anticipated trouble, and as a result the riot fences were not in place, nor had adequate numbers of protective police been assembled in advance. The mob, carrying Stu along with them, reached and crossed Pennsylvania Avenue. The police could be seen, still assembling on the inside of the White House fence.

The advance phalanx of the crowd reached the fence. Then, as Stu continued to push his way closer to a gate, he heard a shout go up to his left, and then the crack of gunfire. He caught a brief glimpse of someone on top of the fence, hanging there, arms dangling loosely on either side. As Stu watched he saw another marcher, then a dozen more, attempt to scale the fence, and, to his horror, he saw the police shoot them down. The crowd roared with anger and again surged against the fence. Stu could not get away and was borne along with them, thankful for the dark night, which had so far kept him from being noticed by the people around him.

Just as Stu was convinced that the mob would force the gates and be massacred, he heard the sound of sirens from behind him. The crowd briefly moved forward, but then broke, as the riot police began clubbing their way through.

Someone shouted, "Hey, there's whitey!" Stu turned and saw a man pointing at him. People began to move toward him, ugly and threatening. He whirled around, frightened, and felt something strike his shoulder. He tripped, but was able to scramble to his feet. He was shoved forward, and angry voices cursed him as he threw his arms over his head. He heard whistles and pounding feet and then, suddenly, the people around him began to scatter. Stu ran toward 17th Street, still covering his head, and praying he would not be noticed again.

He slowly worked his way down 17th Street to the Ellipse on the south side of the White House. From there he was, at last, able to make it to the southwest gate, where he was recognized and allowed to slip inside. He went directly to the medical room in the basement of the Mansion. The orderly on duty wiped the blood from the cut on his arm and bandaged him. He took three aspirins and then walked back to his office.

The ticker tapes were now full of the story of the Washington riot, but, worse than that, they also carried foreboding stories of developments throughout the country. Negro violence was erupting everywhere. The murder of Charlie Jefferson and the incitement of Nina and Mamba's speeches had apparently dissipated all restraint in the ghettos. Militants were openly preaching violent revolution, and riots and looting were reported in over a dozen cities.

For the next two weeks Stu did not leave the White House. The trouble that had started with the march on the White House had steadily increased in intensity, not only in Washington but throughout the nation.

The killing of seven marchers at the White House fence reverberated through the city. For two weeks the rioting continued, and despite the massive efforts of the city government and the President, Washington was an armed camp. Troops were everywhere but could do little more than protect vital government installations. Outside the protected perimeter the looting and fires continued unabated. Only the most essential government employees were able to get to work, and most of those were forced to sleep in their offices. On Capitol Hill, special sleeping facilities had been set up in the congressional office buildings, and the police were strongly advising the congressmen and senators that, when they came to the Capitol for the opening sessions of Congress, they should not plan to leave. The troops could not guarantee their safety if the congressmen insisted on leaving at the end of each day's proceedings.

Black anger at the killings at the White House had ignited riots in twenty states. National Guard troops were called out everywhere and the President was using every possible federal unit to aid the local authorities. However, the massive nature of the uprisings, and the fact that they occurred simultaneously in so many places, simply overwhelmed the available forces. The President reacted by calling up the reserves, and as the new year came, he was seriously considering recalling a half dozen divisions now stationed overseas.

The new Congress had formally convened on Friday, January 3. Shortly before noon on Monday, January 6, Stu Brady and his secretary, Mary O'Brien, made their way to the Family Gallery overlooking the floor of the House of Representatives. It had

258

been a difficult trip from the White House to Capitol Hill. They had been stopped a half dozen times despite their White House car. On each occasion their identification passes had been carefully scrutinized by nervous police and army personnel.

As they watched, senators and representatives filed into the House chamber for a Joint Session of the House and Senate. Their first business would be to officially count the results of the Electoral College vote, a mere formality, since no candidate had received a majority. Then, immediately following the conclusion of the electoral count, the Senate would leave the chamber and the House would start on its task of electing a new President.

Stu had been sent to the Hill by the President to observe the first day's balloting and to aid John Kelly and his staff whenever possible. Mary would help by telephoning periodic reports to the White House, since the rules of the House of Representatives prohibited direct television and radio coverage of the sessions.

The galleries were packed despite the tight security restrictions. To his left, Stu could see that the Press Gallery, along one entire side of the chamber, was so crowded that reporters were sitting in the aisles and between the chairs. Every other gallery was jammed with V.I.P.s and staffers from the Hill. As a matter of fact, it had taken the personal intervention of the President with the Speaker to obtain even the six seats the White House wanted.

As the senators were solemnly announced, and walked onto the floor to their assigned places, Mary asked, "What do you think is going to happen today? Do you think Senator Harrington can hold the Democrats?"

"I just don't know," said Stu. "No one has any idea how it is going to go."

That was the truth. Never before had the House of Representatives been pressured with the intensity that had been exerted since the Electoral College had met. The President had thrown every ounce of know-how he possessed into the battle. Nothing had been left undone. No piece had been left to chance. Everything that the President's lifetime of experience brought to his mind, every wile his potent political mind could work out, every power play his vast power could generate, all of it was brought to bear on the Democratic congressmen.

Stu had done his share. He had been assigned the states of Washington, Missouri, Arkansas, and Louisiana and had called each Democratic member of these delegations to ask how he stood. He had told each of them of the President's strong desire to elect Senator Harrington, and had followed these phone calls by personally visiting the members as they returned to Washington during the past week. He had worked throughout the weekend, spending long hours in deep conversations with every Democrat who was his responsibility. Stu had been well armed for these meetings. The federal departments had given him a complete list for each of his assigned members, with a thorough rundown of the pending items of federal business that related to each congressional district involved.

Stu, along with every other available member of the President's staff, had tramped the halls of the house office buildings and talked with the congressmen. They had argued, cajoled and begged for votes. They had offered everything possible in their arsenal of patronage. However, since the F.B.I. had not yet completed its investigation of Parker, they had been specifically prohibited from using the adverse information that had been leaked to the White House by Parker's ex-secretary. It had been rough going. Although on most issues the power and prestige of the President could be reasonably decisive in his own party, this was no longer the case. The President's influence was rapidly waning, and on an issue of this magnitude the congressmen had their ears tuned to the shrill voices from home, not to 1600 Pennsylvania Avenue.

Stu had started with the state of Washington, which had been easy. Its congressional delegation consisted of five liberal Democrats and two Republicans. The Democrats had unhesitatingly endorsed Harrington, and Stu reported a firm vote from that state.

Missouri had also been firmly behind Harrington, though his conversations with the members had been more troubled. The delegation consisted of nine Democrats and one Republican. The four Democrats who represented St. Louis and Kansas City had strongly endorsed Harrington. However, the remaining Democrats represented areas of varying degrees of rural, conservative constituents. These members had hotly argued with Stu over the Negro riotings, and had been highly critical of the President's handling of the Oakland affair as well as of the present state of disorder. Nevertheless, after Stu had politely listened to all of them, two of their number had given unequivocal promises to vote for Harrington. This was enough to control the delegation, and, in the end, Stu was able to report that all but one of the congressmen would probably vote with the Democrats. This last member, a stubborn old gentleman from southern Missouri, who simply did not give a damn about anything the President had to offer, was apt to do anything, and Stu so reported to the President.

Arkansas and Louisiana had both been extremely difficult.

The Arkansas delegation consisted of four members; three Democrats and a lone Republican. If any of the Democrats voted with the Republican, the state's vote would be a tie, not counted, and the Democrats' precious twenty-six state total would go. Furthermore, under the rules of the House, if one Arkansas congressman voted for Parker, then the resulting total of two for Harrington, and one each for Nelson and Parker would still prevent Arkansas from voting, since a majority of those voting was necessary to cast a state's vote. In all events, this state, like every one of the twenty-six controlled by the Democrats in the new Congress, was essential to Harrington's victory.

The Arkansas Democratic congressional delegation consisted of two bright, young lawyers, Burns Robertson and John Slagin; and one old and established senior member of the House, a powerful committee chairman who wielded immense influence among his peers.

On the previous Thursday, Stu had journeyed to the Hill, passing through armed columns of troops guarding the streets every foot of the way. He had flashed his White House pass at the C Street entrance to the Longworth House Office Building and taken the elevator to the fourth-floor office of Congressman Burns Robertson. The congressman's outer office had been almost deserted, with only the administrative assistant and one secretary busily typing. They had both stopped to give Stu a warm greeting as he walked in.

"Just wait here a second," the assistant had said. "I'll tell the congressman you're here." He had then gone into the inner office, shutting the door behind him.

"Did you have any trouble getting to work?" Stu asked the attractive, blond secretary.

"It was just awful," she said, shaking her head. "Three of us were supposed to be in today, but I'm the only one who made it. I live only a few blocks away, but it took me half the morning to get here, and I wouldn't have made it at all if I hadn't talked a policeman into personally escorting me all the way to the door."

"Was there much trouble around where you live?"

"Terrible. There have been a lot of people running around on the streets every night for two weeks. Sometimes there are just two or three of them, but often they roam in large groups. There has even been some shooting. It's like we're prisoners in the apartment. We can't go out on the street at all."

"How are you going to get back tonight?"

"I'm not," she said, pointing to a small suitcase on the floor. "I guess I'm here for the duration."

Just then the assistant had come out and motioned to Stu, who followed him into Burns Robertson's private office. The office was small, furnished with three deep-cushioned leather chairs, a leather couch, and file cabinets stacked against one end of the room. The walls were covered with pictures of political luminaries and events, with many warm inscriptions to the congressman.

"It's been too long, Stu," Robertson said, bounding from behind his desk as Stu walked in. "I figured now that you White House guys are leaving office you just don't care very much about us poor congressmen who are forced to stay on in this business."

"You know better than that," Stu replied. "I'm always glad

to see you, and as for the President, I guess I don't have to tell you we've got one more little matter to twist your arm about."

"I thought that with this new Congress I was going to get away from this rubber-stamp label," Robertson said with a laugh.

"Just one last time, Burns," Stu said. "I don't have to give you any bull about this one. This is it as far as we are concerned, and we need you."

"Look, Stu, you know I want to help you," Robertson replied, becoming very serious. "As far as that's concerned, I am all for Harrington. The trouble is that not only did my state go for Parker, but my district went for him almost two to one."

"That bad?" Stu asked.

"It's really worse than that. Parker was in Little Rock a couple weeks ago, just after these riots started, and he really raised some kind of hell. The people almost knocked the walls down cheering him on. Now, don't get me wrong. I think he's a no good son of a bitch, but the folks back home sure don't look at it that way."

"I can understand your problem. All I can say is that it would be disaster if the election went to Parker."

"I'll buy that," Robertson replied. "But I really don't think there is any chance of that happening. After all, Parker doesn't control a single congressman."

"What do you think you will do on the vote?" Stu bluntly asked, leaning forward in his chair.

"I really don't know," Robertson said, half to himself. "Let me tell you what Parker has been doing. When he was in Little Rock he met privately with a bunch of the state's fat cats. Since then they have really been turning the pressure on me."

"What could they do to hurt you?"

"Plenty. I was surprised how much my own contributors have been listening. If I can believe my own people, money is going to be tough to get next time, at least it will be if I vote for Harrington. And if I ever decide to run statewide for either senator or governor, it will be even rougher."

"So where does that leave you?" Stu asked again. He had

known that Burns Robertson would make up his own mind and would be honest with him. Stu never even considered pulling out the list of federal goodies he had available for Robertson's district. The congressman would have been offended, and it would have been a mistake to have made the attempt.

"I don't know how this will finally come out," Robertson said. "It is impossible to predict how many ballots it will take, or what kinds of pressures are going to be created, but I'll promise you this much: I will vote for Harrington on the first ballot. After that, I'll have to look at it again. Now will that help you a little?"

"I can't ask for more than that. Will you let me know if you are thinking of changing your vote?"

"Of course. You know I never make a move without you. At least that's what my enemies back home say, and I would hate to disappoint them."

Stu rose to leave. "You're a good man, Burns. If there is ever anything I can do for you, all you have to do is ask."

"Thank you," Robertson said.

Stu spent the remainder of that day and the entire weekend roaming through the House office buildings. He thought bitterly that it was just as well that he and Sari already had split up, since the demands of his job for the past weeks had taken every moment and every ounce of his personality. Their marriage could never have survived it. By Monday he had managed to see each of the Democratic congressmen on his assigned list except for the powerful Arkansas committee chairman, who had sent word to the White House that he would speak to no one but the President on this subject. The remaining Arkansas Democrat, John Slagin, newly elected this term, had been friendly enough but had finally said that he felt obligated to vote the same way as the chairman, who thus became one of many key pieces in structuring Harrington's possible victory. Thus, as far as Arkansas was concerned, Stu could report only one solid Democratic vote out of the three needed to control that state.

Louisiana had also been difficult, but by the time Stu had

completed his round of conversations, he was convinced that the state would cast a solid vote for Harrington, at least on the first ballot. All of Louisiana's eight members were Democrats, and although six of them were quite conservative, most held firm views on party loyalty. Nevertheless, in Louisiana as in Arkansas, Senator Parker had been very active in recent days. He held a public rally in New Orleans and a private meeting with many of the state's powerful personages, both calculated to generate maximum pressure on the congressmen. Balancing this pressure, however, was another factor: four of the Louisiana congressmen had acquired great seniority and would normally be granted committee or sub-committee chairmanships in a Democratically controlled House.

It was this factor of Congressional seniority, and how to use it to advantage, that led the President, during the week before the House convened, to call a meeting with the Speaker, the Majority Leader and the Majority Whip.

The meeting began without the normal pleasantries, and the President came straight to the point with the Speaker: "I want to know what we can do to deny seniority to those who won't vote with the party on the presidential election."

"It is up to the Democratic caucus, Mr. President," the Speaker answered respectfully. "As you know, committee chairmanships, as well as the other perquisites of seniority, are strictly a matter for the Democrats to grant or withhold from their own numbers as they alone see fit. It used to be a power of my office"—the Speaker sighed in mock regret—"but the members didn't want to concentrate that kind of authority. Now they control it themselves."

"Can you get the Democrats to agree to take away those 'perquisites' from those who don't vote with the party?" the President asked impatiently.

"I really don't know, Mr. President."

"A majority of the Democrats can determine what they are going to do, can they not?"

"Of course," the Majority Leader responded.

"Well, a majority of them are liberal L for Harrington,

and therefore it can be done," the President insisted. "That is, if you are willing to call them together before the voting begins."

"We will call a caucus if you wish it done, Mr. President, but we cannot guarantee how they will vote. It is one thing to vote loyally for the party's nominee, but it's something else again to bind the party in advance to strip away seniority from all who may wish to dissent."

"It is your job to force them to do precisely that," the President said. "I am doing all I can from this end of the Avenue, and you must carry your end of the load."

At the end of the meeting the Democratic leaders went scurrying to the Hill to work on their party caucus, which they had agreed to call for the Thursday before the opening of the Congress. The President had been in a nasty mood when they left.

"How can they call themselves 'leaders'?" he had rhetorically asked of his staff. "If I had run the Senate as they do the House we could never have accomplished a damn thing. They have to be led every inch of the way and they don't even have an accurate count on how their people will vote."

The staff stood mutely by, merely nodding. The President then turned on them. "What in the hell are you all doing standing around there with your thumbs up your asses when there is work to be done on the Hill? You should be making those contacts. Now get to work."

The President, however, had been wrong about the ineffectiveness of the Democratic leadership. They had called the Thursday caucus and after five furious hours of debate had emerged with a resolution backed by a slim but workable majority of the House Democrats, to the effect that, in the organization of the House, no committee chairmanship would be given to any member who did not vote for his party's presidential nominee. The resolution provided further that, except for the election of the Speaker and the other necessary officers of the House, no further action would be taken regarding committees until the new President had been elected.

The Speaker then called the President and proudly reported the results of the caucus.

"How solid is it?" the President had asked.

"It is binding unless there is another caucus, which, of course, can always reverse what has been done," the Speaker replied. "However, there is one ominous possibility. There was a lot of threatening in the caucus from the Southerners that they would vote with the Republicans to organize the House. Of course, if they do make that kind of a deal, then the Democrats won't have any say over the chairmanships."

"Do you think they will go through with that threat?" the President asked in a subdued voice.

"I believe that they will vote for my election," the Speaker answered, "but if the caucus starts to implement its resolution, then I would say that all bets are off. The party will be blown apart."

"I understand what you are going through," the President told him. "Let's hope that the threat of taking away seniority will be sufficient, and that they will hold together long enough to elect Harrington."

"I hope that will be so, Mr. President."

Now, at noon on Monday, Stu and Mary O'Brien watched the historical events begin to unfold below them on the floor of the House. The congressional leadership had labored long to work out the rules that would govern these proceedings, in a bipartisan effort to arrive at fair rules. Their only precedent had been the rules adopted by the House in 1825.

These rules were now readopted by the House, but with two notable changes: Though the 1825 balloting had been secret, and though there was pressure from Senator Parker's forces to keep the vote closed, the advocates of secret balloting were eventually outvoted by a majority of the joint leadership, and backed by the House as a whole. The reasoning which prevailed was that the public had been led to expect a roll call vote by the House of Representatives, and that to hide votes in these traumatic times would be a serious, perhaps a disastrous, mistake.

It was decided that the roll of the states would be called alphabetically rather than, by the old procedure, in the order of their admission to the Union. The delegation from Maine, which under the old rule would have had the honor of voting first, tenaciously fought the change, but the modern tradition, as followed by both major political parties in their nominating conventions, carried the day.

The Electoral College vote was formally counted and the outgoing Vice-President announced the final official tally: Harrington, 233; Nelson, 178; and Parker, 127. "Therefore," he intoned, "since no candidate has received the necessary 270 votes, under Amendment Twelve to the Constitution of the United States, the House of Representatives shall choose immediately, by ballot, the President; and the Senate shall choose the Vice-President."

The joint session then adjourned and the senators quietly left the House chamber to separately meet and elect the Vice-President from the two candidates who had received the highest electoral counts, i.e., the Democratic and Republican nominees.

Then, the Speaker ordered that the gentlemen of the House would be seated separately by states, rather than in the traditional arrangement of Republicans to the Speaker's left and Democrats to his right. The Speaker announced that while the Sergeant at Arms was completing this task there would be a thirty-minute recess in the proceedings.

Stu took advantage of this break to telephone the White House. They used the facilities of the House Periodical Press room, just a few steps from the gallery where they were sitting. As always, the older man and the attractive young lady in charge were helpful to the White House personnel who were informally permitted to use this convenient facility.

Then Mary and Stu took the elevator to the Capitol basement, intending to have a quick cup of coffee. The House restaurant was full but Mary and Stu were hailed by Burns Robertson, who was completing a telephone call at the cashier's counter. The young congressman invited them to join him, and escorted them into the private Members Dining Room. At their table he introduced Mary to John Slagin, the young freshman congressman from Arkansas, and to Warren Mathews, a member from Louisiana who, within the limits of the political realities of his district, had always managed to be cooperative with the White House.

"How does it look to you?" Stu asked them all after coffee had been ordered.

"Arkansas is going to be just fine," Robertson said. "The chairman will vote for Harrington, and that makes it easy for the rest of us."

"It's still not exactly a cake walk," Slagin said. "You can't imagine the kind of hell they are raising in my district. Parker has really been moving around back home and it seems as if everybody and his brother has been wiring or calling me about this election, and all of them for Parker."

"How are you going to vote?" Stu asked.

"I will go with Harrington for the time being," Slagin answered.

"I don't know about you fellows," Mathews offered, "but they must have paid for over a hundred people to come to Washington from my part of Louisiana. The only good thing about these riots is that they have caused my good constituents no end of difficulty in getting to the Hill to bother me."

"Is your vote still with Harrington?" Stu asked Mathews.

Mathews answered with a grin. "I figure I don't much like Washington anyway. I'd rather be back home making a good honest living for a change. So I guess I might as well go down the drain voting with you guys like I always do."

"There is one thing you ought to know, Stu," Robertson said, breaking in. "These riots in Washington and around the country are upsetting a lot of fellows on the floor. They are really angry. I've never seen anything like it."

The other two congressmen vigorously nodded their agreement. "They are mad at the blacks, at Mamba, and at that woman who was with him. But mostly they are mad at the President," Mathews said.

"They say he let it happen," said Slagin. "He didn't move fast enough on the Oakland business. He saw Mamba. He didn't lock him up. And now the violence is spreading all over the place."

"Is that what you believe?" Stu asked, getting a little angry himself.

Slagin shrugged his shoulders and Stu had to restrain himself from blurting out more.

"We are with you. You should know that, Stu," Robertson said. "But John here is telling you the truth about what is happening on the floor. Believe me, it's ugly."

The time had come for the House to reconvene. As they all walked up the stairs, Robertson dropped back and took Stu by the arm. "You mustn't mind Slagin," Robertson said. "He really is a good man, but he's frightened. They have been pouring it on, and it doesn't look too good."

Stu and Mary left the congressmen at the closely guarded doors to the chamber and trudged up the remaining flight of stairs to their gallery seats. The galleries were strangely quiet as the members somberly took their newly assigned places. Every one of the 435 House members was present, and they, too, were singularly subdued as they waited for the session to begin.

"The clerk will now call the roll of states for the election of the President of the United States of America," the Speaker announced, banging the gavel on the podium before him.

"Alabama," the Clerk called out, and, as he read the roster of the eight members from that state, each announced his vote. They all voted with their party. The five Democrats voted for Harrington and the three Republicans voted for Nelson. Alabama's one vote was thus cast for the Democratic nominee.

"That's a great sign," whispered Stu, suddenly feeling enthusiastic. "Maybe we will get the entire South. If so, Harrington will have his twenty-six states and win. Call this vote in to Alvin right now, will you?"

Mary got up and hurried to the telephone.

"Alaska," intoned the clerk. Its lone representative, a Republican, voted for Nelson. Next came Arizona, also Republican and for Nelson. Then it was Arkansas' turn. Stu's optimism mounted as he proudly saw that the state that had been assigned to him voted three to one for Harrington, with every Democrat standing firm.

California, Colorado, Connecticut and Delaware likewise voted precisely as their congressional delegations were divided between the two major parties, with the first three going for Harrington, and the last for Nelson.

With Florida, the roof fell in. Its three Republicans went for Nelson; the two liberal Democrats from the Miami area voted for Harrington; but the remaining seven Democrats, constituting a majority of the state's twelve congressmen, voted for Jack Parker, thus capturing Florida's vote.

Stu sent Mary running back to the telephones to report the disaster, which meant, assuming that all other states voted according to their party divisions and the tied states passed, that Harrington could only get a maximum of twenty-five states on the first ballot, one short of the absolute majority of twenty-six necessary to elect him President.

The roll call continued.

Each state voted along straight party lines, except for Mississippi, which cast a unanimous vote for Parker despite the fact that all of its congressmen were nominally Democrats.

Thus, the tally at the conclusion of the first ballot was: Harrington, twenty-four states; Nelson, nineteen states; and Parker, two states. The five states with evenly split delegations—Illinois, Maryland, Montana, Oregon and Virginia—did not vote.

The Speaker immediately ordered a second roll call, but there was no change in the voting. Six more roll calls were taken, and, finally, at eight P.M., with the House still deadlocked, the weary Speaker announced that, without objection, the House would adjourn until noon on Tuesday.

CHAPTER TWENTY-ONE

The President summoned the House Democratic leadership to meet with him and Senator Harrington in the Cabinet Room. It was Monday night, following the adjournment of the deadlocked session, and Alvin Morgan, John Kelly, Sam Baker and Stu had been asked to join the group. The meeting did not start until almost ten o'clock and everyone present looked exhausted.

"We came awfully close, Mr. President," the Speaker said, as they took their seats around the Cabinet table. "Just two states away from victory."

"We took eight roll calls, and not a vote changed," said the Majority Leader.

"Well, at least the Senate came through and elected a Democratic Vice-President," said the President. "That means if the House continues its deadlock until January twentieth, he will be acting President."

"I don't think the House will hold still that long," the Speaker said, his voice thin and tired. "I can't think of anything more we can do."

"That is why we are here, gentlemen. I believe there are some things that can yet be done," said the President. "Just listen to this," he said, extracting a single typewritten sheet from the inside pocket of his coat. "This is a report from the F.B.I. Director. I want to read it to you." He put on his glasses and began: "January third. TO: The President. FROM: Director, Federal Bureau of Investigation. SUBJECT: Senator Jack Parker.

"At your request we have conducted an intensive investigation regarding possible violations of the Federal Corrupt Practices Act by the above subject. Initial source was information furnished by Miss Janice Pruitt, former secretary to the subject. Although the Bureau's work is incomplete, we can now report, on a preliminary basis only, that sources known to the Bureau to be reliable and in a position to know, verify that funds totaling in excess of one hundred thousand dollars have been transferred to campaign organizations controlled by and supporting the subject. These funds originated in Argentine and Swiss banks, and have been traced to individuals and organizations known to be ultra-right wing in nature and, in at least two instances, having direct connections with the former German Nazi party. The investigation is continuing and the Bureau will keep you informed as you requested."

The President then extracted another typed paper from his pocket, and added, "That's not all. I've got a full statement here from the Janice Pruitt the F.B.I. mentioned. She says that Governor Nelson made a deal with Parker to give Nelson the Presidency in the Electoral College in exchange for appointing one of Parker's lackeys Attorney General."

The President looked around the room, peering over the top of his glasses. "She also says," he went on, "that Parker had been bedding her down for quite a while, although that apparently came to a sudden halt a few weeks ago. There is a lesson here somewhere, I would venture."

Self-concious laughter filled the room.

"What do you propose to do with that information, Mr. President?" asked Senator Harrington.

"Release it, of course," answered the President.

"You mean, do it yourself?" the Speaker asked, sounding concerned.

"That is precisely what I propose to do," said the President. "I am calling a press conference for ten tomorrow morning and I will give the nation the facts at that time. Perhaps some members of the House will be listening and may even pay attention to the truth."

"May I say something, Mr. President?" asked Harrington.

"Go right ahead, Jimmy."

Harrington looked down at the table for a moment, idly doodling on the scratch pad before him. The room was silent, while everyone waited for him to speak. Finally, in subdued contrast to his usual buoyant style, he began.

"I stand to gain more than anyone else in this room from the matters that we are speaking about this evening. Therefore, I have the most to lose by giving up any action we might take. Please take what I am about to say in that light, Mr. President."

Harrington paused and the President's smile was instantly replaced by a hard, calculating look. The others fidgeted uncomfortably as Harrington returned the President's stare.

"I think it would be a mistake for you to personally make those charges, Mr. President," Harrington continued.

"Don't you know you are about to lose this election?" the President angrily broke in. "Don't you know that you are in desperate shape and if we don't move boldly it is all going to go down the drain?"

"I agree that it looks bad, though it certainly isn't hopeless," Harrington answered calmly. "My point is that nothing is worth doing damage to the Presidency, and I believe that if you jump in with that kind of accusation, the office will be badly hurt."

"I think I am the best judge of that," the President replied. "You will also recall our agreement," he went on, scowling at Harrington.

"Yes sir, and I have been abiding by it. But I think you should listen to what I've got to say. I think you will see my point," said Harrington. "You see, Mr. President, I feel strongly that the Presidency cannot afford to lose any more good will. It is a precious commodity and in these days there is none to spare. The real power of the President lies in his public acceptance, his credibility with the people, if you will, and I feel that for a President to become so personally involved in this unholy mess would be harmful. Frankly, I would rather not be elected than see you do this."

Harrington sat back, his steady gaze never wavering from

the President's face. Stu felt a deep, wrenching empathy for Harrington.

The President, however, was unimpressed by Harrington's speech. "Do you have any alternative suggestions?" he asked.

"It occurred to me that we should meet with the Republican leadership and try to work something out."

"Absolutely not," the President shot back, and then added, "Perhaps we will eventually be forced to that, but I am dead set against it at this moment. For one thing, it is not yet necessary. For another, it weakens one of the major charges I am going to bring against Parker. And, most importantly, it would destroy the very foundations of the two-party system."

"Then you are determined to go through with the press conference tomorrow?" Harrington asked.

"I am indeed. Furthermore, I expect you to remain silent. I don't want a public repetition of what you are saying here tonight."

"I wouldn't do that, Mr. President," said Harrington, then added, pressing forward, "but I beg you to reconsider your decision. At least sleep on it until tomorrow."

The President abruptly swung around to Sam Baker, who was sitting against the wall directly behind him. "You set up that press conference for ten A.M.," he ordered. "I want full live coverage. You can announce it now."

The meeting ended then, and Stu returned to his office with Sam Baker. Mary O'Brien was waiting along with two other secretaries. The four of them pitched in to make the necessary calls to the press and network representatives. It took over an hour to complete the notifications, but by midnight the television technicians were already busily at work setting up the equipment in the East Room.

The President's personal staff, including Stu and Mary O'Brien, took this particularly late assignment in stride. They had been sleeping at the White House since the riots had made street travel hazardous and often impossible. The First Family had invited the girls to sleep in the Mansion's bedrooms,

275

but the men on the staff had not fared so well. For them, the Mansion's downstairs rooms—Library, Diplomatic Reception, China and Silver rooms—had been pressed into dormitory service. The only consolation was that they had also been offered the use of the swimming pool, together with its shower facilities. If the events that caused these arrangements had not been so grim, it would have been a fascinating experience for all of them. Even so, the natural exuberance of the staff did assert itself and, despite the seriousness of the times, their morale was boosted by the graciousness of the President and the First Lady, who throughout it all treated them like valued, invited guests in their home.

At eight o'clock the following morning, a meeting had been called at a church deep within the Washington ghetto. Eight A.M. was the earliest Washington's nighttime curfew permitted anyone to legally move on the city's streets and, though no outdoor gatherings of more than four people were permitted anywhere in the heavily patrolled area, there was no rule preventing a church meeting.

People approached the church, quickly walking up the steps from the street looking neither left nor right. The police, together with a dozen jeeploads of troops, had been forewarned of the meeting, and they nervously watched from their vehicles surrounding the ancient building.

Nina Moran and Mamba stood in a small passageway behind the pulpit, watching the pews fill with people, most of them young, predominantly male, and all, of course, black.

"There may be some shooting, you know that, don't you?" Mamba was saying to Nina.

"I understand the risks," she said, her voice hard. She was still wearing her khaki uniform, rumpled and dirty. "I will be marching at the front."

"And I'll be right beside you," he said. "I might as well be arrested another time. It will be just one more bail bond for me. If they ever changed the law so that they could keep me in jail because I'm apt to commit another one of their 'offenses' then I'd be in for it. As it is, they've got to let me go out on bail as long as I show up for court." He held up his hands. "So I'll be right there with you."

"You know something, Mamba," Nina said with a sarcastic smile. "I think you are the least bit jealous of all the publicity I've received since coming back here. I called this meeting, but you had to show up. It bugs you, doesn't it, that all of our good militant friends are beginning to listen to me? Does that make you feel a little less of a man by any chance?"

A look of rage flashed over Mamba's face, and he briefly moved toward her. Nina didn't flinch, and he did nothing. "You really are a no good bitch, you know that?"

A few minutes later the church was completely filled, with people sitting in the aisles and standing along the walls, packed three and four deep. Nina strode to the pulpit, with Mamba following behind, but it was Nina who spoke, her unaccented voice firm and easily heard.

"Up at the Capitol they are trying to settle which of their bigots is going to lead their parade of oppression against us," she began. "They tried to make that decision in November, and they failed. They tried again in December, and failed. Now they are trying in a different way in January. I say that their whole system has failed; that it is rotten to the core; and that we must show them the truth."

The crowd responded. "Give it to them, sister!" someone shouted. There was a roar of approval and raised, clenched fists were everywhere.

"I say that we shall march on them. I say that ten thousand black people, and more, shall walk up that Hill to glory and freedom," Nina cried, grasping the rostrum with both hands.

There were more shouts of approval.

"They will try to shoot us down," she went on. "Will that stop you?"

"Hell, no!" came back from the crowd.

"They will kill some of us. Will that stop you?"

"Hell, no!"

"Will you march up that Hill with me today?" she screamed, her small hands upraised, tightly clenched.

"Yes!"

"And tomorrow?"

"Yes!"

"And every day after that until they have been taught the truth?"

"Yes! Yes! Yes!"

At ten o'clock that same Tuesday morning the President held his press conference. He made a slashing attack on Senator Parker. Without revealing the basis for his remarks, he accused Parker of receiving foreign funds from neo-Nazi sources. He repeated his charge of Parker's deal with Nelson, but was now specific about the promise by Nelson to give the Attorney General appointment to Parker's assistant. However, he made no mention of Janice Pruitt or of Parker's affair with her.

Prior to the press conference every available member of the White House staff, as well as the congressional liaison personnel from the major executive departments, had been dispatched to the Hill with explicit instructions to talk to every Democrat in the House, repeating and emphasizing the charges that the President was leveling against Parker. In addition, Stu had been requested to contact Jeff Taylor and several other reporters to plant—off the record, of course—the story of Janice Pruitt and the senator. The hope was that this story would circulate during the day and appear in the afternoon editions.

As noon approached, and the second day of balloting was about to begin, no one knew whether the effort to destroy Jack Parker would succeed. The members from the two key states, Florida and Mississippi, were not talking to anyone from the White House, and, as the President had wished it, there had been no communication between the White House and the Republicans.

At eleven, Nina Moran and Mamba led the first contingent of marchers toward Capitol Hill. Two thousand people had somehow managed to assemble, and they now approached the Capitol from the southeast, walking down Pennsylvania Avenue toward the House of Representatives. The authorities were ready for them, and although the troops were unable to react quickly enough to prevent the formation of the march, they were able to disperse it before it could get close to the Capitol. No one was killed or even badly injured in the skirmish, but some blood was spilled and a good deal of tear gas had to be used. This gas managed to seep into the congressional offices just a few blocks away. The House members, their eyes burning, were made painfully aware that there was trouble outside.

Nina and Mamba escaped arrest, but now they were both sought by the police. Though they went into hiding, they were not inactive. By afternoon, word had spread through the city that there would be another march the next day, an even heavier assault that would escalate the difficulties caused to the police, the troops, and hopefully, to the Congress.

By 11:45 that Tuesday morning, the hallway outside the House chamber was crowded, and Stu had a difficult time pushing his way through the crowd to the Speaker's office. The place was jammed with lobbyists, congressmen, and police. Stu had one argument with a Capitol policeman who refused to accept his White House credentials, and he would not have been allowed near the Speaker's office except for the intervention of one of the House doormen who happened to recognize him.

The Speaker had called a last-minute get-together of the House Democratic leadership and had invited John Kelly, Stu Brady and three other members of Kelly's congressional liaison staff.

The Speaker was nervously smoking a large cigar. The Majority Leader, his small form almost swallowed up in the deep leather chair where he sat to the Speaker's right, was quietly talking on the telephone. The Democratic Whip was intently studying his membership roster, making short notes by several of the names.

"That march outside is murdering us," the Speaker was saying, as Stu entered the room. "The President's speech this morning was magnificent, and I think we had them going, but now those Negroes are trying to storm the Capitol and everybody around here is up in arms about it. I just don't understand those people," the Speaker went on, shaking his head. "If they would just use some common sense, we could work this out together. Instead, it seems like they are doing everything possible to ruin our chances."

"I guess they look at things from a completely different perspective," Stu commented.

"But look at all the things we have done for them," the Speaker said. "There is all that social legislation, the civil-rights bills, all of that. We Democrats have done that for them. We conceived those programs and put the laws on the books. Why, I have been for every one of those bills, and I hardly have a Negro in my district."

"I think they want equality, not handouts," Stu said quietly.

The Speaker raised his eyebrows and peered at Stu. "That is an odd remark from someone on the President's staff," he said.

At that moment the Majority Leader hung up the phone and turned to the Speaker. "Parker has just issued a statement," the leader said, frowning. "He categorically denied everything the President charged. He also attacked the President. He said he has a signed statement from an agent at the F.B.I. to the effect that the White House put pressure on the Bureau to move against Parker for political purposes. He says that the President and the Democrats have staged these marches to intimidate the Congress, and he prays to God that the House has the courage to stand up to them."

"That is quite a mouthful," offered the Whip, dryly.

"It's an emotional statement, all right," said the Majority Leader. "Apparently, Parker is all over the networks reading it, and copies are being distributed on the House floor right now."

"What do you think the effect will be?" asked John Kelly.

"To be blunt with you, John," answered the Speaker, "the President's prestige has fallen so much since that Oakland business, and especially since these riots began, that the best we can hope for is a stand-off between the President and Parker. People are apt to think that all we have got here is two politicians sounding off at each other. Together with everything else that is going on, the Parker scandal is going to be drowned out by the rest of the noise."

"I agree," said the Majority Leader.

The Whip said nothing, but his downcast eyes as he scratched on his note pad was answer enough for Kelly.

"Well," said the Speaker, standing up. "It is nearly noon. Let's get to work, gentlemen, and see what we can salvage out of this." He nodded goodbye to the White House aides and strode out the door.

Stu made his way upstairs to the gallery, to a seat Mary had saved for him.

The Speaker now convened the House, the Chaplain offered a brief prayer, and the second day's voting began.

"Alabama," intoned the clerk, starting the ninth roll call for the election of a President. "Parker," called out the first congressman from that state, a Democrat. With his vote, Stu knew that there was bad trouble ahead. When the second Democratic congressman also voted for Parker and the third representative, a Republican, did the same, it was obvious that the state was going to go for Parker, and that a disaster was in the works.

Stu sent Mary rushing to the telephone to report to the White House that Alabama had switched from Harrington to Parker.

Alaska and Arizona held for Nelson, and Arkansas, to Stu's intense relief, remained with Harrington.

Florida again voted for Parker. However, this time its congressmen, Democrats and Republicans alike—except for the two liberals from Miami—cast solid votes for Parker.

Then Georgia went the way of Alabama, and unanimously. Kentucky stayed with Harrington, but Louisiana, which had gone for Harrington on the previous day, now tied with four for

281

Harrington and four for Parker, and thus was unable to vote. Since Louisiana was one of the states assigned to Stu, he felt this switch like a physical blow.

It was clear that in the South, at least, the Florida senator had managed to smash through traditional party barriers.

Mississippi remained with Parker.

Both the Carolinas and Tennessee swung to Parker, as the South now completely broke the traces.

Virginia and Maryland, previously tied between Harrington and Nelson and thus having not voted on Monday, now swung to Parker, joining the other Southern states.

At the end of this ninth ballot, the count, as announced by the Speaker, was as follows: Harrington, eighteen states; Nelson, nineteen states; Parker, nine states; with four states—Illinois, Louisiana, Montana and Oregon—tied.

Harrington had lost six states since yesterday's voting, all of them from the South, and Nelson had held his own. Now, Nelson was the front runner, with Parker coming up fast. However, twenty-six states were still needed to elect and, as yet, no candidate was in clear sight of this goal.

The Speaker announced that there would be a thirty-minute recess before the next ballot began. The Speaker's clerk, standing on the House floor, looked up at the gallery and, catching Stu's eye, signaled that the Speaker wanted the White House personnel to come to his office. As soon as they arrived, John Kelly picked up a telephone to call the White House. Kelly was as agitated as Stu had ever seen him when he gave his report to Morgan.

Just then the Speaker walked in, closely followed by the other two Democratic leaders. "Those marches are what did it to us," he said, sitting down behind his large desk. "I've never seen so much anger on the floor. Everybody is mad, but the Southern boys are incensed, and there is no stopping them from going to Parker."

"What about the rest?" asked Stu.

"The remainder of our party is pretty much standing pat,

but don't think for a moment that they aren't burning up too," said the Speaker.

"And the Republicans?" asked Stu.

"It looks like they are just sitting back, waiting for the whole business to drop the Presidency right into their hands," the Speaker answered.

Kelly was still on the telephone. Now he cupped his hand over the receiver and turned to the Speaker. "The President wants to know if you can cut this session off without any more voting today?" he asked.

"Impossible," snapped the Speaker. "The Republicans would never go along with that and I couldn't get enough votes from the Democrats to enforce such a move."

"The President would like to meet with the leadership as soon as possible," Kelly went on. "He would like you to come to the White House before it's too late. What would you suggest be done?"

"The best we can do is go out on the floor and shore up what we've got left. If we can stop any further deterioration for a couple of ballots, maybe we can talk them into adjourning until tomorrow. But it is going to be difficult. Parker is turning his big guns on Arkansas and Kentucky, and it will be damned hard for them to hold out through the day."

Kelly turned back to the telephone and reported this to Morgan. "I'll work on Kentucky," he said, hanging up. "Mr. Speaker, if you and the Majority Leader will get to the Arkansas chairman, Stu here will talk to the two younger Democrats from that state, Robertson and Slagin."

"That's fine," said the Speaker. "I would also suggest that we take no more recesses until we adjourn for the day. There is no point in giving Parker any more chance to turn the screws."

There were no smiles as the meeting broke up and the Speaker returned to the House floor to commence the tenth roll call.

The voting continued, but there was no change. The Speaker kept the House in continuous session and ten more roll calls were taken without any further break in the Democratic ranks. By two o'clock in the morning, the House, its members utterly exhausted, finally agreed to recess until noon. Nineteen roll calls had been taken since Monday, and still no President had been elected.

At eight o'clock on Wednesday, the Democratic House leadership, tired and dispirited, met with the President, his staff and Senator Harrington for breakfast at the White House.

"It is not over yet," the President said in a firm, confident voice as they took their seats around the dining table. "The way I see it, Harrington is still as strong as any other candidate, and there is plenty of room to maneuver."

"I don't see how we can hold our own through the day," the Speaker answered, his face sunken with fatigue. "It is chaos on the floor, and we have no control over what is happening."

Breakfast was now being served. "Just fill yourselves up with some of this good food," the President said. "The whole world will look brighter on a full stomach."

Only the President ate with any gusto. The others hardly touched their breakfast. Finally the President pushed back from the table. "The time has come to deal with our Republican friends," he said, plunging in. "Isn't that right, Jimmy?" he asked, gesturing at Harrington.

"That is what I suggested Monday, Mr. President," Harrington replied sardonically. "I am still of that opinion."

"You are quite right," said the President, continuing without reaction, speaking to the others present. "Jimmy and I had a long talk last night while the voting was going on. We reached some conclusions. You tell them, Senator."

"I am willing to offer Nelson the position of Secretary of State," Harrington responded. "I am also agreeable to permitting the Republicans to name the Cabinet posts of Interior, Commerce and Post Office, in exchange for their support of me for President."

"What will that do to the two-party system?" asked the Majority Leader.

"It will hurt it. How much or little is impossible to gauge. But we have no choice," said Harrington.

"Must you give away State?" asked the Whip.

"Actually, it is not such a costly move," answered Harrington. "Nelson has had a great deal of foreign policy experience, as you know, and is very qualified. Besides, after this election crisis, a bipartisan foreign policy is almost mandatory for the nation's stability. Even without a deal, I would seriously consider offering the job to Nelson."

"Do you have any reason to believe they will agree to such a proposition?" asked the Speaker.

"No, we don't," broke in the President. "However, the realities of the situation are such that an understanding such as we are proposing, or one similar to it, is the only rational way out of this crisis. The Republicans are practical, reasonable men, and I am confident that they will look at it the same way we do."

"What makes you think they won't make the reverse of the proposal to Harrington, and ask the Democrats to give them the Presidency?" asked the majority leader.

"They might do that," said Harrington, "but I think I have the stronger hand. After all, except for the Parker situation, the Democrats control the House."

"But what will you do if they make such an offer to you?" the Majority Leader persisted.

"Refuse it," said Harrington. "As I say, I am convinced that my position is stronger than theirs."

"Well, that is certainly a matter of opinion," the Majority Leader replied.

"What about making a deal with Parker?" asked the Whip.

"Never!" the President angrily replied. "We will never do business with that son of a bitch."

"I agree. That is the one thing that we must, at all costs, prevent from happening," said Harrington in a decisive voice.

CHAPTER TWENTY-TWO

Kansas Congressman Thomas Meistler, although only in the House for one term, had made a name for himself. Disdainful of the traditional reticence of freshman members, he had deliberately embarked on a program to make himself known. As a Republican under a Democratic administration there had been no lack of targets, and he had made the most of each opportunity on the premise that any publicity was good publicity. Newsmen had quickly learned to approach Meistler with a suggested response whenever there was a controversy. He almost never refused the bait. And, by the end of his first term, he had begun to receive some national notoriety. It was not surprising that Tom Meistler had been in the forefront of those criticizing the President after the Oakland affair. He had, much to the chagrin of some of his party's elders, unhesitatingly joined in Parker's call for the President's impeachment.

Meistler was a large, florid-faced man whose gray hair was cut close to his scalp. He had a mercurial personality, and his smile could instantly turn into stubborn anger. He was never placid and had the somewhat distracting habit of jerking his head and arms when he became excited. He was not especially liked by his colleagues, but they tolerated him as an effective and necessary gadfly against the administration.

Congressman Meistler had been enraged when the Capitol police had politely requested that he sleep at his offices during the House election and not attempt to commute from his Chevy Chase home. They had carefully explained that the riots in

Washington created great danger to anyone on the streets and that they could not guarantee his safety. Meistler had thrown the officers out of his office, saying that they were typical of what was wrong with law enforcement; that the police today were so afraid of the criminals that they preferred instead to harass law-abiding citizens. Meistler had angrily told the officers that no one was going to order him around, that he was a member of Congress, and that he was free to come and go as he "damn well pleased." The shocked policemen shrugged their shoulders and hoped that it would all work out.

It almost did.

Meistler had secured pistols for himself and two of his male assistants, and, since the House session began on the previous Friday, these two young men had driven him between office and home in his heavy Lincoln sedan, windows shut and doors tightly locked. There had been no incidents and, although they had been stopped a number times by troops and police, Meistler had merely flashed his congressional identification and been allowed to proceed.

At eleven o'clock on Wednesday morning, an hour before the third day's balloting was scheduled to begin, the three men rode through the nearly deserted streets of Washington, traveling down Connecticut Avenue, past the Washington Monument, and on to the Southwest Freeway as they proceeded toward the parking garage across the street from the House office buildings.

At the same moment that Congressman Meistler had started his trip to the Hill, Nina Moran and Mamba, with over ten thousand marchers massed behind them, once again began to move toward the Capitol. Security forces were waiting for them, but as the marchers streamed toward the Capitol, the authorities were amazed at the massive turnout and were prepared only for the two thousand marchers of the previous day. But now, demonstrators appeared to come forward in endless numbers, all of them purposeful. They approached the House side of the Capitol and suddenly broke ranks, spread out and moved fast in an attempt to surround the Capitol. As the troops responded with tear gas, the marchers fell back for a moment. The soldiers called for emergency help, then fixed their bayonets, and with gas masks on, charged into the mass of people.

About a thousand demonstrators managed to reach the west side of the Rayburn House Office Building and tried to force entry. A platoon of police, stationed behind the high balustrades of the building, easily repulsed the assault and the attackers fell back toward the southwest, disorganized and angry. In their frustration they streamed across the streets leading to the House garage, aimlessly running back and forth and blocking access. They yelled catcalls to the police and to the motorists who were thus prevented from getting off the Southwest Freeway.

Congressman Meistler was at that moment driving down the exit ramp of the freeway. It was just after the milling demonstrators had managed to block the street that Meistler's car entered the short tunnel leading to C Street and the garage. The driver turned on the short curve and then suddenly stopped as he came upon the halted cars jammed up in front of him.

"What is going on?" Meistler angrily demanded from the back seat.

"I think there's some trouble up ahead," said his driver as he pounded the horn.

"I'll go see what it is," the other assistant volunteered. He walked ahead several hundred feet, and then returned. He was coughing and holding a handkerchief to his watering eyes. "There's been another march on the Capitol," he said, quickly slamming the car door closed. "It's like yesterday, only now they're on this side of the building too. It looks pretty confused, and the police are using tear gas."

"What in the hell are we supposed to do?" demanded the congressman.

"I think we'd better just sit here and lock the doors," said the assistant. "It looks like we're now blocked from behind, and we can't go forward. We'd better just wait."

"Like hell we will," Meistler exploded, his face deeply flushed. "I am a member of Congress and I am supposed to be at the Capitol, not locked up here like some sitting duck. I'll be goddamned if I'll stay here."

"But there's no one to escort us through," the assistant urged. "The police are protecting the building and we would have to walk right through the rioters to get there."

"Well then, that's exactly what we're going to do," snapped the congressman, jerking open the door. "You two just make sure you have your guns handy in case anyone tries to stop us. Those sons of bitches will back down once they see we mean business."

"I'm not sure it will work," argued the assistant, looking over at the driver, whose face had blanched as he tightly gripped the steering wheel.

"I'm walking to my office," Meistler said, stepping out of the car. "If you two want to stay here and quake, that is up to you. I'm leaving now."

Meistler started to walk forward and, after the briefest hesitation, both of his assistants joined him. He impatiently jerked his hands at them, and they exposed their pistols, nervously holding them at their sides as they slowly walked past two dozen stalled cars, ignoring the amazed looks of the drivers at their drawn guns.

About fifty young black men were standing on the street in front of the first car. They were shouting taunts at the cars and several were sitting on the hoods. For the moment, they were not attempting to get at the drivers, frozen behind the steering wheels of their locked cars.

As Meistler and his two escorts approached, someone laughed and yelled, "Lookee here. Some of the white boys have some guts after all. They going to try to come through."

Meistler didn't say a word and motioned his assistants to follow him as he stepped past the front car and started toward the Rayburn Building several hundred yards away. "Get out of my way," he snapped at the young men standing in front of him.

"Hey, man, they've got guns," someone shouted.

"Just let us through," said one of the assistants. "We don't want any trouble."

"You got it already, honky," said a tough-looking black, planting himself directly in front of them.

For one tense minute everyone stood his ground; Meistler

glaring at the men who were blocking him, and the Negroes refusing to budge. Then the young men started to taunt, and, in another moment a large number of black demonstrators had converged on the scene. The congressman backed up a few paces so that he was standing between two cars. It was now obvious to him that he was not going to get through unless he ordered his boys to start shooting, and, suddenly fearing his great danger, he saw it would be a disastrous mistake to start anything like that.

"Let's go back," he said to his escorts, reaching into his pocket for a handkerchief to wipe his burning eyes.

"He's going for a gun," yelled someone. "Stop him!"

Meistler hesitated, his hand still in his pocket. He started to explain, but before he could utter a word, someone jumped over the hood of the car to his right and struck him hard on the side of the head. The congressman was knocked to his knees, and his head exploded in pain. He vaguely saw that he was being rushed from all sides and that his assistants were struggling. He was hit again and again, until he lay on the pavement choking on his own blood. He desperately tried to cover his head. He saw a foot swung at him, and the blow caught him in the side. Then he was kicked again and though he tried to roll away, he was losing consciousness. If they would only stop now, he prayed. But he knew, in a last flash of thought, that they would not.

Stu Brady was in the House restaurant having coffee with Burns Robertson. It was close to noon and Stu had been earnestly beseeching the Arkansas congressman to stay with the Democratic presidential candidate.

"We are trying to do something with the Republicans," Stu explained. "If you can just stand pat for another day, I think we can take the pressure off."

"How can I do that, Stu?" Robertson asked in a pained voice. "They will destroy me back home if I'm isolated on this. Slagin is voting the same way as the chairman, and if he switches that would leave me naked as a jaybird."

"The Speaker is working on the chairman," offered Stu.

"Well, let's hope he can hold him."

Bells now rang, announcing that the session was going to begin. Stu and Robertson sadly shook hands and Stu disconsolately trudged up the two flights of stairs to the galleries. Policemen were everywhere, and guards had been trebled at each of the gallery doors.

Stu saw that there was a great deal of agitation on the House floor. Members were bunched in excited conversation. The Speaker, looking shaken, mounted the rostrum as the Sergeant at Arms placed the mace in its stand. The Speaker banged the gavel and continued to bang it for several minutes, asking, then begging for order on the House floor. Finally, the members became sufficiently quiet for him to proceed, though over a third remained on their feet.

The Speaker began. "It is my sad duty to announce that a dastardly murder has taken place. One of our members, Congressman Thomas Meistler of Kansas, has just been beaten to death by the mob which has been trying to intimidate these constitutional proceedings."

There were shouts of anger from the floor, and the Speaker again fought to regain order, until, finally, he could be heard again.

"Out of respect for our fallen colleague, and without objection, the House will not vote today, but will stand in recess until noon tomorrow." Then, looking very old, he descended the short stairs to the floor and walked rapidly out of the chamber.

Stu sent Mary scurrying to the telephone while he ran down the flight of stairs to the House floor level. He stationed himself by the House doors, intending to pick up as much comment as possible from the members.

They came out slowly. All those who stopped to talk to Stu expressed great anger. It made no difference whether they were liberal or conservative, from the North or South, the rage was the same. Many were beyond reason in their expressions of disgust at the blacks. Stu listened, feeling shock and then fright at what he was hearing.

Burns Robertson was one of the last to come out. "Some of the boys want a caucus of the Democrats this afternoon," he said. "It's going to start right away. Why don't you go on over to my office and I'll meet you there when it's over. Then we can talk."

Stu waited in Robertson's office for nearly two hours, checking the White House several times. Everything was quiet, ominously so. The marchers had been dispersed. Two hundred arrests had been made, but Mamba and Nina Moran were still at large, despite a gigantic manhunt now turning the city inside out. Meistler's body had been recovered almost immediately after his murder. He had been horribly beaten, but before the police had been able to get the body to the morgue, an Associated Press photographer had been able to get pictures of the bloodied corpse. These photos were now all over the afternoon papers, and they were certain to hit the nation like a bomb.

Though Alvin Morgan had been necessarily circumspect over the telephone, he had managed to inform Stu that, so far at least, there had been no contact between the President and the Republicans. Despite the frantic efforts of the White House operators to reach Governor Nelson, he had not as yet responded to the calls. Thus, except for the developments on the Hill, matters stood pretty much as they had this morning.

Finally, Congressman Robertson returned to his office. "I am sorry you had to wait so long," he said as he flopped down on the couch. "I just couldn't get here any sooner."

"What in the hell happened in the caucus?" asked Stu.

"I've never seen anything like it," Robertson said, shaking his head. "Everyone was angry, from the Speaker on down. I didn't hear one moderate voice during the whole meeting. Not one member so much as mentioned the causes of so much violence, or the responsibility of the government."

"What about yourself?" asked Stu.

"I'm damn mad, too, though I didn't say anything at the caucus. But I think that this kind of thing just has to stop. We can't let a minority of militants push us around like this. This country is either going to be run according to law, or it isn't. As far as I am concerned, I'll fight them with everything I've got.

And I think that the new President had better be thinking along these same lines."

Stu studied Robertson's intense features, and fleetingly thought of Charlie Jefferson and Nina as they had been in Oakland.

"Did the caucus do anything besides talk?" Stu asked.

"Not in any formal sense," said Robertson, "but the Southern boys sure tried. They really are swinging over to Parker now. What they said was that all of this has come about because the President has been coddling the Negroes and playing footsie with people like Mamba. They say that if Parker were President, the marchers would never have been permitted to form in the first place, and that if they had ever tried to storm the Capitol, they would have been shot, driven off, and every last one of them arrested."

"What did the liberals do about that kind of totalitarian talk?" Stu asked, feeling sick.

"I'm telling you that absolutely no one spoke up to defend what is going on or to try to explain it. Even the New York guys had nothing to say. Stu, this killing has done something to the House. It's not the same body it was yesterday. I've never seen emotion like this."

"But you say the caucus took no action," Stu said, leaning forward in his chair.

"That's right. The Speaker was able to stop them from taking any kind of vote. What I'm saying is that if they had voted, I wouldn't guarantee how it would have come out."

"Jesus Christ," murmured Stu, shaking his head. "It's as bad as all that?"

"Stu," Robertson slowly went on, "I'm going to have to vote for Parker tomorrow. The chairman has switched and I just can't do anything else." As he turned around, his face clearly showed the pain of his dilemma. "I'm truly sorry."

Stu understood that Robertson could do nothing else except at the price of his own political destruction, and he felt he had no right to ask that of any member.

"Maybe we can move things around a bit before tomorrow

noon," Stu said in a tone more hopeful than he felt. "There are still some things the President can do. So keep your options open, will you, buddy?"

"Of course I'll do that," said Robertson, grasping his hand firmly. "There is no need for me to issue any kind of statement before I vote. Goddamn, but I hope you guys can do something."

"The Democrats are breaking," Billy Dan Reeves exultantly exclaimed, as he burst into Jack Parker's inner office.

"I just got that same word from the Florida chairman. Now, you just calm down and listen to me for a moment." Parker got up from his desk and glared down at Billy Dan. "The Democratic caucus went well, but they stopped a long way short of endorsing me. The Speaker stopped anything like that, and by tomorrow they will have those fuzzy-headed liberals back in line. The President will see to that."

"But the meeting was all yours," Billy Dan argued.

"The Southerners are mine now, that's true. But the big states will not budge and I'll never be elected going down that road. But I've got something I want you to do. Walk over to the House and have a little chat with the Parliamentarian and the Sergeant at Arms. We are going to have a busy day tomorrow, and I want you to get us ready for it."

Parker then explained in detail what Billy Dan was to do with the House officials, and Billy Dan, taking furious notes, nodded in wide-eyed agreement. When he left the inner office, Parker placed a call to California, and in ten minutes, the governor was on the line.

"I think the time has come," Parker said, without preliminary.

"What is it like out there?" asked the governor.

"The House is in a complete uproar," Parker calmly responded.

"Excellent," said the governor. "I take it you want me to move now."

294

"That's right. Do it this afternoon. I want you to make the calls just as we planned. I'll make my moves tomorrow."

"Whatever you say," said the governor.

"I won't forget what you are doing," said Parker.

Governor Maynard Nelson had taken over the entire fourth floor of the Congressional Hotel and, since the balloting had begun on Monday, had taken personal charge of the Republican operation. The hotel was conveniently located across the street from the House office buildings, and a constant stream of congressmen and party officials had flowed through the headquarters.

Nelson had not been disappointed with the first day's voting. He had been elated when Harrington had not been able to hold Florida and Mississippi. Even on Tuesday, when more Southern states defected to Parker, Nelson had felt quite pleased, despite the fact that his own total state count had not changed.

It was now late Wednesday afternoon and Nelson, along with the Republican House leader and some of his assistants, were meeting in Nelson's bedroom to discuss the effect of Meistler's death, the marches, and the Democrat disarray on Nelson's chances. Nelson had informed them that the President had been attempting to reach him all day, and they had all agreed that the call should not be returned until they decided upon their course of action. But they had not reached a decision and everyone was getting tired and more than a little edgy.

"Let me try to sum it up," Nelson said. "Everyone seems to agree that there is a strong tide now running in Parker's favor; that the riots and the murder have helped him immeasurably, maybe even in our own party. Harrington is losing ground and I am standing still. The dilemma is that, on the one hand, the liberal Democrats whom Harrington still holds will not go for me or Parker under any conceivable circumstances, and, on the other hand, Parker has not yet peaked and therefore it is premature to make him an offer. That is where we seem to be. Now, gentlemen, the question is, Where does this all lead us?"

The Republican House leader stood up, looking rumpled and weary. "It means we should stand pat and let matters settle

295

down for another day or two. I've been telling you that all afternoon. Believe me, it is all we can do."

"But can we take that risk?" Nelson went on. "I feel in my bones that inaction could be disaster, especially in view of how volatile matters now are."

"You just pointed out why you cannot move yet," the Minority Leader continued. "If you jump in either direction now, and it doesn't work, then you are stuck with an alliance you may not want and which may not work. Timing is everything in this business, and it is just too damned early for us to move. I think you will eventually be able to re-establish a deal with Parker, but you certainly can't do it yet."

Nelson sat silently for a moment, his arms tightly folded across his chest. "All right," he said. "We'll wait. But I think all of us had better pray that we are doing the right thing."

"What are you going to do about the President's call?" Jerry Greenberg asked.

"Ignore it," snapped Nelson. "The President and I have nothing to say to each other, at least not yet."

Shortly before noon on Thursday, the day after Meistler's death, Stu and Mary O'Brien wearily took their places in the House gallery.

The President had been trying without let-up to reach Governor Nelson and finally had asked Stu to call Jerry Greenberg. When that had proved equally fruitless, Stu had been dispatched to Nelson's Congressional Hotel headquarters in an effort to personally see Greenberg and convey the urgency of the President's wishes. Stu had spent two hours Wednesday evening at the hotel, but the doors to the Republican suite had remained closed to him. The only message given to Stu by the sheepish secret service agent on duty had been that neither Greenberg nor anyone else inside was available. He had returned to the White House, discouraged and empty-handed.

At breakfast this morning with Harrington and the Democratic House leadership, even the President's great energy had appeared sapped by the week's frustrations. Only Harrington had seemed to have any verve. He had jumped in with a half dozen ideas about what should be done. Some of them, such as the President's requesting a joint House-Senate session so that he could address the nation and make a public offer of accommodation with the Republicans, had been rejected out of hand. Then Harrington suggested that the Speaker be authorized to convey his offer to the House Minority Leader, who could then relay it to Nelson. This plan was eagerly accepted as a method of making contact, but despite Senator Harrington's best efforts the breakfast had broken up in a pessimistic mood. The President and Harrington were to continue their efforts to reach Governor Nelson, and the House leadership, with whatever help the Executive Branch might give, was to now spend "every available chip" to keep the rest of the Democratic party in line.

Stu spent the rest of the morning with the delegations from Washington and Missouri, the only non-Southern states assigned to him. He had run into some trouble with the rural, conservative Democrats from Missouri, but it seemed that Harrington would nonetheless retain a shaky majority of the state's delegation. Washington, on the other hand, had been no problem at all. As a matter of fact, the liberals from that state had expressed anger at the Southern attempt to take over the party. They had recovered from their first shock at Meistler's murder and were now willing to openly state their mounting concern over the reactionary, anti-Negro mood of the country and their fears that the House might bow to it. If the Washingtonians reflected Democratic liberal sentiment, the Northern wing of the party should remain committed to Harrington.

The Washington delegation, however, had been the only good news in an otherwise dismal morning. Stu had not been able to start for the Hill until almost eleven-thirty. He had been certain he would be late for the opening session and, because of the marches, might not be able to make it at all. However, except for the troops and police everywhere on the streets, there wasn't a sign of trouble. Meistler's murder had apparently cooled things off temporarily.

The floor of the House was jammed as the Speaker called

the session to order for the twentieth ballot for President and the clerk commenced the call of the roll.

"Alabama," called out the clerk. The state stayed with Parker.

Alaska's lone Republican again voted for Nelson.

"Arizona," called the clerk, and Stu started to whisper to Mary that maybe it wouldn't be so bad. Before he could get the words out he heard one of the two Republican congressmen from Arizona firmly call out, "Parker." Stu whipped his gaze back to the floor in time to see the second Republican from that state also vote for Parker. Arizona was thus casting its vote for the Florida senator, and the House erupted in a startled roar. Mary, with no need for directions from Stu, rushed from the gallery to telephone the White House.

Stu stared down at the chaos on the House floor, unbelieving. It cannot be happening, he thought. The Republicans would never do it. The Speaker, pounding his gavel, finally regained a semblance of order.

"Arkansas," called the clerk, and as Burns Robertson had predicted, the state voted for Parker. The lone Republican joined the three Democrats to cast a unanimous vote from that state.

The clerk called for California's votes. Stu was relieved to hear the Democrats from that state continue to vote solidly for Harrington, but this relief turned to a sickening dread as he saw that most of the state's Republicans had now switched to Parker. Nevertheless, the state's twenty-one Democrats, holding firm, maintained their four-vote majority and California's vote was cast for Harrington.

Colorado and Connecticut stayed with Harrington.

"Delaware," intoned the clerk. The House was utterly still. "Nelson" called out the state's lone Republican congressman, and Stu let out a sigh of relief.

There were no further changes from the Tuesday vote until the clerk reached Idaho. The state's two Republicans switched to Parker.

The Midwestern and Eastern Republicans continued to hold for Nelson. Kentucky held its precarious one-vote margin for Harrington, but Parker broke through Louisiana's previously tied vote and gathered in the state.

The clerk continued the roll of the states, and by the time he reached New Mexico there was no longer any surprise that the state's two Republican members voted for Parker.

The pattern was now clear. Parker had somehow cracked through the Western Republicans and was now getting almost all of the votes of the largely conservative congressmen from these sparsely populated states.

Finally, with the Republicans from Utah and Wyoming following suit and voting for Parker, the twentieth ballot came to a close, and the Speaker announced the results to a stunned House: Harrington, seventeen states; Parker, sixteen states; Nelson, fourteen; with Illinois, Montana and Oregon still tied.

No candidate yet had the twenty-six states needed to win, but Parker had picked up seven additional states since Tuesday, Harrington had lost one state, and Nelson had lost five. The House had been thrown into a three-way deadlock as it prepared to start the twenty-first roll call for President.

The Republican and Democratic floor leaders were now at the Speaker's rostrum. They ignored the shouts from the floor demanding a start of the next ballot, and they huddled in intense conversation. Then the Majority Leader walked rapidly to his table, pulled the microphone to him, and asked that the House stand in recess for one hour. The Republican leader rose to join in the motion. The Speaker instantly called for those in favor to say "aye" and those opposed, "nay." Then, to the accompaniment of an uproar of objections and calls for a roll call, the Speaker declared that the ayes had it, the House would be in recess. Banging his gavel, the Speaker walked from the House floor while the members helplessly called, "No! No! No!"

Stu rushed to the Speaker's inner office, placed a call to the White House operator, and told her to alert Alvin Morgan for a report.

Then, Stu looked toward the Speaker, who appeared distraught as he ran his hands nervously through his thin white hair. "I spoke to the Republican leader just before we convened this noon," the Speaker began. "I told him we wanted to do business with Nelson. He wasn't interested. He wouldn't even listen to what I had to offer. He just walked away from me."

The Speaker reached for a cigar, but put it down, too upset to smoke. "After the vote," he went on, "he came back. He told me that something terrible was going on in his party, that the governor of California had managed to get the Western Republicans to switch to Parker. Apparently the governor made some kind of deal with Parker as long ago as the Oakland riots and has been setting this up for the past month. From what the Republican leader could learn, the governor of California put together one hell of an organization and managed to get the Westerners to agree to go with Parker if Nelson ever ran out of gas. When Meistler was murdered on top of all these God damned marches, he was able to get them to switch to Parker."

"What about the rest of the Republicans?" Kelly quietly asked.

"The Republican floor leader thinks he can hold them for Nelson," the Speaker continued. "But he needs time to regroup. That's why he agreed to force through this recess. He wanted a firm proposition from Harrington right now. I told him I was authorized to offer the position of Secretary of State to Governor Nelson, and the cabinet posts of Interior, Commerce and Post Office to the Republican party. He wants to pursue it, and he thinks that if we can keep this thing as it is for the rest of the day, maybe something can be done tomorrow."

"Can you stop any more voting today?" Stu asked.

"No. This one-hour break is all we can possibly get done. We won't be able to get away with it again."

Stu flashed the White House operator and reported what had happened to Alvin Morgan.

Morgan's reply was terse. "Tell the Speaker that Governor Nelson just called in and spoke to the President and Senator Harrington, who is in the office with him. Nelson is ready to do business. He is on his way down here now. All you have to do is hold that vote steady until we can reach an agreement. I think the

Minority Leader is right. We will need at least until tomorrow to put it all together. Do you think you can hold it that long?"

Stu turned to the Speaker and repeated Morgan's question. "All we can do is try," the Speaker replied. "At this stage there can't be any guarantees."

Forty-five minutes later Stu returned to his gallery seat. It was five minutes before the next roll call was scheduled to begin. The House floor was jammed as the Speaker entered the chamber and walked to the Minority Leader's side. As they were talking, Stu heard some commotion from the back of the House floor. The noise grew louder and members began to look, then move toward the rear doors. Stu strained to see what was happening, but could only detect increasing excitement as the congressmen began to stand on the seats and shove toward the center aisle. Someone ran to the Speaker and whispered in his ear. Both he and the Republican leader looked startled, and the Speaker walked rapidly to the rostrum, followed by his Republican colleague. The Majority Leader was already there, waiting. The three of them turned and looked toward the rear of the chamber.

Then, suddenly, the rear doors of the House burst open and, to a frenzied roar from the members and the galleries, Senator Jack Parker walked in and stood on the floor of the House. He stood alone for a moment, holding himself ramrod straight and without expression. Then the members surged toward him, shaking his hands, touching him, shouting their approval. The noise was deafening as the House went out of control.

Stu sat silently, feeling helpless. Over half the people in the galleries were on their feet, screaming their support. Parker now moved partway down the center aisle and stood accepting the adulation.

The Speaker called for order, but he could not get it. Then, in a gesture of control that Stu would long remember, Parker raised both hands high over his head, and the House, as if a switch had been pulled, became silent.

A congressman from New York jumped to his feet, grabbing a microphone. "Mr. Speaker," he said in a voice choking with anger. "I demand that the rules of the House be enforced and that the senator from Florida be ordered off the floor immediately."

"I am sorry," the Speaker responded, "but House Rule thirty-two quite specifically provides that floor privileges are granted to 'members of Congress.' This includes senators, and therefore the senator from Florida is within his rights in being here. I must overrule the point of order."

Now the liberals were erupting, yelling objections and invectives. But there was nothing they could do. The rule, old and often used, was precisely as the Speaker had explained it.

Mary, who had gone to phone the White House, now whispered, breathlessly, "Alvin wants to talk to you right now. He is waiting on the phone."

Stu ran up the steps to the Periodical Press Room and into the small phone booth. There was a click on the phone and then the familiar voice of the President came on the line. "Tell the Speaker to stop the vote," the President said, hard and flat.

"Yes, sir. I'll try," said Stu.

"You'll do more than try, Brady."

"Yes, Mr. President."

"Tell the Speaker that Nelson just walked in here and we are going to reach an agreement. I don't care how the Speaker does it, but he has got to stop that vote."

"Yes, sir," Stu replied.

Stu ran back down the stairs to the House floor level. He spotted the chief doorkeeper and told him to get the Speaker for him, that he had an urgent message from the President. The doorkeeper hesitated and then told Stu the Speaker could not be disturbed. Stu angrily insisted and, finally the doorkeeper walked slowly into the chamber. Stu waited nervously. He saw John Kelly and quickly told him the President's orders. "We have got to get to the Speaker," Stu said. He was perspiring heavily, and his head felt as if it was about to break open from the tension.

The doorkeeper reappeared. "The Speaker can't come," he said with a smirk. "They are starting the roll call now."

"My God, he can't do that," implored Stu.

"Well, my good friend, he sure as hell is doing it," drawled the doorkeeper in his deep Southern accent.

Stu turned away in disgust. "Keep trying," he said to Kelly. "Get the Majority Leader, the Whip, anybody out here, and give him the message."

Stu ran back up the stairs to the gallery. He stood just inside the door and watched.

"The clerk will call the roll of the states," the Speaker said. He could barely be heard. Parker was still on the floor, surrounded by ecstatically admiring members. He was moving slowly from delegation to delegation, smiling, talking to the congressmen. He went from one state to another, sure of himself, persuasive, rallying the House to his side.

The Speaker, his voice now hoarse, ordered that the aisles be cleared and the members take their seats. Still no response. The Speaker then directed the Sergeant at Arms to clear the aisles and enforce order. Parker, smiling benignly up at the Speaker, took a seat in the Kentucky delegation, talking earnestly to the members. He then moved to the Kansas group located just behind Kentucky.

Now the clerk called out, "Alabama," and Stu knew the roll call would not be stopped.

The balloting went quickly and decisively. First, Alaska broke to Parker. Then Iowa and Kansas did the same. With their votes, it was clear that the Midwestern Republicans had burst loose. Next Kentucky, always marginal for Harrington, lost one of its Democrats to Parker and he, together with the state's three Republicans, were able to vote the state for Parker.

The clerk continued the roll call. North and South Dakota went for Parker, and so did Wisconsin.

When the clerk reached Wyoming the count stood: Parker, twenty-four states; Harrington, sixteen states; Nelson, seven states; and three states tied.

Parker was only two votes away from victory.

There was a pause as the Speaker prepared to announce the final tally of the twenty-first ballot. Before he could, the Democratic congressman from Montana grabbed a microphone. Senator Parker was standing beside him.

"Is it too late to change my vote?" shouted the congressman. The Speaker consulted the parliamentarian. "No, it is not. You may change at any time before I announce the results. Do you wish to do so at this time?"

"Yes, Mr. Speaker. I now vote for Senator Parker."

"The member from Montana votes for Parker," intoned the clerk, yelling to be heard over the uproar on the House floor. "Inasmuch as the other member from Montana earlier voted for Parker, that state's vote is now cast for the senator from Florida."

That made it twenty-five states. One short of victory.

The Speaker was now attempting to get order and was urging the clerk to hand him the official tally so that he could announce the vote and cut off this roll call. But now another congressman was at the microphone, demanding recognition.

It was the lone congressman from the state of Nevada. A Democrat, newly elected this term, he was a brash young lawyer from Las Vegas, the first ever chosen from that city. Now he stood at the microphone, and in a voice not to be denied he called out, "Mr. Speaker, Mr. Speaker!"

The Speaker paused, peered at the congressman, and, taking a deep breath, finally said, "The gentleman from Nevada is recognized."

The congressman turned his head and smiled at Parker, standing across the room. Then he spoke to a hushed House. "I proudly change my vote and the vote of the great state of Nevada to Senator Jack Parker."

The noise was deafening as the members erupted in chaos. Parker was lifted to the shoulders of the Florida delegation and carried triumphantly down the aisles.

The Speaker called for order, then gave up, and in a tired defeated voice, unheard by anyone, announced the final vote.

"Senator Jack Parker of Florida has received the votes of the following twenty-six states: Alabama, Alaska, Arizona, Arkansas, Florida, Georgia, Idaho, Iowa, Kansas, Kentucky, Louisiana, Maryland, Mississippi, Montana, Nebraska, Nevada,

304

New Mexico, North Carolina, North Dakota, South Carolina, South Dakota, Tennessee, Utah, Virginia, Wisconsin and Wyoming.

"Senator James Harrington of Rhode Island has received the votes of the following fifteen states: California, Colorado, Connecticut, Hawaii, Maine, Massachusetts, Missouri, New Jersey, New York, Oklahoma, Pennsylvania, Rhode Island, Texas, Washington and West Virginia.

"Governor Maynard Nelson of Pennsylvania has received the votes of the following seven states: Delaware, Indiana, Michigan, Minnesota, New Hampshire, Ohio and Vermont.

"The states of Illinois and Oregon, not having cast a majority for any candidate, are not counted.

"Therefore, under the Constitution of the United States, I declare that Senator Jack Parker of Florida is hereby elected President of the United States."

APPENDIX ONE

STATES POPULAR VOTE (rounded to thousands)				ELECTORAL VOTE		
	Harrington(D)	Nelson(R)	Parker (I)	H	N	P
ALABAMA	196,000	147,000	691,000			10
ALASKA	36,000	35,000	10,000	3		
ARIZONA	167,000	256,000	45,000		5	
ARKANSAS	183,000	187,000	237,000			6
CALIFORNIA	3,187,000	3,409,000	482,000		40	
COLORADO	336,000	409,000	61,000		6	
CONNECTICUT	662,000	570,000	79,000	8		
DELAWARE	95,000	88,000	28,000	3		
DISTRICT OF COLUMBIA	130,000	29,000	2,000	3		
FLORIDA	624,000	677,000	887,000			14
GEORGIA	333,000	366,000	535,000			12
HAWAII	141,000	91,000	3,000	4		
IDAHO	89,000	164,000	36,000		4	
ILLINOIS	2,137,000	2,008,000	385,000	26		

STATES POPULAR VOTE (rounded to thousands)				ELECTORAL VOTE		
	Harrington(D)	Nelson(R)	Parker (I)	H	N	P
INDIANA	806,000	1,058,000	243,000		13	
IOWA	477,000	617,000	66,000		9	
KANSAS	300,000	468,000	87,000		7	
KENTUCKY	190,000	395,000	459,000			9
LOUISIANA	318,000	260,000	537,000			10
MAINE	213,000	165,000	6,000	4		
MARYLAND	428,000	421,000	430,000			10
MASSACHUSETTS	1,458,000	762,000	86,000	14		
MICHIGAN	1,567,000	1,331,000	320,000	21		
MINNESOTA	807,000	621,000	67,000	10		
MISSISSIPPI	149,000	88,000	414,000			7
MISSOURI	786,000	808,000	205,000		12	

STATES	POPULAR VOTE (rounded to thousands)			ELECTORAL VOTE		
	Harrington(D)	Nelson(R)	Parker (I)	H	N	P
MONTANA	109,000	130,000	19,000		4	
NEBRASKA	164,000	304,000	43,000		5	
NEVADA	59,000	72,000	20,000		3	
NEW HAMPSHIRE	131,000	155,000	11,000		4	
NEW JERSEY	1,325,000	1,264,000	262,000	17		
NEW MEXICO	129,000	168,000	26,000		4	
NEW YORK	3,357,000	2,980,000	349,000	43		
NORTH CAROLINA	457,000	490,000	619,000			13
NORTH DAKOTA	94,000	139,000	14,000		4	
OHIO	1,785,000	1,692,000	469,000	26		
OKLAHOMA	302,000	450,000	192,000		8	
OREGON	403,000	356,000	49,000	6		
PENNSYLVANIA	1,992,000	2,203,000	368,000		29	
RHODE ISLAND	239,000	116,000	15,000	4		
SOUTH CAROLINA	197,000	211,000	260,000			8
SOUTH DAKOTA	118,000	147,000	13,000		4	
TENNESSEE	350,000	421,000	467,000			11
TEXAS	1,267,000	1,227,000	582,000	25		
UTAH	157,000	239,000	27,000		4	
VERMONT	70,000	85,000	5,000		3	
VIRGINIA	322,000	444,000	596,000			12
WASHINGTON	562,000	520,000	86,000	9		
WEST VIRGINIA	373,000	307,000	72,000	7		
WISCONSIN	749,000	810,000	128,000		12	
WYOMING	45,000	70,000	11,000		3	
TOTALS	30,571,000 (42.4%)	30,430,000 (42.2%)	11,104,000 (15.4%)	233 (17 states and D.C.)	183 (21 states)	122 (12 states)

APPENDIX TWO

Political Party Division of the House of Representatives

STATE	DEM.	REP.	STATE	DEM.	REP.
ALABAMA	5	3	MONTANA	1	1
ALASKA	0	1	NEBRASKA	0	3
ARIZONA	1	2	NEVADA	1	0
ARKANSAS	3	1	NEW HAMPSHIRE	0	2
CALIFORNIA	21	17	NEW JERSEY	9	6
COLORADO	3	1	NEW MEXICO	0	2
CONNECTICUT	4	2	NEW YORK	26	15
DELAWARE	0	1	NORTH CAROLINA	7	4
FLORIDA	9	3	NORTH DAKOTA	0	2
GEORGIA	8	2	OHIO	6	18
HAWAII	2	0	OKLAHOMA	4	2
IDAHO	0	2	OREGON	2	2
ILLINOIS	12	12	PENNSYLVANIA	14	13
INDIANA	4	7	RHODE ISLAND	2	0
IOWA	2	5	SOUTH CAROLINA	5	1
KANSAS	0	5	SOUTH DAKOTA	0	2
KENTUCKY	4	3	TENNESSEE	5	4
LOUISIANA	8	0	TEXAS	20	3
MAINE	2	0	UTAH	0	2
MARYLAND	4	4	VERMONT	0	1
MASSACHUSETTS	7	5	VIRGINIA	5	5
MICHIGAN	7	12	WASHINGTON	5	2
MINNESOTA	3	5	WEST VIRGINIA	5	0
MISSISSIPPI	5	0	WISCONSIN	3	7
MISSOURI	9	1	WYOMING	0	1

SHERWIN MARKMAN, *at present a member of a Washington law firm, was White House Assistant to the President from 1966 through 1968, a Deputy Director of A.I.D., Campaign Director for Senator Harold E. Hughes of Iowa, and a member of Adlai Stevenson's campaign staff in 1960. He lives with his wife and three children in Bethesda, Maryland.*